THE PHOENIX FEATHER I:
FLEDGLINGS

THE PHOENIX FEATHER

1

FLEDGLINGS

SHERWOOD SMITH

Book View Cafe

THE PHOENIX FEATHER 1: FLEDGLINGS
Copyright © 2021 by Sherwood Smith

Published by Book View Café Publishing Cooperative
304 S. Jones Blvd,. Suite 2906
Las Vegas, NV 89107
www.bookviewcafe.org

ISBN: 978-1-61138-971-5

Cover Design by Augusta Scarlett
Interior Design by Marissa Doyle

AUTHOR'S NOTE

When I first encountered Chinese television series and novels, with their complex manners and customs and long braided stories and the underpinnings of a yearning for beauty in all things, I was dazzled. Even as a kid I loved braided tales, with characters growing and changing in a world both breathtaking and strange, where striving to become the best one can be matters. (And how that gets defined is what drives the story.)

After six years of happy immersion in Eastern history, language, literature and art, last year when we got sequestered in our homes, and American culture was polarizing, I wanted escape into such a world, so I began writing *The Phoenix Feather* as a *xuanhuan* (an offshoot of the far older *wuxia* genre, which borrows freely from various mythologies), just to see where it would take me.

This is the result!

IT IS SAID THAT tales are like rivers, always renewing as they flow out to join the endless waters of the sea. I think tales are more like the streams that feed the rivers, for they must have a beginning.

My tale begins with a monk and a child, who sat on mats under the low eaves of a thin-walled cottage. A single candle illuminated the young face and the old, throwing shadows against the bare walls of a room empty of other furnishings except for the neatly rolled bedding in one corner.

The child who was generally known as Little Third in the village, and Mouse within the family, exclaimed, "I get to hear a story all by myself?"

"Yes," said the monk. "This story will not be like those I usually tell you."

"How is it not the same? I hope it will have heroes, at least." Mouse dug bare toes into the mat, knees pulled to chin.

"This story does not concern the acts of gods, demons, or ghosts. As for heroes, you will see. There was an imperial prince—"

"Oh, princes," Mouse said on a sigh, suspecting a lesson hidden behind this story. As if lessons didn't happen all day. "They're like gods and demons and ghosts, all so very very far away."

The monk replied calmly, "Is this going to be your story about my story, or will you listen?"

"Sorry," Mouse said contritely.

The monk cleared his throat. "Enjai was one of several imperial princes. Unlike his various imperial siblings and cousins, some of whom were reputed to be handsome as long as the gifts kept coming, he truly was handsome . . . If you're going to make rude noises, I will leave you to entertain yourself."

"Sorry, sorry," Mouse said, and then to the monk's surprise, dropped face down, moaning, "This unworthy one deserves death—"

"You do not deserve death. Bad manners do not deserve death," the monk replied tartly.

Mouse bounced up again, dark eyes round. "It's how everyone talks to nobles in the hero tales."

"You have picked up some regrettable expressions from reading those hero tales. Perhaps I ought to stop bringing them back—you are not the one who needs encouragement to read."

At that Mouse looked very contrite. "I just thought it would sound extra sorry."

"Do you see any nobles here?" The monk lifted a hand callused from hard work. "Didn't think so. You are right that it is the humble speech expected by some nobles and imperials, which can be as false as the plainer speech of commoners like us. Show your contrition by listening politely, please."

Mouse bobbed eagerly, and the monk cleared his throat once more. "When Second Imperial Prince Enjai turned twenty, as a second son—and a favorite of the empress—he was permitted to leave the imperial palace . . ."

The light from the single candle flickered over the round, unprepossessing face of the child, and smoothed the wrinkles from the monk as he went on to describe how Imperial Prince Enjai's father had died when the prince was young, so he was much indulged by a loving mother as well as by the empress. No one had ever said no to him, the monk added, and Mouse thought, here come the lessons, though *we* aren't spoiled.

But instead, the monk went right on with his description of the prince, who, being young, restless, and hot-blooded as many young people with too much wealth and too little opposition tend to be, decided to marry. Eyeing his small charge, the monk was vague about how the prince could (being a prince) summon up female companionship at the snap of his fingers, but he knew that imperial marriages required the assembly of the most beautiful and talented among the possible choices. He wanted the most beautiful and talented consort . . .

The monk paused. "Did you say something?"

Mouse had groaned, thinking that a romance was coming—even worse than a lesson. Too many romances ended with the woman drowning herself, especially in the older stories. "My stomach was rumbling." Then apologized, half-expecting the monk to stop the story because of bad manners.

But he started right up again. "All the noble clans were required to send a well-born, properly trained, comely daughter between the ages of sixteen and twenty, if no previous marriage treaty had been contracted, but you can be sure that the most ambitious discovered auspicious signs in ten-character birth lines, and found ways around betrothal treaties."

Mouse said, "The families wanted their daughters to marry a prince."

"Not just the families. The provincial governor of Butterfly Island decided that one of the twin daughters of Scholar Alk Bemti would represent the honor of the island, as they were well-born and beautiful, with features considered perfect, eyes the much-prized shade called teak. If they had one flaw, it was the color of their hair, which, though black, was not the true blue-black considered to be the pinnacle of magnificence."

Mouse had heard that before. If there was any tinge of red in it (like Mouse's), it wasn't considered perfect hair. Though the monk went on to say that in every other respect their hair was like silk. Of course it was, Mouse thought.

One daughter had chosen the temple path at an early age and vanished from worldly life. The scholar's second daughter, Alk Hanu, was required to travel all the way to the imperial island, a long and difficult journey. But she was not alone, for other girls traveled as well, many of them wealthy. She fell in with some of these on the boat during a slow, treacherous passage. Though the Alks had been connected to the imperial family five generations before, she had not been raised to insist upon being first, and as a scholar's daughter, she was full of entertaining stories, so she was welcomed by the other candidates.

A storyteller? Mouse sat up straight.

The monk went on to describe the journey, which was of necessity slow. The sun was warm, and as young people will do when time hangs heavy on idle hands, their mouths kept busy. They talked a great deal, and Hanu began to learn how young nobles behaved. She did not think of marriage at all.

Mouse was liking this Hanu better and better. Except if that lesson was lurking somewhere. "I thought nobles all want to marry princes or princesses."

"Not this one."

"I *do* like her," Mouse declared.

The monk explained very briefly that Hanu's mother, the last of the Alk clan, had dutifully taken a consort in order to have an heir, but she had chosen a man a step lower in rank so that there could be no clan trouble when she parted with him after her daughters' birth. "Scholar Bemti preferred the world of books to the noise of the outside world, and had raised her daughters to reflect that preference, one leaving the world entirely —"

One of Mouse's shoulders jerked up. Here came the lesson about the Importance of Scholarship — as if those didn't happen every single day from Mother.

The monk, interpreting this reaction, cut himself short (he had been about to describe how much the Alk daughters had prized learning) and resumed the story. "Hanu only wished to fit in rather than stand out, but such was her beauty that she stood out anyway, especially as she observed the others closely, for she had been trained to notice detail. Quietly she shed her rustic customs along the journey, for she was filial, and did not wish to cause ill reflection on the Alks.

And now we come back to Prince Enjai and his bodyguard Danno. Imperial guards are forbidden to marry during their time of service, except for Spring Festival babies, who are always considered auspicious —"

"I don't get why everybody says it's terrible when babies come if people aren't married, except for Spring Festival babies," Mouse said.

The monk eyed his small charge, deciding to keep it simple. "Many believe that if the gods decide to slip a soul back into the world as a result of Festival celebration, that child will be lucky, especially if it's born right on the new year. Even if it comes a few days early or late, tradition is firm about considering it inauspicious to go against divine mandate."

Sure enough, he saw Mouse promptly lose interest in the subject.

He went on. "Danno's mother having been an imperial guard, and Danno a Spring Festival baby, he was given over to Imperial Prince Enjai's mother's household. Danno and Imperial Prince Enjai shared a milk nurse. Danno was to be Prince Enjai's bodyguard, his only purpose to protect the prince with his life, and consequently became his closest companion . . ."

He went on to relate how the prince's guards trained every day in the training court. Part of the day Prince Enjai trained with them. The rest of the day, the prince was tutored in scholarship, poetry, the arts, and imperial annals, while Danno continued his martial exercise — for the personal guard of a prince or princess must be among the best.

Mouse's entire demeanor brightened. "How different is it from our training?"

"That you shall discover. Danno's skills and talent showed early. By ten he could beat all the other boys in the court, and by fifteen, he was winning competitions against the lowest rank of the imperial guard. The Golden Armor General who commands the imperial guard even tried to lure him away, but he was loyal, and refused to go. And Prince Enjai would only trust the safety of his body to Danno. Before Danno turned twenty, he had twice been acknowledged the best swordsman in the imperial city, and twice he had saved the prince's life . . ."

The monk said that when Prince Enjai was given his own household within the city, Danno, also twenty, was appointed head of the prince's bodyguards. Usually an older, wiser man was given this stewardship, but Enjai did not want old men around him, and he extolled Danno as his brother.

Mouse said cautiously, "He doesn't sound bad. If he was loyal to Danno, too."

"That, you will discover. To resume. The prospective consorts and aunts assembled in the imperial city as the prospective brides arrived to be examined and tested.

"Some girls were rejected out of hand for being too tall, or too short, too thin, or too fat. This one's nose was too prominent, and that one's too undistinguished; this one's eyes too close together, that one's too far apart. One smiled too much, displaying her gums. The imperial consorts and aunts rejected anyone with what they considered physical flaws, for the sake of the family: they did not want such traits passing down to imperial children and tarnishing the purity of the imperial name. All those girls were sent back home. At the third round of tests, more candidates were sent away for ill-made letters, or clumsy stitches, or dull answers, or poor dancing. Finally they were down to those considered perfect in every way."

Mouse scowled in perplexity. "How do they actually judge beauty once all those flaws are done away with? Second Brother says beauty is—"

"How indeed? By this point in the selection, judgment becomes more subjective, a matter of taste, and of political necessity, and finally the mystery of attraction. All were praised for the perfect melon-seed oval of their faces, the willow line of their brows, the smoothness of their skin, and so forth.

"Though the imperial consorts favored this or that daughter of important ministers or nobles, it was Hanu whom no one could find a flaw in, except for her lack of an influential clan. But her birth was distinguished enough to make up for it. And though she had not been trained in all the subtleties of the court bow, and how to command movement from room to room, she won favor in the royal consorts' critical eyes not just for her polite manners, but for her thoughtful brow, and the way she did not giggle or flirt her fan or hair ornaments. The choice was at last reduced to five, at which time the prince was summoned to converse with the prospective brides from behind a silk screen, looked on by his mother."

What the monk could not relate, but I can tell you, is that the first daughter of the Household Minister made languishing eyes at Imperial Prince Enjai, and flattered him with dulcet tones. The fifth daughter of the Minister of War managed to loosen her garments and tried to peek coyly behind the screen, for you have to remember he was very handsome as well an imperial prince, and she was desperate to get away from her crowded home where pride in a distinguished family history was about the only commodity in plenty.

The daughter of the Governor of Five Rivers Island waited complacently to be chosen, for she had been told from birth that she was more beautiful than the Morningstar God, and that her family — the Su clan — was destined for imperial rank.

The daughter of the Harbormaster from Crescent Moon Bay giggled incessantly, even when the prince's mother asked her to sit down, and would she take a cup of scalded gold leaf?

In contrast, Hanu sat with her head lowered, replied in the voice of a scholar's daughter, and employed no arts to attract or allure. They talked of books, then of history, of poetry and music, and he admitted to finding himself hard put to keep pace with her.

That led to a second interview without the screen.

Such was Hanu's lack of experience with people she did not know — and the fact that she never looked directly at Prince Enjai — that she missed the clues to the fact that her manner had the opposite effect of her intent. It could be said that Prince Enjai found her elusive, which was perhaps more intriguing than the most expensive perfume, or jewels, or flirtatious behavior. He left that interview more determined to get her to look at him, and smile.

Meanwhile, the prince's house was decorated with red bunting and streamers and banners with golden characters for good luck, longevity, and family. And the day considered most auspicious for a wedding dawned, the prince having made his decision.

The monk said, "To everyone's surprise, including Hanu's — especially Hanu's — she was told that the prince had chosen her. Hanu found herself summoned before the consorts and told that she had won. A parade of maids brought in a beautiful red dress embroidered with gold, with a jeweled headdress, and because she had no dowry, she was presented with ten bolts of silk, two cups of pearls, and a purse of gold to take with her to the wedding."

Without listening to anything she tried to say, the consorts lectured her on proper behavior in a prince's household as she was dressed in red and gold. She was conducted to an imperial palanquin and carried with great parade to Imperial Prince

Enjai's manor, where she was met by him, dressed as a bridegroom in red and gold.

The imperial relatives had all gathered at the prince's manor, except for the empress, who never left the imperial palace. But the imperial relatives were intimidating enough. Hanu tried to protest that she had never sought this honor, but no one listened, or they put down her quiet words to modesty. Because she had been taught not to speak to her elders and those in rank above her until spoken to, she had to go through the bowing ceremony, and the next thing she knew she was sitting in the bridal chamber. This was when the prince did not find the amenable bride he expected.

At this point, the monk began generalizing as Mouse listened half-comprehending.

"Hanu repeated what she had said from the start, that she had come because she was summoned but had not expected or even desired to marry. She had no wish to marry, she only wished to return to her mother, Scholar Alk Bemti, and her life on Lighthouse Promontory on Butterfly Island, and finish her scholarly training. The prince first laughed, thinking she made a joke; then he was offended."

"Why didn't he just let her go? There were all those others who wanted to marry him, is that not right?" Mouse then nodded, and with the air of one solving a mystery, observed, "You said nobody had ever said no to him, so he had a temper tantrum?"

"Even princes can lose face," the monk said. "To be refused by a scholar's daughter was an insult not easily recovered from. Especially when he had done her the honor of choosing her. And imperial law was very firmly on his side. It was his house, the servants his, and he had bestowed honor on her and thereby her family. As you know, the laws against all forms of slavery had changed under the Sage Empress, but tradition is still strong, especially in imperial households, and so, had he wanted to be more, ah, insistent, any objections Hanu might make would have been as disregarded as if a night bird wailed."

"Huh?"

The monk recollected his audience, and said hastily, "Never mind that. My point is, Prince Enjai believed that a reluctant bride was an insult. She must come to him with gratitude and appreciation for the honor he'd done to her. When she remained steadfast in wanting to go home, he had her locked in the Justice Wing at the other end of the training court, which housed little stone cells not large enough for anyone to stand. They were furnished with nothing but old straw. There she was to stay until she came to him on her knees. Each day Danno was to open the door long enough to put in a jug of water and to ask if she had come to her senses . . ."

Mouse listened in increasing indignation as the monk described how, each morning for five days, Danno opened the cell, which was until then only used for miscreants, and took out the empty jug, for she drank half and used the other half to wash. And each of four mornings she sat on the limp, dirty straw that she had neatened, her form erect and proper, and she remained silent. But each day her eyes were duller, her pallor worse, and on the last morning, when Danno opened the door, he found her lying insensate, for she had had nothing to eat for six days — including that first one.

Meanwhile the entire household walked with silent step, and fled at the sound of the angry prince's approach, avoiding his inner chambers unless summoned.

When the prince heard that Hanu lay on the stone as if dead, still clad in her bridal gown of red and gold, his anger changed as the wind in a tempest, and he threatened the entire household with being boiled alive if she did not revive.

A physician was called, who administered congee by tiny golden spoonfuls, and when Hanu roused, the entire household breathed again.

"She woke to awareness of her situation," the monk said, "but she was no longer bewildered. She was angry. However, she had come to understand the difference between a prince being angry and a scholar's daughter being angry, for tradition, and power, was all on his side. When Prince Enjai entered this room while she sat there still bedraggled, she betrayed no shame at her disarray, for she did not believe herself at fault. She knelt with her back straight and her hands folded, and gave him the same answer: she did not want to be married, but to go home."

What the monk could not know, was how the prince looked at her there, as she waited in her ruined bridal gown, pale and thin and determined, and many in that household thought that at this time he became truly intrigued. He had always won every contest he entered—though there was still the great struggle for the throne, which must be won by wit as well as by prowess. Perhaps he thought that if he could not win over a slip of a girl, what would that say about his chances of winning the throne?

And so he changed his tactic. She was given a fine room, and handmaids to tend her. The bridal finery was taken away, and she was offered costly robes of a wife, but she insisted on wearing the clothes of a scholar's daughter that she had arrived with.

He began to show her great respect, the bow of husband to consort when they met, even if she returned the maiden's bow. At every turn she was to see benefits of living in an imperial prince's household. Every meal was served on gold and the thinnest, most luminous porcelain, always twenty-five dishes to choose from. He brought in musicians, and these she enjoyed, and scholars, and these she listened to, though she refused to speak before them.

The monk said, "Like most nobles, Prince Enjai had been given a fine library. Hanu understood that this library had just come to him and offered to catalogue it, and he granted her wish. I expect that each was mistaking the other: she thought she was offering him a valuable service instead of herself, and perhaps he would find another candidate for marriage and send her back to scholarship, whereas he was amused, and indulged her because he thought it would win her to his side. When each night before they parted Prince Enjai asked what she desired, she said it was to go home to her mother.

"This went on until he ran out of patience. On the last night, he asked what was so special about life with her mother that could not be bettered as the consort of an imperial prince. When he spoke she saw the signs of anger in his eyes, and the smile that showed even white teeth, but she did not suspect what was to come next."

"You promised that this was not a tragic lesson," Mouse

interjected here, voice thin, scraping the edge of tears. Mouse hated injustice, and besides . . . "Mother doesn't want me reading any of those ancient stories in which girls sacrifice themselves for someone else's good."

"And I wouldn't tell you one," the monk promised. "Be patient, and listen. Imperials are raised to believe that the lives of the common people are theirs to use, reward, or dispose as they wish. There came a day, dark indeed, when Prince Enjai informed Hanu that Scholar Alk had slipped on the rocks and fallen to the sea below, so that there was not even a body to be buried, therefore no proper gravesite to be tended. Scholar Alk had been replaced by a new scholar who had a primary husband, two side-consorts with their own consorts, and all their children, who filled the entire house. Hanu had no vestige of a home to go back to.

"She collapsed at this news, and begged for mourning cloth. Perhaps Prince Enjai felt remorse, or perhaps it was only that he did not want to lose face, for we must remember he had the succession duel among the imperial princes and princesses still to be fought, and there was much speculation, even wagers, going on among them. At any rate she was given the least room on the servants' side of the manor overlooking the training court and the Justice Wing, to be guarded only by Danno and his most trusted men during her mourning. Then Prince Enjai rode off to attend the spring hunt with the imperial family, hosted by the First Imperial Prince, who was renowned for his military prowess."

What the monk could not know was how, during the mourning period, while Hanu was in this small room with one window, she could unlatch it and peer out each warm spring day and see Danno training with the elite guard, when he returned from where he had been sent away on orders.

She recognized Danno by now, though the bodyguards of the elite all wore black instead of the brilliant colors reserved for the imperial court. Even their headbands were plain and black, no decoration signifying rank, much less nobles' headgear.

Danno's manners were impeccable, as were all the servants'. They obeyed without murmur; they never spoke unless asked a direct question. They demonstrated less emotion than did their masters, but she was beginning to descry that they had their own thoughts.

There was nothing brutal in Danno's actions as he tended her. By now she had heard tales of brutality in other elite guards belonging to other houses. Young as he was, Danno did not tolerate it in his own guard, or toward the weak and lowly. He looked out for those under his command, and she could see that though all were loyal to the prince's house, it was Danno who had their personal loyalty.

The monk said only, "When Prince Enjai returned from his outing, he was busy with court ritual most every day, for the imperial court was in the midst of negotiating a marriage for the crown princess that involved foreign princes and matters of state. While Hanu watched Danno and the elite guard in their daily training, Danno brought her meals, and took away the dishes, and stood over her while she washed out her mourning garb by herself, so that certain of the servants could not torment her."

"So the bodyguard was her friend?"

"Gradually they began to speak. Danno had not been forbidden to speak to her—he was so silent by habit that it probably never occurred to Prince Enjai that they might talk. And even if he'd thought of it, who could predict that a short conversation about the weather, how long things took to dry, and then small questions about the training, could lead to friendship in each of them?"

The monk said "friendship" to suit his audience, but he did not quite comprehend how friendship could warm to something else. The truth was, though Prince Enjai was handsome, to her he could never be as appealing as Danno, his eyes well-spaced above the strong bones of his face. It was an interesting face to Hanu, and she began to feel rewarded as cups and pearls and gold could never match when she chanced to break Danno's habitual impassivity and make him smile, however briefly. It was his eyes that smiled, rarely his mouth.

It became interesting to her to try to divine Danno's thinking. Why he would choose to follow Imperial Prince Enjai, whose temper could change like the winds? She began to understand that Danno had been raised as a shadow brother to the prince, though he was the best swordsman in the imperial city.

Skill was important and admired, but rank was power. Hanu finally understood that the day would come when Prince Enjai's patience would end, and so would her life. For living as she did with a view of the Justice Wing, she had also seen people go into those cells and not come out alive. Not all of these were thieves or petty criminals; a death was not considered murder when an imperial decreed it.

And so, alone in her room, she began to mirror what she saw in the training court, day after day. At first, her efforts were laughable. But not for long. As a girl she had daily clambered up and down the Promontory, and had danced all night at festivals. Though she'd been forced to be sedentary since her imprisonment, her muscles remembered how to move, and then she began the painful process of building new muscles, until she could mirror what the men did, though of course she had no weapons. But she brought to her study the determination she had brought to cataloguing that library — to which we will return.

"Hanu," the monk said, "had come to the conclusion that she had two choices if she didn't want to be carried out wrapped in white cloth like those victims from the Justice Wing: give in, or run. And if she ran, she must be strong and fleet enough to stay ahead of pursuit."

Mouse had been curling into a small ball, but sat upright in hope. "Now I'm beginning to like this story."

"The day she dreaded arrived at last, perhaps sped by Prince Enjai sensing something between the two, though he never saw either of them speak to the other. But as you have been taught, the language of muscle, of eye, is sometimes so subtle that the unobservant person still knows by instinct that there is hidden meaning. At any rate one night, after Hanu said once more that she wished to return to her mother, the angry prince said to Hanu, 'Danno, tell her how her mother died. You were there to see it done.' Then he walked out."

"That's horrible," Mouse wailed.

The monk, seeing the sheen of tears, said, "I promise it will get better, but you must hear what each said."

Mouse was caught up in the tale by then, thirsting for justice, as the monk related Danno's speech to Hanu. "'I did not find your mother at the lighthouse,' Danno told her. 'I sent my armed escort to search. Word soon was reported back that Scholar Alk Bemti stood on a cliff beside the waterfall, awaiting us. We proceeded there to confront her. She said only that she foresaw our coming, and that she would choose the manner of her own death. I stepped forward, drawing my sword, for I had been given a direct order, but I also knew that I could make the beheading with one stroke, which is as merciful as anything in the situation. But she stepped back and flung herself off the cliff.'

"Here he stopped, and gazed at the door instead of at her. When Hanu said to go on, he did. 'We moved to the cliff and looked down. It was difficult to make out anything past the vapors rising from below, but there are those among the household guard who believe they saw her take wing and fly away. Others insisted that they only saw the streaming of her scholar's sleeves and gown when she fell. I saw neither, and so I had to climb to the rocks below, with half my men. But search as we might, we found nothing aside from the treacherous water, and the sharp rocks.' And then he dropped to his knees, and bowed forehead to the ground before saying, 'I am sorry.'"

"What did she do?" Mouse asked, grinding chin into knees.

"While Danno told his tale, Hanu had been thinking very fast. The shock of her mother's death was long over. There had to be a reason the prince had insisted on Danno telling her this story now. And she suspected that he would be asked to repeat her words. So she said only, 'You were under orders.' She knew by now that his choice, too, was to obey or die. Prince Enjai let five days pass. As they rode to an evening at an entertainment house given by one of the ministers, Enjai told Danno that on Harvest Moons Day—"

Perhaps craving a little distance, or relief, Mouse exclaimed, "When Phoenix Moon is biggest and rules the sky! I love moon cakes best of anything!"

The monk nodded. "It also signals the end of summer. Danno was told that the prince would put the question for the last time to Hanu, and if she proved recalcitrant, Danno was to strangle her, and they would give out that she had died of illness. The prince would try for another bride the following spring. After all, such stubborn stupidity would be an ill trait to pass down to his progeny. Danno bowed, as always, but his heart had turned to stone, for he had come to care for Hanu as she did for him . . ."

And now the monk leaned forward, talking fast. Danno, he explained, still had not been forbidden to speak to Hanu, so he warned her what was coming, which grieved them both. Seeing their grief mirrored in the other, at last they spoke their hearts.

They decided to flee, for his heart had so materially changed that he was willing to give up his entire life rather than kill her, and they laid careful plans. That much the monk knew.

What he did not know was why those plans did not succeed. That is because Danno was as inexperienced as Hanu in recognizing desire or intent. When dealing with the household servants, he'd quite properly avoided the gazes of the women, and paid no attention to those who would have gotten closer to him if they could.

There was one maid of the wardrobe with a nature as vindictive as it was ambitious. When he'd failed to respond to her advances, she had begun to spy on him, and discovered how long he remained in that room at the end of the Justice Wing. So she was watching when Danno took from the laundry area the dull blue and undyed garments worn by servants, to which he had no right.

As soon as she was certain the two had departed in disguise, she took time to dress in her best and do her hair becomingly before she went to the prince and fell at his feet, crying out her discovery. Enjai, infuriated both at the escape and in the delay in the telling, scarcely listened to her protestations of loyalty and devotion; in anger he ordered out horses and swordsmen, but he paused long enough to tell one of his guards to strangle the maid, for he would tolerate no spies in his house whom he had not set there himself.

"Though they had most of a day's head start, they had no horses, of course, and run as they would, they were caught up by the next morning. Danno could feel their approach under his feet as they ran, and though the cause was fairly hopeless, he would not surrender their lives easily. He watched for a likely spot for defense. And now we come back to the library."

"The library?" Mouse exclaimed.

"Hanu had made her own preparations. While cataloguing the library, she had discovered that much of it was trunks of very old scrolls and books that had been passed along the generations on his mother's side. In some, the writing was in the ancient script—"

"I know that script!"

"Yes, you are learning it. And now you will discover how it can be useful. Alk Bemti, having been one of the islands' foremost experts, had taught her daughter about the mysteries of Essence, which is . . ."

"Inside all living things," Mouse said impatiently, wanting to get to a good ending. "That causes us to live, and that powers the sun, the moons, and the world that is invisible as well as the visible world."

"Correct. Before departing with Danno, Hanu had slipped into the otherwise unused library and written certain charms out on hoarded scraps of Essence paper found at the bottom of one trunk. "

"Did she remember to use the oldest paper?"

"Indeed! She knew that the older the paper, the more Essence it would have accumulated over the years, so she trusted these to be powerful charms indeed."

"Good!" Mouse breathed in satisfaction.

"But even the most powerful charms are useless if not used effectively, and few will retain the presence of mind to apply them when confronted by an angry prince with armed men at his back. The pursuit had taken them all outside the city, Danno and Hanu's goal having been to take the river road up to one of the temples for refuge, until they could figure out a destination . . ."

Danno understood very well that Prince Enjai was the more angry for the sense of betrayal he felt, added to his rejection. How could his own sworn brother turn on him? And how could this woman who had refused him, an *imperial prince*, claiming she had no wish to marry, then turn to a no-clan bodyguard who had not ten words to say for himself?

"The prince," said the monk, "dismounted to vent his feelings, keeping his men well back. When Hanu dared to answer his question that love was like lightning—it struck when it would—he retorted, did she not understand that Danno was an assassin, with bloody hands. Her mother had been among his victims.

"She replied that the sword was not the murderer, only its wielder, and that Danno had been wielded by Prince Enjai as surely as Danno had wielded the sword. At which time Prince Enjai lost his temper entirely, and claimed that he would defeat Danno before killing them both with his own hands. He might have believed himself to be the better swordsman—"

"What strokes did they use? Did Enjai try the Serpent's Sting? I'll bet he only thought he mastered it—"

"This is not a sword-lesson story," the monk reminded Mouse, trying not to laugh. "Unless you wish to take over and make it one? I'll listen courteously."

"Sorry, I'll listen, I'll listen."

"Prince Enjai was good, as I said before. Good, perhaps very good, especially for a royal, but not great the way Danno was. No doubt Danno had let him win from time to time in their practices, if he deemed the prince's efforts worthy, but Danno was by far superior. Prince Enjai soon knew it, they all could see it in his eyes, as sweat rolled down his face. But Danno could not entirely overcome a lifetime of training, and could not kill his prince, who was very near weeping, for they had been like brothers. All this Hanu saw, and was glad she had prepared . . ."

As the fight progressed, the guards staying well back at the direction of their prince—and in truth, they probably did not want to be the one to kill their former captain, to whom they had been loyal, and with whom many might have secretly sympathized—Hanu darted in a circle around the duelists, wailing and throwing up her hands. Each time she lowered her hands, she dropped a charm along the folds of her robe to the ground, then trod it into the dirt.

When the circle was complete, and the prince desperate for breath, Hanu suspected that the guards would soon be ordered to cut them down. She released the last charm into the air, a light ribbon of paper, and fog rose out of the ground, entwining horses, men, trees, shrubs.

Danno, seeing what Hanu had done, reversed his weapon and clubbed the prince across the back of his head. The two escaped into the fog, led by Hanu, who had marked out a path of retreat.

The men, enfogged, had to wait there for their silent prince to give orders, for they could not see that he lay unconscious on the ground.

"And they didn't want to chase Danno and Hanu, did they?" Mouse interrupted.

"Some, perhaps. Others might have hoped for promotion or reward. We do not know their stories. Only that they were under orders to remain in that circle, and remain they did. Meanwhile the two made it down the cliffs to the river, and there they exchanged Hanu's fine hairpin, which her mother had given her, for a small boat . . ."

The boat carried them straight to the sea, where they were first becalmed, and then overcome by a fierce storm. Behind them, the prince roused, and seeing in the dissipating fog that the two had fled, ordered a search, but he thought only of roads; when the storm overtook the searchers, nearly driving them off the road, they returned empty-handed to the capital.

Danno and Hanu spent days driven before the demon winds, desperately fighting to keep their craft afloat until their strength failed. Both expected to die, and at last fell into one another's arms at the bottom of the boat, too exhausted to fight any more.

But the craft remained on the water, and they woke up at last on a beach amid the washed-up remains of their boat. While Danno struggled ashore to seek sustenance, Hanu crawled on her knees down to the tumbled wrack, until she found a stone studded with the remains of shells. This she took in both hands, and scraped it across her face. Then she took sandy salt water and rubbed it into the bleeding wounds, before she collapsed, not just from pain — she had already been in pain — but grief for her parents if they looked up from the underworld to see how she marred the body they had given her.

"It was then," the monk said solemnly, knowing what

reaction was to come, for he had told this story twice before, "that Hanu and Danno were discovered by the Sweetwater fishers going out to sea."

Mouse gasped. "Here? OUR island? Wait, is that about my own mother and father? Is that how Mother's face got ruined? I thought it was fire."

"You shall hear what was said, and why. Danno was also near collapse, for they hadn't eaten for days, and had only drunk rainwater. But he roused himself, staggering, to try to protect her with his bare hands, thus winning conditional respect before he, too, collapsed.

"They were nursed back to life. When left to rest, they held a whispered conference, deciding that their own names had brought them nothing but ill luck — and might even bring death, if Prince Enjai put them on a criminal list. Hanu would give up her claim to her family name, though she and her sister were the last of the Alk, five generations ago connected to the Empress Lam, who had married the first emperor of the Jehan Dynasty. They settled on Iley, or Dawn, for her, and he became Olt—"

"Which means carver in the village tongue! That IS Father and Mother! But I thought they came from the south, and her scars were from a fire . . . no, sorry, go on."

"—which means 'carver', for the villagers had assumed that his calluses were due to toolmaking. Iley and Olt built a story about migrating from a crowded island suffering from drought, far to the south, which had too many people and not enough food, and escaping after a fire in which your mother's face was burned by a flaming piece of roof that fell, and when the villagers assumed they had come from Anan or Min people (the first most common in the southern islands, and the second known mostly in the Eastern islands, but spread everywhere), Iley and Olt did not deny it."

"Father! Mother," Mouse whispered. This wasn't just a story, it was *real*.

The monk went on to explains that, as the two regained strength, they learned the island language while hiding as much as they could the fact that they both spoke Imperial — she the ancient form often called scholarly, as well as the modern form, and he the accent and idiom of the military — though there was small chance the islanders would recognize it.

But all it would take is one person who did. They tried to repay their rescuers with work. It was soon observed that neither of them knew anything about cooking, or the making of cloth. But Olt, on recovering some stamina, proved to be very strong, and as he was exceedingly good with his hands — he was an expert at spear fishing by the end of his first day — he was much valued, and soon mastered wood-working.

Iley claimed to be an assistant to a ninth-level librarian, with herb-wife skills, which explained her lack of homemaking skills. And though she was deemed ugly, she was respected as a scholar; she freely shared her herb-knowledge, as there is no trained physician here, as you know. She was also willing to work the Pillars of Destiny for village births, though she was no augur, but as the villagers agreed, one small shrimp is better than a handful of seawater, and so the pair was welcomed into this village.

Mouse burst in, "And this is where *you* came to us, and make the best food, and teach us as well as tell us stories."

"Not quite yet. Because island custom has it that all families must be sealed before the Snow Crane, God of the Abandoned, there was a village wedding which also made them part of the community. And when a phoenix feather dropped between them during the ritual, the shaman interpreted it as a sign that their union was blessed, and surely one of their children would bring greatness to the world, and the shaman appointed them a new branch of the Afan, or Feather clan, to acknowledge the propitious sign."

"A real phoenix feather? Can I see it?"

"A real phoenix feather. You can, but you must ask your mother if you may, for she keeps it."

"A phoenix feather. Of course it is an omen of greatness! Is that why everyone calls First Brother the future great one? I thought it was because he was born the Year of the Dragon. And all the heroes in the tales seem to be born the Year of the Dragon, or the Year of the Tiger."

"It is indeed the real reason. Though you will not hear the phoenix feather talked of directly, for everyone who witnessed it falling that day agreed that to boast of it would be to invite bad luck for temerity. So it became a village secret."

"I won't tell. I have never told anyone about our lessons with Father in defense."

"I know. Which is why you are hearing this story now. As for what happened after, Olt and Iley made their living as healer and a carver. And ten years later, their family began to increase, one, two —"

"One, two, and me."

"One, two, and you."

"First Brother Muinkanda. Mother told me it's because of him we have 'Kanda' as our generation name, for Kanda who first wrote The Twenty-Five Virtues, and Muin with the pronunciation for 'strong tree'."

"And so it is."

"Nobody in all three villages is better than First Brother with the wooden knife, except Father. And First Brother is as good with a spear as anyone, even the boys so big they're getting hair on their faces — he once spread a fish as long as he is. The whole village feasted off that fish!"

"I remember. It's good that you are proud of your brother. He is worthy of that pride."

"Second Brother Yskanda, born year of the Horse, got 'Ys', which means in the old language 'blessed'. Mama wants him to be a scholar."

"It is so. Your second brother has clever fingers, and a very fine eye."

"And I am me, Arikanda, with 'Ari' for peace, but I'm not very peaceable, which is why everyone in the family calls me Mouse. Born Year of the Dolphin. We will help First Brother on his path to greatness."

"You help one another because that is a virtue. But you ought to remember that the shaman never said 'their firstborn', though everyone assumes it because that is tradition, and as you say, the Year of the Dragon is always regarded as auspicious for those with ambition. So it could very well be First Brother whose path was signified by the fall of the phoenix feather, but his story is his story, not told yet. This is your parents' story, and my story is my story. Which someday you may learn, but not tonight."

"That was a good story. I'd like to hear it again. Especially the last part, when they escape the evil prince."

"Perhaps again, but there is a lesson after all. Which is: this story, and the phoenix feather, are your family secret, like your self-defense lessons. The three of you now know the truth about where you came from, and about why your parents never leave the village. Which is why, if anything should happen here and you find yourself separated from your family, you must make your way to any Snow Crane temple, and they will help you get to the great temple at Burning Rock Island. Remember that, the temple of the Snow Crane, God of the Abandoned, at Burning Rock Island. Remember, but never speak of it."

"I'll remember."

"Keep that vow. You have learned how people in the village all know what everyone else does, says, or thinks, if they've once told someone. Because if one person talks, and the second person only tells a third, and the third tells only a fourth . . . before you know it village gossip is overheard by someone who is paid to overhear such things, because nobles and royals tend to have very long memories for insults, and the deep purses to fund their grudges. Your mother will never say so, but her dreams are haunted by the fear of the Imperial Guard showing up and hauling her and your father off to be executed in Lotus Blossom Square, and you children forced to your hands and knees to scrub up their blood before being sentenced to bondage for the rest of your lives."

"I was going to ask if I could see the phoenix feather, but now I don't even want to. I like knowing Mother and Father were heroes, even better than all the tales of the gallant wanderers, but I won't talk about it ever, ever, ever.

ONE

MOUSE WOKE THE NEXT morning after dreams full of terrible images—her parents being chased by shadowy figures led by one wearing gold, and her mother kneeling in the surf with blood pouring down her face.

But they were heroes! Her father fighting a duel against an evil prince, that was heroic. Her mother putting the charms down to raise the fog, that was heroic, too. Also clever. Mouse had grown up hearing her mother called Ugly Iley, so the two words ran together. It was never mean. Her mother was well liked. The word "ugly" had become part of Mother's name, like Grandma Old Iley four houses away, and gossipy Auntie Fox-Ear Iley over in Autumn Sweetwater, the village on the other side of the big stream.

Mouse scowled up at the barely visible lashed bamboo poles holding the walls, and the layered fronds above, on which rain rustled and tapped. The noise was enough to cover the sounds of her brothers' breathing. She turned her head, and discovered that she was alone, their bedding folded away on the shelf.

In a heartbeat she flung off yesterday's shirt and pulled on the soft, much-washed shirt and pants that had been handed down to her from her brothers. She was small for her age, and ordinary in appearance. The village seldom saw her except when tagging after her brothers, so she was referred to as often as not (if she was spoken of at all) as Little Third by them. She had vague memories of hearing her name constantly when she was ill, *Arikanda, Arikanda*. Mother had told her once that they had done that to bring her luck and keep her in the world, but Mouse just remembered hearing that anxious calling while she was so ill. She much preferred being Mouse, which had no bad memories.

She pushed aside the door and looked out, smelling rain-drenched trees and soil. In the distance, the rice farmers sang as they planted.

Tax time! There was the hand cart that Ul Keg would take down to the boat. He'd be gone all day to take this half of the year's tax to the governor's manor, which meant cold food today. She might as well forage for wild fruits in the forest.

She stood in the open doorway, peering across the mushy red soil as she tried to shake the mood of those dreams. That story had already happened, except the last part, which was a warning. Nothing in her own life had changed. Work was always waiting, or as Auntie Fox-Ear Iley said, "Put down the rake in order to pick up the broom."

There was Father, helping to load baskets onto the cart, and Mother was at the other end of the house shaking out bedding. Though her back was bent, her face turned away, Mouse could see the rough, dark red scarring down the side of her face, corrugating as Mother smiled a greeting at two aunties lugging a basket between them, red mud caked up to their ankles.

Mouse tipped her head back. A few stars still shone there between the clouds. Did their alignment might indicate an auspicious day? "The stars only do so much," her mother often said. "You must do the rest."

Ul Keg said the same. Mouse's gaze strayed to the wiry monk who worked in spite of his sodden undyed garment sticking to his bony limbs, his muscles making his shaman tattoos writhe on his skin beneath his rolled and tied sleeves. The story rushed back into her mind as she sketched morning greetings in her father's and tutor's directions, then slunk up to her mother's side. It wasn't often her mother was alone.

When Mother's eyes turned her way, Mouse touched her

fingertips to her bowed forehead, the quick gesture of greeting customary in the villages—the brevity and carelessness of which grieved Iley in her secret heart. But she had braced herself to accept island ways before the scabs fell off her scars all those years ago.

"It seems you've something on your mind," Mother said softly as she caressed her daughter's broad, round forehead above the thick, straight brows so like her husband's.

"Ul Keg told me the story. Because I can keep secrets," Mouse whispered.

Mother's smile, which was never broad because of the scarring, vanished. "I know. Did you have a question?" Mother expected her daughter to ask to see the phoenix feather, as both boys had done.

But Mouse was thinking, *a* question? She had a thousand! She knew better than to spew them all out at once.

"*You* did it," Mouse whispered, as if the words could call forth imperial searchers from the broad-leafed trees surrounding them. She touched her cheeks. Her eyes stung—she knew that Mother's face sometimes hurt, even now. "You. Not a fire. Why?"

Mother's teak-colored eyes were still beautiful, though Mother only had one eyebrow, the other having been scraped off—it had never grown back. She dropped her head, and Mouse's next question withered inside of her: *Why didn't you tell the story?* The answer to that was obvious—because Mother hated it.

Mouse was going to take back her first blurted question, because it had hurt Mother. But then Mother spoke. "I will give you a true answer, though it might be like Second Brother's robe." Mother touched Mouse's shoulder. "Overlarge. To be grown into over time."

Mouse shivered a little, without knowing why.

"There are two reasons I did that, and neither of them is a *good* reason. First, I was desperately angry. You know what I have taught you about anger."

"That it is like fire, hot inside and destructive outside," Mouse said, hoping she wasn't about to be ordered to write out a passage about anger's fire from the ancients. She knew all those passages. Her memory for the written word, like Second Brother's, was excellent. Once she read a text and comprehended it, it stayed with her.

Mother raised a hand, and Mouse interrupted herself. "But Mother, it was not your fault!"

"There are those who would disagree with you, all of them in the imperial city," Mother said, and because she was a scholar, she could not resist making this a teaching moment. "What did the First Sage Empress write about the sun and moons?"

Mouse recited, "The three together make up equal sides of a whole, just as do night and day, each with its own strengths. Men are like the sun, women like the moons, both with powers that balance the world."

Mother nodded. "Therefore, they ought to be equal before the law, to bring balance to the empire. And so she gave women the right to sit to the Imperial Examination, to own a house, land, a business—and to take a consort, or not to marry at all."

Mouse suppressed a sigh, hoping Mother would get past what she'd already heard so many times, and get to why she had hurt her own face.

Mother said, "You must remember that Kanda's teaching about order and hierarchy, placing the father as the king of the household, is tradition with the weight of centuries. Very hard to overcome, all these years later. Especially when tradition is so important in all other ways. And few wish to relinquish power."

Mouse listened, struggling to comprehend.

Mother saw that, and though she loathed the entire subject—it never failed to make her feel sick with residual guilt—she forced herself to speak, lest her daughter inherit that guilt. "Now that you understand that, we come to my reasons for doing what I did. One of the traditions the First Sage Empress tried to end is the belief that a woman's most important quality is her beauty. There are those who still believe that. And not just men," Mother added. "When we landed on the beach that day, all I wanted was to get rid of mine, for it had ruined so very much."

"But that was that horrible prince, not you," Mouse said,

her voice quavering.

Mother cupped Mouse's face with her hands. "I am so very glad you understand that. But there are many grown people who believe *me* at fault. And so I did what I did, and our true origins must remain secret." Mother's voice was husky.

Mouse struggled against this new riptide of emotions. She could see that the question hurt her mother, and so she reached for another of those many questions—one that wasn't about the prince, or Mother's onetime beauty. "Can you tell me about Scholar Alk Bemti? My grandmother." She tasted the word in wonder. Other village children had grandmothers and grandfathers and blood-uncles and aunts. The Afan children didn't.

Only now, it seems she did. Or had. "The story. About the wings. Is it real?"

Mother smiled a little as she lifted her gaze to the distance, as if she could see beyond the shoreline hidden behind the dense forest. "How could I know? I was not there. This I do know," she said, looking down at Mouse. "Your grandmother was born the Year of the Eagle, and she had great Essence strength."

Iley touched hand to heart and forehead. "It is the Alk gift, which is rare. If anyone had the strength to work a transformation charm, it was my mother. However, if she became a bird, that shape would be forever, for a bird cannot work a charm in reverse. I hope that if she did work a charm and flew away, she made it to another island to dwell in peace—and I have waited ever since for a dream to tell me that I ought to perform the rituals for her death, but it has not come. So I pray for her life in the world, that it be peaceful and long."

Though they had a small shrine in their house, as did everyone, Mouse already knew that they alone of the villagers had no actual graves to pray at when that time of year rolled around, but she'd always heard that that it was because her parents had come from an island farther south, where their ancestral shrine was.

Mouse thought of her own jumbled, confusing dreams. "Would she come in a dream?"

"I think so," Mother said. "I remember she used to have

dreams in which her own mother spoke to her. And my sister grew up talking more to ghosts than to the living." Mother looked down into Mouse's earnest face and added quickly, "Many thought my sister mad, and that my mother's dreams were mere wishes, though she was a greatly respected scholar. Since there is no proof either way to point at or to hold—"

Mother had never ceased looking around. She stopped suddenly, and smiled as a village woman came their way, clutching her stomach. Obviously needing medicine.

"I won't tell," Mouse whispered. And she pelted off, the mud warm between her bare toes as she sought her brothers.

There was so much to think about! But a lot of it was grownup stuff, like that about beauty, which Mouse knew she did not have. Nor had she ever wanted it. She had once overheard one of the village aunties saying that Second Brother had it for all three of them. People sometimes stopped him to pat his cheeks or caution him to be careful of scars, which he endured patiently, while some of the village children snickered. And there was a beautiful girl in the northern village who had to stay inside, and never run free lest she get scrapes that might leave scars. She was being taught dull things like how to flirt her fan and to embroider, for Mouse had heard that her parents hoped to make a fine marriage for this girl among the wealthy merchants in the town.

Boring! Mother was right. Beauty was stupid.

She caught on furtive movement at the other end of the cottage, which was no more than a frond-roofed string of rooms, each with its door to the outside, as were all the village cottages. She turned her head in time to see First Brother dragging Second Brother behind the cottage.

A plan? A prank? She ducked around the corner, gathered her inner fire, and leaped. One, two light touches of her bare feet to the spreading branch of a banyan to guide her, then to the ridgepole. She ran lightly along the pole, avoiding the overlapping fronds of the roof lest her footfalls be heard below. She ducked around the rain collectors with her head low, so that no one below would catch her silhouette.

Two years ago, Spring Festival had been livened by entertainers from another island, kin to someone in one of the villages. Mouse was elated by the girl her own age who walked a single strand of lianas strung between two roofs while juggling torches. If Mouse could learn that, she might be able to balance on a flying sword—like in the hero tales! Later on, Mouse found the girl eating candied hawthorns, and asked if she could learn that.

The girl laughed. "The elders put us on a plank as soon as we start walking. When you can balance one leg, then the other, on two metal chopsticks side by side, you can start learning tricks. First leaps, then a somersault. When you can do those, you can start working with objects, and then get rid of the plank and walk the lianas."

Easier said than done! At first she had fallen a lot, inevitably ripping the worn clothing she had inherited from both brothers, but Second Brother had patiently mended the tears for her, for his thin fingers were so nimble.

Mouse practiced on a bundled segment of three inter-twined lianas that had crashed down in a storm. She'd hauled it to rest on two boulders in the forest, and though—after much failure—she could run along it, and even leap and land, she couldn't do a somersault along it without falling, much less swap the pole out for anything as narrow as two eat-sticks.

But though she was no closer to being able to juggle torches while suspended over the village gathering square, she'd found that her balance had so improved that she could do things like run along ridgepoles, and leap to the roof of Father's work shed adjacent to the family house, landing lightly enough not to thump on the overlapping fronds that covered the roof.

First and Second Brothers never looked up. Mouse crouched down as First pushed Second against the shed wall, talking earnestly. "You said you want new brushes and books. Ayah, here's your chance to choose one yourself!"

"But . . ."

"But what? We know we're as fast in our boat as any fisher, with both of us working. We'll certainly be faster than Ul Keg in the village boat weighed down with all the tax baskets. If he can go and come in a day, so can we."

"But we're forbidden . . ." Second Brother said softly, torn between awareness of the rules and a longing to go.

"We're forbidden to do a lot of things we do anyway. Dive from Giant Rock? We've been doing that for *years*. They say that so the babies don't try, and crack their heads on the rocks below. We've taken out the steel, and haven't killed ourselves sparring."

Here Second Brother sighed, for he loathed weapons practice. He only sneaked the steel because First Brother and Mouse wanted to.

First Brother went on, "They forbid it because they think we'll get lost, but if we keep Ul Keg in sight, how can we get lost?"

"First Brother, I don't know . . ."

First Brother said in a coaxing tone, "Think of all those new books to choose from! And inks that you don't have to make yourself. Imagine choosing one you *want*. Not something they think is good for you."

First Brother waited, and it was as clear to him as it was to Mouse up above that Second Brother was wavering. Born the Year of the Horse, Second Brother had what Ul Keg called the horse's sees-the-wind eye when it came to the subject of drawing. With the perfect timing honed after a lifetime of coaxing Second, First Brother said, "I'll give you my moon." He sketched the shape of a brass coin in the air. "*Think* how much you can get for that!"

Mouse's jaw dropped. She understood now. They were going all the way to the island's capital, the harbor at the island's southern tip? *Without her?*

Oh, no, they weren't.

She dropped down, startling both. First Brother scowled her way, aware that once again, she'd managed to sneak up on them, though he'd been on the watch.

"I'm going, too," she stated—bobbing her head in respect to her elders, but her tone made it clear she was opening negotiations.

"No, you're not, Mouse." First Brother's heavy, straight brows drew together into a line. "You're too small."

How she hated hearing that! Her own heavy, straight brows—the only feature she shared with First Brother—met in a line over her nose. "I helped build that boat. I should get to use it, too. And I'll bail. Both ways. Won't ask to touch the sail. And you two can have my tinnies."

She was not a good saver. The fact that she had a couple of the smallest bits of money — it took a lot of tinnies to equal one moon — left from her last birthday was simply because she had no way to spend it. But any time there was a chance of someone else going where money could be spent, she asked for good things to eat.

First Brother, knowing that, scowled in perplexity. "That will leave you with nothing, so there's no point in going if you can't buy any of the snacks they sell on the street. Why do you want to go?"

"To *see!* I want to see the ships in the harbor, and any dancers or clowns, and look at all the people." Maybe there would be gallant wanderers, like in the hero tales!

First Brother, fighting a retreating action, muttered, "You'll get us caught because you'll be behind in lessons."

She negated *that* with a swipe of her hand. "Done. Actually ahead."

First Brother turned suspiciously to Second, who said, "True. It's sloppy," he added, his artistic soul harrowed at the waste of ink on the bark-and-rice paper they made so laboriously.

"I hate writing," Mouse stated. "It's so slow. Once I read a thing, I know it. I don't need to copy it out. I do lessons ahead so I can play, and they think I'm working."

First Brother sighed. Mouse had never been Little Sister, though everywhere else on the island, a young sister was either Little Sister or her number, if there were more than two sisters. First and Second Brothers treated her as a third brother, so she'd always just been . . . Mouse.

He was not given to reflection about such things, but he was scrupulous about an elder brother's duty. Sister or brother, it was his responsibility to look out for the younger ones. But he would be fifteen next turn of the year, practically a man, and in his nearly-a-man eyes Mouse was a liability, being the smallest.

Yet what she said was also true. She stood there frowning direfully, wearing clothes he and Second Brother had cast off, her hair invariably bound up in a boy's topknot, which was easier to drill in. She was the quickest of the three in evasion and escape, but her feet were small. Her wrists were small, instead of knobby and bony like his and Second's. Yet you couldn't call her weak, as she held her own in scrapping. She could even beat Second Brother, who tended to get distracted by some bird, or the patterns of sunlight through leaves. Though she was five years younger, somehow she was harder to watch over than Second, three years younger.

He sighed out his frustration, hating it when things weren't clear one way or the other. So, as was habit, he treated her as another brother, and turned his glare onto her. "You bail. Both ways."

Though she knew her arms and shoulders would be screaming by the end of the journey, especially if the wind got up — and that would be the least of it if they were caught — she bounced on her toes for joy. Adventure awaited!

As it was, their adventure nearly didn't happen, as Ul Keg had not waited around once the last basket of tightly rolled floor mats was loaded into the hand cart. He'd pulled the harness over his shoulders, a couple of men gave pushes from behind, and he was off down the gentle slope toward the inlet where the village's bigger boats bobbed, anchored to the sea floor by bound rocks.

He reached the broad beach, testing the wind absently. A good sign that the Phoenix Moon god favored his journey — and his decision to stay quiet. The wind imps were blowing at a promising angle; he seldom put out fruits to propitiate them, as did the fishers who followed the Snow Crane God, but he saw no harm in that practice, as those fruits fed the weaker among the winged population. He liked to see the thriving of all living things.

He shoved the cart into the gentle ripples, and hauled the baskets one by one over the gunwale. The floor mats, which were the primary production of the village for outside trade, were made of the tough, waxy blue-weed that grew in the spring estuaries emptying to the sea. Cultivated for centuries, they grew in a variety of colors from a deep indigo to the pale blue of a summer dawn, and were woven into pleasing patterns. Once they'd provided their tax, any extras brought a decent price from their seller in the harbor, which enabled them to purchase the rare items they couldn't make.

Ul Keg worked quickly, his long monk's braid tied around his forehead with a cloth to keep it from getting caught under his elbows or between baskets. He distributed the baskets evenly along the gunwale on both sides, and set sail before the sun had moved a finger above the sea. A tug and his sail clattered to its full length. He tied it off, and the overlapping slats caught the morning breeze, pulling the boat to the water. It began to surge out beyond the inlet. Once the individual trees merged to a dark green whole, he pulled a bamboo hat over his head, and peered under its brim—

And there it was, as expected, the boat he'd been watching the children build all season. Letting out a sigh, he pulled a seaweed-wrapped roll of rice and dried fish from his shoulder sling, and ate as he mentally reorganized the day.

The three children had also set sail. Their boat, made by themselves, was filled with slow leaks that they hadn't been able to find and patch.

Mother and Ul Keg had taught the children about Essence, but it had only taken with Mouse, and that during a terrible fever. She seemed to be the only one with the aptitude and the interest—and her interest was, at best, sporadic. Mouse had been scamping her Essence studies as she was impatient of discipline and outright loathed the grinding repetition that mastering Essence charms required. Now she regretted not knowing any charms for water, the toughest element to control. Light was the easiest, however useless for much besides entertaining her brothers with flickering images.

The wood of course still floated, but letting water build up was not only uncomfortable to sit in, it dragged the boat. Mindful of her promise, Mouse picked up the half-gourds and began bailing, as First Brother skimmed the boat close to the shore in hopes they would not be visible from the water the way they would if they pushed out farther into the sea.

No one in the village knew of Ul Keg's altar on one of the highest points of the rocky hill at the very north of the island. When he had shown up, blown ashore by a storm, his welcome had been assured when he made it clear he was willing to bow to the authority of the Shaman of the Snow Crane god.

From his private shrine, where he could sing his Sun Sutras in peace, he saw many things—such as the children building their boats over the last year (three sank upon being launched). He saw Olt travel once a month down to a secluded place on the shoreline to practice with the fine steel sword he'd gone back to find at low tide after his and Iley's recovery, and secreted in a hollow tree midway between his house and that secluded training ground. More regularly Ul Keg saw Olt take all three of his children there to learn self-defense, unknown to the rest of the village.

Two

ON THE GREAT IMPERIAL maps, the empire is shaped like a dragon.

Imai Island is a speck of ink amid a scattering of specks as countless as a field of stars, southwest of the great islands that make up the empire's middle section. As island scholars say, Imai lies somewhere in the middle of the great dragon's left hind claw. The island boasts one good bay, which is both harbor and provincial capital.

Imai is one of many such outposts considered career death for the ambitious, but its governor, who preferred an easy life as far as possible from the imperial court, was content to be assigned there.

The silent chase took most of the morning, the children hugging the coast, partly to remain as unseen as possible, but also to avoid the bigger waves farther out. Their boat was the biggest they could contrive, but it required two to sail. Their arms were not yet long enough to tend both sail and tiller, much less bail.

First Brother watched sea and sail as he tended the latter, the favored job. Second Brother worked the tiller, his attention distracted by the deep waters below, but he obediently guided them as First Brother commanded. Though First Brother's palms were callused from sword drill, tending the hempen rope raised blisters on his hands by the time Ul Keg's boat was seen curving between larger boats as he headed into the small harbor. He cinched the clattering sail up, then dabbled his hands in the salt water as the tide carried the boat up to the shore.

That harbor might look small to those used to the grander islands, but to the children it was magnificent, like a wide-mouthed bowl filled with all manner of ships.

They prudently decided not to enter the harbor directly, but instead chose to beach just outside the northmost promontory. There was no chance they'd go unnoticed, much less be permitted to leave their boat at the pier reserved for tax payers.

It was three tired, hungry children who dragged their boat up onto the strand, the custom among islanders from the sparsely populated north end. They looked back at their boat, which was well above the high tide mark, then started the long walk along the curve of the peninsula that sheltered the harbor.

Presently they crested the last hill and saw the entire harbor laid out below, with two actual streets running parallel to the shoreline, bisected by a number of very short streets more or less perpendicular. In the center rose the governmental manor with its sweeping rooflines stacked one above the other in the manner of nobles' palaces. At each up-tilted end small figures of mythic animal guardian statues posed, the maximum amount permitted the governor's rank. Mouse stared, awed by the strangeness of tubular roof tiles instead of the fronds she had grown up with in the three villages. Second Brother also noticed the glazed roof tiles, his gaze lingering on the graceful, textured patterns they made — and how the governor's manor stood out with its tiles of both gray and blue.

The garrison would be nearby, First Brother thought — he had no interest in roofs, other than to keep out rain. "We need to watch for Ul Keg's boat," he said.

"I see it." Second Brother pointed to a haphazard jumble of craft to one side of the official pier, where those bringing taxes were permitted to anchor.

"We all do," First Brother said. "I meant, when he leaves, we need to be right behind him, or we'll be caught for certain."

They knew being caught meant a beating for breaking bounds. Even worse — for those rare thrashings never really hurt much — the real disappointment in Father's voice when he lectured them beforehand. Mostly they tried to avoid trouble, but today all three understood that they would accept the risk.

First Brother spotted the Imperial Army garrison behind the manor. Turning to his siblings, he said, "Remember what I said." And he pelted away, mentally shaking them off.

Second Brother had already forgotten him. He bounced up and down, trying to spot signs or banners for the scholars' street. The bright light scintillated off the humid haze, winking off rare bits of metal, distracting him. He needed to get closer, so he, too, began to run.

Mouse waited until First Brother had rounded a curve, then set out after him. While she wasn't as fast in a short sprint as her brother with his lengthening legs, none of them — including Mouse — had ever noticed that she was able to keep up with them, despite as often as not being lumbered with weapons, or baskets, or tools as she trailed behind. That had been the usual agreement these past couple of years: if they included her, she was stuck being the porter. As a result, she had built up endurance, enhanced by her conscious focus on maintaining Essence in her belly and core.

None of them had been to the harbor, due to their mother's anxiety about being discovered; each had a primary goal. First Brother's was to find the garrison, and watch the training to figure out, if he could, why he still was kept at home though nearly fifteen, when most boys aimed for the Military Examination and army or navy command went to be tested for training. Fifteen was as late as they would take anyone, which meant he had only one year before it would be too late.

Mouse knew that, and as she wanted to see First Brother set his foot upon the path of greatness, she shadowed him with all the stealth she'd been learning since the older boys began leaving her behind whenever they wanted to do something she deemed interesting. Interesting invariably meant anything they considered her too small for.

First Brother ran hard until the last slope, where traffic began to thicken, then slowed to a walk as he caught his breath.

His attention remained entirely on those walls, so he never noticed his sister ten or so people back, her head swiveling constantly as she took in the carts full of fascinating items, the people wearing not just the cotton and hemp she saw every day, but cotton interwoven with silk.

They both eyed the guards walking about in pairs, the captains in blue, their broad hats with long feathers and tassels bobbing. The governor believed that his guards' appearances bolstered his face. A governor with face enough to inspire awe, he said often, was the best method of deterring crime. And the captains cooperated with the enthusiasm of those who liked tassels dangling from their hats and their sword sheaths, the way nobles wore them.

Mouse veered out of their paths, as did everyone else. To her, they were now the inimical eyes of that terrible prince, who would catch and kill her parents if he could.

She dodged around slow carts hauled by oxen, and adults burdened with baskets and rolls of goods. She saw two horses, both ridden by captains wearing side-slashed long robes with broad sashes. They did look very dashing. Perhaps First Brother might be one of these one day, and perform some deed so heroic he would be granted an imperial pardon for their parents, living up to the promise of that phoenix feather. She couldn't imagine any greater merit, outside of the fantastic exploits of the hero tales. But she had never actually seen a hero. Or a ghost. She heard about them, she warded them like everyone else, but aside from Grandma Kau, who talked with ghosts every day as she worked in her garden (and Mouse had over-heard some gossipy neighbors saying once she had been demon-struck in the head as a girl), no one in the village had seen one.

Mouse was so distracted by these thoughts and the interesting sights that caused them, she nearly lost sight of her brother—and her goal. But then he stopped at the public fount-ain to slurp up handfuls of water. When he moved away, she bolted to the fountain to drink as well, then pelted after him, slowing when she spotted him moving adjacent to the high wall on the north side of the governor's manor, where the garrison was attached.

Behind the back gate, a training corral had been set up, marked off by a bamboo fence. First Brother slowed when he looked into the yard and saw boys lined up in rows, wooden swords in hand as they moved through familiar sequences.

Mouse slowed, ducking and eeling around elbows as she neared the fence. She expected — as did First Brother — to see amazing martial displays, but what she saw was drill, and disappointingly slow at that. In fact, the sloppiness would have earned cuffs from Father for any of them.

Losing interest, she ran off, as First Brother watched with growing resentment. Those boys looked older than he was, doing drills he'd mastered by the time he was seven. *Mouse* could take any two of these boys, without even trying! So why was he being kept back . . .

We will leave him simmering in a welter of questions he could not answer, as we follow Mouse around to the east side, poetically termed the autumn side by those above a certain rank, and then to south or summer side, which was — like nearly all manor houses — the front entrance.

She stopped at the fountain again, hand suspended as she blinked at the ice-blue glow of a powerful charm purifying the water that sprayed up from beneath the ground. She dashed her hands into the cool liquid and drank, making a conscious effort to fill her empty belly with water. Then she chose a spot from which to survey the world.

There was the Justice Building with its gigantic gong that anyone seeking justice might ring, but woe to anyone with a frivolous complaint. She glimpsed two of the guards on duty, with their hooked spears that could be reversed and used to beat those sentenced to punishment.

Her gaze swept past the throngs to the scintillation of working charms everywhere, and to observe the street hawkers and the parade of important people going to the Summer Gate of the governor's manor, as on the west side, off the main street, Second Brother stood before a shop, entranced with brushes of a fineness he had never seen. He made his own brushes, of course. In the remote villages, they all did.

Books were forgotten. Here were brushes that begged to be used for fine letters and decorative elements, the part of scholarship he loved most, as most of the people around him spoke Imperial the way his mother and tutor spoke during lessons. Second Brother thought of it as the scholarly language, a marvel to hear it in other voices besides Ul Keg's, Mother's, and occasionally Father's.

And here beckoned pots of colors in a range he had not been able to imagine, no matter how far he ranged, and how many herbs, minerals, shells, or bark he harvested and pounded and mixed to experiment with. Ink stones, too, providing ink of a silky smoothness that made his throat hurt to see.

Over against one side the ultimate seduction: a table for scholars to test a small array of brushes and inks. He lurked about, suspecting (rightly) that if he presumed before any of these grand people in silk, he would be chased away, and probably booted for his temerity.

But patience rewards those who wait, so Ul Keg had cautioned them. Eventually the table was abandoned as a knot of teenage scholars-in-training stood about, admiring a calligraphed wall hanging.

Second Brother chose a brush, dipped it in the pure-hued ink, and tried a character. The ink bled and smeared. It was so much smoother than his own inks, he understood that he had to gather less on the brush and sketch with a quicker stroke. He paused to breathe properly, and moving from the shoulder in the proper form his mother had instilled in him, he began anew.

The character for water. It came out so smooth, so elegant! Then that for sea, even finer. Building on those, the characters for rain, then for tempest — the ink began to dry out just when he wanted it to, so he twisted the brush before lifting, leaving a gracefully articulated tail, each individual hair differentiated —

"Get out of here, urchin," a teenage voice cracked in the island language. "Who do you think you are, bringing your stinking commoner dirt in a place for —"

Second Brother ducked his head into his shoulders, and the hand he'd expected swatted the top of his head, instead of clapping his ear. He turned to bolt, but an older, more authoritative voice ordered, in Imperial, "Wait."

The big apprentice in blue and gray shut his mouth before

he'd finished his insult, and the teenage scholars in their plainer gray-blue robes faded back, heads bowed, hands pressed to thighs.

To Second Brother's amazement, a bearded scholar with purple edging his silver-gray robe stepped up, stroking his pointed beard as he eyed Second Brother's letters, then asked in Imperial, "Who taught you to write?"

Second Brother bit back the words, *My mother*. He had always thought it unfair that Ul Keg was regarded as his master, though it was Mother who conducted most of his lessons.

That was until he heard The Story. "My master, Ul Keg, Monk of the Phoenix Moon," Second Brother replied in the same scholarly Imperial, using servant-to-master form, and hastily bowed low.

The master *hmm*ed again, a higher note of approval. The urchin's grasp of Imperial was slightly quaint, but excellent, and he had good manners, even if his clothing looked like something that would shame a rat catcher. "This is court hand, and a very fine style. The tail on *tempest*, this dashing stroke on *rain*, almost arrogant, but just short of it. Was your monk palace-trained?"

"I don't know, esteemed master," Second Brother replied. "All we know is, he is in our village on his Wander."

"Ah," the master exclaimed, looking more closely at Second Brother.

Under the dirt, he was well made, even beautiful, with glossy black hair and eyes the color of teakwood. "That explains it. The wind-sweep in the tail of your tempest is quite fine. I could point out many small errors, but there is no doubt: you have good training, perhaps even Talent." The listeners could hear the capital letter. "Where did you say you were from?"

"Sweetwater North," Second Brother said. "My family wishes to send me to the Temple of the Way next year," he added.

"Archive scholars," the master said, eyeing with disapprobation Second Brother's worn, carefully mended clothing of hemp and cotton. "You would be wasted there, for you'll end up making copies of *The Five Elements* and *The Dialects of*

Enlightenment for monks whose only interest in art is the 'art' of forcing as many words onto a scroll as possible to save a bit of paper. No, no, you must talk to the head of your clan, and if he sends you to me soon, I will waive the apprentice fee, if you contract to give me five years after you pass the Imperial State Examination. Which you surely will, if I have the training of you soon, before you settle into bad habits that I must waste a year undoing."

"I am unworthy," Second Brother managed, bowing even more deeply.

"That's for me to determine," the master retorted, but in a genial voice. Someone had taken the effort to teach him proper manners, though he was obviously from one of the many tiny, squalid villages pocking the island. His good manners, his talent, and his beauty would guarantee employment from the upper ranks, who were notoriously choosy when hiring scholars. "Your name?"

"Afan Yskanda."

Afan, a good, solid name, numerous in the various branches of service but rarely high, which the master regarded as more of an attribute than not. He had enough presumptuous pups of nobles on his hands. But no low name, either, which would inevitably cause dispute among the competitive youngsters when his back was turned. And "Kanda" as a generation name suggested a conservative family, well versed in the rites and rules. "Your father?"

"Afan Olt."

"A carver, eh? Ayah, put the question to him, and come find me at Bankan Manor, fifth house on the Street of Orioles, west of the governor's manor. I am Chief Scholar Bankan Evnet."

Second Brother bowed again, more deeply, and on seeing so many eyes on him (not all in approbation, especially from those competitive teens) he bowed again and again, retreating a couple steps each time, until he could turn and run.

Float, actually, or so it felt. Five years! He had a vague sense that five years without pay—that is, anything he earned going to his master—would put him all the way into his twenties before he could earn enough to buy his own brushes and paper, but . . . at the temple, he would have earned next to nothing all his life, the tradeoff being a library always there to be explored, and supplies ready to hand.

He wafted past the displays of books, his mind filled with brushes, and colors, and when he reached a more modest display whose brushes were not as exquisite (but still far better than his), he stopped and pored intently over each one in the ceramic vase labeled with the price he could afford.

That purchase at last made, he crossed a narrow alley and began working his way back toward the governor's manor along the parallel street, until a display of silken tassels caught his eye. These were strictly forbidden to any below a certain rank, none of whom lived at the north end of the island, so Second Brother had never seen an actual tassel, though he had seen many illustrations.

He slowed, lingered, and touched, shivering at the cool slither of silk over his fingers. As he peered closely at the glistening twists, he was vaguely aware of a shout rising from scarcely a hundred paces away — where, unknown to him, First Brother was learning a very hard lesson.

First Brother had initially found himself hemmed in at the fence by the sudden arrival of a group of teens a year or so older than he, who began commenting disparagingly on the form, strength, brains, and even looks of the boys sweating under the drill captain's merciless eye. The boys all spoke with the same accent Father used, the military version of Imperial — quick, blunt.

Their pungent critiques were all prefaced by names, or nicknames, which First Brother shrugged off, having come from the end of the island where everyone was known to everyone else by name, if little else.

All he knew was, these criticisms were just. Maybe even too easy. "That one? You say he's had two years of drill? I would have thought two weeks," he commented as the boy he scorned dropped his wooden sword, earning a whack across the shoulder blades from the drill captain.

First Brother offered two more similar comments before he became aware that he was the only speaker. He glanced to the side, startled at the narrow glares of affront and outright anger.

The loose crowd had drawn together into a pack. First Brother took an inadvertent step away.

Too late.

"So, you're an expert, are you? A hero sent by the gods to instruct us all?" the leader said in a light tone that First Brother did not mistake for friendly.

"How about a demonstration. Teach us, O Hero," said another.

"I . . . I . . ." First Brother swallowed in a suddenly dry throat. "I don't have practice weapons." He made a fair assumption at bravado, but his voice sounded high to his own ears.

The boys' laughter crashed against his ears, harrowing his heart.

"Oh, surely a hero needs no weapons," one boy cooed from the back, as the group moved to ring First Brother.

And with a shout of "Let's give him a lesson in proper manners," from their leader, they charged, yelling a war cry.

Second Brother didn't hear it, but Mouse did.

She was already boiling with fury.

She had gone down the street away from the manor, enthralled by the spectacle around her. She was drawn first to the sound of a storyteller who had quite a crowd gathered round. The man gestured as he chanted his tale . . . of a gallant wanderer! A woman sat nearby with a drum and a small gong plus a variety of other items which she struck or stroked, evoking sounds as the man related the end of a fight between the famous wanderer Waoji Lion's Mane and an evil villain of some sort.

Unfortunately, by the time Mouse had squeezed and elbowed her way into the crowd the story was just ending — and the storyteller and partner were passing the hat. Mouse had nothing to contribute, of course, so she could hardly ask for another story. She turned away, but promised herself to come back.

She moved away, and found herself alone in a world of fascination, from the charms to the trained songbirds in wicker cages to the richly decorated palanquins moving back and forth, some with servants in matching silk walking before, with banners, drums, and a man in front banging a loud gong. Behind the palanquin marched rows of men wearing bright silk military robes with broad sashes, and carrying spears.

It was before one of these last approached that the world changed, drawing her from theater to real, when the man with the gong was not satisfied to bellow, "Make way! Make way!" as he clashed his gong with a metal mallet.

He kicked a crippled blind beggar who wasn't moving fast enough from the street below a shrine to the Snow Crane, sending the person tumbling over the paved stones, a tangle of thin limbs. Then the man uttered a hoarse laugh as he walked on by.

Mouse stared, burning at the injustice. In Sweetwater North, aiding the disabled was a sure merit, smiled on by gods and ancestors. There but for fortune could go you — if not in this life, surely the next.

Mouse could do nothing for the beggar, now crawling painfully toward the shrine. She bent over and said, "Can I help you?"

She repeated it two or three times before the beggar turned milky-white eyes her way, then scuttled in the opposite direction, toward the relative shelter of the shrine.

Mouse had been holding her breath against the beggar's stench. Feeling foolish, she backed away. As the gong echoed down the street, she wished she knew charms for boils, or itches, or windy guts. Whoever was in the palanquin did not so much as lift the curtain by a finger, which made Mouse add that unknown person to her internal curse.

She had no incense, nor so much as a tinnie to buy a thumb's worth, but she bowed hastily five times before the shrine as she whispered a prayer to the Snow Crane, God of the Abandoned, on behalf of that beggar. Then she scooped all the indignation still simmering inside her, and sent it after that man with the gong with an unspoken curse for him to suffer a dose of watery bowels.

After that she ran, remembering her initial errand to follow First Brother. She slowed when she reached the garrison and spied movement through the bamboo fencing at the north end. Well used to avoiding local bullies around the Sweetwater villages, she recognized the gloating anger in the voices: some-one was getting tromped.

She was used to First Brother being the toughest in village boy scrapping. This last year he'd finally bested the three villages' worst bullies, the two big, mean sons of a fisher from Sweetwater East at the island's tip.

Shock burned through her, hot, then cold, when she rounded the fence corner and spotted First Brother in the midst of . . . seven, no, nine. Nine against one! First Brother's clothes were covered with dust, and the dark splatter of blood from his nose.

Mouse swept her gaze over the attackers, seeing blood in two faces. So First Brother had gotten in two good hits. But he was swaying—he'd clearly taken too many. Nine against one!

Tucking her head down, she began to run.

THREE

UL KEG ALSO HEARD the yelling, though it was faint within the first court of the manor. The long line had been shuffling forward in the hot sun as the tax collector's agents inspected every offering, and then passed the bearer to the scribes for an exact accounting to be written up in the Imperial Account Book, a copy of which would be duly sent along to the capital, once the tax gatherers had taken their share, and the governor his.

Ul Keg had passed the time watching people come and go, until he drew near to the broad wall on which official notices were posted. It never would do to demonstrate too much interest in those posters given pride of place at the end of the display, each poster edged with the bright yellow that represented imperial gold.

The most avoided of all was the Capital List. Though according to law everyone from high to low was expected to be on the watch for, and report, anyone on that list, common people for generations had passed down the hard-won wisdom that it *never* brought good luck to get involved with noble or imperial affairs, especially turning in "criminals" whose crimes smacked of politics.

Ul Keg had been in charge of village tax delivery since his arrival in the three Sweetwater villages, as everyone trusted monks. Usually with reason, as they were forbidden to earn or own money. He had been able to scan the capital list each half-year.

Forgiveness was rare. Capital crimes tended to be forever, one's name removed only at death. The list was long. But the island's governor was lazy, dedicated to his comfort. Ul Keg had seen within a couple of visits that the governor would make the least possible effort—such as only posting only the first page of the list as new names were added, and older names dropped down to later pages. After all, a sizable portion of those he governed did not even read, and in any case the vast majority of capital crimes were committed in the imperial city, or on other islands at unimaginable distances.

On Ul Keg's first tax trip, his heart had hammered sharply when he side-eyed the list and right there, midway down the second column were the names Danno and Alk Hanu, the list of crimes headed, as usual, with treason.

The next year, the names had dropped off, replaced by a new crop of names.

But twenty years ago, news had reached the outer islands that Empress Teyan had died, and there was a new emperor. Ul Keg had scarcely breathed as he read past the glorious rhetoric surrounding Emperor Guiyan's declaration of the new era name that would begin with the next New Year's Two Moons: Peaceful Endeavor. There, at end of the proclamation, was the new emperor's birth name, which would never again be used in public: Jehan Enjai.

With a renewed fervency, Ul Keg had searched the capital list, to see if the new emperor had restored the names of Danno and Alk Hanu.

They were not there. He read it through twice more, slowly. Still not there. Though it would never do to become complacent. It was only practical to assume that in the duel for the succession, in allying with, imprisoning, or contriving the deaths of the rest of the imperial progeny, Enjai had forgotten his old grudge.

The names had not reappeared on that list. Ul Keg wiped his sweaty face, hiding a smile of relief.

That was when he registered the angry bray of boyish

voices. His attention sharpened. It probably had nothing to do with his charges, but the age range of those voices matched the Afan children, and he knew youth. If there was something going on among their peers, they would no doubt be drawn to watch.

He debated leaving the line, then was beckoned forward.

"Ah," exclaimed the Chief Tax Inspector, a short paunchy fellow whose carefully cultivated mustaches hung down below his jowls on either side. "The Phoenix Moon Monk from the north, is it not?"

Ul Keg put his palms together and bowed. "Chief Inspector."

"You're still here?" the man asked cheerily. "I thought when you monks were sent a-begging as ul-seekers, it was only for a year or two."

"We wander as our god wills," Ul Keg said, too gently to be perceived as correcting the man. "Some for a year, some for twenty. Each follows a different path. I have not been called back."

The Chief Inspector had no interest in temple matters of any sort, but he liked monks because they never argued or gave him trouble. He turned to his assistant with a lordly air. "The mats sent by the northerners are always the best quality. Merely count them. No need to take them all out to inspect each one. It's late, the line is long, and virtue ought to be rewarded, eh?"

Ul Keg, being a monk, was not expected to offer bribes. But he knew a hint when he heard one, and at once thanked the Chief Inspector, bowing three times as if to a lord, and the Chief Inspector beamed at this mark of respect before the line of waiting eyes.

The result was, the inspectors bowed to their chief and turned to the next tribute, the scribe stamped the Sweetwater villages' entry, making it official, and Ul Keg was free to take the rest of his delivery to their middleman, who would have their earnings from last autumn's delivery, from which money he would buy items the villagers had asked for.

But first he would take a quick look. Just in case.

He withdrew, trying not to be hasty enough to catch idle eyes. The noise had come from the training yard outside of the actual garrison court, which he was fairly certain had been First Brother's destination.

This was about the time that Mouse charged.

She slowed a couple of steps, taking an extra breath or two to assess the ring of attackers. Three hard years of being the smallest, the tag-along, the target for those Sweetwater East boys, and hard training from First Brother and Father had taught her a lot about the most often used attacks and defenses. She had also seen how those attacks and defenses acted upon others.

She had very little Essence left in her core after that long morning toil, and her prayer, with nothing to eat or drink since morning. There wouldn't be much Essence in her blows.

So she had to make what she had count. And — as a couple of the big boys slapped First Brother back and forth — she saw how to do it.

She began once again to run, picking up speed before she hunched her head down into her shoulders and stiffened her arms at her sides. A glance, a side step to adjust her angle of approach, and . . . *smash!*

She head-butted squarely into the lower back of the leader, at an angle that knocked him into two others standing shoulder to shoulder. The three went down in a squalling tangle of arms and legs as she staggered, then whirled to kick out the knee of an attacker on her right.

Knees were a weak point, Father had taught his children, and almost nobody remembered to defend them. The boy went down with a shriek. That was four. The rest yelled a war cry, and that's when the drill captain finally became aware of the battle shaping up outside the fence, which more than half of his charges were sneaking peeks at.

He spotted the dust rising from wild motion, and scowled at the man with the gong, who began beating the brass cymbal, raising a satisfying crash of sound.

First Brother, half-blinded by blood from his nose and the rapid swelling around his eyes, had fallen, curling in on himself as three pairs of feet began stamping and kicking. Mouse darted about frantically as the five (soon including three of those she'd dropped, limping slightly but red-faced in rage) hemmed her, closing in step by step.

She whirled, assessing possible escape between elbows and knees — and then a miracle happened, and her assailants froze. Gasping for breath, she became aware of the crash of the gong (barely audible above her own heartbeat) and then the hoarse bawl of the drill captain. "What's this? Dak! Parig! Brawling like common rabble *right here?* Is this the respect you show me, right outside the drill court? Report to the Justice Chief for punishment!"

The man looked down at Mouse, who stared back, and he surveyed First Brother, who was picking himself up, his clothes liberally splattered with blood. "You land rats take yourselves off before I send the guards to haul you to prison for vagrancy!"

First Brother stumbled away as fast as he could. The pain sending lightning shards through his head with every beat of his heart was so intense that he tolerated Mouse at his side, steadying him.

He leaned on her until they were safely out of sight, then stopped to catch his breath. Neither spoke, she light-headed from hunger and her burst of exertion, and he in too much pain. By mutual and silent consent they stopped at the fountain for a long drink, then began the long, weary trek up the slope toward the promontory toward their boat.

Once they reached the summit, both were remembering Second Brother. She hoped First Brother wouldn't send her back to find him, and he was ready to do just that, when the sound of footsteps pelting up behind them caused them to move to the side of the path.

It was Second Brother. "Sun is . . ." His free hand sketched the character for mid-afternoon, the time of day when one's shadow is one's true size. His other hand had closed over the mouth of his sleeve.

Euphoric with relief, Mouse said, "What did you buy? Not a book." There was no bulk in that sleeve.

"A brush," Second Brother said reverently. "Have you eaten?"

They all knew Mouse had no money, but First Brother also muttered, "No." He did not want to admit that his precious coins had fallen into the dust somewhere when those jackals had attacked him for no reason.

Second Brother carefully removed some pan-fried honey bread from his dust-marked sleeve. "It was your tinnies," he said to Mouse. "Put together with what I had left after I got my brush."

He saw the hunger in his siblings' faces, and tore the pan bread into portions. First Brother gulped his in two bites in spite of puffy lips. Second Brother, who had already eaten a bread while crossing the harbor, offered First Brother his share; Mouse forced herself to take tiny bites of hers, rolling it over her tongue then letting the bread dissolve to mush in her mouth before swallowing it. Maybe she could fool her stomach into thinking it was more.

"What happened?" Second Brother asked, touching his own nose.

"Jumped by jackals," First Brother said plummily.

"Nine of them," Mouse added.

First Brother shot her a broody look, but she said nothing more. She was too busy with her bread. Second Brother gave a mental shrug. He had no interest in fights.

Beyond the promontory the path abruptly narrowed, with fewer people on it. Unconsciously they sped up a little, each very ready to sit down.

But as they walked along the beach, they wondered, how far *was* their boat?

"I thought it was here," First Brother muttered finally, nearly out of strength. "I don't remember coming this far."

Second Brother, who viewed the world in terms of art, said, "I marked that we left it right below that crag with the tree." He pointed behind them to a feather-leafed lychee clinging picturesquely to cracks in a rock.

First Brother and Mouse scarcely glanced at the tree. Both realized sickly that they had passed that crag. It lay behind them some fifty paces.

And so the three learned another difference between village life, where everyone is known to the others, and a city full of strangers: theft.

First Brother stared at the empty strand. What now?

Mouse's stomach lurched, and she shoved her piece of

bread into her sleeve, wondering if it was the last meal she would ever have. Already the shadows were lengthening! They would *never* get home! Second Brother turned in a slow circle, devastated — but then he pointed. "Isn't that Uncle Keg?"

They peered out beyond the rippling tide, toward the familiar boat with the familiar figure in it. As they stood in a row, mouths open, Ul Keg, who had sailed close in to shore to make certain they had departed, pulled up the sail in a racket clatter of bamboo ribs. "Come along," he shouted. "The wind will die altogether on this side once the sun goes down, and no amount of praying will bring it up."

As one they pelted down the strand and dove into the water, Mouse pausing long enough to shove her bread into her mouth.

Soon, dripping wet, they clambered aboard the boat and bowed, awaiting judgement. They had no defense. They were thoroughly out of bounds. It seemed a miracle that the monk had somehow spotted them.

He waved them to sit in the broad belly where the tax baskets had been stored. They dropped down beside the baskets containing items Ul Keg had purchased.

"Thank you, Master Ul Keg," First Brother began, wondering if they could wheedle him into not tattling on them.

They did not realize as yet that that ship had already sailed. The monk leaned into the tiller. "Never mind the formalities. I'm Uncle Keg right now, not Master Ul Keg. I expect there will be trouble enough at home. Let's just get you there safely."

First Brother hunched miserably. The pain was beginning to settle into his muscles, and he knew worse was to come.

Second Brother had taken out his brush and examined it anxiously, worried that the salt water had damaged it. Mouse collapsed against the gunwale, staring back at the harbor, which still had so much left to see, though she hadn't spotted a single gallant wanderer, much less a hero. At least, she thought wearily, she would not have to bail.

FOUR

THE EXHAUSTED, STARVED CHILDREN trod wearily home once Ul Keg anchored the boat. The anxious father took the two boys in one direction to be interrogated, and the mother took her daughter.

While Iley checked her perfectly healthy daughter over with the habitual anxiety of a parent who had once nearly lost that child to illness, Mouse gave a tangled, impassioned description of her day, lingering on the vast unfairness of the beggar and the gong man. "I promised to light an incense and pray again to the Snow Crane God for that beggar, but really, what I want is to rain down curses on that man."

Iley sat back on her heels and rubbed absently at her cheek. "I can understand that. And it grieves my heart to hear about the beggar, who was surely once someone's beloved infant, sweet promise of a new life. Whatever fate brought that person there, at least you did not add to their misery, even if you did nothing to help."

"I want to help by begging the Snow Crane God for a curse!"

"That," said Iley, "helps no one, except perhaps to bring ill luck to *you*."

No bad luck that Mouse could see ever seemed to come to

those Sweetwater East twins, who cursed morning noon and night, Mouse muttered under her breath, as her mother added, "Justice is safer to leave to the stars and the gods."

Mouse accepted that. In all the stories, it seldom did any ordinary person any good to catch the inimical eye of the immortals. She said nothing, and was glad she'd said nothing when her mother added in The Punishment Voice, "The fact is, the three of you were willfully disobedient. You know that your father and I are considered lenient by many, as we do not believe that fear is the right guide to the Way of Enlightenment. But disobedience to such a degree makes me worry that you have forgotten the First Virtue—"

Mouse's eyes burned with tears as she whimpered, "But we do respect our parents, we do, we do, we do, it's just . . ."

"Go explain to your father. I'm afraid I will be too harsh if it's left to me," Mother said sternly, her disappointment, and residual fear, more painful to Mouse than any mere swat. "Go."

Mouse met First and Second Brothers on the way, both grimacing as they rubbed their backsides. It was now her turn.

After Mouse got her swats, and they morosely compared notes, they decided Father must have worked too hard all day, for it wasn't nearly as bad as they'd dreaded, considering the magnitude of their rule-breaking.

First Brother had gotten the worst of it, as the eldest, who should have known better. Two sharp whacks expressed their father's seemingly endless hours of horror once a child from Sweetwater Spring tattled self-righteously having seen them sailing away that morning.

But two smacks and Olt's worry-driven anger was spent, after which the hits were mere stings, not that First Brother noted it at the time, full of aches as he was. When it was over, they tumbled together into the pool behind the house where they had dammed the spring for a summer bath. The water felt good on tired bodies and stinging posteriors—Second Brother, as usual, wanting to float there like a dead thing until his skin was all wrinkly. First Brother hauled him out; they were fed plain rice, and sent to bed. Nobody would get a story that evening.

There they dropped into the profound sleep of the young.

That left three emotionally worn-out adults to gather at the other end of the house, pulling the door shut, though it was still warm and humid inside, the heat from the day having nowhere to go. Even opening the transom under the ceiling did little to disperse the heat. As a result, Iley did not light a candle, but sketched one of her charms, forming a soft glowing ball of light that she sent over their heads so it wouldn't distract them. Olt dragged the mats closer together, and they sat knee to knee in a triangle.

Iley was still shaking from residual terror, and beneath that, old resentment. To her orderly, scholar-trained mind, the children's unruliness was the direct result of lack of proper ritual. Of course, they had had to adapt to village ways. The children could not put on their formal robes to greet their parents in the morning because they had no formal robes. And to perform the relatively simple ritual customary for scholars, far less the elaborate rituals she had witnessed during her brief stay in the imperial city, would have made them the objects of gossip and wonder on the island.

But she had no doubt that First Brother's taking the children to the harbor without permission, and Mouse's lamentable lack of discipline in her studies, were all attributable to this lack.

So she allowed herself a low-voiced, "I trust you made them feel it."

"I did," Olt said. "But . . . we knew this day would come. If First Son is truly destined for greatness, is he not going to attempt forays away from the safety of home?"

Iley suppressed a sigh. To her, greatness was synonymous with wisdom and scholarship, not feats of arms, but this was an old argument. Alas, First Son had early on proved to be no scholar. He'd screwed up his face as a small child, mistaking characters and acting out in frustration. His writing was worse than his reading. Here was First Son's father, once deemed the greatest swordsman in the capital—whose scrawl was scarcely legible, and who read so slowly it was painful to hear. Like father, like son.

Perhaps it was true that the gods disagreed with her, and pointed First Son toward greatness in military expertise and leadership. And that included leading his siblings on a foray . . . to? "He had a purpose, then?" she asked.

Olt had listened to all three before delivering justice. "He wanted to evaluate the training of the boys his age at the garrison."

All right, that did suggest leadership. But! "That should not have gotten his face battered," Iley stated.

"He learned that outsiders' opinions are not welcome. Unless they are praise, and his wasn't," Olt said. "A hard lesson, one that perhaps can only be learnt through experience. I think he was more disturbed by the fact that he lost his head completely. If Mouse hadn't shown up and gotten in a lucky blow, he might have suffered far more severe damage."

"Arikanda!" Iley exclaimed, and not in approbation.

"She displayed a vestige of tactical sense," Olt said. "According to Ul Keg, she had the time. First Son was taken by surprise. That's what grieves the boy most."

Here, Ul Keg nodded, rocking back and forth on his mat. "True. I saw the end of it, having heard the uproar just after our tax was officially accepted. She also evaded the worst of the subsequent retaliation, though they were closing in fast before their captain called them to order."

"Oh, Arikanda." Iley let out a sighing breath as she and Ul Keg exchanged glances, each acknowledging the other's comprehension. "I have always regretted your teaching her fighting. I realize it is a way to teach the discipline she sorely lacks, but the time she spends playing with weapons ought to be spent in reviewing *The Five Essences* or studying her affinities and nerve-conduits."

Olt spread his hands. "It's not fighting, it's self-defense. I still believe it's a good idea to teach them to defend them-selves — which is about all the protection we can give them be-cause of our past, other than secrecy and eternal watchfulness."

Iley bowed her head at that; she refused to teach Mouse any lethal pressure points until she was old enough to understand what she was doing. Olt, raised as a bodyguard, taught them what he knew best.

Olt continued, "Mouse wants to keep up with her brothers. Better she get correct form from me than incorrect from them.

And you know that First Son cannot really practice unless he has someone who can give him at least a small amount of challenge. Second is not that someone."

Iley sighed again. Was she a monster in her last life, that all her children were conspiring to bring her white hairs before her time? When she'd had a daughter at last, Mouse fell terribly ill with a disease that had landed only lightly on others in the village, burning so with fever that no charms or herbs had worked. Iley was still not certain Mouse would have lived had it not been for Ul Keg sitting with her through the night, holding her hand and talking to her in simple words until she — somehow — was able to breathe with him. And once that happened, she had — somehow — heard enough of his explanation of Essence to open her own nerve-conduits to help abate her fever.

But on waking, did she wish to pursue this study? No. Mouse — who unlike First Brother was quick to learn and reproduce characters — was easily distracted, and loved nothing more than running with her brothers, or off by herself, the moment she recovered enough to go. It had been that way ever since. The most stringent punishments, or flagrant rewards, did not swerve her resolve.

And the worst of it was, Iley suspected that Mouse might, *might*, have inherited the spiritual Essence of the Alk clan. Oh, not to match Mother's talent, and whose self-discipline had been legendary. But even a sliver of the Alk gift ought not to be squandered in mere brawling!

Ul Keg saw Iley's conflict in the downward turn of her mouth and her averted gaze. He said, "At least your names remain absent from the Capital List."

Iley raised both hands. "That does count for something against today's ill luck."

"Ill luck?" Olt repeated. "Are you forgetting Second Son's encounter? He kept his wits about him, and claimed that Ul Keg here was his master, just as he ought."

"But Chief Scholar Bankan, for all his fame, is no more than a scribe, making pretty papers to paste on walls for the wealthy. He is not a true scholar, and Second Son caught his eye by drawing court hand, not writing in ancient script," Iley said, hands pressed to her cheeks in an old gesture of worry. The pain in her face had long ago abated to mere twinges now and then, but the memory of the abrasive stone cutting deep, followed by the agony of the salt, still throbbed whenever her heart knotted. "Second Son doesn't cherish ancient script; he never thinks of it unless I require it of him. Perhaps I am the guilty one. In my pride, I have tried to make a scholar of him. I did want something of my mother to live on."

"I believe he did well in the circumstance," Ul Keg pointed out in a soothing voice. "Surely a village child knowing the ancient script might raise more interest than you wish?"

That was *a* worry, but not her *chief* worry. She closed her eyes. How to explain? Second Son had bought a brush for painting instead of a book. That he was truly more interested in decoration than in the wisdom of the text was proving to be true.

But it was also well known that Chief Scholar Bankan was a lavish host, which drew traveling scholars to visit him, a rarity in these tiny islands. Many visitors brought books and even old scrolls, and the rich ones often left them behind, whence these artifacts made their way to the booksellers. Perhaps Second Son might meet a sage among these visitors who could lure him away from scribbling drawings.

"If he is serious about an apprenticeship, then it might be a lucky thing," she said slowly. "This and our remaining off the Capital list. As it should," she added with low-voiced bitterness. "From all the rumors, Enjai as emperor has packed that imperial palace with consorts and favorites. The pair of us ought to be long forgotten."

Olt, who had grown up side by side with Enjai, remembered the utter betrayal in his former foster-brother's face when the prince confronted the two of them on that road. He had seen in Enjai's face, as clearly as if they had spoken, *Why you? Why not me?* Because the prince's feelings had been more complicated than mere lust, which drove the knife of rejection deeper.

But Olt had kept that to himself all these years, knowing it would only disturb Iley's peace. At every festival and ancestral offering he prayed they would never again see the new emperor, and his days were spent in part striving to make it true, so what matter if she believed Enjai as wayward as the wind? Perhaps he had become so since those days. After all, as the poet said, no stream ran straight. And there were all those palace consorts, favorites, and flirts lavishly illustrated in court gossip scrolls whose more spectacular details eventually trickled to the villages.

Iley was aware that her worries had kept Olt from sending First Son off to training for the Military Examination. She knew very well why Ul Keg had brought up that list. First Son was already past the youngest age they took candidates. If another year passed, he would be too old, and his likely future would be as a city guard. Was this turning one's face from the promise of the phoenix feather? Inauspicious, to say the very least!

She drew in a deep breath, thinking of that feather hidden away up in the eaves. The truth was, from year to year, usually on festival days, she sometimes took down the hidden box to reassure herself with a glimpse of the phoenix feather, still softly glowing like a scrap of the purest dawn. Only it had slowly diminished to translucency at the tips. Phoenix feathers did not rot in the way of ordinary birds' feathers. They . . . dissolved.

Faded or not, it was still a promise from the unseen world, and she would be deservedly condemned in her next life if she willfully got in her son's way.

And so she gave in at last. "Perhaps it is time to let them both go."

The two men gazed at her, knowing what that concession cost her.

"Yes." She nodded once. "Do not tell them right away. First Son ought not to deem himself rewarded for breaking the very few rules we laid down."

"I agree," Olt said, rejoicing in his heart. Not one, but two sons, at last beginning a promising road to life? Perhaps the day had begun terribly, but it was turning out to be a blessing.

Still. "First Son is going to *earn* that chance to test at the Spring Festival. Oh, yes, he will. We'll send him along with the spring taxes. By then whatever notoriety he might have earned today will be long forgotten."

"Excellent," Iley said, and she really smiled, for the thought had occurred to her that if Olt began a more intensive training regimen with First Son when other work didn't call them, he would have less time for teaching Mouse what would not serve her future in the least. That would leave more time for scholarship, and Essence studies.

Iley snapped away her charmed light, and Olt slid the door open to slightly cooler air. Iley turned to take down and spread out the bedding as Olt said, "I'll check that First's nose isn't bleeding in his sleep, then be right back."

Ul Keg bowed a good night. The two men walked out.

Ul Keg said, "I feel I ought to point out that your wife seems to think that First's new training will leave Mouse out."

Olt sighed. "I know. But he needs a practice partner when I cannot be there. Second Son is too likely to be distracted by some flower, or a rock with interesting colors, and end up brained through inattention. Mouse doesn't get distracted. A result, I'm sure, of being the smallest. She has always had to scramble to catch up. She can go back to her books after First Son passes the test."

Ul Keg said, "It is only right and proper that Iley should wish her daughter to follow her as a scholar. And Mouse is an excellent reader."

Olt slowly shook his head. "It must be the Alk blood in her. I remember she was reading as fast as First Brother by her fourth Spring Festival. Faster." He sighed heavily. "While it's true that Mouse remembers everything she reads, our girl resists all the memorization and practice of affinities and charms that my wife says are necessary. That is not a likely quality for a scholar. Poor and common-born children always have a more stringent set of standards to pass. There are too many nobles' third and fifth offspring out there competing for scholar placement."

Ul Keg shrugged off the problems with nobles and their drive to accumulate (or buy) sufficient merits to retain their rank. He was thinking that Mouse was impatient with repeating the basics when she already thoroughly understood the concept they were building toward. If she conceived some prank or idea, they could scarcely drag her away from the books until she found what she wanted, as she demonstrated a thorough grounding in how to use those basics.

But this was her mother's realm. He knew better than to encroach.

Olt said slowly, "Perhaps if I train her, she might learn enough discipline to bring to her proper studies, once First Son goes off to training."

"I think," Ul Keg said, "she will spar with First Brother anyway. Giving her the good grounding is better than risking the children causing actual harm to one another out of ignorance. And what you say about discipline makes sense to me."

With that, the two entered into a conspiracy of silence, to preserve Iley's peace of mind.

The next morning, before Father and First Brother went off ostensibly to seek choice wood (which they would also do) and to train, Father beckoned to Mouse, and surprised both children by saying, "First Brother must drill harder if he is to test creditably, come Spring Festival. He will need a partner. So I am going to teach you the sword."

"Mouse?" First Brother said at the same time Mouse exclaimed, "Me?"

"Mouse," Father said, and at First Brother's skeptical glance at his small sister, he frowned. "What are the Four Pillars of defense?"

"Balance. Control. Speed. Strength," both children replied.

"What is the first of the pillars?"

"Balance," First Brother said, drawing the word out in question.

"Exactly. I've told you time and again, a finger can move an iron spear if it is applied in the right place. Deflection and redirection are more powerful, by far, than mere strength, which is why it's fourth and last. Mouse," he said, "I think is going to surprise you, once she understands the form." Here he turned a stern look her way. "But there will be no lessons for you unless you complete, to your mother's satisfaction, your daily studies."

Mouse sighed, and promised.

She kept that promise, rising early so that she could get

through her divination assignment as fast as possible. Her mother was gratified—until Mouse ran off as if she were an arrow shot from a bow—then sighed. She reminded herself hopefully, if Mouse kept up that determination, she would get an excellent grounding in the complicated study of affinities at last. Time to add in more herb-studies and memorization of conduits . . .

As Mouse walked with her brothers down the steep, twisted and root-tangled path toward the village's inlet, her father told her the true story about how he had had to sneak down every low tide to search the wreckage of their boat until he'd found his sword, and then he'd had to hide it.

When they reached the sand, they walked in the rilling, lapping water so that their footprints would vanish, and made their way up along the coast, past a tumble of ancient volcanic rock, to their private beach.

Once they were there, Mouse looked hopefully into her father's face, saying, "Is this a secret form?"

"Yes. Ayah, it was. The imperial guard had to be better than anyone else."

"So could you fly on your swords?" she asked, pointing to the steel blade.

Father burst out laughing. "Fly!" he exclaimed in disbelief, but then he remembered some odd rumors when he wasn't much older than First Brother was now. Rumors, he reminded himself. "That's for the hero tales," he told his daughter. "Like Essence, they might be true, they might not. What I'll teach you will always be right there, ready to use if you are serious about your practice."

Mouse tried to hide her disappointment, and said, "I'm serious."

"Steel," Father said sternly, to reinforce the difference between the real world and the foolishness of stories, "as I've told you, and will remind you once more, is strictly forbidden to commoners outside the military, or guards belonging to a noble, and they must always wear livery if they carry weapons. If you're caught with steel, that will earn an instant and painful public death, and possibly your entire family as well, if whoever catches you is angry enough."

"What about the gallant wanderers?" Mouse asked.

Olt—palace raised, then confined to island life—waved them off. "Again, those are mere stories. It's easy to call a brigand a hero in a tale told round a fireside. The lesson here is, this sword is never to be removed from this place, ever, no matter how much you're tempted by those two young jackals over in Sweetwater East. Your brother had to swear an oath as well: swear on your honor and heart's blood that you will never take this sword away from this place, or reveal to anyone in Sweetwater the drill I am about to teach you."

She swore, giving no sign that First Brother had taught her very basic blocks and thrusts with the sword—but he had refused to teach her the *real* drill. Now at last she would get it!

Father said, "You know the basics of most martial arts, which was enough grounding for the simple defenses you have already learned. Heaven and Earth is the drill for imperial bodyguards. Watch me first."

Father stood quietly, head a little bent, as Mouse's brothers took up positions about five paces from Father. All three assumed the squared stance called the Tiger Readies Himself Breathing, and she fell into the breathing pattern without thinking.

Then Father stepped forward, the sword humming upward in a strike, then flicking away, as quick as a hawk on the wing. Mouse forgot about her unarmed brothers as she watched, enchanted: Feint, thrust, block, turn. The sword sang as Father fought upward against four imaginary mounted enemies in front, behind, to either side. That was the heaven part. Then came the earth part, fighting against enemies on foot. He paused, his feet in the exact place he'd begun, tossed the sword up and grabbed it with the other hand, then performed the entire drill in reverse.

"That's what you will work up to. As always, we begin with the warmup sequence—which you know, but now you'll understand how the two fit together."

Then, instead of offering her the sword, he used it to describe a circle in the ground, with the S divider, one side for the powers of sun and masculine strength, the other for the powers of moons and feminine strength. One smaller circle at each end of the S, evenly divided, then two more along the curves, all evenly spaced.

"Footing is important. Vital," Father said. "We will begin with footing, and when you know that well enough to never have to look at the ground while placing your feet correctly, I will teach you the rest. Your second brother," he added, nodding at Second Brother, who was at that moment crouched on a rock, gazing down into the surging seawater, "knows the drill—I saw to that—but he never mastered it enough for me to put the sword into his hand."

Second Brother looked away from surging breakers, his smile sweet and a little absent. He longed to explore the world under the sea, though everyone knew it was dangerous. He cared nothing for swords.

But Mouse cared! She bowed the way Mother had taught her, for it seemed like the moment required it.

Father said, "This time, watch only my feet."

He went through it with her until she understood it not just with her mind, but with her body. And within three days, she never had to look down again.

Father watched her perform correctly three times, then said, "Now for the rest."

She held out her hand, but Father did not let her pick up the sword. He set it aside and tossed her a practice knife.

She swallowed her disappointment and took up a ready stance, mirroring Father. First Brother worked by himself a ways away as Father taught Mouse the complex movements of Heaven and Earth. He made her repeat it again and again—first with her preferred left hand, then extra drills with her right until it was equally comfortable. She repeated it until she was drenched with sweat and wobbling on her feet, but didn't have to think about the next movement.

The next day, the same thing, though she protested she knew it.

Father shook his head. "Next week we'll try with the sword. But you need to practice it until your *body* knows it, just as you did with the footwork. Do it every day, before you do anything else."

And then, after a water break, he beckoned First Brother

over, as Second Brother walked away, relieved to have his share of the hated exercises over with. He'd spotted two or three color-drenched blossoms on the walk to the shore, something new to experiment with. The others' voices faded behind as he wandered gratefully away.

"Now, Mouse, you and First Brother will practice working against each other with this combination . . ."

FIVE

ILEY NEVER TOLD ANYONE that when she was her children's age, her mother had done her best to direct her interest toward ancient tests and the mysteries of Essence. It seemed unfilial to her mother's memory, whether she was alive or dead. But Hanu had wanted to become a healer, not a scholar of the ancient mysteries. When she reached the age of fourteen, her mother had at last given in—and so she had had two years of healer studies before she was sent to the imperial city.

Those two years, plus her own experiments, and whatever appropriate texts Ul Keg could find for her in the harbor booksellers' shops, were what she brought to the villagers. Sometimes she regretted not having had longer to study. This seemed unfilial, making her regret her mother being taken from her without being able to say farewell. So she tried her best to interest Second Brother in Scholar Alk Bemti's studies—and when he resisted, Mouse. While still teaching Mouse the rudiments of healing.

Mouse kept her promise and diligently did her studies, but in her own secret heart, she wanted to be a gallant wanderer.

And so the season wore on, each day hotter than the previous until the air seemed to be saturated with boiling water. Harvest Festival followed, then the rainy season was upon them, with cool weather at last.

They gave up the pool bath on the chilliest days. During the (mild) southern winters, if they wanted a hot bath they first filled a bucket from the cauldron always on the simmer in any kitchen, for use in cooking and making medicines or drinking tea. Then they lugged the steaming bucket to the bath house out beyond the water wheel, got up on the stool to pour into the huge rainwater cistern to warm the water a bit, soaped all over, then pulled the string that opened the cistern spigot and let the lukewarm water rinse them off. Mouse liked to bathe with her brothers because that meant three buckets of hot water, which rendered the water deliciously warm. But then there was all the cold air. Even Second Brother got chilled, so they dried and dressed fast.

Training happened whether it rained or not. Father and First Brother sparred with swords in the early morning while Second Brother and Mouse were at their studies. But afternoons, while Second Brother roamed about looking for new colors to experiment with, or observing shapes and textures, Mouse worked with First Brother, or when he was out fishing with the village men, she worked on her own secret project.

Mouse hadn't grown a jot, but Olt said that this was an advantage: a smaller target would refine First's aim. For strength, of course, he sparred with his father, but then came back to Mouse without anyone, including Mouse, noticing that as he gained in strength, Mouse kept pace. He still outmatched her, of course, but that margin had not widened. In fact, it began to narrow.

This was because she began using Essence, shortly after the Year of the Horse changed to the Year of the Eagle.

She knew the principle of drawing on one's innate Essence—she had learned that from Ul Keg as she lay in pain from the internal fire of fever. Ever since she had grasped the first principle—so difficult for most—she'd been using Essence for jumping and climbing. But concentrating on opening her nerve-conduits to draw on Essence while fighting was far more challenging than balancing on a bamboo pole.

Ul Keg had warned her that not everyone could master what was effectively concentrating on two very different things at the same time. Mouse struggled until one especially hot, stuffy day she made a discovery.

It was a hot morning, and she was grinding her way through forcing a wad of nearly impenetrable text to memory.

The divine world is connected to the world of living things. If a seeker understands the affinities between stone, rock, tree, water, doe, and star, the seeker begins to perceive that there the world is not chaotic, but ordered in patterns. Understanding the events of the stars reveals clear connections between all the living things of Earth. To reach harmony, the seeker must understand balance as well as affinity, the equal pull between all things . . .

Her eyes stung. She wiped them on the back of her sleeve, realizing she'd lost the sense of what she'd been reciting after the words "ordered in patterns."

She let out a groan, her entire body as well as her brain one big itch longing for freedom. Promising she'd come back to it, she escaped upward into the trees, running along the twisting lianas between the old banyans, so that she never left footprints in the paths below.

She knew from Mother's lessons that Essence could be very powerful, but that was for grown and trained shamans, augurs, and healers. Those powerful figures were the ones responsible for the great Essence charms that soothed the fire dragons deep underground, so that when they moved it was slowly, gently, instead of in great bursts that caused mountains to spit molten rock, and the ground to shiver so badly that houses crushed people and animals, and rivers jumped their banks to flood the countryside on the islands large enough to have rivers.

But those were mighty wielders of Essence. Not someone like Mouse, with no more talent than a gnat. The storm broke, and with it the oppressive heat. She lay along a tree branch as a fast-moving thunderstorm briefly cooled the air. She stared upward as the foliage tossed and rustled.

Wind.

Though it was full of imps and invisible minions of the gods, there had to be something to carry them, right? The wind was a power all on its own, bringing and sending storms, rain, the hot airs of summer, the cooler winds of winter.

She could push wind with her Essence! Couldn't she?

At first she was only aware of the tingle, as if thousands of tiny insect feet danced over her skin, that signaled the presence of Essence. By habit she breathed, letting it find its balance within her, and as lightning branched high overhead, flickering above the treetops, she pushed from within, thinking, *Wind!* And threw the Essence skyward.

Then she watched in amazement as the lightning burst into a shower of tiny lights that winked out in a heartbeat.

Had she done that? She tried again, but doubt made concentration difficult, and sure enough, it didn't work. So maybe it had worked, maybe it hadn't, but if it had, even if it worked sporadically, then it was true that Essence control applied to *everything*. Including pushing wind imps!

After that, she brought her Essence awareness to the secret training ground each day, her idea to test its limits. Not that she could use Essence tricks against First Brother. That would not help him train for the garrison test. The army did not train in Essence, which was too rare and too volatile, Olt had said. To the army, a sword was always a sword, an arm an arm. The arm needed to learn to wield the sword. Nothing rare or tricky about that.

So she practiced that on her own, setting up husks and empty pods on rocks and working over and over to bring up Essence from her core to mentally thrust a spurt of air, until she could blow the husks over with a snap of her palm from two paces away.

In one of the legends Ul Keg told, a hero had learned by ringing temple bells with Essence. She fashioned bits of wood to clatter and hung them up in her secret dell, working until she could get them all dancing and rattling. She also discovered that Essence could help her master the somersault on her lianas-pole, the goal that had been eluding her for nearly three years, if she concentrated on lightness. It never worked long—she could not fly—but she could leap, and balance on narrow things. Though it took far more effort than pushing wind imps.

Elated with her small successes, she went spelunking through the tattered books that the villages had preserved for generations, as well as those Ul Keg had brought back for Iley at her request.

They weren't enough. There was more out there—she began focusing once more on the ancient script that Mother had tried unsuccessfully to teach First Brother. Second Brother had dutifully learned it, but Mouse, watching him struggle, had resisted as much as she could. But now she wondered what interesting secrets might be found in really old writings. She soon discovered tantalizing references in the oldest, grubbiest scrolls, which she hid under the hated practice sheets of Imperial court-and-scholarship handwriting. And she set up a classic text as a shield.

Iley, seeing her daughter poring over her studies, assumed contentedly that Mouse had returned to memorizing the *Five Essences*, and began to hope again that her wayward daughter was coming around at last, and she'd make a scholar of her yet.

When at last Spring Festival drew near, which meant Ul Keg taking the taxes to the governor's manor, Olt planned to go along to see First Brother test at the garrison after he delivered Second Brother to Master Bankan's scribe house.

Mouse begged to be allowed to go with them so that she could look at books. Iley surprised everyone by readily consenting. She even rewarded her daughter for her good behavior and diligent studies with a silver moon for a book, and tinnies for a meal.

Iley was teary, and anxious, at the prospect of her family breaking up, but she told herself it was foreordained. At least she would have Mouse to herself, now, which meant no more sword foolery. It was time to refine Mouse's scholarship.

She would miss her boys, but she hoped they both would return with wives someday, so that her house would be full again, with grandchildren—one of whom might be born with the Alk Talent.

The day they were to set out, she brought a slip of charm paper to each boy, saying, "I don't dare etch protections into your skin, for those will call attention, but you can wear these next to your skin—"

Olt took her hands, saying gently, "Second Son, perhaps. But First will be searched before he even tests. He has to learn to protect himself before he can protect others."

Iley's eyes filled with tears as she handed Second Brother his protection. And as he put it within his inner wrap, Iley then issued her own condition: that Olt not go to see the testing, but remain behind.

Here she was adamant. In a low voice she slipped from island dialect to the pure Imperial of scholarship as she said, "I know you'll say it's unlikely, but it's *possible* that an imperial guard or army captain of your generation traveling on imperial orders might chance by to watch the competition, too. Someone who will recognize you as Danno, the swordsman who won all the imperial competitions in his day. Your looks have changed little. And though Ul Keg says our old names are no longer on the Capital List, that doesn't mean that they aren't remembered."

She then turned to Mouse. "This will be your first book chosen by yourself. I'll give Ul Keg your coin, so that he can approve your choice. Choose well. Think of your future," she cautioned, and Mouse bowed, fingers to forehead, knowing what her mother wanted.

She would obey, but first she could *look* at some hero tales, and commit to memory as much as she could!

The children's spirits were high when they set out.

Ul Keg's thoughts were complicated.

He had done his best to educate the children through the stories he had told them at night. Ul Keg believed that stories before sleep became lessons in dreams.

First Brother, in truth, had begun falling asleep halfway through the latest stories, exhausted by his intense lessons. He slept dreamlessly, but then he, like the rest of the family, believed his future had been foretold by the phoenix feather. He had only to work toward it.

Second Brother's dreams pulled images from the stories and spun them into detailed images drenched in enchanting color.

Mouse dreamed entirely in stories, almost always of great heroes and mythic figures. These heroes had most often worn First Brother's face as they accomplished great deeds of martial prowess aided by impressive exhibitions of Essence power.

This time the children were permitted to help sail the boat, and as children do, the three departed with high hearts and no look back, their minds full of beckoning adventure: the boys looking forward to a new life, and Mouse a day of fun in the harbor, with the prospect of spending all her wealth before returning to home and grinding through the ancient language and lists and lists of affinities and nerve conduits and herbs.

At least, Ul Keg thought as First Brother hauled the sail around easily with one hand, his muscular arm straining against his worn sleeve, there was plenty of time before Mouse would be sent to temple testing. Alone of the three, she recollected all the details of the heroic stories she loved so much, but unlike her brothers, who seemed determined to step onto their life paths, she had no thought to the future.

She was young. It would come. Along with Iley he had let himself hope that she would go to temple testing; though he recognized his secret heart's desire, he was too honest to try to lure her toward the Phoenix Moon, and intended to take her around to the various temples' schools, in hopes one might inspire her to a life of peaceful immersion in the greatness of the past, and sharing it with the next generation.

Mid-morning they spotted masts bobbing on the sea ahead. Mouse scrambled to the forepeak of the boat. There were actual ships in the harbor, with two tall masts each, and holes down the side for the long oars.

Ul Keg's wistful mood sharpened to watchfulness, then wariness as they were beckoned into the pier reserved for boats bringing taxes. Along the quay, warriors in gray and brown walked in groups, or stood watching. Captains in blue were everywhere, both the dark blue of the imperial army, their hats decorated with a kingfisher feather, and the gaudy, over-decorated blue of the governor's own guards with their peacock-feathered hats.

A few moments after Ul Keg and the children stepped onto hard land, the mass faded back due to some unseen impetus, leaving a brief, uninterrupted view of a military man in a commander's purple. Gold winked at the binding around the tassel hanging down from his broad-brimmed black hat, and around the two tassels dancing at his sword.

Someone who had to have been in the capital at least long enough to be awarded that sword with its golden-bound tassels. He appeared to be about forty, which would make him old enough to have met, or at least seen, Danno.

Iley had been right not to tempt fate, Ul Keg thought, but out loud he said, "It's rude to stare. You all know what you're here to do. First Brother, you report to the garrison gate. Mouse, would you like to go with him to watch the testing, or come with me to deliver Second Brother to the Chief Scholar? We can shop for your book once your brothers are where they need to be."

Mouse thought for the space of two heartbeats: the scholars might bore in with speeches and bowing, whereas the garrison testing at least would furnish something interesting to watch. "I'll go with First Brother," she said.

"I'll meet you there when I'm done," Ul Keg said.

The brothers smiled absently at one another, each expecting to see the other before too long. Mouse tugged impatiently at First Brother's sleeve. She wanted to see the testing, but there were also Spring Festival sights beckoning!

First Brother and Mouse took off, but slowed when they neared the garrison. "Remember last time," First Brother muttered.

"Polite and quiet," Mouse returned, scanning the faces of anyone near their age for familiar features from that terrible day.

While they made their circumspect approach, Ul Keg and Second Brother worked their way through the crowd of gawkers, keeping a respectful distance from the grand sight of so many imperial officers—there as guard to an imperial relation, who was entertaining himself while their ship took on supplies. No one expected anything of interest on this boring little nonentity of an island before setting sail at the turn of the tide.

The crowd only seemed to get thicker the farther Ul Keg and Second Brother went, increasing the heat and humidity. But at last they reached the Chief Scholar's manor.

Here, Ul Keg noticed a pair of banners hanging to the right of the manor's carved sign, indicating the presence of honored guests. One of these banners carried a dragon, which drew the eye, as that indicated a relation of the emperor. No one but the imperial family could add dragons to their banners.

Ul Keg paused for a heartbeat, interpreting the symbols. There was no tiger-eye of the Jehans, instead a topaz symbol carried in the mouth of a small silver dragon. The banner had only two swallow-tails hanging down, which meant the visitor was descended from the dowager empress's sister — Enjai's mother having been promoted to empress dowager on her son's accession. The three marks below the small dragon indicated a third son.

So this visitor was a third cousin to the emperor, which should be safe enough . . . and anyway, the two liveried household guards at either side of the door were looking at them expectantly.

Let's not beat the grass to alarm the snake, Ul Keg thought to himself, and bowed as he said, "This child, Afan Yskanda, was summoned by the Chief Scholar himself. Have we come to the right place?"

The guard at the right grunted assent, and passed them within; others would check the truth of that statement, and mete out the appropriate punishment for presumption or false claims.

The double doors opened onto a vast mural of an illustrated poem in the ancient tongue, written vertically right to left. Ul Keg looked past, scanning the crowd inside for the Chief Scribe. As a monk, used to solitude and accustomed to the slow rhythm of life in small villages, he was bemused by the mass of people moving about what appeared to be randomly as he sought the robes of a scribe.

One of those he failed to notice was a man who sat, screened by fragrant shrubberies, in a comfortable spot from which to view the comings and goings, that he might sketch those who interested him.

Beauty always captivated him. He observed Second Brother's encounter with the mural and the wonder that transformed an already arresting face. He rose, a servant hastened to pick up his brushes, ink, and paper, and as everyone around the illustrious personage bowed, this personage followed Yskanda at a discreet distance.

Ahead, unaware of this small stir behind him, Second Brother was vowing that if life here would teach him how to make art like that mural he would never would leave, ever, ever, *ever*.

He was subliminally aware of Ul Keg halted by someone or other. He was grateful to be able to look back at the green, blue, and black ink drawings around the text, here and there highlighted with what looked like *real gold*. Suddenly the colors he had labored so painfully to emulate gold seemed garish and flat.

He scarcely heard the low conversation between Ul Keg and the servant; his mind was entirely on the glory of that amazing illustration, which managed to combine high mountains, forests, tumbling streams, right down to a small village along the edge of a river, and a skillfully detailed fisher — every bit as detailed as the eagle flying high above.

Then they moved again, led to a small room containing little more than guest mats and a tiny, bare table. But the room boasted a window looking out into a garden with raked sand and stones in interesting groupings, partially obscured by gnarled trees of a type Second Brother — now Afan Yskanda, apprentice scholar — had never seen.

Everything about the scene bespoke order, but nothing was symmetrical or grouped in arrogant lines, which made it too easy for demons to use as a pathway. Yskanda was too fascinated by the scenery of this garden to notice the passage of time as they were kept waiting.

Ul Keg reflected on the density of the crowd, and comforted himself with the notion that it would surely be equally slow for First Brother among the candidates for testing. So, from long habit, he shut his eyes and composed himself to meditate.

Neither was aware of the eyeholes in the bamboo-patterned wall opposite the window, behind which the artist — who, being maternal cousin to the emperor, could stop this entire household at a gesture — sat at leisure in order to sketch the boy.

Once he was satisfied with his drawing, he left the little

chamber and resumed his place off the main entry so that he could once again observe the comings and goings, which in turn released everyone else into action.

An apprentice in dull gray-blue opened the door to the waiting room, and the Chief Scholar himself walked in. "A new apprentice?" he said to the two waiting.

Of course they must pretend there had been no wait. Ul Keg with the humility of the dedicated monk, and Yskanda with the fervency of a bedazzled youth, were sincere in their thanks for the Chief Scholar's time and attention.

At the Chief Scholar's elbow stood First Apprentice Fei, who watched Yskanda narrowly for the slightest hint of conceit after having caused the entire house to come to a halt so that the exalted guest could sketch him. This was a flagrant upsetting of the proper order, and she loved order very dearly, the more because she had worked grimly to attain her present rank among the scholars. She also had a temper like a weathervane — those apprentices she frowned on led miserable lives, and those she smiled on were fawned on by her followers.

It occurred to her that this new boy was utterly unaware of what had happened. And so, as the Chief Scholar spoke the formal words accepting the apprentice and then turned him over to First Apprentice Fei to be settled in, she decided in favor of this newcomer. He was appropriately humble, and besides, she had always liked a pretty face.

When Ul Keg saw the supercilious apprentice in blue smile kindly on Yskanda as she led him off to his new life, he bowed his way out.

SIX

ON THE FAR SIDE of the governor's manor, First Brother and Mouse made their way to the training grounds without spotting any of their attackers from the summer previous.

First Brother, who had been pondering his future since the day Father had said he could test, turned to Mouse the moment they were alone, and spoke in the elder-brother voice that meant he expected to be obeyed. "I'm not going in as Afan Muinkanda. I'm going to be Ryu Muin," he said in a fierce undervoice. "From one of the Small Islands."

He named the scattering of islands sometimes visible on very clear days from the promontory at the island's end beyond Sweetwater. Having no bays large enough for ships, and being so small, they had no imperial presence, so their inhabitants brought their trade to Imai Harbor.

"Ryu? Why? The shaman gave us Afan as a clan name."

"Afan is a good name, but it's only our family. There are no ancestors to be insulted if I use another name to disguise myself."

Mouse tipped her head as First Brother went on, "Father's closest friend in his training was named Ryu, for a clan in the north, Father told me once. The Ryu clan tends to go into the army and navy. Which means, if I do become famous, then no one can come here looking for Mother and Father, right?"

"Oh-h-h-h," Mouse said. "That's right. It protects Mother and Father."

"And forget the 'Kanda,' as generation names are mostly given by scholars and the nobles. I mean to win, which means they'll ask questions, and I don't want to have to say anything about our parents. I was trained by a gallant wanderer. Understand?"

Mouse slapped her hands flat to her thighs. This absolutely made sense to her. Hiding Father's training behind a mysterious hero appealed to her sense of adventure, and as for names, Muin was a common village name. There were two in their village, both named after heroes among the gallant wanderer tales. Ryu Muin was a good name for First Brother to start with. He'd bring his own fame to it along his path to greatness.

"Then come on, I see the line."

There were no politer youngsters among the candidates that day than these two. They bowed to anyone who looked their way. Once they were pointed to hardpacked ground at the side to wait, they knelt properly instead of flopping down cross-legged the way most of the others had, and kept their hands flat on their thighs rather than fingering everything in sight.

They soon observed that the captain in charge of the testing preferred taking the military offspring first. These boys and girls were obvious by their sober clothing, not much different from what their parents wore for daily training.

Nobles' sons were second for preference. To be expected. Rank would always come first; besides, it was clear that almost all had training. Left to the last were those like First Brother, clearly sons of common folk, who at most could hope to become guards, unless they demonstrated extraordinary talent.

As Father had promised, there was an orderly in a gray robe who held something in his palm as he ran it swiftly through the air in front of each candidate. This happened while a military aide in dun asked questions she couldn't hear.

The person doing the search with the charmed object reacted only once, and Mouse — intensely interested — didn't see what warned him, but he said something to one of the dun-coated guards, who jerked the child out of line for a rough search.

A guard handed something that glinted with Essence to the one in the robe, and Mouse bounced on her tiptoes, frustrated at not being able to see or hear. The child was dismissed untested, and everything carried on as if nothing had happened.

The testing progressed rapidly, sometimes no more than two or three passes of the wooden practice blades before a candidate was directed toward the largest group—those future guards—or to the smallest group, consisting of those who would be put in training for captains, or sent away altogether. A few of these were told to return in a year or so, and a handful of head-bowed, dejected youngsters were dismissed with a terse "Try apprenticing to someone else."

Unlike the rest of the muttering, sighing line, First Brother never made a peep when two very well-dressed boys arrived late, then pushed ahead of the line with the arrogant confidence of rank. Neither he nor Mouse so much as smiled when the first of these boys dropped his sword and wailed during the very first pass—nor did they react when the second boy swaggered out, lounging with an air of bored hauteur, then returned the instructor's easy attack with a fury that almost knocked the weary, surprised man off his feet.

The supervising captain scowled, but motioned the boy to the captains' training. Talent and birth must always be accepted. The noble boy sauntered that way. His servant, who had waited at the side, head lowered, scrambled after him.

Finally First Brother was beckoned to the square.

As the one slowly waved the charmed thing in front of him, the other asked in the bored tone of someone who has repeated the same question too many times to count, "Are you familiar with *The Way of the Blade?*"

"Yes," First Brother said cautiously, uneasy at this unexpected question. "I thought there was no written examination except for scholars."

The man uttered a dry laugh. "This is the *army* examination for training. The written Military Examination only happens in the capital, if you rank high enough to be sent there after your five years of training. So, give me a quotation from the book. Any will do."

First Brother snorted a breath, his mind blanking from sheer panic. His eyes turned toward Mouse, his reading partner, as her lips shaped the word 'strength'."

First Brother was not much of a reader, but Father seen to it that what reading he did was from the old books on strategy. Muin said quickly, "'Strength lies in the defense, victory in attack.'"

"Close enough, youngster. Go on to the field."

An instructor in a dun fighting robe belted over darker trousers waited with a wooden practice sword. First Brother settled into the proper stance, shoulders straight, eyes on the instructor's weapon. Mouse held her breath, wishing Father could be there to see.

The instructor, instantly recognizing good training in First Brother's stance and poise, straightened up a little, and made a more complicated first move than usual. First Brother met it with a snap, then pulled back to await the next. No showing off, no flourishes, no unnecessary moves.

The instructor already knew that they would take this boy, but decided to provide a demonstration to the rest of the candidates, including those noble boys over there, and so he came in at the attack.

High, low, pressing, retreating, he brought out First Brother's clean style, his expertise in the basics. The entire field was silent, watching as the instructor spun out this test.

The captain in charge grunted, as the single woman there turned to him. "That's imperial guard training," she stated. She would know. She was there to scout for girls to be trained for duty in the capital, guarding princesses and female consorts.

The instructor decided his lesson had been successfully delivered, and described a circle in the air before dropping his point, a sign of approbation.

First Brother flushed (more, as he was already red in the face), bowed, and returned the wooden sword to the rack.

The captain in charge said, "You. Name? Age?"

"Ryu Muin. Born Year of the Dragon."

"Who trained you?"

First Brother stated without pause, "A passing hero shipwrecked on our shore, in trade for food and shelter, taught whoever would be taught before sailing away."

The woman nodded; not all those who began training in the imperial style were kept, for various reasons. Many turned up in the wandering world as would-be heroes, earning their way by teaching or fighting. Those who didn't become brigands, or worse.

The supervising captain grunted in disappointment. He would have been willing to send a patrol to the other side of the island to hire that hero that day. But wandering heroes were wandering heroes. "You'll join the captains' training." He pointed to the side. And when First Brother headed that way, the captain turned to Mouse impatiently. "Don't dawdle, grunt."

First Brother and Mouse both sent bewildered glances from the captain to each other and then to the captains' training group. Every boy and girl there had a servant at hand.

First Brother turned to Mouse, unsure what to do.

But Mouse knew exactly what to do. At least five of the *Exemplars of Filial Harmony* under the Second Virtue of the *Twenty-Five Virtues* concerned siblings, one of which was stepping away from their own path to help an elder sibling. This was First Brother's beginning road to greatness. He was not going to be turned away from what the phoenix feather had promised because no one in Sweetwater had servants, nor knew how to get them.

She bowed quickly, and scurried to First Brother's side.

Meanwhile, the captain had cast expert eyes over the remainder of the land boys, seeing nothing in the yawning, slumping, scratching candidates anything likely for his chosen elite. He already had seven, two more than the usual quota, and meanwhile the signal had come that the tide was turning.

So he nodded to the waiting orderlies while the female captain peeled away the promising girl candidates. These vanished in one direction, watched thoughtfully by Mouse, before First Brother's group of seven (servants walking behind them) was lined up and taken to the dock, where, to the utter surprise of First Brother and Mouse, they approached the ramp leading up into a ship.

And so, when Ul Keg arrived breathlessly at the testing ground, no matter where he looked, he could not find either of his last two charges.

SEVEN

ON THE WHARF, BEFORE the ramp, the seven halted. The only one who noticed the decorated ship flying the banners of the dowager empress's relation as it set sail for the east was the tall noble boy, an expression of longing on his face that smoothed into irritation when one of the military men said, "One servant only."

"I've *always* had three servants! How am I expected to make do with one?" he began in pure court Imperial.

"You'll make do, or go home," was the flat answer.

He turned to his three waiting servants, muttered something at them, and two departed, one with a quick look back that Mouse thought was mostly relief.

Then, leading his single servant, the noble boy raised his chin, twitched at his clothes, which were finer than anything Mouse had ever seen, and swaggered up the ramp, his silken sleeves and the back panels of his embroidered silk over-robe swinging. While Muin evaluated what he'd seen of the noble's fighting style, Mouse's considering gaze took in what appeared to be the leader of the military sons, a brawny, pale-skinned boy who eyed the noble's son in a way that Mouse recognized: the born bully who recognizes another bully—or a target.

Muin—no longer First Brother—and Mouse were last in

line to board. Lagging a couple of steps back, he whispered uneasily, "You can't be here. It's all men!"

"Sure I can," Mouse whispered back. "That captain yelled at me to hurry up, not to go away. Nobody's even looked at me twice."

Muin shifted from one foot to the other. From various tales that he'd overheard from the adults, he'd learned that servants were invisible to their masters unless given an order, and to everyone else most of the time. Mouse was just Mouse, his sparring partner. Who fetched and carried. Wavering, he muttered, "What if they see you . . . not being a boy?"

"They won't," she said, shrugging. To her, used to running with boys, such distinctions were irrelevant. "Anyway, it's only until you find a servant." Mouse let out a short breath. "*I'm* not going to be the one to get in the way of your destiny, and be reborn as a worm!"

Muin gave in, relieved. After all, how could he be expected to find a servant when he had never seen one? Village people didn't have servants. And he'd much rather have Mouse there than some stranger.

They fell silent when beckoned up the ramp, and onto the broad weather deck of the ship, where they found a host of boys already gathered. These sat at one end. The seven moved toward the only available space, the noble and the brawny captain's son moving with confidence, expecting others to give way.

When Muin and Mouse, the last two, topped the ramp, Muin eyed the knotted rope at the belt of the man who took up position on the opposite side of the rail. He was clearly in command, at least of the boys, if not of the ship, the way he looked them over. The way the military sons cast him speculative looks and then sat down near the quiet rows reinforced the impression.

Muin had seen the challenge in both of the tall boys. Back in Sweetwater, he would have rushed to meet those challenges. It was the only way to keep the twins from preying on Second Brother and the rest of the smaller ones. But he was no longer in Sweetwater. Everything had changed.

So he sat next to Mouse, unconsciously assuming his father's patient pose, knees together, back straight, butt on heels so that if needed he could rise in a heartbeat.

He didn't sit long.

The man with the knotted rope bawled an order and the boys formed into lines, the servants waved off to the side.

Then began a day of exercises. Anyone who slowed, or yawned, or looked around, got a crack of that rope. The exercises weren't hard, but they were repetitive, and the day passed slowly as Muin and those around him got more and more sweaty.

At last they were released to sit down. Most of them sank directly to the deck.

Muin looked around wearily, and here was Mouse, carrying rice balls made with fish and cabbage, served on a cabbage leaf.

Ravenous at the sight of food, he pounced. Then mumbled through a huge bite, "Where were you?"

"I was watching what the servants do. Glad I did," she whispered. "They went over the ship to learn where things are, and I followed. The privy," she said next, forestalling his first question, "is behind that hanging door, either side. I was looking below when someone yelled, 'grunts to the galley,' which meant us." She smacked the front of her now-grubby smock and tipped her head toward another servant. "We line up outside the kitchen to get the food."

Muin finished off the last of the cabbage leaf, slurped the water down that she brought in a wooden cup, and as he licked his fingers, "Can you get more?"

"They said no."

"Did you eat?"

She patted the front of her smock. "In here." She thought of that feather, and forced herself to add, "Want some of mine?"

Muin wanted very badly to say yes. It seemed he was always hungry these days. But he gave his head a shake. If he got whatever everyone else got, then it was probably a matter of discipline, and the sooner he got used to it, the better. "Eat your share," he muttered gruffly. "You have to be as hungry as I am."

She didn't deny it, and took out a rice ball, which had begun to crumble inside her grimy garment. It still looked delicious to him. So he gazed out at the rippling water rushing by as he said, "This is a good enough spot, now that I'm used to the smell. At least we can sleep on deck."

Mouse's nose wrinkled. "I heard one of the sailors say that there's rain on the way."

Now that the sun was vanishing, the air was pleasant, and Muin suspected it would be stuffy and uncomfortable below, but sailors ought to know the weather on the sea.

Grumpily, he followed Mouse into the hold that stank of fish, pickled cabbage, and sweaty feet. She had already spied out a spot near coiled ropes. They made themselves as comfortable as they could, squeezing up when thunder rumbled outside the ship, followed by a rush of angry voices as wet, tired boys crashed their way below.

In the murky darkness, scarcely broken by one swinging lantern, the hissing and grunting of a scuffle broke out. That only lasted a few heartbeats before the crack of the knotted rope on flesh called an abrupt halt.

"Silence," a deep voice grated.

Muin and Mouse remained where they were as bodies pressed up on either side. Neither spoke, but her sticky hand stole into his, then both fell asleep to the sound of rain drumming on the deck over their heads.

Muin fell asleep without realizing it, his head bumping gently against a barrel, until he was woken by a persistent poke. He winced, straightening his stiff neck, and wiped the drool off his chin as Mouse held out a leaf with three fish-and-rice cakes on it, and a gourd of water.

He scarcely had time to wolf it down—she'd obviously been shoved to the back of the line to get food—before the rope knots cracked against a bulkhead and that man roared, "On deck!"

Mouse hastily shoved a tiny cup into his hand, from which a brief scent of stale steep momentarily overcame the aroma of the hold. "Rinse your mouth with that, and spit it in the privy, or over the side," she said urgently.

Muin sniffed the sharp scent, suspecting that this was his first taste of tiger leaf, the tea that was reserved for the military. He filled his mouth and swished the liquid between his teeth, relishing the subtle tingle of the morning rinse charm as he ran. At least his teeth would feel clean, though the rest of him was itchy from sleeping in sweaty clothing.

Once everyone had gathered on deck in the roaring rain, the boys discovered they were expected yet again to line up for calisthenics. To the nobles' affronted faces, "No one asks for good weather when called to battle," the instructor roared.

Muin and Mouse exchanged covert glances across the width of the deck.

So, while the boys were put through a set of somewhat more complicated calisthenics until their muscles trembled and their breath burned in their throats, the rain perforce gave them a bath while laundering their clothes. Muin found it a relief, except for the drip in his eyes. He suspected from the set looks in the military boys' faces that this was to be expected, a contrast to the ill-concealed disgust and discomfort betrayed by the wealthy, whose clothes were sorry, sodden messes, their cherished silken tassels bedraggled.

At the end of a very long day, nicely calculated to bring them to the brink of dropping from exhaustion, they paused long enough for water and a meal. Then they lined up again, this time to be instructed in military etiquette: which kind of bow went to whom, when. A salute on the battlefield in full armor was a different matter than the morning salute to one's captain or commander. And very different from the knee and opposite fist to ground of a salute to the emperor.

"Once you set foot in Loyalty Fortress," the trainer intoned, "you will be expected to note each person's rank, and salute accordingly." He cast a narrowed glance at the well-dressed boys as he added, "You are all first-year cadets, at the very bottom of military rank. No other rank matters here. You will also salute one another when under orders. Errors earn a flogging to aid you in remembering."

And so it went for three days, until they stopped at another harbor to take in what proved to be the last group of new candidates. No one was permitted to leave the ship, and they set sail again once the tide had turned.

Rain or shine, they exercised until they could scarcely stand, they ate, they slept almost the moment they took their last bite. Not a single weapon had made an appearance, but their training had most definitely begun. As they strained and sweated, rules and regulations were repeated by the instructor in a hortatory tone, followed by the inevitable penalty for inattention. The rope dealt out mere stings for what were considered less serious misdemeanors, such as speaking when not asked a direct question. Those who ignored an order or harassed another cadet earned weals; everyone watched one another.

With an eye honed by several years of contention with the vicious twins of Sweetwater East, Muin noted during the training who was strongest and fastest, and who was spoiling for a fight as soon as they could find space away from those watchful eyes. Competition was inevitable, but he didn't see any reason to invite trouble before it came to find him, and kept a prudent distance from those wearing increasingly grimy silk, and the leader of the military sons.

Mouse had noticed her first day aboard the ship that those who knew each other moved in groups. The servants of the wealthy boys ignored her as if she didn't exist. She stayed out of their way, instinct warning her that to be so thoroughly ignored meant she was noticed. She slept during the day, and mostly explored at night, when the boys dropped into exhausted sleep.

She wasn't the only one awake besides the night crew. As she roamed about the ship, listening to muttered conversations, she understood that everyone saw everyone else in this tiny, confined wooden world with its clattering batten sails and its colorful flags meant to ward demons and dragons, surrounded by the vastness of the sea.

The best part of her day was when the sun sank, creating a path of molten gold over the water. The sky filled with color, and the horizon varied as they threaded between islands, some no more than a single point, others like combs with upward juts of broken teeth.

Each day's end, the sun always sank somewhere to the left, occasionally forward, mostly toward the rear, which meant they were moving steadily into cooler waters to the northeast. She already missed her parents and Ul Keg terribly. It comforted her somewhat to waken before the sun, and find a relatively isolated spot where she could face the southwest and salute each of the three of them, and again before sleep, once it was safely dark.

One morning Muin woke himself early enough to get ahead of the line for the privy, and he caught her at her salute. "Why do you do that?" he asked. "They can't see you."

"I know. But I think of them as I bow," she replied, touching fingers to her forehead. "I send the bow."

"But they can't *see* it," he argued. "It's not a proper bow if they don't see it. They can't know if you greet them or not."

"It's like bowing to the ancestors. Or at an altar to a god," Mouse said, uncomfortable as she groped mentally for the right words. "Ul Keg, and the shaman of the Snow Crane God, both said no one has proved the ancestors are watching. Or the gods. But no one has proved they aren't. And things happen that—"

Muin waved off myths, legends, and miracles. "Proper honor will be what I'll bring home." He put two fingers together, the sign of a feather. "That's what we have to think of. Go get our congee, will you? If you're first, maybe you can finger some extra when they're not looking."

They were always looking. But she went anyway, thinking that he was probably right, at least for him. He did have to think of the feather, for that would indeed bring honor to the family. But she had no such future, and it was comforting to bow in the direction of home before sleeping and on waking, thinking of Mother and Father and Ul Keg's smiling faces as she did.

At last came a morning when the servants rising before dawn were in time to see one of the boat crew bring forth a wicker cage, and send pigeons flapping into the air.

The word whispered through the crowded ship that that meant they'd soon reach their destination.

The horizon looked exactly the same day after day, but finally they were all roused early, the remainder of the food stores prepared and shared out. This morning, as a chilly wind tangled with hair and clothes, they were told to line up on deck. All of them. For the first time since they came aboard, the servants with their masters.

They stood in disciplined silence, dirty and rumpled, eyes straining in the slowly lifting darkness to make something of the uniform shape humping on the horizon ahead.

As they drifted near, the rising sun began to paint the emerging contours with light. Muin, as did most of his cohorts, scarcely gave the island a glance once they noticed the watchtowers of the fortress set up on a plain between a steep, rocky set of mountains jutting toward the sky, and a smaller, rounder set of hills terraced behind the bay.

Mouse divided her attention between the emerging landscape and her fellow servants. Ul Keg, who loved all living things, had taught them as much as they would listen to about the world visible and invisible. The latter Mouse had learned about with her scholarly studies, so she took in the orchards behind the village in its square, the new trees, wildflowers she could not name, some she could, birds different and familiar.

She longed to explore, but first she had to survive being the very lowest in the entire hierarchy: a servant, youngest and poorest. What had begun as an adventure had become a question of survival. She, too, had noticed who was spoiling for a fight. They and moving groups were always to be avoided.

At last the sun topped the horizon behind them. Mouse was one of the few who noticed the small village belonging to the dock workers built just back of the shoreline, and the much larger village below the terraced hills, lying to the east of the fortress, divided off by a stream plunging off the low mountains further inland. The new cadets and their servants gazed at the fortress built of mostly red stone, reinforced with mighty timbers. Towers stood over the gate and at each corner. Sentries patrolled along the walls — all boy aged.

The sign over the gate had, in imperial script, *Loyalty Fortress.*

The new arrivals had become wary of moving without orders, so even when the ship had been snugged up against the wharf, they remained where they were, gazes darting every-where, occasionally whispering if no leaderly eye was per-ceived, until a captain in a purple robe appeared at the top of a rise, beside the road that led to the fortress.

The first one over the side was their instructor, who had

never given them his name. Bodies visibly relaxed as he strode away, the knotted rope at his belt gaining distance with each step. Eyes watched avidly as he approached the captain in faded purple, and saluted properly: they knew that salute.

What they didn't know was that the instructor had assessed them with far more expertise than they had him. He handed off a scroll bearing the names of the recruits, saying, "Captain Instructor Fumig. You've got Yulin, grand-nephew of a governor, a tax collector's son, and the son of a noble scholar."

"Any of our own?" Meaning, of course, progeny of military officers.

"Six. Falik from—

"Supreme Cavalry General Falik," the captain cut in, a brief almost-smile easing his weathered face. "Trained, I take it?"

"Very well trained. The other five from captains. All show the expected rudiments of sword, most with knife."

The captain grunted. "How many barefoots?" Commoners, that meant—unlikely to have ever seen a horse, much less ridden one.

"Five."

"Any with promise?"

The instructor pointed to two names, one of these being Muin's. "As for possible trouble, I'd watch these." A thick finger jabbed names—Muin's not among them.

Captain Instructor Fumig's mouth tightened. He knew how to deal with troublesome boys.

"Finally, the one whose moves promise sword talent is a barefoot." Now another tap to Muin's name.

A grunt of approbation in response. The captain knew the commander would be pleased that the one with most promise (or best training) was from a humble background, which usually meant a lot less arrogance to be sweated out. Their commander was justly proud of his reputation for turning out captains who were as dependable and obedient as they were excellently trained.

The two then saluted, and the instructor was dismissed to his well-earned rest before his next journey, which has nothing to do with our tale, and so he passes from our notice.

Captain Instructor Fumig, who in his many years at

Loyalty Fortress had seen countless boys go by him, sorted the newcomers according to the sparse hints he'd heard. By the time he reached the commander's quarters where orderlies waited in expectation of being assigned to integrate the new arrivals, he had mentally assigned the boys to various huts.

To those still waiting on the ship, the wait seemed an eternity, but it was scarcely a turn of the glass before two aides in dun emerged from the fortress gate, a steward in gray behind them, and marched toward the ship.

"When I call your name, come down and line up," an aide shouted, and ran swiftly through the list.

The first ones down were divided from their servants, who were motioned into a clump off to the side, under the watchful eyes of the balding man in gray. Muin and Mouse came midway through the list. She found herself standing with the other servants for the first time, instead of hiding in various cubbies on the ship when she wasn't in line for meals.

When the last servant had joined them, the man in gray said, "I am Steward Pand. You will continue to do your master's laundry and bring his wash water in the mornings, and see to his boots and weapons, but you will take your orders from me, and from any other steward, officer, or aide."

His hard eyes traveled over the waiting faces, and came to rest at a point between the two best-dressed of the new servants. "You lot are at the very bottom of all the ranks, right above the pigs. You will bow to those above you." He demonstrated, hands on thighs, eyes lowered: slight bow for the cadets, deeper for officers and stewards, and a very deep bow for the commander. "Which, I repeat, is everyone. You bow when you encounter them, you bow to acknowledge orders, you bow when dismissed. You will remain silent unless asked a question by a superior—if you ever speak without being spoken to, it had better be to utter a wise saying from *The Twenty-Five Virtues*. If you have a question, your right hand to your heart, and wait to be acknowledged. Follow me."

He whirled and began walking fast, talking as he walked. They hustled after him, crowding behind in order to hear as he led them inside Loyalty Fortress on the heels of the candidates.

They soon learned that all fortresses were constructed

along the same lines, not unlike manors: south was for command and the mess hall off the kitchens, west the instruction halls and the domiciles for the staff, east for supplies, laundry, and the bath house (as there were no women in training here), as well as their own huts; the north belonged to the cadets, and behind their huts, the various training fields stretching back to the far walls.

Yes, huts. This was the main difference. The army had barracks, but anyone could get used to sleeping halls. When on the move, the army slept in tents, and so, to learn tent life, the cadets and their orderlies slept in huts, permanent buildings otherwise constructed to be the exact size and shape of army tents.

"The actual practice tents, I need hardly say, will be yours to set up, break down, and carry," Steward Pand barked over his shoulder. "You will drill with the tents in all weathers, night and day. You will also serve the camp, which means the fortress, in the time you are not seeing to your master's person, clothing, and eventually his horses, his armor, and weapons."

As they crossed the clean-swept parade ground immediately behind the south-facing gate — this parade ground also serving as punishment ground, they were warned — Mouse stared at the huge sundial. She'd seen pictures of them in Mother's books. Of course they would have one if they honored the Sun God, like most of the military. No water clock in sight here, she saw as she skipped between thrusting elbows of larger boys, listening and staring about.

She caught a glimpse of Muin among the cadets lined up before a table, where stewards in gray measured each, then sifted through waiting piles of neatly folded clothing to find items, all dyed brown, that more or less matched each boy. Each item was duly written down.

Then they were dispatched toward the rows of huts over on the north side. How was she going to find Muin?

As if reading her mind — or knowing the first questions anyone would ask — Steward Pand then said to the clump of waiting servants, "Once you are assigned a bunk in your own quarters, you'll be informed where your master is, and tomorrow morning you will begin your duties with wash water and sweeping out the huts, no later than Tiger Five. During the dry season, you must carry your wash water to the kitchen garden. Otherwise, you can dump it in the rain gutter behind the hut."

Fifth gong of Tiger Watch? That meant getting up in the dark before dawn, the hour many called the Ghost Gong. A groaned curse escaped one of the servants with fine clothes, which ended abruptly when Steward Pand's head jerked around.

He made a sharp turn, taking them through the mess hall and the kitchen adjacent, firing information at them at a fast clip. Then to the baths and laundry, as he explained in the fast voice of someone who has repeated the same words for years, that the baths were located underground, off a hot spring that mixed with the stream that came down off the hills on the east side of Loyalty Fortress, dividing it from the village. He told them that some summers that stream dried up, which meant hauling up buckets of cold water from the well, but the hot spring never went dry. Farther up the stream Mouse spotted a huge water wheel, and a windmill on its own hill.

Onward to supply, with even more directions. Mouse, used to memorization from her lessons, kept repeating bits to herself, reaching for mental reminders, as the steward did not slow, nor did anyone dare to request him to. It was clear from his picked-up pace that that curse had annoyed him. Exchanged glances and mutters made it equally clear that Mouse was not the only one wondering if they were all going to pay for it.

Steward Pand banged through the back door, and at last they had reached their own territory: the area closest to supply was reserved for the stewards. The huts beyond — grouped in fives along the fortress's east wall — were for the cadets' servants. And *of course* (someone muttered, echoing Mouse's unspoken thought) the last hut, farthest from everything except the horse barns (and their smell), was theirs: North-Three, west door. They saw that the hut had a wall down the middle, dividing them from the east door's side.

"You will move up to better quarters each year," Steward Pand stated in that wooden voice. "The southmost hut of each year goes to those with the most honor marks. Part of your master's honor merits will be the state of his person and weapons."

"Do we get honor merits?" tall Amna — servant to the noble Cor — asked.

"You're orderlies, not warriors," the steward said. "You earn duty merits, or lose duty marks. One of which you just now lost, speaking without bowing and asking permission after you have *just* been instructed. You will sweep the parade ground directly after the meal."

As Amna flushed, bowing jerkily, Steward Pand went on, "Losing duty marks always has consequences; lose three in a week and there will be a beating to help remind you of duty, in addition to other tasks. Earning duty merits is based on diligence, obedience, and cooperation as well as a job well executed," he added heavily.

They lined up to receive their new clothes, which were an undyed kerchief for tying over the head in hot weather and over the ears in cold, two shapeless tie-shirts of an undyed material the color of light dust, sashed by a thin strip of the same fabric, two robes dyed a sort of dreary light gray for colder weather, one thicker than the other, underclothes and stockings, loose trousers, over which long pieces of fabric tied the lower leg to keep stockings and trousers in place. These were attached to their shoes, and must be *neatly* — he emphasized that word — tied.

Shoes.

Mouse had never worn shoes. No one wore shoes in the village until their feet finished growing. She stared helplessly at the low hempen shoes — for servants' shoes did not reach above the ankle. Then to the other servants, all of whom wore some sort of footgear. The wealthiest at least didn't have the ties. Their shoes were also low, but well made, more like the boys' boots.

Mouse took hers, the smallest pair they had, intensely aware of looks of scorn sent her way. Steward Pand said that they would be expected to be dressed properly before they could eat, and everything had to be done before Horse Watch's First gong, which was when the boys would gather for their first meal.

"You have a single gong to get cleaned up and dressed," he said. "This is the only time you will ever have the bathhouse to yourselves at this time of the day, so don't get used to it. It's for our comfort, not yours. You stink."

With that he turned his back and left them to sort out the bed areas.

The hut was of course one big room, designed for five sleeping pallets to a side — beyond the wall, ten more. There was no obvious preferred place besides avoiding the spot immediately next to the door, which would get all the noise and air of comings and goings. Otherwise, the shelves against the wall, each containing rolled bedding on top and a shelf below for pillows, winter blankets and other oddments, were exactly alike.

Mouse tried to dive for a bed at the far end, but a hard hand caught her by her grimy, messy topknot and she was jerked so violently backward that her neck crackled and she found herself landing painfully on her butt, her armload scattering.

Someone let out a short laugh. Another muttered, "Peh! I hate village rats."

By the time she'd picked herself up, she saw all the bed spaces taken but the two either side of the door. She dumped her things on the closest one as her neck throbbed, and she breathed hard, angry with the others, but also at herself for being unaware. Never again, she vowed.

The bed spaces were divided by a plain wooden clothes rack, which, Mouse was relieved to see, made a kind of partition if you hung your towel and extra garments right. There wasn't much you could do about the person sleeping across from you, or comings and goings through the door, but at least she could dress with her back turned.

The elder boys stampeded for the door once their sleeping places were claimed, and Mouse remembered that they were to wash up and dress.

Another agony! What would the baths be like?

She never expected that this might be the thing that ended her career as a servant. Which would destroy Muin's chances . . . no. She had to think ahead.

She snatched up her new clothes (plus her very own towel!

no more waiting for her brothers' damp one while she dripped!) and bolted after the others, peering fearfully over their shoulders to see the worst.

The outer chamber, tiled in ceramic and walled with polished wood, was where people dried and dressed. The bathhouse lay down a long curving stair cut out of living rock, from which wisps of steam emerged. She was not the only one to refuse to undress all the way, as modesty is one of the Twenty-Five Virtues.

She followed some boys down the stairs, and felt the tingle of Essence charms, recognizing them as protection against mold and dankness—the charms had been carved right into the stone.

Around the corner at the bottom, they entered a world of steam. Vague shapes in various colors of brown, and many feet, were scarcely visible. At one end someone had worked wooden conduits of bamboo poked with holes at regular intervals, through which small streams of water spilled down. A few seemed to prefer bathing under these, but the rest went into the pool, where myriad heads bobbed about, dark hair drifting about them like sooty seaweed.

She spotted a space at the far end of the conduit that was mainly steam, no feet visible, and ran to it over the warm, wet stone, her hands shaking as she divested herself of her clothes. Then she plunged into the pool a few steps away. Along the edges of the pool were dishes carved in the shape of shells containing soap. She scooped up a handful. It was gritty with fine silt, smelling of olive and lime, not unlike the soap that Father made at home. He must have learned it in the military, she thought as she soaped herself all over, then ducked under water to rinse free of it.

Then she hauled herself out of the water under one of the streams. She would have loved to stand there, but not naked. While she knew from growing up with brothers that she looked like them from the back, anyone might poke in front of her and stare. She wrapped herself in her towel, grabbed her filthy home-clothes, and hesitated, wondering if she ought to risk a deflection charm.

But there were no scholars or geomancers or augurs or

suchlike in a military camp who would detect Essence being used for a charm, surely. For that matter, she wasn't even certain the charm would be effective as she hastily sketched the signs on her body and whispered the chant. Essence could be that way, wayward as the wind.

If this charm did have any effect, it was as close to being invisible as one could get, diverting attention. It would break if she did anything to draw attention.

She forced herself to move quietly behind two chattering boys back upstairs to the bench where she'd left the rest of her things. No one so much as glanced her way as she pulled on the new underclothes under her towel, and the trousers.

The worst was now over. At halfway to eleven years, she was still as flat as a fish in front, above the waist no different from the others.

Over her body went the loose shirt-tunic, too short, falling above her knees, to be a robe. This was much like what she'd grown up in. And the sash was too thin to store ward-stones or other items in, a reminder she was in the military —

Mother's, Father's, and Ul Keg's voices came unbidden, Mother saying that while ward-stones could be charmed with Essence to ward specific types of demons, the nasty articles, mostly from once-living creatures, that were supposed to ward swellings and itches and suchlike were all quackery.

I saw it myself, she'd said once, with a frown. *In the village where I was born, a man had carried the finger bone of an infant to ward infections, but he tripped and fell, the brittle bone pierced his stomach like a knife, and he died after a terrible infection developed. I always wondered how that baby died – if the gods had dispensed justice.*

Ul Keg had said, *Another reason the goddess Suanek forbade blood sacrifices, and the eating of all creatures who feed their young from their own bodies: that violence is loosed into the world to beget more violence.*

After which Father had said, *Such stuff is forbidden in the military. You're supposed to be strong enough to defend yourself.*

The memory brought a hard knot of grief to her heart. She shivered as she tied the sash, then wound up her wet hair and clasped her topknot. She pulled the stockings on, which felt confining to her toes. She glared at the shoes, then pulled them on. They were made with flexible fiber, knotted loops joined to a larger loop that pulled together over her foot by the ties, to make it fit. That much she could do. But getting the tie up her leg utterly failed.

She was fighting tears when someone poked her shoulder. "You."

She looked up into eyes a lighter brown than often seen, in a face marked with freckles. Those freckles, and his thick, coarse dark brown hair gleaming with a reddish sheen meant he had outlanders somewhere in his heritage. Like Mouse herself. Though she had never seen a mirror, she'd examined her hair in the light once or twice, and seen the brassy sheen in her dark brown hair that her mother had pointed out she'd inherited from her grandmother Bemti.

She recognized the freckled boy as one of the military boys, about Second Brother's age. He said, "I'll teach you in trade."

All right, trade was something she understood. But . . . what did she have to trade? "What?" she said belatedly.

"You're kinda stupid, aren't you?" he retorted, but not unfriendly. "Or is it just that you've still got mother's milk on your lip." When she didn't answer, he said plainly, "You do my morning hot water bucket for a week."

Of course! It was like home, then, trade for work. She was about to bargain, noticed they were last, and bit it back. "Done."

After all, she had to fetch water anyway, and she was at least used to hauling buckets.

"There's a trick to this," he said, kneeling down. "Your mistake is in trying to wrap it straight, like you'd wrap a board. Your leg is not a board. You turn the tie as you wrap. Like so."

He worked rapidly, the ties crossing over her ankle and calf, and tying off in back. Then he flicked the tie loose with a finger, unraveled it, and said, "Now you do it."

She bit back a protest. This was actually good — if he didn't abandon her.

But he stayed there until she'd more or less reproduced what he'd done. "That'll do," he said critically. "For the first day. There's always someone who either wore silk shoes or straw. Don't give the tassels reason to mark you, and they'll overlook a little mess until you get it right. But my guess is, they'll be looking at that Cor bigmouth."

Cor — that was the clan name of that arrogant noble boy.

"Tassels?" she asked. "You mean the officers?"

"Instructors, officers. Who else wears sword tassels?"

She ducked her head and slapped her thighs in acknowledgment. He turned away. She followed more slowly, figuring they were done until morning, but he paused at the door. "You belong to the tiger with the caterpillar brows, eh?" He touched his own brows.

"Tiger," she had learned by listening, could be a compliment or an insult, depending on the tone, and on what words came before it. Someone who thought too highly of himself could be a golden tiger, or a paper tiger for one who boasted without any proof. Both were equal for scorn in tone. But to be called a tiger usually meant someone fast and strong. Prowess.

"My brother?" she asked. "Is he the one you mean?"

"Brothers. Thought so. You got caterpillar brows too. He's a dragon where you live, eh?"

Tiger. Dragon. This was definitely a fishing expedition. "Everything is new for us," she said, navigating around the rocks. "Our village is very small."

Freckles gave a grunt, then said abruptly, "What's your name?"

"Mouse," she said automatically, then fought a grimace. She'd thought about names! But she hadn't had a chance to settle on one with Muin.

She waited for scorn, but to her total surprise, the boy thumped his chest and said, "Among *us*, I'm Colt. But out there, I'll be Grunt Bian."

"Grunt?"

The word for grunt was one character-stroke from *de*, pronounced in a lower tone, which the lowest form of laborer, usually given to street sweepers or farm hands hired by farmers to do the scut work no one wanted, like night-soil gathering and spreading on crops. "We're not stewards or orderlies?"

"No. Just as who we serve is a cadet, not a warrior. Our rank will rise as our masters rise, as long as we don't do something that gets us kicked out. Who're you with?"

"Ryu Muin. So I guess that makes me Grunt Ryu," she said, to get used to it.

Colt punched her shoulder. "Better run."

They caught up with the rest of their group. Mouse flung her dirty clothes in a corner of the bed shelf, and trailed the others to the mess hall, which had long tables with mats much like the ones made in Sweetwater. Here they found fish grilled with spices and spiced vegetables to ladle onto their rice. There was tonic tea to wash it down, and barely enough time to eat it before they were herded through to the kitchens, where, they discovered, some of them would be put to work washing the bowls once the cadets came in, then stacking things to be ready for dinner.

"As for the rest of you," Steward Pand stated, "you'll begin your chores today. The new grunts always rotate weekly on night-soil duty, as well as general sweeping, as you don't know how to do much else. You'll be collecting and hauling night-soil for longer if you lose three duty marks in a week." He then eyed the servants of the noble sons, who superficially looked like everyone else now, and said, "When I call your name, you will step forward."

Mouse held her breath — and sure enough, Steward Pand's flat voice pronounced with the barest hint of relish, "Grunt Cor."

The tall, sharp-chinned servant with the soft hands actually hissed in a breath of affront.

Pand stopped, and eyed him. "You have something to say, Grunt Cor?"

"My name is Amna —" the unsettled boy began, then shut up, his lips white.

Steward Pand gave a tiny nod, and went on to distribute the jobs, which this first week would rotate by day, so that everyone learned everything. The three nobles' servants had the first day, but there was little time for anyone else to gloat.

Just as well: Mouse heard that she would have night-soil duty the following day, along with Colt.

She made certain her face didn't betray her, but shrugged inwardly. It was nothing new, after all. She and her brothers had had the job of carrying the night soil to the garden since they were small. As Steward Pand finished speaking, she peered past him at the kitchen garden through the back windows. There wheelbarrows with flies buzzing about them waited at the head of the path, obviously collected that morning.

Pand dismissed them then, Mouse hearing a whispered, "Watch Amna cover himself in shit."

EIGHT

HERE IS A LITTLE about North-Three Hut, west door, as they began exchanging names.

Mouse learned that Colt hadn't been surprised at her being called Mouse because apparently all servants — that is, most except for the rare ones from powerful, established clans — didn't have names; they had nicknames as names.

As was common everywhere, most big households numbered servants of a given generation in birth order. These numbers might turn into a name, given by someone or other higher in rank, not necessarily parents; whether careless, cruel, or kind, those names stuck.

Pigear served a general's son, Weed the nephew of a governor. Those she learned the first night, as Weed bragged about his connections. Colt and Vin both served captains' sons. And Dun's servant, Trickle, was obviously Dun's brother. Cadet Dun and his brother Trickle looked a lot more alike than Mouse suspected she resembled Muin.

She also discovered when she passed the week's duty roster board that she and Colt had gained a duty merit next to their names. It was written in green ink, which they learned meant "cooperation." Her hauling Colt's hot water, and Colt teaching her the shoe ties, had been noticed, and approved of as cooperation; what it meant was, they still had to sweep around the huts and other buildings, but they were exempt from sweeping the parade ground for that week.

She soon saw that Colt and the others who had grown up in barracks were used to the invisible rules of military life. She decided to watch them for clues.

Her experience contrasted with that of Amna (who until that day had been quite proud of being Cor Kenek's personal servant, as his family had served the Cor clan for generations), who regarded this journey so far as the worse experience of his life.

He had been promised an exalted position as personal aide to Cor Kenek, who of course would rise to army command as fast as a comet crossed the sky. But no one had told him what would happen to him before then, beginning with losing the underservants on the very first day, followed by a filthy journey in a stinking ship, crowded next to commoners, and now *this*.

Night soil duty meant collection from the huts, consolidating it into big jugs, putting it on wagons in threes, then dragging it through the east gate. Half went to the farmers, who used it to augment the sandy soil of the island, and the other half went to the pits to make gunpowder for training the fifth years. Then they had to use the hay-colored sand to scour out the big jugs and return them for the next day's use.

They were told that detouring to the kitchen garden to dump it would mean instant punishment—and every year someone tried it. They carried the scars for the rest of their lives.

He gagged and retched, slopping the contents from the huts into the big collection jars. No matter how hard he tried, he couldn't control the splashes. Then when it came time to scour, he just threw sand in and dumped it out, ignoring the long sticks with bristles on the ends.

Miserable and furious, Amna looked over to discover the others stuck with duty already done with their jugs, or else working in twos. No one looked his way.

And so Amna had to work alone, swearing all kinds of wild revenge the moment he got the chance. By the time he finally finished, and trod reeking toward the hut to get his second set of clothes (as he wondered what he would wear on the morrow), he was relieved to notice that the others were nearly as bespattered as he was.

"They stuck us with it on purpose," he muttered, catching up—and trying not to resent how they stepped away from him. Yes, he stank. But so did they.

"Nothing we can do about orders," one said miserably.

"But there is something we can do about *that*," Weed said, making an obscene gesture back toward the vegetable garden. "We just have to find the right person to serve *us*."

That got Amna's attention. "How?" he asked with a skeptical grimace. "No one will trade for shit duty."

Weed grinned. "If we stick together, we can make it happen. We just need a leader." He turned to Amna, who betrayed a flush at what he thought was a compliment.

Well-honed by three years of avoiding the Sweetwater twins, Mouse watched everyone. She saw Amna's speculative glance, and Weed's contemptuous sneer when they were at the laundry scrubbing out their old clothes as well as their masters'. She knew neither expression was caused by admiration for how well she used a clothes paddle to beat and scrub the dirt out. She was the smallest, which meant she was going to be a target. The Sweetwater twins had *always* made targets of anyone smaller, until they turned up with allies—like First Brother.

She finished hastily and fled back to North-Three west, very last of the grunts' domiciles, to unroll her bedding. She longed to go to sleep right then—her eyes burned—but she forced herself to practice the shoe ties a lucky ten times, to train her fingers.

She was asleep two breaths after her head hit the pillow, waking as soon as the first ones stirred around her. It was still dark. With the habit of a lifetime she sensed that it was third or fourth gong in Tiger Watch.

She quickly made her bows, then scrambled into her clean outfit, her hands faster as she did up her shoes. Then she ran out, wincing as the shoes rubbed against the sides of her feet.

The pails for the hot water were no larger than those at home. She walked with Colt, whose master had been assigned to the same hut Muin lived in. Colt carried the masters' clean clothes so that Mouse could lug the two pails.

Muin looked so *different*, in his sashed brown military robe, with the neat headband around his brow. But there was his familiar face — far more familiar than her own, which she had never seen — as he watched her with a grimace of pain. She first filled the mouth-rinse bowl, with its bit of powdered leaf at the bottom, then, as he swished that around, she filled the big bowl for him to wash in. As he did, she whispered in their island dialect, "Are you all right?"

In silence he pointed his chin at his feet, where she saw blisters worse than her own. Her eyes went to his boots, with their rings worked in to turn steel, and the straps for holding a knife, and the hard soles with the heel made for catching on stirrups. At least her shoes had give in them. "You?" he asked.

"Same," she whispered. "Do they have a medic? For ointment? I can make you some if they don't," she added.

"I'm not the only one," he muttered, sliding a glance at where Trickle and his elder brother bent over Dun's equally raw feet, the brothers' black hair the same crow-feather shade.

"I'm not going to stand out by whining," Muin whispered. He spat into the bucket, and then she poured the dirty wash water in on top of it, and took it and his dirty laundry out.

And so began her new life.

Each morning she woke to the sound of the night patrol passing on their last round. In the thick darkness of the hut she faced the direction of home and bowed to parents and tutor, then soundlessly scrambled into her clothes before getting out of bed: she was not used to the cold of the mornings.

After getting up and running to fetch the hot water, she was awake, at least, and hot congee, plain except for some egg, warmed her. The work was no harder than any job she'd done at home, but it was all drudgery — carrying, scrubbing, and always the endless sweeping lest malicious imps and demons gather in the dust and dirt and spread bad luck. Aunt Fox-Ear Iley's old saying about putting down the rake to pick up the broom had become her life.

By the end of her second day she found herself actually missing her scholarly lessons, but worst was the itch from missing practice. She had been doing Heaven and Earth every day before sparring with Muin, most of the time under Father's exacting eye. How was he going to excel if he didn't have her as partner?

She tried to spy out Muin's training as she ran back and forth on various tasks. But the first year cadets were mostly at the farther fields. North-Three, being the last hut, had its north window looking into the riding ground, but all she saw was dust.

For Muin, those dust storms were the result of humiliation: learning horseback riding. Until now, the only time he'd seen a horse had been those brief visits to the harbor, and he hadn't come within fifty feet of one.

At the other end of the riding field, Falik, Yulin, and Cor galloped and wheeled their mounts, looking like proper warriors. Muin, Dun, and a handful of others who all felt like two-year-olds were carefully instructed in horse safety and how to mount properly. Then they were led in a circle on what were obviously older horses, an instructor whapping thighs and back and arms to get the boys into a correct seat.

Obviously he would earn no honor marks there.

The next time Mouse saw Muin was in a miserable lineup outside the medic's door, with Dun and an assortment of city, farm, and merchant family boys. The reason was clear the next day when she brought Muin's wash water and took away his dirty clothes, including bloody stockings. At least the healers had ointment, which meant she wouldn't be expected to find time to scour the unknown fields outside Loyalty Fortress in order to seek the means to make some.

Presently she found enough of a rhythm to think ahead of ways to do her tasks faster, leaving her bits of time. She also knew the territory enough to have figured out where no one was likely to look for her. It seemed Muin was with those boys all the time, so it was up to her to find a good spot for them to continue practicing Heaven and Earth once he did get a little freedom.

She ran downwind of the kitchen garden, which ended at a lot of scrub brush and some wild apple trees with small, sour fruit that no one gathered except to add to the compost heap.

The trees grew around a grassy area that had once held some sort of building, screening it from the fortress's east wall as well as the kitchen buildings.

As she had hoped, there was plenty of space in the clearing. Yes, it stank — which meant she could use the garden as a privy, making sure to blend her waste with the soil the way it was done at home, once the kitchen workers tending the garden were elsewhere. That meant she could avoid the regular privies, which were basically holes in a board above the collection buckets, set in a row so everyone could see one another. In the baths at least there was steam to help hide her.

Reminding herself to bring a kerchief next time, she pulled her tie-shirt up over her nose and worked through Heaven and Earth. Because she had no weapon to practice with, she obeyed Father's injunction and did handstands on the grassy verge, and then found a good branch of the apple tree and pulled her head to it over and over, whispering some of Ul Keg's and Mother's favorite poems because counting was boring.

Another time, she finished hanging laundry, bent to make sure there were no feet visible among the rows, then drilled again, aiming Essence at hanging stockings and underthings. It was satisfying to watch them flutter. Then she hand-walked between the rows of clean things, making certain her feet touched nothing, or she'd have to wash it anew. It was a good test of balance.

So it went. When she could drill, she reveled in the familiar rhythms, even if inevitably she never made it twice through, interrupted by the gong that sent her hurrying to her next task.

She avoided her fellow grunts as much as possible, but she felt stares from time to time, and at night she heard the suppressed breathing of anger. It was easy to guess what was going to happen, most likely before their next stint at night soil duty.

She had no friends, and she was youngest and smallest. Father had even said that certain types of people always threw their anger at those lower in rank, smaller, or lesser in their own eyes.

One cold morning toward the end of the week, she was not surprised when she came to that turn in the shortcut that was out of sight of all buildings, to find Amna and Vin, servant to a boy from the rich, influential Pol family, standing in her way.

When she backed up a step, a crunch of rubble behind her caused her to glance back to discover Weed, servant to Yulin, the grand-nephew of a governor, sauntering out to block her way.

She began her warrior breathing, though her heart hammered against her ribs in a way that had never happened before practice, no matter how arduous. She flexed her fingers among the folds of her gray robe, glad she'd been drilling, and put her hands on her thighs the way servants were supposed to salute everybody.

There was no responding politeness. Amna, the sharp-chinned tall one with the tight smile of expectation said slowly, "I hate rising early. I hate the cold. I hate being here."

He stopped there, as if he expected an answer. Mouse wasn't going to oblige him.

Thick-set Weed snickered behind her, a sound that made her hackles rise.

"Here's how it's going to be," Amna said even more slowly, and she understood that he thought she was stupid. Or was pretending she was. "You farm wallowers sleep and eat in filth. You're used to it. So you are going to take night soil duty for the three of us. A simple task, everyday for you, I'm certain. Do it quietly and well, and the rest of your day is yours to enjoy."

For the space of six heartbeats she considered how much simpler life would be if she gave in. It wasn't that the work would be that much harder . . . she already had to get up early, and fetch and carry. What material difference between one and four?

But then she took in those narrowed eyes, and Weed's licked lips of anticipation, and Amna's quick breathing. Weed had placed himself behind and slightly to the left—away from what he probably assumed was her strongest hand.

"Speak up," Amna said. "On your knees, kiss the ground in promise, and all you leave with is a reminder. Otherwise . . ." He held out his hand flat, and then slowly formed a fist.

She understood then that this would not end here. They

were enjoying it far too much. If she gave in, she would end up doing all their scut work.

She drew in a slow breath, feeling the tingle of Essence, as she half-turned, assessing them. First strike from Amna. Vin next, Weed ready to hit from behind, maybe a sweep.

All last season she'd mentally gone over that fight at the garrison, reinforcing what Father had always told them: the only way to come out of a fight against superior numbers was to attack fast, winning yourself enough time to run.

So she dropped to her knees, head down as she watched their feet. Sure enough, the two in front relaxed their stances in anticipation of her humiliation. Weed snickered behind her, giving away his exact position. She laid her hands flat on the dusty ground, then tensed all her muscles. A leap, a thrust of Essence-wind as she opened both her hands full of dust directly into Amna's and Vin's faces.

They cursed, staggering back. She whirled, kicked to the side, her toes connecting painfully with Weed's left knee. It hurt even through her shoes, but the pain was far worse for him. He crumpled up, howling. She pelted past him, turning a corner out of their sight before leaping to the top of the supply roof, and then dropping down safely between the rows of laundry hung up on lines.

She heard them cursing as they chased, their noise diminishing as she bolted away for the safety of numbers.

Amna and Vin chased after, rounding the back supply hut in the direction they supposed their target had gone, and thus smashed straight into a group of older servants lugging freshly washed laundry toward the drying lines.

One basket flew as its owner tumbled to the ground. Clean clothes slapped into the dirt. The sudden encounter staggered Amna mentally as well as physically, leaving him open-mouthed with horror as angry hands were laid upon him.

Weed limped painfully into sight then, and the infuriated senior servants put together a likely but erroneous picture that Amna had the wit not to deny: it was apparent that he and Vin had just ganged up on Weed.

The result was both immediate (Amna and Vin had to rewash all the dirtied laundry on top of their undone chores) and prospective (Steward Pand assigned them night soil duty, beginning the next day, for a week).

The grunts' portion of the mess hall was full of the story, which had grown in the telling. Amna and Vin suffered in silence. Weed as well, for he found it far better for everyone to believe he'd been ambushed by two than taken out in a single kick by the smallest and youngest of them all.

NINE

MOUSE KEPT WATCHING MUIN as often as she could. She was lurking behind the horse barn when Muin and his hut at last got some free time, after the evening meal. She hovered at the extreme edge of their territory, trying to catch his attention, but Muin stayed right with his hut, where a set of battered metal vases with long necks had been set up. Each vase had a pair of tubes, called ears, attached to either side.

As Mouse slunk along the verge, she discovered that this was a game. Arrows were unfamiliar in Sweetwater. The boys tossed these, calling out points if they managed to land one within either of the ears or in the equally narrow opening of the pot, called the mouth.

Muin, of course, was terrible at it. He never even looked up, though Mouse waited as long as she dared. Even when the boys laughed, or jeered, he kept trying.

She finally left, fighting a sense of loneliness. As if she'd been cast adrift. No, that's stupid, she scolded herself. He still depended on her.

She ran back to her secret spot and practiced Heaven and Earth on her own.

Of course the three erstwhile bullies wanted retribution, but Mouse stayed out of their way, and as the days slipped by, tempers cooled enough for them to realize that that little turd Mouse hadn't told anyone the truth. But could have. As Vin mumbled when Weed cut him out and suggested another try, "Mouse could have blabbed. We would have looked like rabbits. Far as I'm concerned, we're quits."

"You *are* a rabbit," Weed muttered in disgust.

Despite Weed's, and Amna's, longing for revenge, further action was prevented by the fact that Steward Pand, who had dealt with boys for years, seemed to be everywhere, watching, at the unlikeliest times—and the next lecture was begun with a reminder of the punishment for three duty marks, following which another third meant expulsion. And expulsion meant being booted out after a beating—you had to make your own way home.

As Amna's temper cooled he ignored Mouse, to her relief, but she felt Weed watching her from time to time, the way the twins used to watch First Brother and the rest of them at festival time, when all the villages got together. And because she listened for them as well as watched for them, she overheard Weed trying to urge, then scorn, Vin into attacking her when she wasn't looking.

"Yes, Mouse is a shit, but if you want him scragged, *you* do it," Vin snapped.

"You're going to let it rest, after he made you limp for three weeks? What next, cleaning his underwear?"

"If you want Mouse scragged, do it yourself," Vin retorted—then they both hastily looked around for Pand and his ever-ready wand.

Mouse had been perched on the roof overhead. She drew back in case instinct caused either of them to look up as well as around, then leaped down on the opposite side of the supply hut.

She watched all three from the time she got up until bed. If she saw either of their familiar heads, Vin's square, his hair darker than Weed's, she went another way, or if they were in a group for instruction, she stayed on the opposite side.

She had enough to occupy her mind. Muin continued to

stay away during his free time — twice she saw him and a couple others from his hut out practicing that boring-looking game with the arrows and the pot, over and over. Pitch-pot, it was called.

The weather got steadily colder. She discovered that if she stayed dry and busy, she could remain warm enough to endure, but as soon as she got wet, she couldn't seem to get warm without burning her inner Essence until she was thoroughly dry again. Getting out of bed was more difficult every day. At least she wasn't alone in that.

"I thought we were going to be issued winter togs," Colt muttered one morning, words that Mouse had been thinking, but didn't dare speak lest they draw unwanted attention.

Sure enough, all the northerners laughed or made scornful noises, and one said, "It's almost summer. If you think this is bad, weak little weanling, just wait till the *real* cold weather gets here!"

The word "weak" ended discussion. As usual.

At least boys were predictable.

The day of Mouse's introduction to the war tents started out better than the past few, with the sun emerging again after those miserable, seemingly endless days of rain and wind. Steward Tolu came through the mess hall as they gulped down their congee, announcing that the stewards' orderlies had brought the tents out. Each hut was to take one wagon to the practice field, where they would be given instructions.

Colt, with an older brother in service, leaned out to whisper, "If we're fast, we don't have to drag the wagon as far."

By now, whatever their private feelings about one another, every grunt in North-Three, west and east doors, had learned respect for anything that aided their unending labors. No one argued. They began slipping out, some cramming the last of their meal into their mouths, eyes tearing as they tried to hastily swallow down their food.

They found that someone had already loaded the wagons full of tent equipment, one tent's worth of equipment to each wagon.

"We have to drag it to the field," Colt said.

Quick as they were, the grunts in North-Two west and North-Center east were faster. But at least they were ahead of the rest. They found the training field empty, the first year cadets having been taken out to the far field to drill in riding and shooting, and the older year cadets away altogether on their endless overnight battle games.

Little flags had been pushed into the ground, marking off the space for four tents. North-Two west was already heading toward the closest one, North-center east right behind them. Mouse's hut mates worked together pushing and pulling the wagon over the bumpy ground on which the mud was already drying fast in the strengthening sun.

When their wagon drew abreast of the logs marking the edge of the field, they looked from their wagonload of poles and long, lumpy rolls of canvas to one to another.

Colt knew generally what to expect; though he and Vin were barracks-raised, they had never been anywhere near any battles or war camps. But Weed, servant to a family connected to a governor, had seen countless tent-pavilions set up for festivals. He liked knowing what no one else knew—and he reveled in everyone having to listen to him. "These rolls on top are the sides, the wood the supports. The roof parts are at the bottom."

He paused, enjoying the undivided attention. Then his eyes fell on Mouse, the smallest, with the always-untidy knot of brassy-tinged dark hair. He saw a way to get back at Mouse without attacking outright and drawing down Pand's wrath. "I've done it a million times," he lied—but he'd seen men carry them. How hard could it be? He knew he was as strong as a man, or nearly. "We carry them, one to each end. I'll go first. Mouse, you take that end."

So far, cooperation had earned them green duty merits. So Mouse moved to the wagon, as everyone else watched to see how it was to be done.

Weed—who was indeed a strong boy for fifteen—gave a grunt and began hauling out the thick, rolled canvas, hefting it to one shoulder. His confidence faltered, but he squared himself up, determined not to show weakness before the others.

Mouse eyed that roll, and when the far end appeared, she

tried to take it so it wouldn't hit the muddy ground, but it slipped through her fingers. Her half of the roll knocked her to the mud and fell on top of her, causing Weed to stagger.

"You're even more of a weanling than I thought," he said corrosively, exulting inside. This had gone better than he'd hoped.

Mouse didn't hear the whispers and laughter among the others. She knew Weed was trying to make her a target, and her greatest fear if everyone scragged her was discovery.

Furious, she summoned all the Essence in her belly, and in the process of wiping the mud off her clothes, whispered a strengthening charm as she sketched quick shapes over trunk, legs, and arms.

Charms worked or they didn't. The one thing she was sure of was Mother's repeated warnings not to spend Essence in anger. Every second page in all the books warned of fire, poison, ash, destruction.

But anger-fueled Essence worked.

She stooped, grunted, and hauled the muddy, slippery role to her shoulder. "Come on," she snapped. "Are we going to stand all day?"

That much speech took far more effort than it should have. She knew the coming walk would tax all her strength. She concentrated on that fire in her belly, tiger-breathing with each step the way Father had taught them all.

She was scarcely aware of an abrupt silence behind them as others began to lift the rolls, or tried.

Weed was slowing as they neared the flat. Ten steps . . . seven . . . five . . . blackness whorled at the edge of her vision. She breathed hard against it, and at two, dropped her end, then bent over, shaky hands on her knees as she fought against the onslaught of lightheadedness.

She was vaguely aware of bawling voices as Steward Tolu arrived at a run, bellowing, "What *idiot* told you to do that? Who ordered those two . . ."

"It was Weed, ah, Grunt Yulin himself," Colt spoke up, saluting smartly. "Said he's got experience. Told Grunt Ryu to take the other end."

Tall, gaunt Steward Tolu stared at little Mouse, still

gasping for breath, and shouted, "It's *three* to a roll. Three! Four, if you're that size, even five! Grunt Yulin, that's a duty mark against you for stupidity, and another for giving orders. *You* will clean every tent when we get them back to Supply. And you will be sweeping the parade ground for the rest of the month to burn those duty marks off."

Weed paled, his gaze still flicking back to Mouse, who had straightened up, once-pallid face flushed. Mouse looked destroyed, but by rights the wretched runt should not have been able to lift that canvas, much less carry it fifty long paces.

Steward Tolu snapped, "The rest of you pair up. Look, everyone else is already done unloading. North-Three west is holding everyone back. Grunt Ryu. You'll drive tent pegs, so retrieve the mallet. You're done carrying for the day. It's a miracle you got that far." He went on scolding and complaining about idiocy as the rest of their hut struggled to get the rolls out.

Three times they had to work the poles into the sides of each tent wall, raise and anchor them, as a team worked on the primary tent pole. Then came the struggle to get the roof on. It was heavy, sweaty, awkward work, while Steward Tolu stalked back and forth along the line bawling orders and reminding them that the weather would *never* be good when they set them up in the field.

As they worked, many speculative glances were sent Mouse's way, and at one point, Colt, nearest her holding the rope as she drove the stake into the ground, said, "What's your birth year, Mouse?"

She was aware of listening ears. "Dolphin."

"Dolphin! You're just a baby! My Third Brother was born in the Year of the Dolphin, but the family said he was too young to—"

"*Anyway,*" Mouse cut in, "there were no auspicious stars or signs. Not that we noticed, as we have no augurs in our village. What we do have is a lot of wood and water to carry."

That was accepted, more or less. There wasn't time for more discussion, as everything was haste, haste, haste. At last they were told to roll and stow exactly as they had found their tent, and then they dragged the wagon back to supply to unload the rolls and spread them out.

Here, Weed, along with three from other huts who had lost duty marks, dismally set about cleaning the mud off the canvas and draping it over the drying racks.

Bed was late that night. Most dropped into sleep the moment they lay down. Mouse, exhausted and aching, forced herself once the lantern was snuffed to sit up in bed and do her cleansing breathing. There was no hope she wasn't going to waken with aching joints the next day, but the breathing would help—that much she had learned when she had worked too hard with Muin, or with her Essence experiments.

Her shoulder still throbbed where she had propped that canvas when she finished, but at least she had a calmer mind for making her bow to parents and tutor—

The door opened. Quickly she lay down as Weed entered with the lagging steps of fatigue. She closed her eyes, willing his attention away.

To no avail. All he'd been able to think about ever since the tent training was Mouse, half his size, carrying something that had taken all his own strength. And Mouse, kicking out his knee so quick and precise there'd been nothing to see but a blur. He'd told himself ever since that day that the kick had been merely a lucky accident. But now he was beginning to think that there was a whole lot more to Mouse than met the eye.

TEN

SPRING RIPENED TOWARD SUMMER, the two moons' parting ever widening as Ghost Moon gathers the souls for leading to the River of Forgetfulness before Phoenix Moon can bring them to reincarnation.

Mouse's world was now filled with the smells of dust and horse drifting in the north window, the long, hot days banishing memories of cold as North-Three Hut was kept on the run. Muin's path to greatness was not going to be easy, she grumped to herself from time to time, especially when chores kept her and her fellow grunts toiling from Tiger Watch's last gong until Dragon Watch's last gong, or even into Turtle Watch, which was when they began tent drill at night.

On days when she fell aching into bed, facing more of the same on the morrow, she occasionally choked back tears as she made her silent bows to her parents so far away in that cozy, quiet house on the island.

She missed home terribly at those times, searching every corner of her memory for her mother's voice as her body performed tedious chores. It was her father's voice she heard during rare free moments, when she escaped everyone, going to the far side of the kitchen garden, where she put up charms warding the smell as she performed Heaven and Earth twice through, right hand and left. And it was Ul Keg's voice she heard when she contemplated what sort of path Muin would be taking on his way to glory, as the wandering monk was the one who had talked most about the world outside the island.

As for her hut mates, Vin ceased to trouble her—he watched warily from a distance, but Mouse never again performed such an astonishing feat of strength. Still, the runt seemed to be too strong for such a small size, until Weed decided *that's* what it was. Mouse was a runt. Probably as old as they were, lying about being born in the Dolphin year to cover being so short. He tried a couple times to ask questions to trip Mouse into telling the truth, but somehow the little turd was always somewhere else, or else altogether out of sight.

Amna had also ceased to trouble Mouse, who kept a prudent distance, never so much as speaking to him . . . unlike Steward Pand and the others, who seemed to be tireless in their determination to pounce on the smallest deviation from orders, handing out extra labors of the most hated jobs as well as whacks from those wands.

It was Weed who waited for the right moment to square accounts, bolstered by the heated mutters of his master, who as one of the Yulin clan, who after generations of middling warrior captains was determined to rise, meant to take the coveted number one ranking by year's end. As was his right! For Yulin, the successes of Muin, Cor, and that swaggering shit Falik, son of a general, were personal affronts. Weed soaked in his master's smoldering anger, taking it back each evening to North-Three west, and cherishing it like a hot coal in a bucket, ready to start a fire.

Mouse's world had narrowed to hard, predictable work. The masters watched them closely, giving them new tasks to learn the moment they mastered the old.

Which now included horse care. That was one of the few chores that most of them enjoyed, especially as it was whispered that the orderlies of those whose masters were being shaped toward cavalry might be taught to ride. They would be carrying his war gear, rather than walking alongside their masters' horses or the baggage wagons in column.

Tent duty continued to be roundly loathed. But at least they were getting better at it.

The routine broke abruptly one day when whisper breezed from lips to eager ears: there was going to be a punishment in the square, the entire fortress lined up.

"Who? What?"

"Theft. It's one of those down in South-One. Turnip in East-Two east says he was caught in the act, and when they searched his trunk, it was full of silver!" That was Trickle, North-Three's biggest gossip.

The tale lost nothing in the telling; the trunk full of silver had expanded to gold, and secret plans, by the time everyone lined up on a hot, windy day to watch the disciplined, deliberate flogging of a wretched boy before he was forced out through the great gate to make his way in the world however he could.

Then they were dismissed, some sick to their stomachs, others thrilled, all with Commander Weken's field-command voice ringing in their ears: "My warriors leave here knowing the truth of the fourth rule in *The Way of the Blade*: they must be able to trust one another, or they are defeated before they ever reach the battlefield."

It was especially painful to some, and puzzling to others, when the word was passed through the grunts' masters that what had actually been stolen was a few brass coins, a silver hair clasp, and a handful of oddments whose owners assumed had been lost.

There was rarely talk in North-Three west at night, outside of a few desultory remarks about the next day's chores. They were too tired, and cherished sleep too much for chat. But this night was an exception.

"Why'd he do it?"

"His mother saw a thief before he was born, of course."

"Bad alignment of stars, and his family too cheap to pay for augurs to ward evil."

"He was a fool. Shut up and go to sleep."

"*You* shut up. What'll happen to his master, what was his name, Erk? Will he be booted out too?"

"I heard they questioned Erk for a full day." That was Trickle, his voice always excited when repeating gossip.

"Ayah, he can't have known. Or there'd be two of them bleeding all over the ground."

"One of the kitchen grunts is going to get lucky now."

Everyone knew that the kitchen, armory, and repair areas were mostly staffed by the villagers, many of whose sons hoped to luck into a chance at serving a future general. A few of them did make up the numbers of grunts if a cadet had not brought one, or something happened to his.

When she'd found that out, Mouse offered to let one take over for Muin, to get a short answer: "No. I can *talk* to you. And when I get more liberty, I want to go back to our sparring."

Mouse accepted that. After all, she had no idea how to get back to the island if Muin turned out not to want her.

The others were still speculating about who would be the new grunt for Erk.

"Not if Erk's family has plenty of money, and sends some-one new. I wonder if that grunt will be with us or start with next year's grunts. And Erk's a *second year!*"

"Shut up, shut up, shut up, I want to sleep."

"*You* shut up."

A brief silence fell, then the first voice muttered, "I don't get why he'd take a *hair clasp*. I mean it wasn't even gold or jade, or one with gems in, and where could you sell it even if it had?"

Mouse remembered a girl in Sweetwater East who took things, even though people knew she was taking things. That girl got awful drubbings for theft, but she didn't stop. Some just had to steal, but she couldn't understand why.

"What will happen to Grunt Erk—no, he was a second year, he was Orderly Erk." That was Colt, his voice husky with drowsiness.

"Talk his way onto a ship, work for passage," Amna stated. "When he gets home they'll put him in the army as a foot warrior. Or, if they have any honor, they'll send him away again. He'll end up in bond-service somewhere for stealing, you watch."

"Won't he love shit-bucket duty," someone else chortled.

"He can steal those," someone else remarked, and after the chuckles died away, they sank into dreams.

But theft, and the lack of it, lingered in the minds of the

more thoughtful among them. There were even a few who began to understand the lesson taken from their first day on tent duty — four carrying a heavy, unwieldy thing did far better than two — and applied this to everything.

From time to time they were heard to suggest variations on, "Look, if we all take a bit, it'll go faster. Like the tents." Faster was always good, and so, by the time the days began to shorten, and the winds brought rain again, they approached larger tasks as a unit.

Which was right around the time word sped among the younger boys: they were being sent on their first battle game.

One army, comprised of all the west doors of the five huts, with green tied around their arms, would be sent to one location, and the east door huts, wearing red arm bands, to another. They would have to send scouts to find their assigned enemy, then try to take one another's camp. Their performance would be judged by the watching instructors, after which their competition rankings would change once again. Everyone was eager to command — or said they were — but that privilege was reserved strictly to those who ranked first.

Which was not Muin, as he, along with the other islanders who worshipped the Snow Crane, had to learn to shoot arrows, and to ride horses. No commoner on their island had a bow or arrows. Shooting any bird of flight was forbidden to worshippers of the peaceful Snow Crane God, whose charge was the weak and the abandoned. This injunction against shooting any creature that could fly was the more easily obeyed in areas surrounded by nearly impenetrable forest.

But Muin was away from the island now, and though he still would never shoot a bird, he had no compunctions about shooting an enemy warrior who was shooting at *him*. He and the others who had never held a bow were trying to learn as fast as they could.

He was aware of happiness as he followed in the tramping, chattering column winding up into the hills before dawn one chilly autumnal morning. It had begun to get cold in the mornings, but excitement had gotten them ready quickly, and walking warmed them.

As the cavalcade followed a train bent around a slope, he glimpsed Mouse at the back of their column, dragging the wagons with the other servants. He could hardly wait for her to see how well he'd do. Though they'd seen each other twice a day, that was in the hut, where anyone might overhear, so they had said little to each other for weeks.

All around him boys speculated about where the enemy had been sent, and who was going to lead a charge. A few quoted from *The Way of the Blade*, as if knowing it would somehow lend them glory.

Muin recognized every quote — they had been discussing it in the instructor's lessons on past wars. But what possible use was that book, really, when words like *The highest skill in war is to subdue the enemy without fighting* were regarded as wisdom? It seemed to him that words like that were only worthwhile when talking about past battles, but what good would they do now?

Or, *The great warriors of ancient days put themselves first beyond the possibility of defeat, and then waited for an opportunity of defeating the enemy*. That was about as easy to get a grip on as holding onto water.

At least he ranked seventeenth, right now, so he was safe from having to command for a battle or two. By now he'd been in enough sparring skirmishes to understand the difference between the hero stories, wherein some great warrior leaped to the front of the fray, rallied the others, and led them to victory, and real life, which was a mess of clacking weapons, dust kicked up, and yelling. The only thing he knew how to do was to beat his way through the mass. It got him lots of honor merits to offset his terrible scores in archery and riding, but it wasn't *leading*.

At the back of the column, short-legged Mouse jog-walked alongside a wagon, waiting for her turn to push or pull, as she listened to the chatter up ahead, punctuated now and then by the chants of someone in front calling out and the others responding in unison.

Everyone was in a good mood. She recognized the language if not all the quotations. When she was seven and eight, she'd read through Muin's worn scroll, to help him with the words. *The Way of the Blade* had been written in the same ancient tongue as *Kanda's Conversations with His Students* and of course *The Twenty-Five Virtues*, as well as many of those old Essence texts Mother had tried to get her to study.

So she ignored the chanted words, and looked at those who were chanting. Most of the yelling came from the direction of the boy wearing a green sash tied around his topknot, who marched in front of a boy carrying a green banner, denoting the fact that he was this battle's commander.

Her mood stayed sunny as the cavalcade pushed on, each hut of grunts dragging a wagon of supplies. They reached their destination by mid-morning, as gray clouds rolled across the sky. The grunt huts competed against each other in setting up the tents, North-Three west only two posts behind North-One west, to their satisfaction.

Equally to their satisfaction, the steward in charge of overseeing them only commented once, on how late they were in getting the cauldron going over the fire. "But you'll learn how fast the hot water goes once they want steeped leaf after the evening meal, and then wash water," he warned.

Mouse was one of those detailed to haul buckets of water from the stream, but that just reminded her of home.

This first battle, the grunts were not expected to cook, which they hadn't really been taught yet. The kitchen had supplied dried fish and sticky rice balls. All they had to do was boil cabbage to serve under the fish and rice, and then dole out the cups of steeped phoenix-well tea, which many proclaimed tasted better made with mountain water.

Because the weather was fine, the grunts were expected to sleep outside, nominally on guard over the tents and supplies (and animals, if there had been any). For the first time in weeks, Mouse fell asleep gazing up at the stars, a sight so vast and harmonious that for once she felt no pangs of homesickness.

She woke to numbing ears, and the crunch of footsteps in a blue, shadowy world. It took all her effort to force her way out of her bedroll into the frigid air; she had to draw on her Essence breathing to warm herself internally before she could get her hands to work in tidying her bedroll and wrapping her shoe bindings. Instinct had prompted her into wakefulness—if a steward was walking around, the grunts had better be, too.

She was right. She had gone to fetch her first pail of water when the steward, apparently warned by some inner gong of his own, went about with his withy wand, whacking the dark lumps on the ground, eliciting yelps and muffled protests.

The grunts had hot water simmering and congee ready before the sun had begun to banish the eastern stars. Then, it seemed between one moment and the next, the silent tents burst into activity, with yelling, pushing, and chattering boys erupting in all directions, fifty combatants looking more like five hundred.

It took both the green-topknot commander's captains banging their gongs repeatedly to get everyone under control (with revealing glances toward the silent tassels watching, and not the boy commander or his captains). As soon as they had settled into lines by hut, the commander said, "Scouts, you eat first, and then go find the enemy. While they're gone, the rest of us will hold competition. We worked it out last night . . ." And he went on to explain.

While he was doing that, the steward in charge of the grunts summoned them over with a hand-wave, and said, "These first battles seldom last a day. My suggestion is to break down the tents now. If you have to put them up again, it will be good practice."

It was an order spoken in the form of a suggestion, a technicality, as they all knew the boy commander was too busy talking about the competition to give any orders about the camp.

Some grunts muttered under their breath about extra work—many had hoped to sit in the sun and watch the boys fighting—but by noon, when the competition had only elimina-ted about the half the green army waiting for the scouts to return so they could get to their battle, the scouts reappeared at a breathless run, yelling, "They found us first! They're *coming!*"

The commander and his two captains exchanged shocked looks. Some quick, random orders ensued, which were useless against the fact that the red armband scouts had found them the night before (mostly by the noise they made) and so Falik, the red army commander, had put together a sneak attack. Meanwhile he, trained by a warrior family, had instructed his perimeter guards to set up various skillful traps, which impressed his men until contact with the angry green armbands. Everything then dissolved into skirmishing, and finally brawling—many insisting shrilly that they'd killed one another—until the chief tassel banged his big gong.

"Strike camp," he ordered. "Form up."

The red armbands retreated in triumph to rejoin their army as the sullen, disconsolate green armbands milled about. Mouse and the grunts were now relieved at their having the tents already laid out ready for loading, which was by far their biggest chore. The rest of the camp was easily packed up, and so began the march back down the small hill, reaching the fortress in time for dinner.

"You're not the worst-ever first battle," an instructor told Muin and his erstwhile army-mates kindly as he rode by on his horse. "That would be the year the red army was ambushed in the middle of their first night, and tapped for dead before they even got out of their bedrolls."

That did little to cheer the future captains as they trooped into the mess hall for their meal. As for Mouse and rest of her green army grunts, because they had returned so swiftly, they were given an unprecedented evening of liberty. Some got food; others played games, or slept.

Mouse vanished, covering the fortress's broad space in a streak to get a start on Muin's wash. She finished hanging her laundry roughly the same time the boys finished their meal and marched to the instruction hall. Here, the two armies, with their instructors, had gathered to hear the results of their evaluation. The shutters had been pulled to against a damp, chilly night, but not fixed tight. Mouse crouched down below a window, hands tucked between her pulled-up knees and her chest, listening to the voices filtering between the wooden slats.

"Red army gains two honor merits for a successful attack at the enemy camp," the instructor began. "But takes a mark for complete failure to follow orders once first contact with the enemy was made."

A rustle meant boys were standing and saluting, hoping to be called on.

"Luyin?"

"Our orders were to attack them in their tents! They were all right there!"

"Cor?"

"We were not in our tents! We had our weapons, and we defended our camp!"

"Which is why their win is two points out of a possible five. And that brings us to evaluations for the commanders and captains," the instructor said imperturbably.

Nothing Mouse heard was a surprise. The red command ought to have had a plan in case the green army wasn't still in their tents — which, given the time was midday, was only to be expected. But the green commanders got the most criticism, first for permitting so much noise in their camp that made scouting their location easy, then for waiting for daylight, when they'd been practicing night stalks for a month.

"To sum up, it wasn't the worst I've seen, and there were individuals who managed to do great damage in spite of adverse circumstances. Yulin, Dun, Muin, you three each gain an honor mark for individual excellence, but no more than that as none of you thought to rally and counter-attack. As it is written, *The successful general sees a superior force, and has two choices, to attack or to flee . . .*"

As he went on about rallying to break the enemy force, Mouse slipped away, thoughtful as she considered what she'd seen. She still didn't understand much about commanding, but she didn't have to. The heartening thing was that she'd seen most of those individual battles. She knew she could have defended herself against any of them, at least long enough to run away.

That meant she was still a worthy sparring partner for Muin, which renewed her sense of purpose. Any number of night soil duties could be endured as long as she was still able to help him on that uphill Path.

ELEVEN

A LAST BURST OF summer, and then the sun seemed to drop more rapidly in a world becoming more alien to the islanders. Harvest Festival meant a feast and then competition games, without being counted.

And so the days fled. Unnoticed, Mouse's eleventh birthday came and went as the north huts were initiated into the skills of camp cooking. The cooler the weather, the harder it was to get up in the mornings unless she lay in bed working on Essence breathing to raise inner heat. The cold was still thoroughly unpleasant, and she was now glad of the shoes she'd once cursed.

Muin's fellow first year cadets went on their second battle, this time for the full two days, a sleety storm overtaking them as they set up camp. It was the first time the grunts cooked, but they were given supplies for an easy menu — once they caught enough freshwater fish.

The grunts came away feeling good about their efforts, especially having successfully gotten those tents up in rising wind with stinging sideways rain. Muin's hut, not so much. This time they were part of red army, and they lost the battle.

"At least I got top kills," Muin said to Mouse that second evening, orders having been passed to return to the fortress in the morning. No night marches yet, at least not until they'd had more practice at night maneuvers, particularly under the threat of bad weather.

The losing army had night patrol, and Muin was given the midnight watch. He told Mouse to join him so that he'd stay awake. It was always a relief to find a few moments alone, during which they could revert to the dialect of childhood, safely unheard.

He said, "I've jumped up in the rankings, and the first twelve have had their chance to be either captain or commander. Next command will be mine, everyone says. It comes after a big rank jump."

"You'll be great," Mouse said with loyal conviction.

"No, I won't," he muttered. "Being good with a sword is being good with a sword. Not with planning a battle."

"Is there anything in the book that you can use?"

"If there was, would I be asking you?" he retorted, crabby because he foresaw no way out of humiliation, the way he knew their commander was feeling right now. "It's all so . . . so general. Like the kind of good advice the elders give you, but none of it is what you actually need."

They walked in silence, crunch, crunch, as Mouse turned over this new idea in her mind. She was used to searching in her mother's books for whatever she needed to learn. "I wish I could help," she said finally.

"You can," he responded. "Look, I'm always in the middle of it. All I see is the next blade I have to beat back. Everything else is a mess. You get to be outside of it all. I noticed you grunts all watching. What did you see?"

Mouse stared up at the peaceful stars, considering. She had no idea what the instructors were looking for. She was able to eavesdrop on too few of the lessons—and of course she had no idea what the instructor was talking about when he said "this hill here" or "this pass" because she could not see the sand table that the boys gathered around, with its hills and valleys and moss representing forest.

But she could always go back to what Father had taught them.

She nodded. "From what I saw, you all push *that* way when

you're attacking," she gestured. "Most, I mean. Most of you are right-handed, and it's just as Father told us. You defend the weaker side. I saw them all doing it, kind of . . . oh, in a big slow circle that nobody really noticed." She waved an imaginary sword with her right hand." She smiled. "So maybe you make a plan to go at them from the other way?"

Muin scoffed, "What use is that? If they see us coming, they just turn."

"Not if you do like we did that time against the Sweetwater twins. You remember. You got Second Brother and me to be the tigers and make a lot of noise, in order to lure the snakes out of the hole."

Muin grinned, remembering how his father had talked about using Chase Tiger Lure Snake in his own training days.

But. "That worked because we knew the terrain. You and Second Brother lured the twins to the spot where I had the trap waiting. I won't know what terrain I've got. None of us do, we have to scout it, half the time at night." He scowled into the darkness. "But . . . what you say about the weak side. If we flank them?"

Mouse yawned. "What's flanking again?"

"You know, coming at the side. The weaker side."

She yawned again, her eyes watering. "Makes sense to me."

They talked what-ifs for several more rounds, until the drum tower rumbled the watch change, then went off to sleep, he for a full watch, and she for half.

A week later, once a series of storms passed through, the fortress emptied of the first, second, and third years as the fourth years attacked the fortress and the fifth years defended it.

This time, Muin was indeed in command, and even better, his army won. His Chase Tiger Lure Snake plan worked. Mouse went about the arduous labor of packing up for the return march feeling as buoyant as Muin was, marching at the head of the column as winning commander, directly before the captain jubilantly bearing the banner.

But Muin's elation over having at last figured out the mystery of leading lasted until the next battle, in which both commanders used variations of Chase Tiger Lure Snake, one more clever than the other.

"Of course they'd think of ways to use my plan," Muin complained to Mouse later that night, when he was once again a sentry—having been on the losing side. He ached from where Yulin had jabbed him viciously from behind, but Yulin's aggression was so much a part of everyday life it wasn't worth mentioning.

"Isn't it an old plan? Which is why it has a name," Mouse pointed out. "It's just that you were the first to use it."

Muin waved off her words impatiently, unable to utter the real problem, which was his uncertainty that he could come up with another good plan. "What did you see?"

"Mostly mud flying," she said. "Trees in the way everywhere, and the surprise attack was behind the rocks down in that gulley where they tricked your charge. We could hear the yelling. We knew it was a surprise attack, but we couldn't see anything."

Muin scowled at the ground as they sloshed a few more steps, then turned. He said, "If you could get up high, like the chief tassel. Not like a scout, of course, or you'd get scragged if the enemy thought you were one of us in disguise, there to signal. Nobody cares if the grunts are watching. You could tell me later what you saw."

Mouse ducked her head. She'd expected to get ahead of her own tasks, but she remembered her purpose. If he needed her to watch the battles, she'd watch the battles—and, she thought with an inward gloat, she could practice Heaven and Earth without anyone seeing her, and without a kerchief tied over her face to mask the stink that her Essence-charms never quite entirely eradicated. "As soon as I'm done with orders, if there is a tree or hill to climb, I'll do it," she promised.

By now winter had settled in. New Year's Double-Moons saw out the Year of the Eagle and welcomed the Year of the Dolphin with another feast and more competitions—only the fifth years could go into the village to celebrate the festival.

To the islanders winter was relentless, though others insisted it wasn't bad at all, and you should see winters in the big islands to the north. Mouse began using her inner fire even in

her sleep, which increased her appetite. She was always ravenous. There was a lot of chaffing at how much she ate, but
everyone knew that appetite meant growth spurts, and indeed,
having to get new shoes and shorten the hems on their clothes
was a regular occurrence.

No one noticed that Mouse had scarcely grown—and that
included Mouse herself. They were far too busy. All she noticed
was that her constant use of Essence to warm herself put a strain
on her command of the wind imps during her lonely drills of
Heaven and Earth, until she slowly began to gain incremental
progress again.

The next battle was ruined by a blizzard that came on suddenly
when they were halfway to their designated place. The tassel in
charge halted them in the lee of a slope and gave the signal to
set up camp there.

This time the army had to help their servants with the tents,
as the wind threatened to turn the sturdy canvas squares into
madly flapping bats. It took everyone to get the tents set up and
secured at last; Mouse was shivering so hard she was afraid her
chattering teeth would crack. She had long since lost feeling in
fingers and toes.

Feeling returned, painfully, once they got water heating.
Then they set about making hot food and drink as the tassels
tried to use the time effectively by giving the boys a tracking
assignment in close proximity to the tents.

The following battle took place under a clear sky that
melted the snows on the south side of the slopes. A wisp of
green scent on the cold wind made Mouse's eyes tear up, it was
such a relief. Muin's army lost that battle, too, resulting in
another cold march at night. This time Muin began outlining
the tassels' lectures on strategy, quoting from *The Way of the
Sword*, and he and Mouse discussed them, trying to tease out
practical advice from such general wisdom. Thus Mouse
learned some of the basic ideas of strategy, and its language.

TWELVE

BACK ON IMAI ISLAND (or "the island" to those who were born, lived, and died there), a message passed to Afan Yskanda that he had a visitor.

Everyone in the room where the first-year apprentices worked to grind and mix colors looked up in surprise. He'd never had a visitor before.

Many looked curiously on as Yskanda put away his materials and fetched the scholar's heavy finely woven wool cloak he was so proud of, until word whispered belatedly back that Handsome Afan's visitor was merely a monk.

Yskanda's heartbeat quickened when word reached him. He crossed through three courtyards, each boasting its spirit screen either painted by, or carved by, an illustrious former student. His supreme ambition was to have one of his own screens chosen for display there.

At last he reached the little reception areas off the main entry, and here was Ul Keg, more grizzled than Yskanda remembered, but he was smiling, so that couldn't mean bad news.

He also carried a bundle tied over one shoulder, something Yskanda didn't remember seeing before. He was about to blurt out a thousand questions about the family, but the monk said,

"Let us walk outside. It's a perfect day. A little cold, but the sun is out. Have you had a chance to see any of the New Year's sights?"

"Nothing except the bowing for the ritual."

"Tell me what you saw."

People had lined the street for when the temple palanquins passed, bowing as they chanted the prayers for the ghosts crossing the Sky Bridge between the two moons. They celebrated in Sweetwater, of course, but never as long or as elaborate. To Yskanda it had been worth it to stand shivering in the cold air in order to see the symbol-rich, skillfully articulated ritual canopies and fans borne by the various shamans, to sniff the incense, and especially to see the glowing lanterns with names of departed loved ones floated out on the water like a field of stars.

And then out came the colorful banners and streamers decorated with dolphins to welcome the new year, as people prepared to celebrate.

Encouraged by Ul Keg, he explained that he'd watched until his eyelashes nearly froze, trying to memorize colors and shapes of the fireworks, but as yet his attempts to capture the beauty and awe were disappointing: his sketches looked like nothing so much as orange, yellow, and crimson bugs crawling on a midnight blue backdrop.

When they reached the street, and had passed out of earshot of Chief Scholar Bankan's liveried guards, Yskanda interrupted himself. "How is everyone? What is Mouse doing?"

Ul Keg had expected Yskanda to chatter about himself. He was not ready for that question, but memory flashed through his mind, first last spring, when he spent the entire day and late into the night searching for Mouse. Then confessing his failure to Olt and Iley, and seeing his own sorrow and defeat in Iley's horrified eyes—until Olt said, *I think I know what happened. You didn't see First Son among those at the garrison, am I correct?*

You are, Ul Keg had admitted. *I was so desperate I thought that little Mouse might somehow have elbowed her way into the test, to stay with her brother at the garrison.*

I don't think you are far off, Olt had said. *I very much suspect that First Son was offered the chance to train as a captain, instead of staying local. In my day the officers had orderlies from the start. Probably still do. Of course she would go with him. When has she not trotted at his heels?*

But Mouse is a girl, Iley had protested.

To which Olt had said, *She's lived her entire life as a third brother. If the army trainers find her out, they'll send her to a temple. The important thing is, our two seem to have remembered to use a false name, if Ul Keg here couldn't find any trace of Afan Muinkanda at the garrison. A new name will protect them, wherever they are, until they can get back to us.*

But Iley had looked unconvinced, and ever since that day had been lighting incense at the household shrine and praying for Mouse — and Ul Keg prayed daily at his altar.

Which was part of the reason he was here now. It was Iley's worry that lingered, and her whispered, *Tell Yskanda nothing that will distress him*, before Ul Keg had set sail that ran through his mind now as he handed Yskanda the two carefully hoarded silver coins Iley had pressed into his hand. "Everyone is well." He sent up a silent prayer that it was so, then added, "And busy, now that they have embarked on their own paths. Your parents asked me to give you these coins. They thought you might need them."

"Silvers," Yskanda exclaimed appreciatively, then his brow puckered. "Isn't that all they have?" He knew his parents were mostly paid in kind, but sometimes villagers gave his mother tinnies, a moon rarely after the successful birth of a boy — the old ways still persisting in some places.

"Your parents said you should have them. As you get older, you will need your own money to spend, without having to justify it to anyone. How are *you* doing?"

"Ayah, very well," Yskanda said, reluctant to take the coins. "I can earn something on my own, grinding ink and making paints for the senior apprentices," he said, his gaze straying in question to Ul Keg's bundle.

Ul Keg did not misinterpret the glance. "I have been Called away," he said, not mentioning that his having failed to find Mouse meant he no longer had anyone to teach. "And you know that monks do not carry coins, so I'm afraid these silvers are yours or I will leave them at a temple."

To reject a thing from his parents' hands seemed unfilial, so Yskanda took them, mentally promising that one would go to the shrine that housed the beggars and abandoned as Ul Keg said, "If there is anything you wish to talk about, regard this as our last lesson together."

Yskanda began with painstaking care. "I'm grateful. For everything. I am learning *so, so much*. But it wasn't easy, at first. I didn't know so many things, and they all thought I was stupid."

He paused, considering his early days. They had to rise early each day and perform a set of movements that got the blood flowing through the nerve-conduits, hated by most everyone. But Yskanda had been astonished to discover that they also considered it hard. Heaven and Earth was hard. What the apprentices did was easier than what Father had first taught Yskanda and his siblings as very small children.

But that had been the only easy thing. He'd endured the derisive looks, the smirks, the comments when he asked questions that he had not realized sounded stupid to everyone else until one day one of the more temperamental seniors stomped into the dormitory and kicked apart his neatly folded clothes while telling him so.

Yskanda had apologized, folded his things again, and after that went silent, listening in order to learn. "It helped a little that First Apprentice Fei favored me for two seasons, before she got hired over at the governor's palace, for her neat hand. She also reads aloud to the governor's wife."

Ul Keg knew a little about the governor's wife, who, it was said, enjoyed delicate health, while sending physicians hither and yon in search of an elixir to grant her eternal youth.

"Go on," Ul Keg said encouragingly as they strolled down the street with its dancing dragons and phoenixes, the tumblers and fire-breathers and storytellers.

"I'm so happy when I can be in the world of color, and line. Everything is graceful and harmonious," Yskanda said, opening his hand outward. "But . . ."

"One has to live," the monk said gently. "Am I right?"

Yskanda nodded soberly. One must come out of that inner world of grace and beauty to the ongoing competition among his peers for notice, for praise, for place. "I had to learn that what—people—say is not always what they think, or mean." He paused again, trying to describe First Apprentice Fei's brief, ironic admonishments to observe the trick of eye, the flex or turn of a hand, and how it might belie a ready smile. *Truth,* she had said, *is often revealed in the skin around the eyes. And in the hands.* And Ul Keg himself had told them to be wary of those with angry eyes, when they first encountered the Sweetwater twins.

"Mouse told me once it's like the stinging flies," Yskanda said in a rush of words. "Insults won't kill you, but enough of them hurt. So I have been learning to see, and hear, the truth under or behind the smiles, the words." He had covered his sketchbooks with hundreds of quick drawings of the corners of eyes, the angle of jaw, the curve or tightness or shadows of mouths, and hands in every position, tense, relaxed, tightened, posed. The more he observed, the better he understood what was really being said—and consequently, even if his efforts to capture the ineffable were uncertain, his drawings of people had taken an exponential leap in skill.

Yskanda gave Ul Keg a sober glance. "I found that it's easier to let the others think me slow," he admitted. "And strange. During summer, when we were given liberty, I found that when they go to swim in the sea, what they mean is splashing about on the shoreline. We are forbidden to swim into the deeps, just as at home. I just want to *see.*"

"There are undersea creatures who would regard you as a meal," Ul Keg reminded him sympathetically. Yskanda's fascination with tidepools, forest streams, and of course the sea was long known to him—but after all, there was plenty to draw on land. "I think your mother, at least, would be reassured if you have made friends among those you will work with in your future life."

"I try," Yskanda said, honestly. "But they still think me slow."

What Yskanda's fellow apprentices could have told Ul Keg was that nobody really understood Yskanda, who was so unlike the others. Some instructors read instructive texts to them as they worked, and Yskanda listened instead of passing covert notes, or whispering. But other instructors allowed them to chat while working—then Yskanda's mind seemed to go somewhere else altogether, especially if he was painting.

Once a big boy, passing by his desk, and noticing the big girls whispering and admiring Yskanda's oblivious profile, reached down to swat Yskanda off his cushion, just to get the girls' attention. But to his astonishment, Yskanda had snapped his forearm up in a block. Then he blinked, and went right back to work. The girls glared at the big boy, who retreated.

On another day that same boy put a spider on Yskanda's back while he painted. The entire class watched it stealthily as it clambered slowly up his skinny shoulder blades working away under his robe, then up his glossy hair in its half topknot, to the crown of his head, before it plopped onto his page.

But instead of yelling insults, or jumping up, or even crushing it, he had carefully carried it to the window, where he tipped it out into the courtyard. It was then that the others understood that he was a follower of the Snow Crane, and somehow, by degree, that made him an unworthy target.

His gaze widened in question. "Is that cowardice, to let them think me slow? First Brother always said it was. But he was so much like Father, a protector. Mouse, in her way, too."

Ul Keg looked down into Yskanda's face, which was just beginning to shed the rounded contours of the little boy. The bones emerging strengthened the promise of beauty to come that had been his, all unknowing, since babyhood—and that, he suspected, gave people pause more than that earnest, utterly guileless expression. "Not cowardice at all," he said slowly. "But you are talking to a monk. Our way has always been to wait, if we can. To permit the heavens to restore their natural order in their own time. Humans," he added, "do not always have the patience of eternity, I fear."

Yskanda laughed. "I also hate destruction. Especially of art, and humans are art, in their way. Every living thing is art. To see it destroyed, it hurts."

"I don't see any of your thoughts as cowardice," Ul Keg said as reassuringly as he could. "At least here, you live among people who value art. This is a good place for you," he added firmly—for the third reason he was going was the troubled dreams he'd had of late, difficult to interpret. He knew only that it was time to move on.

"Tell me more about your days," Ul Keg said, and Yskanda readily talked about his classes and projects, his enthusiasm unmistakable. Ul Keg listened with real pleasure. Truly, this was the right place for Yskanda, who had never made much claim on Ul Keg's attention. That had mostly gone to Mouse, as he'd striven to heed Iley's desire to turn her into a scholar.

He paused when the great gong before the palace shivered on the air.

Ul Keg smiled at him. "I'll tell Granny Anise to carry your thanks, and your words, back to your parents. And should you like to, I can ask her to come by when she brings the taxes to hear how you are doing, and to report on your family—you know your mother would never risk writing a letter." Seeing Yskanda's eager nod, Ul Keg went on. "Granny Anise was selected by the headman as new tax carrier for the three villages. She came with me to see where and how it is done. I've got to go meet her before it gets much later, so that she can get back to Sweetwater before dark."

Yskanda made a deep, protracted bow.

"Be well," Ul Keg said, tracing a protection talisman on the boy's forehead, as he breathed a prayer to the Phoenix Moon. "Be well, and flourish."

Far to the north and then eastward, the new year was celebrated more elegantly on the Imperial Island, specifically in the perfect horseshoe bay that had been created, it was said, by battle between gods and demons that began with the eruption of Lir, King of Red Dragons centuries ago. Lir the Fire Dragon was said to be quiescent in enchanted sleep deep beneath the snow-topped mountain that now bore his name, beneath the imperial city built along its lower slopes.

The imperial capital was decorated with dolphin streamers, and everywhere people bought dolphin-decorated lanterns, and lotus lamps to be launched on the water, and fine strips of calligraphed sayings to be affixed to doors, all to bring them luck in the new year.

Vendors filled the streets selling musical instruments, drums, and books, both fixed and folding fans, hair clasps and pins, and all manner of good things to eat. The savory, pungent smells of foods changed every few steps, the cries of those hawking their wares chanted in song.

Most elegant of all was the palace ritual as all the court was gathered in their finest robes of brocade to salute the new year and the emperor's birthday. When at last that ended, the imperial court gathered in the Hall of Heaven for a magnificent banquet, as the best entertainers danced, sang, and acted out favorites of old.

The skills of the performers were superlative, yet the greater part of the courtiers' attention veered always toward the dais below the great golden dragon with one claw up holding a Tiger Eye. Here the imperial family sat, with cousins a step below them. On the dais, lower than the emperor, sat his five children by his consorts, four of whom were his, and so whose names were appended with "On," a generation name from a famous poet who wrote during the time of the Sage Empress, who ruled in her own right as she established the Yslan dynasty, and handed down so many new laws.

The first imperial prince leaned back on his elbows, habitually petulant expression eased and eyes closed as he listened to the music. The first imperial princess sat as straight-backed as the step-sister she ignored. Both princesses' faces were modestly lowered, as the second imperial prince flicked chick peas into First Imperial Princess Manon's headdress. Of the five imperial children, only the youngest princess gazed at the dancers, chin on her little fists, obviously enchanted.

The second imperial prince included his second-cousins in his attentions when his half-sister did not react. The cousins endured it because they must, under their elders' stern eyes, but when the adults talked to each other, the cousins both flicked peas back at the second prince. He smothered silent laughter as he used them to renew his attack on his elder half-sister.

The first imperial princess sat still and self-effacing—and when, at last, the emperor noticed, what was happening to her otherwise perfect headdress he beckoned to the waiting servant and — with a brief glance at his second son — ordered a whack with the paddle for every spot in the princess's headdress.

The second imperial prince, aware of what was to come, sat back sullenly, and played with the perfectly prepared meal, making a mess; the first imperial prince was already in trouble, though for him the penalty was further restrictions on his already restricted freedom, after a day of walking the main street and loudly proclaiming his opinion of every scrap of music he heard. (This might have been tolerated if the accompanying guards, both obvious and unseen, hadn't corroborated their reports on the pungent contempt First Imperial Prince Jion had used in his disparagement of what he declared was bad music — behavior Not Worthy of an Imperial Prince, even one dressed as an apprentice scholar.)

The only person sitting on the same level as the emperor was Dowager Empress Kui Jin, trying to remain upright under a headdress that cruelly pressed down on her scalp. She cast a glance at her son's profile to gauge his mood, wondering if she could plead a very real headache and withdraw. Not yet, perhaps; if her second grandson's foolishness had ruffled his mood, he might order the entertainers flung out or even flogged if he thought she was not entertained.

She gazed fondly at her own family sitting down a level, to her left. There was her sister, surrounded by all three of her sons — including Kui Pandan, the wanderer — and their children . . . was that a chick pea?

The dowager empress considered the trajectory. Now that the second imperial prince had been promised signal vengeance, his cousin was using this opportunity to pelt him back. She turned her gaze to the three consorts, catching the anxious eye of the second imperial prince's mother and shook her head slightly, then made a subtle signal to her niece-by-marriage to tend to her boy. Which was done with a pinch that made the urchin's face blanch. He sat up straight, hands in his lap. Excellent.

The dowager empress turned her attention back to her nephew Pandan. He was so clever, always bringing back sketches of a world that the dowager empress would never get to see. She caught her sister's eye, glanced toward Pandan, and her sister smiled back, making a small sign: later.

The dowager empress sat back. Her head still hurt, but anticipation made it bearable. She became aware of eyes, turned, and caught her son's gaze.

She smiled, and he smiled back. All was well.

THIRTEEN

TWO MOONS NEW YEAR at Loyalty Fortress was celebrated separately in the village. Only the fifth year cadets were permitted to go across the bridge—if they had earned sufficient honor merits—to enjoy the village's very modest offerings. After their years of austerity in training, even the wealthiest cadets came to appreciate the homey costumes and the plain fare, for there was always plenty to drink, and young people to flirt with, though village parents were on the watch as everyone knew there was no future to be found among these boys who would soon go away to their illustrious careers.

At Loyalty Fortress, everyone else was given a big feast after the dedication ritual, and then they played competition games for fun, as the rice wine came out.

Mouse had thoroughly accustomed herself to the rhythm of life at Loyalty. Trickle kept their hut in a ripple of laughter, and Mouse won everyone's sesame cakes off them at the Circle game. She fell asleep happy that night, in spite of a stomach ache from too many sesame cakes.

Next day, it was back to training hard, and working harder—for the grunts.

Winter slowly spent itself, roaring back sporadically less and less often as they waited for word of the spring ships.

Spring had begun to fuzz the trees and the edges of the drill field, and the horses were losing their winter coats, when the first pigeon fluttered into the coop, loosed by the garrison on Te Gar Island as the supply ship set sail.

On a windy spring day the command went out to assemble at the parade ground, where the altar had been set up before the sundial. The commander lined all the cadets on the parade ground, with their gear packed and resting by their left side. Once the bowing, libation, and salutation was done, the fifth year cadets, now potential captains in new fighting robes of blue, were called out in rank order. The young man ranked first of that year walked out alone, made his bow to the altar, then to the commander.

After him the four next in rank, all five slated to go the imperial island to take the Imperial Examination this year, and in between-years, to other garrisons to serve under famous captains and hone their skills until the examination year.

All eyes followed these five, awed and envious, though Muin watched with mixed feelings. He craved the glory of being the first in rank. How proud he would be, walking out alone as the commander called his name and recited all his merits! But the yearning dampened when Muin imagined trying to find an excuse not to go to the capital to sit that examination, which might result in his coming face to face with the sinister emperor and his equally sinister imperial court. How could he refuse to go?

Ayah! He had four years to figure that out. There were other ways to greatness, that much the phoenix feather promised.

Mouse, watching from the very back where the newly promoted orderlies waited to carry their own belongings to their new huts, actually shuddered at the idea of that sinister imperial palace and its emperor. But Muin would not go there, which meant she would be safe from ever being forced to enter that terrible place.

After the new warriors were saluted, the changes went more rapidly, fourth years to fifth, third to fourth, and so on down to Muin's year, who were now second years. No one was left to watch them except the grunts as they were assigned their new huts. Muin held his breath — and exchanged covert grins when Yulin was sent off to another hut. Then his name was called, and he found himself with Dun, who had become a friend. Grinning at each other, they followed as all were dispersed to their new huts.

Second year, he thought. New hut. New rankings. But the same problems brought along with their clothes — at least he would have to deal with Yulin's kicks when passing his bed, or listen to his sneezes now that the jasmine back of the target hill was blooming. And new military problems. This was the year that they would begin practicing cavalry fighting, both sword and archery.

"Lan told me that the targets are open at evening meal, and no one is around," Dun muttered as they chucked their belongings into trunks, to be straightened out when their grunts — no, their orderlies, now — turned up later. "Want to go with me?"

"Of course," Muin said, thought without the enthusiasm of last year. After a year of hard work his archery ranking still held him back.

He wondered why future commanders had to know how to shoot. Wasn't that what you gave orders for? But everyone insisted captains had to be better than the men who followed them, or they'd never rise in rank. Not if you weren't a noble's son, or from a wealthy clan with impressive connections.

As for Mouse and the grunts, they were now officially orderlies, and they had been reassigned some precious hundred steps closer to the kitchens and supply. Their hut had been moved as a group, promoted up a step to East-Two east door.

They also got to watch pityingly, or smirking, or indifferent, when the next day, the first of the three spring ships brought new crops of cadets and their grunts — the latter to night soil duty.

But there was no free time, just new duties.

Mouse received Muin's orders to meet him the next night out at the practice field, with something to eat, when ordinarily the second years went to supper. She was to bring him whatever she could find, and she could collect his laundry on the way back.

She wondered why she had to be there, but his orders, given under his breath, meant he didn't want the others in the hut to overhear. So she swallowed her questions until the second night. She had to scant her own supper in order to get something for him, but that was scanting, not skipping. She gulped down a few rice-and-fish balls as she ran, carrying the greater share for her brother.

She found him there with a handful of others, all with bows and arrows. None of the carpentry servants were there, which meant she and the other orderlies were expected to fetch the arrows and run them back. Of course that was why she had to be there — she should have thought of that.

But she was wrong. She gave him his food, which he tore into, mumbling, "I need you to learn to shoot."

"Me? Why? I'll never need that!"

He glared at her, lost somewhere inside his head as she muttered the healing charm into the darkening bruise on his temple. Someone had been teaching Yulin pain points, she thought, then Muin said, "I found out today that the fourth years practice riding and shooting with real arrows, not the blunted ones. And accidents happen. Or what is claimed are accidents."

Mouse's jaw dropped. "You mean someone, here, not an enemy, but *here*, would try to kill you?"

Muin's mouth twisted. "It's always an accident, they say. But somehow an arrow gets in a knee, a hip, and you're out for a season. Or longer, if the damage is really bad, and your ranking drops below the first-years. I need you to learn to shoot at me so I can ward arrows. Father used to ward arrows as part of his drill. But they don't teach that here. You have to find me somewhere I can teach you and not be seen."

Mouse's heart thumped at the ferocity in Muin's face, his white lips. "I already have a place," she said. "Who would actually shoot at you — oh, Yulin? Still? You aren't in his hut."

Muin gave her a sour look. "It's the rankings for the entire year that matter, not the hut rankings."

"He would really do that?" she asked.

"I believe it," Muin exclaimed, aching from toes to ears from the day's sparring, during which he'd been paired with

Yulin, who had hit with extreme ferocity when the instructor's back was turned. No one dared complain, for tattling was equated with cowardice. *We all have to be tough, don't we?* Yulin had sneered once, after stepping on someone's arm deliberately.

Mouse fell silent, hearing Ul Keg's voice in memory, after he'd told a story: *Why do you think he did this? Why did she say that?* Maybe that was something only monks, or scholars asked, as Mother had, too, when Mouse's lessons concerned history tales. "I have a place," she said.

"Then tomorrow, meet me at the edge of the riding field. Take me to your spot from there," he said.

She did.

But first she got up extra early, using starlight to navigate by as she sped to her secret spot and set it all up, dragging together some material for a makeshift target.

The riding field was not far from the orderlies' huts. Mouse found Muin with a pair of bows and a quiver of arrows. He slung the latter to her to carry, and beckoned for her to lead on.

From there it was easy to slip along behind the horse barns and the storage buildings for winter horse gear, then past the armory's secondary storage, to Mouse's solitary practice field.

Here, Muin looked around, hands on hips, his face a comical grimace. "It stinks! How can you stand it?"

"It's worse in summer," she said, holding out her handkerchief. "But no one ever comes here. Here, take this. I'm used to the smell," she lied.

"We'd better be done by summer," he said with a grim smile before tying the kerchief tightly, covering his nose. "Come here. Let's get you shooting. There is no time to lose."

Mouse accepted that, as she accepted everything Muin said. He got her into the correct stance, put her fingers in position, yanked her elbow up and back, and then held her arm when she loosed the arrow so that her forearm snapped back in a line, without waving all around. "Now you're ready to reach back, snag another arrow, line it up, and shoot. If I see that elbow tuck against your ribs, or your hand fly around, I'll smack it," he added. "This arm is your aim, and that's important, but *that* arm is your strength and speed. So don't let it flap around."

He watched narrowly as Mouse drew and shot. Her first few arrows didn't make it anywhere near the target, but he said nothing. His hadn't either.

He let her get a feel for the rudiments, then he picked up his bow, and shot three arrows in what she assumed was a speedy succession. All three smacked into her target.

"Move it back," he said. "All the way to those trees there."

"I don't think I'll ever be that good," she said.

"You don't have to be. But it's something to aim for. I'm only in the middle ranks right now," he added, hating to admit it. "Others have been shooting since they could walk. They're fast. And accurate. That's all the arrows I brought. Bring them back, and let's try again."

Feeling intimidated, Mouse scampered to the target, pulled the arrows, collected her terrible shots lying on the ground, and returned. They kept at it until the gong signaled the end of the watch. "I have to get back," Muin said. "Practice!"

She practiced.

She remembered the bloody fingers her brother had had the previous year, and made herself a hand guard, then sneaked out to her hideaway every chance she could get. First she had to get the stance, then there was learning to judge the wind and the feel of the arrow, and the tautness of the bow. And then she had to add Essence-strength. Why couldn't they just use crossbows? She didn't bother asking that question, as the answer, whatever it might be, clearly would make no difference.

Getting Essence to align with all the other things she had to concentrate on was the hardest. It was like trying to catch a bit of slippery ice when everything else was either numb or equally slippery, but she forced her breathing to calm, and then one day . . . it was all there.

Her aim was not precise, but at least she reached the target with every shot. Rejoicing inwardly, she made herself wait one day, though she knew Muin was getting more impatient by the day—and she saw new bruises darkening on his flesh, more of a goad to urgency than any words could have done.

The next day her shooting was slightly better, and that night she let Muin know she was ready to practice shooting at him.

The following day, he met her at her secret place, and this time he brought the blunted arrows that they used in their battles. Even so, fear gripped her all over again as she aimed at her brother, who stood squarely in front of the target. Those points didn't have steel, but they obviously could hurt, and even put out an eye if one wasn't careful.

"Shoot!"

She shot.

Muin whapped the arrow away — barely.

She shot again. This time he swung, realized he was late, and skipped out of the way. "Again!"

It got a little easier for them both, but she began to notice his shoulder crowding his neck, his arm twisting forward. She debated saying anything, until he lowered his sword and scowled at her in perplexity. "What?"

She said, "Are you still doing Heaven and Earth?"

Muin sighed. "When and where could I do that? I'm never alone. Or wasn't, until this year. I'm skipping supper. We can do that this year. As for alone the rest of the day, no, except in the privy, and you can't do Heaven and Earth *there*. What's wrong, what do you see?"

She closed her eyes, and there was Father, shoulders back and down, arm swinging in that complicated arc with grace and power. She mimed it, and then opened her eyes. "This is what I see you doing." She hitched her shoulder up, her outer arm outward.

Muin scowled more deeply, but not at her. "It's the block they taught us for foot against horse," he said. "I've done it so many times. But it isn't Father's, is it?"

She wanted to say, *How could you have not seen that?* But she didn't know what the cadets' drills were like, or what happened if you did something different from the others.

Muin sighed. "I've gotten used to what they teach here. I'll try to remember what Father said, but it's hard when they're banging the gong to keep us in cadence, and yelling to stamp, step, thrust, block."

On his next few shots, he did try to get back to Father's form, but gradually he reverted to what Mouse now recognized as army form, so she said nothing more.

He got hit twice, jumped out of the way a hand of times, but managed to bat the rest away. "I have to do better," he said when the gong sounded. "At least the days are getting longer."

As he slipped back toward his territory, he promised himself that once he mastered it, he would practice with Dun, who as another "barefoot" was Yulin's target as well. They were brothers in war, facing the same enemy.

One day he was going to lose Mouse, but not yet, not yet. She was so useful. He could talk to her, and she was right about Heaven and Earth, and was he losing his form as he gained strength? But she was Mouse, not Second Brother—and somebody was bound to figure it out. Who knows, there might be a rule and a punishment. There was for everything else.

These and other problems stung his mind from time to time as the days slipped past.

He and Mouse practiced shooting until both began to improve rapidly, she at placing an arrow in the target and he at dodging. He was so pleased at his progress that it never occurred to him to notice that she took to archery a lot faster than he had.

Then the day arrived, right before their first scheduled battle as second years, when she arrived at her secret practice field to find not one there, but two.

She stood silently, looking from Muin to Dun as her brother said, "I warned you about the stink."

Dun shrugged. "Reminds me of home. The children in our family all had night soil duty." He grinned. "The main reason I wanted to try for the army was to get away from it, Third Brother and me both—Second went off to the temple, where he probably ran into more stenches!"

Mouse couldn't help laughing a little, though she hated having her secret spot revealed like that, so suddenly. The little she'd seen of Dun she liked. He had even features and a ready smile that crinkled his dark eyes, making them twinkle. She knew he was an islander as well, though from the extreme southern end, opposite Sweetwater at the northern tip.

But Dun's orderly was Trickle, a friendly, prank-loving boy who was the biggest blabbermouth she had ever met, worse even than Auntie Nim back in Sweetwater North, who everyone called "Five Aunts and Ten Grandmothers" — swearing that she knew gossip before it happened. Mouse was afraid that Dun would bring Trickle next time, and there was nothing she could do. She was going to lose this place she had so carefully tended for over a year.

And Muin saw it. He said, half-surly and half-pleading, "I had to bring Dun. We can't let Yulin see us."

Dun glanced from one to the other, surprised that tough Muin, who scarcely spoke ten words in a day, would feel he had to explain to his grunt. Even if the grunt was his younger brother, which Dun had figured had to be the case, though they didn't look a lot alike, except the eyebrows. Most of the others just gave an order and that was that.

And then there were those like Yulin with their ready fists.

The younger brother — Mouse, Trickle had said he was called — flushed angrily. Why would he be angry? But, quite properly, he said nothing.

Dun said, "Who tied these nut shells and things to hang from this apple tree?" He pointed at Mouse's dangling object for her Essence focus. "It looks like a wish tree!"

"Never mind that," Muin said hastily. Explaining Mouse's playing around with Essence would lead nowhere good. "Mouse!"

Mouse had kept her gaze on the ground as she struggled against resentment. She could understand wanting to surprise Yulin with this defense if Yulin was actually mad enough to shoot at them, but the surprise would not last but the once. She reminded herself firmly that her entire purpose here was to help Muin in his path to greatness. If he needed this spot, he needed this spot.

"Let's show Dun," Muin said. "Shoot at me first, so he gets the idea. Then shoot at us both. As fast as you can."

FOURTEEN

AS SECOND YEARS, MUIN and his fellow cadets would be going farther afield for their battle games. There would also be specific military goals. Simple ones, at first, with safety boundaries, and of course the tassels whose purpose was to see that the rules were kept. And to evaluate the cadets' progress.

What that meant for the orderlies was more free time, if they were fast and efficient with their chores. Their masters spent a lot more time planning, then stalking or laying various types of warning traps, or scouting, and of course then came skirmishing.

Farther afield meant riding, for the first time, which added horse care to the orderlies' chores. Not that there was all that much to be done once the horse picket was set up, as more than half the second years were completely unused to mounted warfare as yet.

Mouse had to saddle and unsaddle Muin's mount, and see that it was fed and watered, which didn't take long. As Muin was not among the best riders, he wasn't sent scouting, so she had time to explore above the ruined wall that someone insisted had been put up in the days of the Golden Dragon Dynasty, two forms of writing ago. It was that heaven-sent dragon, so the story went, who gave gold to his chosen king, which is why emperors were called Heaven's Chosen, and had worn gold in their crowns and their court clothes ever since.

Falik was commanding, once again. As the orderly set up camp alongside a stream, he pulled aside Dun Duan and Muin, saying, low-voiced, "This water is a provincial border river, and we have to defend it. I'll have to spread everyone out, line of sight. But you know what Yulin is going to do as secondary captain. I really need you two to ward him off so I can concentrate on the main defense, especially now that we're using the signal flags."

Dun sighed heavily. "Yulin will find whatever group is smallest and scrag them. Especially if Ryu here and I are in it. We all know it—including the red army commander. What's to talk about. We may as well paint targets on our backs so he can find us easier."

Muin had been gazing around. The "river" was really a meandering stream through marshy country, which was a terrain he knew well from boyhood. He grinned. "I hope he does."

When the other two looked his way, he said, "Let's capture arrows with boats of straw, as Tassel Shaz keeps saying. Don't worry, Falik. I know what to do and even where to do it."

While Falik positioned his army, paying attention to line-of-sight for the signal flags, Muin explained the ruse, without saying that he'd used it successfully against the Sweetwater bullies. As Dun volunteered to be the bait, along with two other barefoots Yulin also habitually targeted, Muin placed his men, chuckling to himself. Who would ever have thought that he'd be grateful to those Sweetwater twins, all this time later?

And sure enough, the plan was a splashing success. "Splashing" as Yulin and his flank attack stormed after Dun and his two cronies, who retreated yelling in fake fear. When Muin and his team popped up on their right, Yulin cleverly veered left, leading his team straight into what looked like a puddle (if you didn't pay attention to the cattails), but was in fact a nasty marsh of thick, stinking mud.

Muin, Dun, and their team watched in satisfaction as the entire red army attack team took headers into the mud, then squelched and flailed as they tried to get out, bellowing and cursing so loudly that birds in the distance flapped skyward.

When they finally got out, there Falik was with half the green army, waiting to capture them.

Mindful of Muin's need for her to witness the battles, Mouse always volunteered for the unwanted setup chores, like digging the jakes, which meant others would be responsible for cooking, which kept them in camp while she had free time.

The heavy clouds had begun to mist, decorating blossoms, grass, and trees with tiny crystal beads as she climbed all the way up the craggy mountainside a ways from the stream. She must not let herself get distracted by the softness of the colors, or the smell of living things thriving in fresh water. She had to find a vantage from which to watch the battle.

At least she could look as she toiled her way up a sharp hill. The ground was covered with wildflowers, and here and there ripe bayberries, which she alternately ate and gathered in her voluminous shirt to take back to camp. She counted nineteen types of flowers and herbs, then her heart really began to race when she lifted her head to see how much farther she could climb, and spotted the distinctive heart-shaped petals of the Longevity Herb, growing freely and unpicked. The area was much more rocky, slippery in the wet. She peered under her hand at the shadowy tree shapes on the summit.

Could that rounded one with the graceful, feathery leaves hanging down like banner streamers possibly be a drooping redbark tree?

Redbark trees, Mother had taught her, were rare in that they breathed Essence from their leaves. They were beautiful trees, often to be found with crane nests in their tops, and thereby sacred to followers of the Snow Crane. The feathery leaves were drawn almost as often as bamboo shoots by aspiring artists.

In spite of her intentions, she forgot completely about Muin's battle as she scrambled upward on her hands and knees, then halted inside the relative shelter of those whispering leaves, blinking raindrops from her eyelashes. She breathed in, her hands out, fingers extended. The subtle sense of Essence whispered over her skin, a delicious feeling akin to the thousands of bubbles bursting over her after a first plunge in the cool, frothing breakers on a hot day.

Ul Keg had called such places sacred. He had built his altar to the Phoenix Moon in such a place, she remembered. There he went to pray to the god who shepherded souls back into the world again.

She performed a deep, reverent bow, then proceeded more cautiously, bent double so that she wouldn't accidentally step on anything those long, thin leaves sheltered.

Like . . .

She knelt down with painstaking care and set aside her bayberries. Here was the rare, very rare Longevity Herb with blossoms of so deep a purple they looked black. This variety of the Longevity Herb was so rare because it grew very slowly, only in certain soils, invariably beneath the partial shelter of redbark trees.

She thought of Mother, upon whom an entire village relied for medical aid, and plunged her fingers into the soft, wet soil, then carefully, carefully, fingered free the precious roots of three plants, leaving the rest untouched.

She gently slid the plants into her clothes next to her skin, tops and all, then regathered her bayberries, wishing she'd thought to bring a basket. No, it was better that she hadn't, perhaps. The bayberries were easily explained—the boys had stripped and eaten some on the march. But how many military boys knew anything about herbs? If she had brought a basket, she was certain to be questioned, and then the questions might go in dangerous directions. Like, why had she had scholar training, and by whom? It was much better for the rest of her hut to think she didn't even know how to read, as was the case with about half of them.

A shout and a gong echoing from below reminded her of her purpose. She scrambled crabwise over the face of the slope, one arm keeping the herbs safely inside her clothes, until she found a good spot from which to watch the battle.

She watched, but her thoughts strayed back to herbs. Ought she to report her find to the physician?

She wavered. Her mother would say it was the responsible thing to do, but then her mother was the chief medicine-maker for Sweetwater. This island was one of several bound over entirely for training. There were far more useful herbs growing wild than they could harvest—from what she'd seen, the village children mostly roamed the hills to the west of the fortress to seek feathers for fletching, rather than herb-gathering, though in season they came back with blue and purple lips from eating wild berries.

The ships brought the rarer, more precious items already compounded and stored, so the healers and their assistants really only had to go abroad for those herbs, roots, blossoms, and so forth needed to cure the scrapes and breaks and cuts common to boys training with weapons. Mouse had been in and out of the fortress medicine storage plenty of times, and she knew what was stored there.

She broke from her reverie when the gong rang, and in the distance the ragged shouting of triumphant boys sounded like crows cawing. She'd forgotten the battle!

When she got back to camp, she handed the bayberries off to those on cook duty, then retreated to her tent, where she tenderly wrapped the roots in her second shirt and stored them in her travel gear. As she did, a piece broke off, which she tucked into her pocket. She might try experimenting with it in hot water.

As Falik's army won that particular battle, Muin had free time after the evening meal, while his opponents were stuck with sentry duty. For the first through fourth years, that meant playing endless rounds of pitch-pot, or Circle, the strategy game played on a nineteen-by-nineteen point board, one player with black stones, one with white as they tried to encircle and capture each other's stones. Though gambling was absolutely forbidden, these games were permitted, the one to improve aim, the other to foster military thinking.

During the rainy season, Father had taught the three children to play Circle, with stones he'd picked up from the seashore, on a board he'd made himself. Second Brother had proved to be the best at the game. Mouse could beat him when she could be got to pay attention, but she'd considered it tedious beyond bearing—too easy to see where it was going, so why bother? She'd rather be outside, working on her leaping skills, rain or not.

Those games had caused inward sighs for Muin. He was the oldest—why hadn't he won? He finally decided it had something to do with why he had trouble reading, but as Father also had trouble reading, he'd settled it within himself that not being good at Circle was not a sign of stupidity, or worse, cowardice. He'd played because Father wanted him to play, but he was glad of those games now. It gave him something in common with the rest of the boys, whereas he was still catching up with pitch-pot.

His mood was good because of the win, and even better when Falik took him aside between games. "I think I've figured something out."

Muin looked a question.

"You know how the tassels keep quoting the Master, saying that without tactics, strategy is the slowest route to victory, whereas tactics without strategy is the clanging gong before defeat?"

Muin shrugged. He had no idea what that really meant in practical terms.

Falik said, "My father also used to say it. I see it now. I see it. You're a tactician, Ryu. I told you to find a way to deflect Yulin's flank attack, and you did. I'm getting better at strategy. I still have trouble thinking out the details. Tactics. Unless I read a battle with exactly the same situation. But you're getting good at those details."

"Tactics," Muin said. And he repeated that a short time later, when he found Mouse tending his horse.

"So that's what tactics is?" Mouse asked, wondering if she'd ever remember. Why should she? Muin was now setting his own foot steadily on the path to greatness. As was right. She grinned. "I'm glad you told me. Not just about the tactics, but about the mud. I'm going to make sure to be around to enjoy watching Weed scrubbing out that mud. I'll tell Trickle, if Dun hasn't already."

They both laughed, then, as usual, Muin asked, "Where were you? I know you couldn't see us in the marshy area."

Mouse carefully reached into the folded-over front of her tunic, and pulled out her precious root. "I found this."

"So?" he said, looking down at it, puzzled. "It's a root."

"It's Longevity Root!"

"Isn't that for old and sick people?"

"This is the purple, very rare. It's worth actual gold, Mother once said. I remember she wanted some, but said she would never be able to get it. It's usually preserved for royalty and their connections, to give them longer life and vigor — some say, prepared with powerful charms when there are falling stars, it confers immortality."

Muin's eyes widened. "Does it confer strength? Can you make up some sort of pill, or charm, or brew that will give me the powers I need for my phoenix feather destiny?"

Mouse shook her head, struggling to find the right words for something her mother had been talking about ever since she could first read. She reminded herself that Muin had always been impatient about Essence once he gave up trying to use it. Or even recognize it inside him.

From the way he was standing, he wanted most of all to be sitting down. Soon. Which meant he didn't want a long speech about how Essence, as far as it could be understood, was absolutely fair. It was how it was used that could be wonderful — or terrible, good or evil. "The books say that the purple pill doesn't work that way. It can destroy you. It's a healing power, not a . . . a *power* power."

"I'd risk it," Muin muttered, kneeling down and pointing at his opposite shoulder, where a harder whack than usual had bruised him. Of course that had come from one of Yulin's followers — not Yulin, for he always jabbed, or went for joints.

Mouse noted that it was right on a pressure point, and breathed out a healing charm as she rubbed the knot for Muin. She couldn't cure a bruise, but she was getting good at working out knots. Presently, she felt the muscle ease as he said, "I need anything I can get."

"But I can't make it."

Muin let out a hissing sigh. "You mean you won't."

"No. I can't. First, I'm not certain I remember everything correctly."

Muin turned to go, then turned back, his expression wary. "That's the first I've heard of you not remembering something. You've looked at one page and recited it ever since you were this high." He held his hand flat below his waist.

Mouse set down the empty feed bucket. As the horse lowered its head and began lipping the ground for any stray bits that had fallen, Mouse shut her eyes, then in a quick, flat voice, recited, "First, I would need to gather ten stamens from winter's pinkest plum blossoms from the highest point of the tree, spring's darkest peonies, gathered from a meadow where no one else trod, summer's finest water lilies from the purest pool that no one bathed in, and autumn's silver lotus blossoms from a mountaintop bathed in cloudy mists."

"Is that all?" But he said it without much conviction.

"*Then*, these would have to be dried in pure, balmy air for at least a spring and summer season. While drying the herbs, I'd have to gather rainwater on the sixth day of the sixth month, dew from the ninth day of the ninth month, and water from snow that has not touched the ground on either the last day of the last month of the year, or else the first day of the first month. And if the weather did not cooperate, it must all be gathered again the next year, while the dried herbs lay wrapped in silk, inside either porcelain or cherry-wood, untouched, with charms to protect them. And none of this during a metal or fire year, only water or wood."

He was about to speak when she held up two fingers. "Not finished. The collected waters would be boiled on an auspicious day that also cannot be metal or fire, as the herbs are ground to powder, while I'm repeating the Five Healing Charms — which I haven't been trained in yet. I barely know the first one, which is the one I say when I work on your knots and bruises."

"Oh."

"*Then* the mixture must be poured into carved pill shapes before being buried to age, with more charms said over the spot. I think. As I said, I might have gotten something out of order, or a wrong measure."

"Ayah." Muin let out a long sigh, working his bruised shoulder. As usual, Mouse had made it feel a lot better. "So why do you have the root? For Mother, of course."

Mouse nodded. "If I can dry it right, and save it, I'll take it home once you are promoted away from here. Surely by then you won't need me anymore."

FIFTEEN

"NOW BOTH THE BAREFOOTS are missing at mess," Yulin Pel said to Weed a day after their return from the battle. He was still angry over the loss, though at least it hadn't been his command.

He and Weed stood behind their hut, in a hard, slanting rain, which meant they wouldn't be overheard.

Yulin said to Weed, "If I follow them, they'll know it. I want you to find out where they're going."

"But I—"

Lightning struck Weed. When he could breathe again, he discovered that he lay face down in the mud, the entire left side of his face throbbing. His wits began to return, as the shock of being knocked down coalesced into pain.

Yulin scowled down at him, snarling, "Did I ask you to question orders?"

Did I ask you to question orders? Falik had said at the height of the battle. That their side lost. Not just lost, but lost because those two farm turds had bulled through the attack, scattering everyone.

Falik hadn't hit Yulin, which would have been preferable to being humiliated in front of their army. Falik had followed up his question with, *If we were in a real battle, would there be time to argue? They're right on top of us!*

"Get up," Yulin snapped, angry because it unsettled him to see Weed lying there. He knew he was wrong to hit Weed so hard, and hated the knowing. There was always memory to justify it: his own father, after every beating, reminding him that no one would coddle warriors in the field. No general reached his rank by tender feelings.

Yulin said, a shade less truculently, "Of course you won't follow them. You follow one of their grunts. Who have to know where they are. My guess is, they get cold food and take it wherever they are. You find where, and come back and tell me."

Weed bowed, head low, hands flat on his sodden thighs as pink rain dripped off his nose.

Yulin whirled around and returned to the hut, getting away from the sight of Weed's face with that red blotch on it, the thin trickle of blood from his nose. He'd slapped Weed plenty of times, but until now had never hit him with his fist.

If only those low-born shits didn't make him so furious. The injustice of two mud grubbers thrusting their way into the elite! And tomorrow he'd be forced to stand there and listen to both of those turds be ranked above him for the month, because of that *stupid* battle that Falik had commanded so badly. Not that Falik cared. At most, because of his loss *he'd* slip down to number two, but that wouldn't last long . . .

Mouse had been uneasy all the next day, sensing unfriendly eyes. No surprise when she caught a covert glance from Weed one too many times. It was hard to read his expression because half his face was swollen, but she didn't need to read it to suspect trouble.

When the mess bell rang, and she headed for the kitchen, she took a couple of side jinks, and when she rounded a corner behind the bath house, she leaped to the roof and crouched, looking down—to find Weed furtively sticking to the wall before peering around the corner.

For her.

She waited, then made her way to the kitchens by a roundabout method, thinking rapidly as she ran.

She found Trickle at the kitchen door where they waited to get food to carry to a master getting extra practice.

Trickle saw her, glanced around, then said breezily, "Time for Camp Reek, eh?"

She bit down hard on a retort that would be sure to draw attention.

She'd noticed, along with the other orderlies, that their masters had a bewildering list of slang terms for not only different drills and instructors among the tassels, but also various locations, like the mess hall being "swill." But since they slapped down anyone who presumed to use their terms, she'd paid no attention to any of it. Her fellow grunts had developed their own slang, all of it shortcuts. Then there were the terms only used by particular friends—such as some arcane military terms used by Colt and Vin and some others who grew up in barracks—and they, too, had a summary way with anyone who used their terms uninvited. She avoided them all, speaking as seldom as possible.

Trickle was the complete opposite. He seemed to delight in making up names, whether anyone used them or not. *He* should have been named Weed, Mouse sometimes thought, looking at his skinny form when he put up laundry. Since he turned thirteen (which he had told everyone about, interested or not) he'd only gotten more weedy.

He stood there grinning at her, kitchen workers laboring not five paces away. Mouse yanked him by the arm around a corner into an area with stacked barrels. His mouth opened to protest, but she said, "Weed is shadowing me. Us."

Trickle puffed out a breath. "Why? I noticed Prince Turd's knuckle prints on his ugly face." He looked puzzled. "You think he's supposed to follow us to Camp Reek, instead of Prince Turd following Muin and my First Brother? Ayah, he said it was bound to happen." He grinned. "I want to decoy him. Let me, please, please. I'll do your hot water tomorrow—"

"Agreed." Mouse really didn't care if she was spared one day of water fetching, but that was the way things were done. "You have to keep him away until our brothers get back."

"You don't think that's the only place that stinks, right?" Trickle snickered. "Don't hurry."

That was the problem. Everything was a game for Trickle. It was only good luck that no one had bothered to ask what

"Camp Turd" was, as she was certain Trickle had mentioned it. He was always blabbing about stuff he found funny, and stinks were at the top of his list of things that were *always* funny. Like farts. And butts.

Mouse got the food and sped to her place, watching in all directions. She made it, and while the two wolfed down the fish cakes and fruit, she reported on her suspicions about Weed.

However silly Trickle might be, he kept to his word. He was still sneaking around the back barns, luring the desperate Weed out around the piles of horse manure the first year grunts had pitchforked out of the stalls, when the gong reverberated off the east wall, indicating the watch change.

Trickle glanced up at the boy sentries on the wall, knowing they'd been watching curiously, and couldn't resist a grin and the flat palm squeezed into a fist that meant a successful prank, before he ran off. The episode, as far as he was concerned, was done. He didn't consider the speculation that went from sentries to huts after the change to night duty with the third year sentries, or how Yulin, catching the gist of it, would take it out on the hapless Weed for not only failing his orders, but making himself a laughingstock while doing it.

The next night a thunderstorm struck. Mouse woke up, turned over, and burrowed down to return to sleep when she heard voices. She sat up, aware of two others sitting up, barely outlined in the weak moonlight coming through the window. She gasped in alarm.

"What's that?" someone murmured, voice thick with sleep.

"Shut up," Amna muttered. "It's an attack on the walls."

Of course it was. Nothing new. The fourth and fifth year cadets staged big battles, one attacking the fortress and one defending, when the first and second years were away. But beginning with the third year, when night sentry duty was a regular thing, parties of fourth and fifth years would try to breach the walls. They all knew it.

Mouse lay back, wide awake now, breathing to calm her banging heart. After a time she recognized what had alarmed her. She had been dreaming that Yulin was hunting Muin, only on their island, and he was somehow two—mixed with the twins who had been such a torment.

She told herself to get what sleep she could, but worry about how Yulin was going to retaliate gnawed at her, and she finally slipped into a brief, restless sleep—just to be jerked awake by the Tiger Watch gong.

Trickle was already up and dressed. He kicked her bed as he walked by. "Go back to snoring," he said cheerily. "Remember I'm getting your water."

She would never stay alone in the hut. She rose to get dressed, watching out of the side of her eyes. Weed followed the rest out, leaving her to breathe a sigh of relief. She decided to get an early start on Muin's laundry, which she hadn't washed the night before as the storm was clearly coming in. She picked up the clothes and headed for the laundry area.

From behind East Three, Weed watched, still furious from the slaps he'd endured the night before when he'd had to report his failure to Yulin Pel. "You were played," Yulin Pel had snarled the obvious, his scorn salt in the wound. "Forget that shit running after Dun. Here's new orders. Tomorrow, isolate Muin's grunt, and choke it out of the runty shit."

Weed had lain awake most of the night, his face still aching, his mood ranging between fury and desperation. Mouse was a runt, yes, but like his name, he managed to hide better than anyone else. Every time Weed tried to pick him out of a group, Mouse always seemed to just vanish, as if he were a ghost, or a demon.

He waited uneasily. Maybe Mouse had gone back to sleep, except that no one had finished washing clothes last night.

He was about to turn away when a quick, soft step brought his eyes back, and there was Mouse, arms loaded with laundry. Fierce exultation lasted a heartbeat, replaced by guardedness. Mouse's hearing seemed to be better than anyone's. Weed had never been able to follow Mouse without being noticed.

So he turned away and ran his hardest the long way about, knowing where Mouse had to be headed.

Equally tired, Mouse watched her perimeter, but perfunctorily. She believed she was safely alone as she reached for a basin—

Then a hard hand gripped her topknot and jerked her around, as a fist struck her in the ribs. She couldn't breathe past the pain as Weed flung her face down in the dirt, her laundry scattering. He stomped on the back of her neck — carefully to keep his shoe on her robe below her bare skin, as any marks on grunts earned instant interrogation from the stewards. Yulin Pel had taught him through personal experience where to hit where it hurt worst, yet didn't leave visible marks.

The hard fingers yanked her hair back. She struggled for breath as Weed snarled, "You're going to tell me where they go at evening mess."

For an agonizing moment or two she was afraid that she was going to die right there, unable to breathe, but then her seized lungs eased enough for her to suck in air. Not much, and not easily, with her head yanked back. Her hands flailed uselessly in the dirt, the shoe pressing hard on the back of her neck.

"Talk!" Weed leaned down and with his other hand, punched her in the kidney.

Pain blossomed through her again, bringing with it the toxic Essence of anger. She breathed against it, tightening her core, and in that instant she remembered Heaven and Earth — and her father's voice, *Upright, sideways, lying, leaping — it always works if you remember to bring up the strength from your hips, not your shoulders.*

Hips. Her shoulders were pinned flat, but her hips weren't. Weed was balanced on one foot, the other on her neck. One hand holding her hair in a grip. Free arm cocked back, then swinging down —

She calculated the arc, jerked her right hip up and her left arm to her side. She felt Weed's balance weaken as his foot slid over her spine, and she torqued hard, muscles snapping her around and up after years of daily drill, her left fingers scraping up a handful of dirt, which she flung straight into his eyes.

He let out a squawk and staggered back. She hesitated, the urge to kick him in the face so strong — to strike with all the Essence in her — but she forced herself to expel it in a furious hiss and scrabbled her laundry together as Weed rubbed his tearing eyes.

She fled around the corner, then up to the bathhouse roof. So great was her pain she almost didn't make it. Only a tremendous effort got her the rest of the way, leaving her trembling as she lay flat, jaw clenched against pain.

She leaned out far enough to watch from above as Weed got to his feet and staggered around the corner in pursuit, without ever looking up. Mouse remained where she was, her breathing shuddering. She wanted to run straight to the stewards, but she couldn't. They'd want to see the evidence, and while she could sketch deflection charms on her skin when everyone was bathing, it would be impossible if she were to be inspected for bruises. Also, since she and Weed had been alone, he could say anything he wanted to, like blaming her for attacking him first. They'd both lose duty marks and be stuck back in night soil hauling for a month, on top of all their other chores.

So she waited where she was until she heard the sound of familiar voices. It was her hut mates, on their way back with their empty buckets to do the laundry no one could the night before.

Though it hurt to move, she forced herself to slide off the roof and land, and then mixed herself among them. She hid the trembling in her fingers by scrubbing, and she knew by the rising of the hairs on the back of her neck when Weed joined them, though he didn't speak until Trickle — of course it had to be Trickle — chortled, "You look like you've been drinking all on your own! What happened to your eyes?"

"Shut up."

Wedged safely between two oblivious orderlies, Mouse worked on without so much as a glance upward.

Weed was watching. As he'd expected, that runt Mouse said nothing. No one wanted night soil duty, and that's what they'd get for fighting among themselves. He turned away, trying to figure out what to say to Yulin Pel.

After a day of anxiety and impotent fury, he discovered he didn't have to. Muin and Dun were at mess, Dun having told one friend about the secret drilling, who told one friend, who told one, and so on until Muin overheard and told Dun they might as well join the rest at the targets. Less smelly. Beginning after the next battle.

This, Weed discovered that evening when he went to collect his master's laundry.

Yulin complained to Weed about the fact that the next battle would be commanded by Dun who'd been (or so Yulin insisted) bragging all over the mess hall, and who by rights ought to be a stable grunt, the orders about Mouse apparently forgotten.

As for Mouse, while she dared not drill at her secret spot anymore, at least she could lay out her precious Longevity Herb to dry in the hot, sunny weather.

SIXTEEN

THE NEXT BATTLE WAS held on a flat stretch, beside a stream that was deemed a river border that one side must breach and the other defend.

The boys' chatter on the march had changed from the year previous, when they had parroted words from ancient writings as if those would confer the military greatness of those generals of old. Now it was all whispered talk, and code words, and sidled looks until they split apart, green army to go to their location, red to the valley they must defend. Dun, the red commander, watched the green army's dust vanish down a trail, then lifted his command tally (a polished piece of wood whose carvings, worn by countless boy hands over the years, had become indistinguishable) and pointed.

His scouts departed to lay some warning traps for enemy scouts, and track the green army—whose commander would, Mouse suspected, have someone stationed to watch for them.

She and the others tasked to set up camp decided to dig the jakes first, before the day got much hotter. Then they'd unpack their food supplies.

By the time the horses were tended and left to munch in their feed bags, and the boys also fed, there was still some light. She used the time to roam the heights above the valley that the red army was to defend. By then the shadows had deepened, bluing the valley below. Mouse looked it over, noting the spots from which she might best see the action—because of course Dun would use that stand there to station a silent attack squad behind, right above the best spot to cross the stream.

Then she turned away, checked her surroundings, and gloried in being able to practice Heaven and Earth in sweet air rather than the stench of her secret place.

Rain spattered their tents during the night, wind thudding the canvas. But it was gone by morning, leaving them a crisp, clean day that promised to be hot later, though when Mouse woke, she could see her breath.

She got through dragging water to the horses, and then was free. Wanting to have time for her own drills before the first attack, she raced up to her vantage. As she began her preparatory breathing, she scanned in all directions, more carefully than usual after that disastrous encounter with Weed—but even so she was startled when she heard the clatter of rocks falling, and along a narrow animal path came a tall man in a faded robe of instructor's blue.

She stared witlessly.

He was about Father's age, with ears like the handles of jugs, and lines around his eyes from so much time in the sun. "Here's a surprise," he said, halting.

She remembered who and what she was, bowing, hands on thighs, eyes lowered.

"This is an isolated spot for a ramble," he went on.

"I . . . I . . ."

"Came up to watch, too?" he said, his smile reminding her of Ul Keg's, as though not quite hiding a mirth she didn't understand. Then his brows lifted. "What made you choose this spot, youngster?"

Most of the time, the tassels ignored the orderlies. Unless you got in the way, or did something wrong. No one wanted to catch their notice. But this one wasn't annoyed, or impatient. If anything, Mouse would have guessed he was . . . bored?

She swallowed, and of course had to speak the truth. "I figured the first attack would be there." She pointed down at the shallow spot in the stream, where silt had built up. "My—

that is, Cadet Ryu likes me to watch, sir. To talk over what happened."

On each point, an encouraging nod kept her going, those straight black brows still lifted in question.

"But they aren't here yet. What makes you think they will be? Do they discuss their plans with you?"

"Oh, no, sir! It's just, this is the likeliest place for the first attack. To keep us, red army, that is, busy until the rest come over the hill. My guess is, that way." She pointed.

"Then you'll run over there and watch?"

"Yes, sir," she responded, her own face radiating the question she dared not ask: *Am I in trouble?*

The instructor perched on a mossy boulder in the shade of tree. "What did you overhear leading you to this spot?"

"Nothing, sir," Mouse said, searching her mind nervously. "Ayah, that is, I thought yesterday, when the scouts were sent, that they would be captured, and I was right, everyone talked about it at supper. And when that happens, the defense commanders usually stay close to defend if they don't know where the other army is, or . . ." She went on in a tangle of words to describe what she expected.

The instructor, named Shaz, had wanted to be a scholar, but his family could never afford the necessary education, and hadn't seen the necessity to try. They were a military family, and the sons went into the military. That was traditional, and respecting tradition was one of the Twenty-Five Virtues.

He'd asked so many questions during his training that he was picked out as a future instructor, which suited him well. His favorite subjects were the great writings and their histories; he never admitted that he was counting off the years until he completed his twenty and he could marry and settle on his own plot of land—somewhere near a temple library.

Until then, he amused himself observing the personalities of those who passed under his eyes.

He'd begun the conversation with the little orderly, hereto noticeable only for being the smallest of the second year cadets' servants. As he listened to that stumbling, halting description of not only Dun's strategy, but how the battle was likely to play out, his interest sharpened.

The strategy perhaps was easy enough to guess. Not even Falik Tan demonstrated much brilliance or innovation, not to be expected at this age. Few of them below were able to predict so accurately; but then, it was also expected at this age that most of them were more passionate about personal heroism than observation of the patterns of maneuvering.

"It seems that First Ryu is a teacher," Instructor Shaz said when Mouse ran out of breath.

"Yes, sir?" It was more a question, with an anxious glance, than a statement.

Instructor Shaz squashed the urge to laugh. "It's fine, perhaps unusual. But not unknown," he added, glancing down as boyish shouts echoed up the steep, rocky cliff from below. "Particularly among brothers. It must seem a hard thing," he added, mistaking the motivation for Mouse's expression of dismay. "To be relegated to servanthood because one is younger. Sometimes I wish that tradition was not so difficult to alter. You do know that officers were strictly drawn from the noble ranks in the ancient days."

Mouse bit back the urge to say that *everything* of importance was drawn from the noble ranks in the old days, and from what she could see and hear it wasn't all that different now. She dipped her head in the grunts' bow.

Instructor Shaz went on in a teaching voice, "It was the first Yslan Empress who changed the law, after the Years of Island Wars. Mostly we had so few noble houses willing to send their sons to train as army or navy captains. And the new law was a success. Your brother has surely told you the stories of great generals who all came of humble birth."

He paused, mildly surprised that the youngster's expression of extreme unease had not altered. So he went on in a kindly, coaxing voice, "For a time they were getting far too many candidates, too often runaways from apprenticeships or homes. So the requirement to come with a servant was preserved, to select for those determined enough to meet it. Though the scouting captains will waive that rule from time to time, if they discover an outstanding prospect among the candidates."

Then he said encouragingly, "But you do know that we

often give younger brothers a chance to test with us, if they show an interest. Ah, I hear our approaching invasion. We ought to return to duty, the both of us." He indicated the stream below, and rose from the boulder.

Thus freed, Mouse bowed to his back and sped away in search of another vantage — safely instructor-free — from which to observe her brother's battle, and to consider what she'd just heard.

The first, overwhelming fact was that Muin could have gone alone!

Maybe. *The scouting captains will waive it from time to time* didn't meant Muin would have been one of those chosen in spite of having no servant. In any case she was here. There was no going back, and anyway Muin wouldn't be able to talk about Father's training, or anything else, with some grunt who wouldn't speak the island language, or care about Muin, or know about the phoenix feather. Her being here surely was part of Muin's destiny of greatness.

She hid in a tree to watch the battle, then returned to duty. When next she saw Instructor Shaz, he was busy overseeing the boys. Good. When the hawk flies away, the mice can play, she reassured herself. She would be far more vigilant about avoiding the tassels.

For her own peace of mind, it was as well that she did not know that on their return to Loyalty Fortress, Instructor Shaz entertained his fellow instructors with the story of the little orderly who predicted the course of the battle game.

Out of the mouths of parrots! Of course the little grunt's grasp of strategy and tactics, rudimentary as it was, could be entirely attributed to Muin's skill.

This brought Muin more attention — and expectation. To close the loop, as colder days closed in, Muin carried his frustrations to Mouse one night when he was detailed to stand at the southeast tower during Turtle Watch, the most miserable of the night watches.

The second years were now expected to master night sentry duty. They all knew that no one would ever attack the island, nor would they, as future commanders, ever have to do sentry duty. But they had to thoroughly understand defense of fort and camp, which meant learning how to stay alert during those night hours, how to listen for trouble, and how to deal with it when it came. They had winter to accustom themselves, and then, as everyone knew, the third years would be making night raids. Being caught flat would set them all back in honor marks, besides being thoroughly humiliating.

Most ordered their servants to bring them something hot; those who did were excused early morning duty, as their masters were permitted to sleep until the Phoenix Watch first gong.

On a cold night, the stars glittering like ice shards, and both moons half visible in opposite parts of the sky, Mouse brought Muin steeped ginger root, tinged with lemongrass that she had picked herself.

Muin slurped gratefully, then said, "They said I'm going to command again."

"That's good, isn't it?" Mouse asked.

"Good, bad, I can't tell. I know I can lead a charge. Defending. Attacking, it's all one. I lead, they follow. But I'm beginning to have nightmares about planning battles. I really hate that sand table."

"Sand table?"

"You know. Instructor Shaz's sand table—it's sand with some mosses and pebbles and things, shaped up to look like various terrains, from how an eagle sees the world below. I always see what they mean after it's all explained, but beforehand, when it's time to plan, it just looks to me like hills and valleys."

"You won the last one you commanded," Mouse said.

Muin scowled, looking unhappy. "I won't say this to anyone else. But that wasn't me. That was Falik, on his own. He said it was within orders, but we all know he took command and saved us from total annihilation, once Cor's assassins took me out."

Mouse had learned that "took me out" meant tagged as dead, preventing the cadet from going back to the battle, or even talking to anyone.

"I should have figured they were coming," he finished bitterly. "Cor *always* wants to run assassin attacks if he's not in command, and I *know* who's likely to let him. But I was too busy trying to see how my defense was going." He sighed, and then the words were wrung from him, "The last one I lost. Everyone expects Falik to come up with good plans. His father has been tutoring him since he spoke his first word. Dun and Cor are better than I at making plans. It was Dun who got the idea to create the false camp after we saw those scouts, and they got away. And Cor loves the sneak, as I said. When is planning going to get easier? I just want to lead the charge. That, I *know* I'm good at."

Mouse of course had no answer. Nor did Muin expect her to have one. What he did expect was a suggestion for a new plan, which she gave him. Wrinkling her nose, she said tentatively, "If you have Cor again. And those who like to be assassins. Why not turn that around?"

"Turn it around?" Muin repeated.

"Yes. It sounds like everyone is expecting them, now. So instead of trying more and more ways to get to the commander, which is just going to get harder, why not let the assassins be the deflection?"

Muin's furrowed brow cleared, his eyes glittering in the torchlight. "So the army still makes noise like they're the deflection, but they aren't. On a signal they . . .what? Decide that when I see the terrain. But the assassins lure . . . oh, what fun." Then his mood soured again. "Why didn't I think of that?" He slapped his own face.

"No, no," Mouse cried. "It's just thinking of opposites. I always do that. I always did, to fool you and Second Brother, when I wanted to follow you and you didn't want me. I think about what's expected, what is usually done, and do the opposite."

"*All war is deception*," Muin muttered. "Is that what that means?"

Mouse shrugged, unsure whether she had helped or hurt Muin. She only breathed easier when his expression lightened, and he went away to pull his assigned captains aside to lay plans.

The ruse worked.

Of course variations on it showed up in subsequent battles,

but in the analysis discussions, Muin was credited with his innovation. Mouse was delighted with his cleverness, and shared his pride when he was moved up in the rankings again—meanwhile, she worked a trade with one of the carpenter's apprentices who badly wanted to learn to read, but had been scoffed at by his peers for such presumption.

He made Mouse a water-tight box to keep her dried Longevity Herb in, while she taught him enough of the basics of the Imperial characters to begin him on the road to reading.

Training progressed.

Muin was not the only one who noticed that he was getting as many command assignments as Falik and Dun. Those who could not accept a barefoot rising above them in rank complained bitterly to each other. It was Yulin who urged the others to Do Something About It.

But what?

They held furtive meetings in one of the privies, behind the barns, and in the space between the weapons storage sheds—most of it was cursing, and *I'd like to*, followed by wild threats. Meanwhile, these meetings did not go unnoticed—Trickle spotted Dun's enemies slinking between the storage sheds twice, and reported it to Dun, who shared it with Muin and the other barefoots.

Then Muin pulled Mouse apart one frigid day, as sleet spat from low clouds overhead. "Remember that time you gave Second Brother and me some 'medicine' and we were in the privy half the day?"

Mouse groaned, hopping from foot to foot as she shivered. "How could I forget that? My hand hurt for weeks after Mother made me copy out the entire Herbal five times, with the annotations about the dangers of poisons, and after that, Ul Keg made me copy *The Twenty-Five Virtues*. All because I heard her prescribing that medicine for Granny Yenk, and I thought it would be good for us. But they didn't believe me."

"They didn't believe you could *read* those books. I remember the fuss," Muin corrected, and waved the entire episode away. "Can you get whatever that medicine was?"

"Why? Are you constipated?" Mouse asked.

"No! I want to slip it to Yulin."

"No," Mouse said. "That's poison, or the next thing to it, and I promised faithfully never to poison anyone again."

"It's not *poison*," Muin said in an agony of frustration. "I don't want to *poison* him, I just want him off in the bushes on this next command of mine, which will be in the snow. I still don't understand snow. We still have to go unless it's a blizzard, and even if *I* think it's a blizzard, the tassels won't, you'll see, we'll be marching up to our butts in slush, and the worst of it is . . ." He stopped for breath. "When they announced today that I'll be commanding—*again*—I saw Yulin going like this." Muin's normally somber, honest face twisted into a hideous parody of a smirk. "You *know* he's going to do something terrible, and the tassels won't see it. If it weren't *snowing* so much, I could find some blooming jasmine and stuff it in his trunk so he'd sneeze himself into his bunk, but there isn't any jasmine blooming now."

Mouse wavered. She absolutely believed Muin, first because he never lied, and second, Trickle had been gossiping to Colt and a couple others about seeing Yulin sneaking around.

Then she thought of the phoenix feather, and said reluctantly, "I'll give it to you. But I won't put it in his food."

"Done," Muin said. He knew that Trickle would be delighted to slip the stuff into Yulin's food, and it would be so much easier to achieve in camp.

Knowing Trickle's penchant for talk, both Muin and Dun had threatened him with dire tortures and a hideous, protracted death if he so much as blabbed a word, but nothing could keep Weed from noticing how Trickle went about his camp chores with the tight jaw of suppressed laughter after his master turned an odd shade of green, then bolted for the jakes. Where he was still in possession, shivering and groaning.

The same day Mouse came near him, and muttered, "If jasmine really does make Yulin Pel sneeze, get him to put at least two petals of hairy stingrose in hot water. But don't touch the stem—"

"Oh, sure, you want me covered with welts, and his insides, too," Weed snarled, swinging a fist at Mouse.

She ducked by sidestepping and gave up. Weed went to complain to Yulin.

Muin's ploy worked. Without Yulin there to exhort his followers into action, his plot fell apart, which in turn caused his army to lose. This disgusted his fellow greens so much that when several gloating reds made fart noises when Yulin sat down, and inspected anyplace he sat before sitting, and sniffed the air when he passed, making exaggerated faces of nausea, the greens acted as if they saw and heard nothing.

Yulin was in a fury for retribution—once his innards settled down again.

The day after they returned to the fortress, winter set in early, and stayed with a series of blizzards. Everyone was grounded except the fifth years, who were caught elsewhere on an extended battle game at the other end of the island.

The instructors kept the cadets busy with mapping projects, studies of the writings of generals, and fierce competitions between the huts, and finally between the various years. The storms ended, leaving a hard freeze that created a glistening blue world of ice-bound danger, making it impossible to venture, especially when yet another great snowfall blew in, hiding the ice. The roads were completely invisible, the valleys impassable.

SEVENTEEN

WINTER WAS HARD IN all the northern islands.

But the stars never pause in their slow dance across the skies, and both moons wound their way together again, facing each other at either end of the Sky Bridge of stars as below, the Empire of a Thousand Islands celebrated the turn of another year.

Everywhere, from high to low, New Year's Two Moons was a time to foregather in family, paying respects to the elder generation, unless one was in service to the empire, or dedicated to a temple. Or on the wander.

Master Bankan's scribe house in Imai Harbor celebrated outwardly with customary rituals, and within the house, with promotions.

Again, Yskanda skipped up two levels. He was now studying alongside students of eighteen, nineteen, twenty. Under ordinary circumstances that might have caused jealousy and even covert retribution, but without trying—possibly because it would never occur to him to try—he had gradually become so well liked that the cheer for him was far more sincere than the cheers for the higher-level assistants being promoted to full scribe.

Yskanda blushed and smiled and accepted invitations to

celebrate with his ever-widening circle of friends, but inwardly he missed his family terribly at these moments of triumph. And his highest ambition was still to make a spirit screen for one of Master Bankan's minor courtyards.

In the palace, in spite of the terrible weather, the dowager empress's family had faithfully gathered to entertain her, with the usual mix of motivations: duty, ambition—there were nieces and nephews hopeful of titles, sinecures, and expensive gifts—and even love.

The emperor, prowling around his palace under banners of dragons and tigers as his mind ranged ahead, considering the latest reports from his eyes abroad, particularly those from the direction of the island kingdom in the northern reaches, west of the empire. Invasion was again imminent—so maintained his Admiral of the Western Seas, while requesting more ships, more supplies; they all wanted more, more, more. Everyone had their faces to the floor these days, palms stretched out in plea, always for some dire emergency. Which meant strain on the treasury.

As his steps passed the manors of his consorts and approached his mother's glorious mansion, he reflected that at least the Spring Hunt was no longer the bloody contest he'd endured as a boy. He'd civilized it. That was one merit, even if no one acknowledged it but him.

On that thought he entered his mother's mansion to greet her, without seeing how the servants along his way curled heads to the floor, whatever they were carrying set before them. He heard the sound of laughter, and was drawn thither to see what pleased her. He was not surprised to discover his cousins there, who he privately thought of as beggars in silk, their metaphorical hands out even as they joked and smiled at the old women who really ought to know better.

His mother sat in the midst of them, papers on her lap.

At his entry, they all rose and made the imperial bow. He waved them back, and bent to kiss his mother on the forehead before saying, "I heard you laughing. Will you share the mirth?"

"It's this drawing of a parrot standing on the head of a monkey, who is riding the back of a sheep — see? This painting is so clever, you can see the motion, the parrot clutching, the monkey leaning over as if about to fall, the fat sheep waddling."

The emperor glanced down at the hasty sketch by his maternal cousin Kui Pandan, finding it jejune at best, but for his mother's sake he smiled. "Very lifelike."

"Here's another, of a little girl dressed up like the Fox Princess in the tale, and balancing on a pole . . ."

As his mother spoke, he idly reached down for the stack of papers she had set aside.

She said, "Oh, those are from his journey last year. I didn't get to see them because Ze Lua thought she was in labor, and by the time I was free again, Pandan was off on another journey . . ."

The emperor rifled through two or three drawings of ships at sail, strange flowers and plants, and was about to put the stack down again when he saw the upper curve of a woman's hair, and one languid eye. His cousin was an idle, gluttonous fool, but it was true that, when he exerted himself, he had a way with a brush. Especially when drawing women. The emperor paused over a sketch of a dancer, her veils and flimsy skirts flying artfully around a body just hinted at in shadows.

With more interest, the emperor glanced at drawings of the dancer from a couple more angles, then came other faces — an old monk sitting on a mat, eyes uplifted, a couple making wedding bows to a gathering, a beautiful boy sketching his own picture, his face bent just so —

Cold prickles ran through the emperor, and he paused, the paper in hand. Then he brought it closer. Those eyes, that perfect forehead, the entrancing arch to brows, the face utterly innocent of the coy, sly arts of pleasing.

His stillness alerted those whose lives depended on pleasing him. Elderly Topaz, who had waited on the dowager empress for decades, noted the subtle tightening of focus in the emperor, and stooped ostensibly to check the vessel holding hot water for tea. His fingers touched the pot but his eyes skimmed the page that the emperor held so tightly. Topaz found that sketched face vaguely familiar; well-honed instinct caused him to turn his head half a heartbeat before the emperor looked up.

Topaz signaled to a young page for more hot water, and the moment passed as memory propelled the emperor back to his first manor, and the sixteen-year-old girl who should have been his bride, sitting in his library over her dusty tomes, her perfect oval of a face dominated by that pure forehead and arched brows, her head bent just so . . .

He turned to Cousin Pandan, and forced his voice to idleness. "Where were you when you did this? Who is the young artist?"

His cousin glanced at the paper and wrinkled his nose. "A pretty face on some grubby nothing of an island, I forget where. My ship was stuck there for the Spring Festival. It ought to say on the back."

The emperor turned over the paper, aware that his hand shook. *First Scholar's House, Spring Festival, scholar's apprentice.* And the date — which meant nothing if Pandan did not recollect where he was.

Kui Pandan, always aware that his expensive journeys were entirely due to his imperial cousin's generosity, made an effort to recall. "Let me glance at the others, to see if I can — yes, there's that odd tree with the purple flowers, which I'm told doesn't grow here in the colder north. It was somewhere in the south."

The emperor stared down at the drawing, knowing that that boy could be anyone. Or anywhere. "The south" comprised over a hundred islands at the very least — not counting those without an official imperial presence, but which he still ruled.

Then, aware of a sudden silence, he glanced up to find them all staring. "Very fine," he said, leafing through another several before adding, "Your talent, Cousin, has only improved over the years. I would like to take these back with me, to look at with more leisure. May I?"

There was only one answer to be made to that, of course.

Kui Pandan, with visions of his own artistic school set up in sumptuous comfort right here in the capital — funded by the emperor, of course — bowed and said enthusiastically, "Take them, Imperial Cousin, they are my gift to you. I am honored you even glanced at my foolish scribbles . . ."

At Loyalty Fortress, the Two Moon New Year celebration brought in the Year of the Dog as a welcome break in a long, grim winter. The commander gave the younger cadets a two-day treasure hunt, and the older ones a rare all-day liberty in the village.

Then it was right back to cold, icy reality, punctuated by periods of wading hip deep through snow, until at last the storms brought more sleet than snow, with clear days between bands of clouds.

After so protracted a period with the boys locked in the fortress, the instructors decided not to wait for the spring ships, but to permit the third years (soon to be promoted to fourth years) to attack the soon to be third years a little early, as they guarded the walls.

Everyone anticipated the advent of those surprise night attacks: the attackers to prove their prowess, the defenders to prove theirs.

And Yulin, with darkness to protect him, could at last wreak vengeance on the worst of the barefoots: Ryu Muin, now tied with Cor Kenek for second place behind General Falik's son.

Yulin was tied for third with Dun Duan.

"The tassels are too stupid to see the injustice," Yulin said to Weed while prowling the wall on his sentry duty. "It wouldn't surprise me to find out they're all barefoots themselves. Sons of street-sweepers."

He peered out in the darkness. "I think they're all asleep, except for the Stick Tassel. And then he goes back to stay warm." This referring to the instructor who prowled silently among the sentries, and anyone he caught having slid down the wall for a nap would be wakened with a crack of the withy wand.

Yulin peered toward the towers, which had partial walls to block cold winds. You could only see heads bobbing above these walls—barely—limned in torchlight. There were also torches over the gate. Between the walls and the gate on either side? Covering darkness.

"Yes," Yulin said, grinning so wide his teeth chilled in the wintry air. "The tassels are bound to send the third years against us when Ryu, Dun, or Falik are on tower watches. They'll want to see how they defend. I hope it's Muin," he added nastily.

Weapons were flogging offenses if they were not issued by the tassels. But Yulin didn't mean to get caught. The whole point was to strike and then retreat under cover of darkness. "I can name five who will beg for the chance to join me."

Not quite true. They actually had to be begged, but only as long as it took to convince them that the plan was foolproof. "How will we even know when to go?" one asked. "The whole idea is for the third years to be stealthy. We're not going to wait up every night hoping they got the orders to go."

Yulin said, "I overheard Falik telling Cor that it would surely be the first night of thaw. The tassels don't want anyone slipping on ice."

"Then what?" another asked. "If the third years see us, it's all over. They'll know their own."

"They won't see us if we stay well behind them. Look, I'll take the first night's watch over their huts, and I can bring you out when they leave to execute the sneak attack. We don't have to go anywhere near them."

"But we have to follow them to know where they're attacking, right?"

"They can't breach the west wall, as that has a two hundred pace drop below it. No one tries the main gate wall — the noise would wake up the tassels snoring right behind it, and anyway it's also got a fifty pace drop. That leaves the east and north walls. I think it'll be the north wall, as the last two invasions came up from Shit Road and attacked the east. Muin is bound to put most of his people along the east wall. The north is a much longer run in the cold and slush, but it also means they're way beyond the targets and the horse barns. Perfect for us. So we just wait until the third years leave, and stay away from the tassel. Then when they strike, under cover of their noise, we go for Muin."

"I get the first whack," Silam stated.

"No, I do," Yulin retorted. "This plan is mine, and I'll do the first watch." He saw mutiny in Silam's face, so he added, "If I'm wrong about the first night of thaw, then you watch on the second. Whoever sits up to watch for the third years gets first whack."

Silam relented then. After all, he could always get first whack on one of the other barefoots presuming to thrust themselves up among their betters.

Thaw arrived at last, the entire island a damp, chilly world of drips and trickles when the team chosen among the third years was given their order to invade. Yulin's prediction — or rather Falik's — was correct.

The third years on the attack team ghosted out of their huts during the second gong of Turtle Watch, the worst stretch of the night. They met, and streamed silently toward the barns, followed by Instructor Vin, the youngest of the instructors, who had been tasked to evaluate the third years' first fortress invasion attempt.

As Yulin had predicted, they left by the east gate and headed up the rocky incline, past the waterfall feeding the stream that divided Loyalty Fortress from the village, to invade from the north wall.

By then Yulin had woken his own team. They stopped to fetch the wooden weapons that Weed had secreted, one by one, over the past week. They also headed for the barns, but turned north, to sneak along the wall to the inner stair, which they knew would be dark and empty. Muin and his sentries would be watching outward.

They'd nearly reached the stair when Yulin turned to Weed. "If he has the runt with him, that's your target."

Weed muttered uneasily, "You want *me* to attack Mouse?"

Yulin snapped his head around, and though Weed could barely see his face, he felt Yulin's fury. "You don't mean to say you are afraid of that runt?"

"He *is* a runt," Weed said quickly, in a pleading whine. "Short, but not weak. I think he's as old as us, maybe even older —"

"That's ridiculous," Yulin whispered fiercely. "I've looked at his ugly face maybe twice in two years, but even I could see there's no hint of beard. He's got baby cheeks. Probably baby *teeth*."

Weed had to admit the truth of that, and muttered defensively, "He's stronger than he looks. Really."

Yulin retorted sarcastically, "You're a rabbit. Really." But then he let it go, aware that he wanted it that way. One of his father's earliest lessons was *Never have anyone stronger than you at your back. It'll be your last regret when they turn on you.*

So he said, "In any case, you'll watch for the tassel and *I'll* scrag him. But Ryu Muin is first, and he's mine." Yulin looked around at the others. "We'll be fast, hit then run. Quiet. The tassel will be busy watching the third years. As long as you're fast, he'll never know we're there."

Mouse was indeed there, having just brought hot spicy ginger-root for Muin.

Her brother laid his wooden sword on the wall and gratefully took the cup in both hands, warming them before he even ventured a sip. Mouse sniffed the air, sure she'd caught the smallest whiff of green stuff. Or maybe it was imagination, she thought wistfully as she took up a stance a few paces from Muin. It had been so very *long* a winter.

As Muin was still sipping, she began Heaven and Earth, grateful not to have to peer around her lest she be caught—the wall hid her from below, and she made certain to stand in the shadow cast by the torchlight, so no one along the wall could see her, in the unlikely chance they looked her way.

Ever since Trickle had ruined her secret spot, she'd had to find places to practice, always with an ear alert for someone approaching. Her favorite had been the laundry, where she could see her Essence wind imps bat at hanging stockings and shirts, but that was the most dangerous place because it was so well-traveled. Perhaps it was good to have to be alert, but she was always alert. What she liked best was to let her mind go to other places as she performed the drill.

She finished right hand, reversed the pattern with her left, then flipped into a handstand to walk in a circle. When she'd completed a round, she glanced up to gauge where she was, to find upside-down Muin watching her over his cup. "I forgot what Heaven and Earth looks like," he said.

She back-flipped upright. "What?"

"Done properly, I mean." He set down the empty cup on the wall, and gestured with his hands. "It's like water, when you do it. Like when Father did it."

"Isn't it the same when you do it?" she replied. "I mean, the feeling inside, like the flow of a river in the sky? It is for me, if I don't have to constantly watch out for someone seeing me."

Muin looked away, not wanting to admit that he hadn't done it for months. Why should he, when there was constant drill anyway? And he dared not let anyone see it, as he'd promised Father. Anyway, the last few times he'd done it, he knew he'd brought the army drill's cadenced jerking and stamping, which made the old rhythm turn awkward. Far too much effort.

He sighed out a breath, aware of cold creeping into his limbs again. "Tell me what I'm doing wrong," he said.

Mouse moved to the wall to watch. As always, it took a while to find the rhythm, and even then it didn't quite feel . . .

"Shoulders are too far forward on the thrusts," Mouse said. "Throwing your balance off."

"The tassels like it," Muin said. "Says it gives our thrusts the extra power."

Mouse shrugged. "Maybe. But I feel stronger like this." As Muin abandoned his pose to look, she demonstrated a turn and a snap from the hip. "This . . ." She mimicked his jerky forward thrust of the shoulder. "It feels wrong."

"Go through Heaven and Earth with me again," Muin said. "Fast. I want to see if I can get Father's rhythm again." At least he'd be warm.

They took up positions, making certain they were a bit beyond arm's reach, but away from the walls of the tower. There was barely enough space for them without weapons, so Muin left his sword on the wall. Mouse noted that the cramped space would keep her from traveling. Father had insisted it was part of control to finish in the same spot he'd begun in.

Together they worked through the form, speeding up until their clothes snapped and popped. He noticed with surprise that hers snapped as much as his, though he was so much larger.

He was going to comment when she stilled. He'd been reaching for his cup, then stilled — and heard it. No more than a puff of breath, the hiss of clothing.

Someone was on the back stair? A tassel, doing an inspection to see if they were awake? The third year attackers were supposed to attack from the front—

A shout rang through the air, coming from farther down the wall, closer to the northwest tower. Cor shouted, "Here!" And laughed — the attackers were busy climbing the outside of the wall. "Tip the ladders!"

Shouts and grunts filled the air, Muin poised to run to their aid if Cor yelled, but holding his position in case of a sneak attack. He leaned out over the wall to look for third year attackers sneaking up—

And heard a step behind him. Instinct snapped him around, sidestepping a heartbeat before a blow glanced off the side of his head, knocking him off-balance. He hit the wall face first. Lightning split across his vision and he fell heavily, aware of the grunts and hisses of a fight very close at hand.

He forced himself to one knee, his right hand groping for his sword. Gone. He froze. What was Yulin doing here? He was not part of tonight's sentry duty.

Before Muin could shake off the dizziness enough to move, he saw a practice sword thwack Yulin hard across the elbow, and when he recoiled, the weapon whirled around and cracked on the point of his right shoulder. Yulin howled. A foot— Mouse's small foot — kicked out his knee.

Yulin slammed flat to the stones half an arm's length from Muin. Mouse stood over him, keening softly.

"Mouse?" Muin croaked.

As if given permission, or maybe it was only the sudden quiet, Mouse broke into wild sobbing, and threw Muin's wooden sword clattering away. Muin forced himself to his feet, his head aching, blood sticky on his swelling face. Farther down the wall people stood as if frozen, faces pale in the starlight, except for round mouths.

With them, a tassel.

Everyone staring at Mouse.

Muin looked back at Mouse, who stood there trembling, her breath shuddering as she wept. Muin then took in the five sprawled figures, all moaning or rocking back and forth, cradling limbs . . . except for the one who had fallen off the wall to the stones below.

EIGHTEEN

COMMANDER WEKEN WAS YANKED out of deep sleep mid-way through Turtle Watch as increasingly wild rumors swept through Loyalty Fortress like fire. But no sooner had the commander grasped the gist of Instructor Vin's incoherent report than he issued a stream of orders: early as it was, the entire fortress was to report to the parade ground. There, with the cadets spaced well apart, the instructors were to work them hard until he understood what had happened and decided what to do.

The wounded went of course to the "sweat beds," the age-old name for the physicians' building, where boys went to sweat out sicknesses or wounds, after drinking medicine bitter enough to discourage the lazy. Each was to be kept in a separate room, and not permitted to come out or to speak to one another. That went for Ryu Muin and Muin's orderly as well, until they could be interviewed.

Tiger Watch had begun, the sun still below the eastern horizon, when the commander sat down with his instructors, the chief physician, and the two chief stewards, balding Pand and cadaverous, somber Tolu.

Commander Weken said, "Instructor Vin. You were the only staff eye-witness. Please repeat for us all exactly what you saw."

Vin had had the remainder of Turtle Watch to get his thoughts in order. He raised his square, earnest face, and said, "I was behind the third year invasion team, whose captain had chosen to advance from the northeast . . ."

He gave a brief description of the team's approach to the fortress's north wall, positioning their two ladders midway along the wall and near the northwest tower. He chose the midway ladder to mount, from which he thought he would get the best view of the invasion and defense, and gave a succinct report on the action.

". . . then I was distracted by yelling from the east tower. I looked that way, though I knew I had the entire invasion team in sight before me. None had progressed toward the northeast tower. In the torchlight I saw a cadet dressed in a black night-maneuver robe leap up onto the wall in order to strike down with his weapon at a small orderly in gray. The orderly blocked the downward blow, and in a backhand move struck the weapon from the cadet's hand. The cadet reached for his weapon, overbalanced, and vanished."

"So Orderly Ryu did not throw or push or otherwise cause Cadet Silam to go over the wall?" the commander asked.

"Correct," Instructor Vin said. "Though I was perhaps twenty-five paces from them, approaching rapidly, the torch burned not five paces from them, and there was nothing impeding my view. In the time it took for me to reach the action, I saw Orderly Ryu knock the remaining cadets in black to their knees. It could not have taken more than twenty moves."

A soft whisper ran around the room, but at a flick of a glance from the commander, it ended.

Instructor Vin went on in his flat report voice, "I reached the wall to check on Silam below. He lay at a bad angle, but he was making noise so I knew he was alive. Five were down: Orderly Yulin, Yulin himself, and three second year cadets, all dressed for night maneuvers. Cadet Ryu was on his hands and knees, the side of his head bleeding. Orderly Ryu, the only one standing, had dropped his sword by then. He wept as he said over and over, 'They tried to kill my brother! They tried to kill my brother!'"

The commander raised his hand, and Vin halted.

The commander turned to the two stewards. "What can you tell us about Orderly Ryu?"

The two exchanged glances, then Pand, as the senior, spoke up. "Though the youngest of the second year orderlies, Orderly Ryu is quiet, clean, and obedient. Always earns full duty merits."

Another exchange of looks, then Pand made a hand gesture and Tolu cleared his throat. "There was an incident. Caused by Orderly Yulin, as it happens." He went on to describe what he'd seen on the first day of tent training. "I still don't understand how someone so small could have carried half that canvas," he finished. "Though he was clearly in pain afterward."

"Thank you," Commander Weken said.

The commander turned to the old physician. "I saw Yulin and his companions when I interviewed them shortly before our gathering here, but I would like you to give us your expert opinion on their status."

The old physician said in his dry, husky voice, "In order of seriousness, Silam has a shattered shoulder and a broken leg, both from his fall. I thought it best to dose him with sleep herbs before addressing his wounds. Cadet Ryu has a knot on his head and a finger-length cut on his face from where he landed against a stone in the wall." He went on to list the bruises and contusions of the rest, making it clear that Mouse had broken no heads or bones, though there were at least two badly bruised joints on each of them. Except: "Weed — Orderly Yulin — seems to be entirely unhurt. Though he claimed Orderly Ryu beat him after taking the sword Cadet Yulin insisted he bring, I found no such evidence anywhere on his body."

"Dropped down and hid his face," the commander commented. "Which is what we'd expect from an orderly-in-training of fifteen or sixteen." He turned to Steward Pand. "How old is Orderly Ryu?"

"According to his records on arrival, he was born the Year of the Dolphin."

"He's a year younger than the age we accept for testing!" the commander exclaimed.

"He's been here two years already," Steward Pand

reminded him. "We do have several orderlies around the same age."

The commander sat back and gazed at the steward as he said, "But not one that can drop five older boys who have been training hard for two years. Unless your orderly training is far different from what we had assumed."

Steward Pand was scrupulously honest, though lacking in a sense of humor. He said stiffly, "The only weapon in that boy's hands has been a laundry paddle. And a broom."

One of the older instructors glanced at the commander for permission to speak.

Commander Weken—guessing what direction the commentary might lead—turned back to Steward Pand. "Thank you. You may return to duty now."

The stewards bowed and turned to leave. Then Pand paused to look back, bowing again as he said, "Commander, do you want to interview Orderly Ryu now?"

"Not yet, thank you. I will send an aide when I am ready. No, strike that. I'll go myself."

As soon as the door was shut, the commander glanced at grizzled Fumig Kanda, who had been an army captain before being reassigned to the training school. He alone of the instructors had seen actual battle. The rest had been selected out to teach not long after their own training. "Captain Instructor Fumig," the commander said. "You listened as I interviewed Yulin and the three cadets still awake. Before I offer my own comments, do you have anything to say?"

Fumig said slowly, "Of those particular boys, I believe the most reliable and least self-serving would be Cadet Pol. He was raised in barracks, and has seen all manner of drill, scrapping, and the occasional duel since he could walk. His description of that young orderly's fighting style reminds me very much of a style I have not seen for many years . . ."

Commander Weken gave a nod. "The imperial guard style from two decades ago. I looked at Cadet Ryu's recruit information. He stated that someone arrived at his island, taught swordsmanship to the villagers in order to fight pirates, then left again. Exactly what might be expected from a former guard who left, or was sent away, and took to the wandering sword world. Ryu's father then taught his boys."

Fumig, who didn't want to bring up the infamous name Danno if he didn't have to, sat back a little. He had not known Captain of Guards Danno personally, but his nephew had been one of Danno's guards, and had talked enthusiastically about Danno. Young as he was, he had apparently been an excellent captain, refining the imperial guard drills and looking out for his men, until suddenly he ended up on the capital list.

Commander Weken said, "We don't even have a name, so there is no use in sending a report that will only stir up useless questions — this happens too often to be of note, except when those illegally trained turn to treason and rebellion, and there are no such reports out of any of those southern islands. Unless there comes an imperial order to the contrary, we can safely let be. What we need to turn our attention to is the dilemma before us, beginning with what to do about this orderly. And Cadet Yulin."

No one spoke, but the blanking of expressions and the quick glances to the side at the name "Yulin" were quite telling. The commander said, "Setting aside the total disregard for orders and rules, if we look at Cadet Yulin's plot strictly as a military exercise, it was competently done. Even excellently. If the little orderly had not been there, Yulin probably would have achieved his goal."

Captain Instructor Fumig glowered. "He sat there and lied through his teeth, claiming it was merely a prank, but from all accounts, his first strike was at Cadet Ryu's head — and Ryu Muin's hands were empty. He'd just been drinking something hot. The cup was there beside him when he fell."

Commander Weken said, "I believe many of us are aware that the Yulin clan has become very powerful, it's said through unsavory methods as well as through service. Yulin's own father, as it happens, was dismissed from the imperial training school around the time we were speaking of previously. He was also evicted from the naval school, on both accounts for excessive cruelty. I mention these things because our decision will have to take the clan reaction into account, however much we might regret the necessity."

He paused to thumb his upper eyelids, as if to press away

a building headache. Then he looked around at his staff. "So, as I was saying, regarded strictly as a military exercise, Cadet Yulin Pel did everything correctly, from scouting the time and place, predicting the movements of the third year exercise, and using it as cover. But against that we must look not only at his intent—at the very least to seriously harm Ryu Muin, if not worse—and his record so far. Which is full of honor marks, always for excess."

Fumig looked up. "Send him to Dragon Claw Army."

Some stirred at this. Nods, even a grim smile or two, indicated approval. Dragon Claw Army had a fearsome reputation. Their banners were more warlike than any, with crimson dragons stitched against a black background, coveted gold edging the dragon, earned by their victories and granted by a past emperor. Their armor, red on black, was famed. And feared.

Everyone there knew that the Dragon Claw Army was where noble clans, and city magistrates, sent brutish young men who could or would not settle anywhere else. There was a reason this army was always at the forefront of any war.

"Yulin Pel has the makings of a future General of the Red Dragon. The youngest the Dragon Claw Army takes prospective captains is eighteen. If we keep him through the fourth year, then send him, with a suitably complimentary letter to his family, that might suffice," Fumig added—what he did not say, but all understood, was that Yulin must not be permitted to damage or endanger their prize cadets. The next Imperial Examination for the military would be coming up after Falik and the other promising cadets in his year finished their fifth. The training center that produced first rank examinees gained tremendous merit. "Through the fourth year for Yulin, to satisfy his clan. But he'll have to be put on oath, and watched constantly."

"That can be done," Commander Weken commented. "In fact, there are two among the incoming fifth years who would do well with exactly such an assignment for this next year, and we can see about the year after. Very well. Yulin Pel will suffer a suitable punishment, which ought to remind our cadets of the cost of ignoring the rules in favor of personal vendettas—eh? What is it?"

This to an aide, who had just entered, and stood silently by, head bowed. "Pigeon, commander." The aide saluted, and handed off a strip of paper.

The room remained still as the commander unrolled the tiny paper and squinted at it. Then sighed. "The first candidate ship is two days from arrival. I want all this resolved, and order restored well before that ship docks. Which brings us to Orderly Ryu . . ."

NINETEEN

MOUSE HAD GONE FROM elation at saving her brother from what she'd assumed was assassination, to shock at the arrival of an instructor seemingly out of nowhere, to dread of what surely would be catastrophic consequences. Orderlies were absolutely forbidden to pick up weapons for any purpose but cleaning and storage.

Her grim imaginings only worsened when Muin was led off with those she'd beaten to the physicians to be treated, and she was told to report to the Chief Steward, who stashed her in a small room she'd never seen before, distressingly near where the staff was housed — forbidden territory.

She sat hunched up in a ball until one of the kitchen aides brought in a bowl of congee she was too distraught to eat. There she remained, her imagination filling with a horrific variety of fates, when entered no less a personage than Commander Weken, with one of the instructors at his shoulder.

By now she was nearly fainting with terror, but managed to get her watery joints to work enough for her to rise and bow.

"Tell us what happened," the commander said, sitting in the chair, the instructor standing behind him.

Mouse locked her knees to keep herself from falling, she was trembling so hard. She gave a report in a stuttering morass of words she was miserably aware were nearly incoherent. She kept returning to the one fact she knew was irrefutable: "I saw Yulin come from the stair, and hit my brother, and I wasn't going to let him kill him."

The commander said, "You were taught by your brother?"

"Yes sir, and my fa—" She gulped.

"Your father? I take it he was one of the island men instructed by a visitor from elsewhere?"

"Yes, sir," she exclaimed thankfully. That was true—or close to true.

"And this man went away again, and your brother reinforced his learning by teaching you."

"Yes, sir, starting when I was little."

The commander's mouth pursed as if he was hiding a smile.

Puzzled—afraid he didn't believe her—she said, "It was a long time ago."

The commander was thinking that Orderly Ryu was so very little now. Yet this small orderly had taken down five cadets who had been working hard for two years. "So Cadet Ryu said. Eat your congee here, before it goes cold. We'll send for you by and by."

They left without issuing orders to leave, so she sank back down again. She picked at the food, then folded up again, with her legs pulled up tight against her churning stomach. Then she put her head on her knees, and was actually dozing off when the door opened again.

Sleep fled as Steward Pand entered, followed by the instructor with the jug-handle ears. Oh yes, Instructor Shaz.

"Orderly Ryu," Steward Pand said. "The commander has new orders for you. You will no longer be an orderly. You are to join the next class of first year cadets. I will personally find you an orderly, who will see to the transfer of your things."

After saying that, he walked out.

Instructor Shaz looked at the miserable face before him, the swollen eyes, and said hastily, "This is a reward, Cadet Ryu. For your excellence in defending your brother, Cadet Ryu Muin. Who will now be First Ryu, and you'll be Second Ryu."

"No, no, no." Mouse jerked into a bow, her hands flat in

negation. All this interest was so very dangerous! "I want to take care of my brother. Nobody can do it as well as I can."

Instructor Shaz said, "You want to be an orderly your entire life?"

"Yes—no—once he's a captain, and then a general, he'll have *squads* of stewards, and I'll go home again. To our little island. To care for my parents. Grandparents, I mean," she stammered. "Very old. As I have no cousins. But *lots* of aunts and uncles. Old, all old," she added, feeling as if she'd fallen into a stream with a fast undercurrent from which she could not get free.

Instructor Shaz laughed. "Very admirable, your filial piety. But you are also in the army, and even stewards must take orders. What is your given name?"

"All I ever heard was Mouse," she stated firmly, determined that no hints about her family, or true home, must slip past her lips.

"Very well, Ryu Mouse," Instructor Shaz said in that kindly voice, mentally consigning her to the vast number of poor commoners who never did get actual names, only numbers, like Second Son, and then some sort of nickname. This new cadet would also be written into the records as *Second Ryu*.

"Your sword skills, the commander feels, would be commensurate with your brother's year, but we understand that might not be the same with your riding and other skills?" At Mouse's violent, if voiceless, negation, he smiled again. "And you are a little young to be joining them. So Commander Weken is giving you the chance to begin with the new arrivals, who will be closer to you in age."

Mouse opened her mouth, considered, then closed it. If there were thirteen-year-olds, or even fourteen or fifteen among the new first year cadets, that would be no more than she'd gotten used to. But the idea of being with seventeen and eighteen-year-olds, those tall young men who might even have beards starting, and their talk among themselves of things she only half-understood, alarmed her.

Her mind began to race. She wouldn't even have to stay five years. Once Muin was done with *his* five years, then she could confess that she was a girl. It wouldn't matter if she was booted out and sent away on the next ship, because Muin would be safely away, and on his path to greatness.

"Yes, sir," she said in a quavering voice. "What must I do?"

Muin had been given a pain elixir after the wound on his face was cleaned and salve smeared on it.

He woke to the physician checking his pulse, and winced against the headache.

"You can remain here, or return to your bunk, Cadet," the physician said. "Either way, you are to stay in bed for two days, and then return here to be examined before I release you back to training."

Muin said, "I guess I'll go back then." He got up, winced against the crashing of pain through his skull, bowed his thanks and left. His mind burgeoned with questions. First, where was Mouse?

He was met outside the building by one of the grunts he recognized from the barns, who tended the horses. This was a boy exactly his height, and appeared to be his own age. A sharp bow, and this boy said, "I am Orderly Fenig In. Commander Weken promoted me to serve you."

The words "Commander Weken" rang in Muin's ears like a gong, and the protest rising to his lips withered and died. Muin felt completely unsettled. But orders were orders, and his head hurt too much to think, so he began the long walk to his hut, hoping that maybe Fenig In would prove to be so clumsy or incompetent he could ask for Mouse back.

At the other end of the building, Mouse stared up at a moon-faced, gangly individual who smiled vaguely out of eyes the color of honey, framed by the longest lashes she'd ever seen on anyone except her mother's. "I am Yaso," said this Yaso. "I'm your new orderly. Ah, this is new for me. You won't mind if I ask questions?"

"I can do for myself," Mouse said, more unbalanced by the moment.

"Steward Pand sent me," Yaso said with a gentle smile and an apologetic lift of one narrow shoulder.

This was horrible! She did *not* want a servant nosing around her! But even more terrifying was the prospect of going

against orders. She looked down at her feet in their straw
shoes—she would have to wear boots now!

If Muin could bear them, she could.

And, she reminded herself, she knew the schedule for
orderlies. And grunts. This Yaso would only be a grunt, if they
were now first years. She knew exactly how the days would go.
She could still keep her identity safe.

And nothing would disturb Muin's path.

She looked up, unhappiness plain in her face. "All right,"
she said in a small voice—as if Yaso were the master, she the
orderly, and this new change was a punishment.

The changes happened rapidly.

The day before the dedication of the fifth years, and
everyone else's promotion and move to new quarters, Yulin
and his companions except for bedridden Silam suffered a
public flogging, while all the rules they had broken were read
out. Silam could hear the sounds, and the cries, from an open
window—knowing what awaited him once he could stand
again.

It was a relief for Mouse to get back to her old hut, even
though everyone's behavior changed. At least they were merely
orderlies, like her. They couldn't bring any moral suasion to
bear by their very presence, and it soon became apparent that
they had been strictly ordered not to ask questions.

That didn't stop the more venturesome from making
comments, from Colt's whispered, "I hope you smacked that
turd Weed real good," to Trickle's earnest, "Watch your back. I
hear Yulin is delirious over there in the sweat beds swearing
he'll kill you when he can."

"I expected that," Mouse muttered.

Colt gave her an admiring grin. "We should have guessed
it that day when you humped that tent canvas. You never *told*
anybody you could fight like a hero!"

Weed turned up then, glowering around and daring
anyone to speak; he, having been ordered to go on the illegal
mission by his master, had been spared the flogging, but he
would have night soil duty, training the new grunts.

The sight of him caused the rest of the hut to hurry toward

the line for hot water, sparing Mouse having to say anything. Weed avoided Mouse, who was glad to stay as far from him as she could.

The orderlies of Yulin's followers had spent the day scrubbing the parade ground clean of blood. The next day, so that no taint of the previous day's blood would render the ritual inauspicious, the fifth years were promoted and everyone else moved up a year.

During that day, as everyone was changing quarters, several of the tassels greeted Mouse, and asked kindly questions. Rather, they asked questions in kindly voices, letting her go when she stammered and stuttered, clearly terrified.

And Mouse's own hut dispersed, without her.

She could tell whose masters hated Muin (and her) and who not, by which orderlies wished Mouse good luck and which passed by with side-glances as they parted to go to their new huts.

Alone in the hut, she took out her box containing the herb. She had worked deflection charms into the box on all sides, in hopes that anyone seeing it would look away again. Everyone knew what happened to thieves, and anyway, there was no coin inside, or jewels, just the dried herb that she was certain no one would recognize.

Still, she wrapped the box inside a summer shirt, walked alone across the parade ground to where the cadets were housed, and slunk along the extreme perimeter until she reached the first year row of huts, beyond everyone else. She'd been told which one she would be in, which was next to Muin's old one.

She had gotten used to sleeping by the door, which made it easier to slip in and out. So she turned toward one of the beds by the door, then started at the sound of a step in the open doorway.

Yaso entered with an armload of clothing. "They said I could fetch your things early, Cadet Ryu."

"Please, just call me Mouse. Cadet Ryu is my brother."

"He is Cadet First Ryu and you are Cadet Second Ryu, I was told," Yaso said cheerfully.

Mouse gave up on her name. There were more pressing

problems, such as the shirt-wrapped box lying at the bottom of her new trunk. "I can put those things away," Mouse said. It wasn't as if such things were forbidden. She was afraid of where questions might lead.

"It's my duty," Yaso replied. This was unanswerable.

Mouse uttered a word of thanks, and went out—then stopped short when she almost bumped into her brother. "Muin!"

"There you are," Muin said in their islander dialect, casting a quick glance around.

"Are you all right? I hope I didn't get you into any trouble," Mouse confessed. "I didn't see that tassel coming, it all happened so fast, and I was so scared that Yulin was trying to kill you."

"I think he *was* trying to kill me," Muin said, carefully touching the side of his face. It was horribly swollen and discolored, the gash nasty. It was obvious he would have a scar. "Are you going to be all right here?" he asked, with a hand toward the hut, and extra meaning in his look and his tone.

"I figure it's not much different than being a grunt," she said quietly. "I mean the living part. I just don't think anyone will take care of you well."

Muin chuckled. "Fenig's all right. He sews better than you do—that I found out the very first day. As for the rest . . ." He looked around. "Everyone thinks I'm some sort of god for teaching you defense. With the third years, we have hut captains. I'm one. At least for a season. We have to look out for those whose ranks are low. Get them to improve. But I'll have a bit more freedom. Next year, we can go out Shit Road to the village when we earn liberty," he breathed. "And look at something besides each other."

"Like . . . what? Flowers? Horses?"

"Girls," Muin said, and at Mouse's incredulous stare, he blushed to the neck. "Never mind that. Here's what I'm thinking. You won't be able to watch the battles for me, but it's time for me to do for myself. So maybe everything is fate. But still, be careful," he warned. "That turd Yulin is supposed to be under orders to stay away from either of us when he comes back, but don't trust him."

"I never did trust him," Mouse said. "He's got what Ul Keg

calls angry eyes. Uncle Keg told us, you have to remember, that people with angry eyes see the world the way we see a reed in water, when it looks bent, but it isn't — "

Muin clapped his hand over her mouth, and glanced desperately around. But they were alone, as the ship with Mouse's soon-to-be year mates was half a day's travel away. "Don't say that name here," he whispered. "Don't say *anything* about home, *ever*. Especially about Father's training."

"I know that," she muttered around his fingers, and he dropped his hand. "Yesterday the tassels kept asking me things, like what are the movements called, and I could tell them I don't know the names. I just learned to do them."

"You can't do Heaven and Earth anymore," Muin pleaded.

Mouse stared at him, shocked. This was the first time she entirely disagreed with Muin. Why would he say that? But she knew why he would say that. She murmured tentatively, "I will learn the drills here. I won't do anything that the others don't do. I want the tassels to forget all about me. Think it was an accident." She scowled. "I guess I'll have to learn that stupid pitch-pot game."

"It'll improve your aim," Muin said. "And it makes you fit in." Muin heaved a sigh of relief, looking around, then back. "You're a good . . . boy." He swatted her shoulder, then walked away, whistling an old charm-song to ward bad luck imps.

Mouse let her breath trickle out in relief. He hadn't said anything more about Heaven and Earth. Which meant she could keep up her practice, the only thing she did completely for herself.

She went back to the empty hut, feeling the need for the privy.

She stopped inside: what to do now? As an orderly, she had had the run of the entire fortress, so she could take care of nature's call away from the others. But Muin and the cadets, as far as she had seen, traveled in groups.

She moved slowly through the first stage of Heaven, frowning. She much preferred her own natural arrangement, finding it in every way superior to boys, who could so easily be wounded down there. Except when it came to the need for a privy. Her Essence ward, along with steam, had been sufficient to keep eyes away from her in the bath. Why not in the privy, too, if she was in the middle of a pack of boys too busy to pay attention to anyone else?

Having grown up with brothers, she was familiar with how boys were made. Well, why couldn't she make something of the sort for herself?

How? Something tube-shaped and hollow . . . oh! Bamboo, of course.

She had one day to figure it out.

There was plenty of bamboo in the supply house, and tools for shaping it. Some trial and error gave her something small that might even look more or less like a boy's natural equipment in the dark, and with both her hands there holding it steady.

She ran to the privy, which was empty, awaiting the arrival of the new first years. There she endured a frustrating, messy interval until she finally got it right. A little practice, and she was ready. She found a way to tuck the thing inside a wrapped-up sock stuck in her underclothes, which gave her the proper shape as well as kept the bamboo from gouging her skin when she tried Heaven and Earth.

She was ready for the new hut mates.

TWENTY

THE NEXT DAY, MOUSE woke alone in her new hut. For the first — and only — time she could rise and bow to the southwest three times without having to be furtive, whispering a greeting to Mother, Father, and Ul Keg.

After breakfast she went to the privy . . . and she was slow, but it worked to pee standing up. Practice, she thought, and left. Now to concentrate on things she ought to know that Muin had struggled with.

She forced herself out to the side of the barn where the pitch-pots had been set up, with a load of blunted arrows. Looking around to make sure she was alone, she grabbed some up, went to the line, and began to throw them.

She was terrible at it. At least as bad as Muin had been when she saw him try it the first time. She made herself do it until her arm ached, and the tedium made her eyes burn, then replaced the arrow. By that time she'd heard random shouts about the ship coming in, so she ran to watch.

When the new arrivals came through the gate, she retreated to her hut. Before long four exceedingly grubby boys appeared, looking around with interest. Two of them were close enough to her size, only a hand taller. Then she saw the third one, and her eyes stayed so she never noticed the fourth.

This third new cadet was not just tall, but strikingly handsome—like the illustrations in the hero tales, except that his clothes were ill-fitting as well as grubby from ship-travel, and worn at elbows and knees. The sleeves were also too short, revealing his wrists. His long, phoenix eyes were black, under slanted brows of the sort the poets wrote about. His hair was like silk, and true black, so black its sheen was blue, even when messily wound up in a lopsided topknot. She realized she was staring when his arrogantly curved mouth tightened with impatience, and she tore her gaze away, taking an instant dislike to him.

"Ignore Shigan Fin," said the fourth, a breezy boy with eyes like crescents of mirth, so narrow you could not see their color. "He doesn't talk to anyone, though he stank worse than anyone *before* he came onto the ship. Who are you? I'm Mo Fuin. How did you get here before us? We were the first off the ship, and first in line to get our duds," he added as he chucked his new belongings into the shelf beside his bed—which was the one next to Mouse. When he noticed her gaze, he shrugged. "My brother Gam can straighten all that when he gets here. He won't have anything else to do."

"Your brother? Will he be your orderly?"

"That's right. It was either that or stay home and make pots. He came along with my cousin and me, but as orderly, since he was too young to test. Just turned twelve. I didn't see you on the ship," Mo Fuin added.

Seeing she could not avoid the question, Mouse said, "I used to be an orderly for my First Brother, but I came over."

Mo Fuin's entire demeanor brightened. "I knew it! At the garrison they said it could happen, but we didn't know if was one of those things that happens every year, or more like every century. Will you tell my third brother Gam when he turns up? He was sure it was only heroes and prince's sons. Though why a prince's son would be an orderly, I still don't understand, but then a lot of the things you hear about nobles don't make a lot of sense. Third Gam came with me anyway. He said toting my sword and washing my underwear was still better than making pots."

Mo Fuin laughed, and though Mouse hadn't spoken, he

went right on to describe how miserable the ship journey had been, packed in tight with boys from a thousand different islands and forced to do ten thousand drills a day, until everyone stank as bad as the haughty Shigan—indicating the back of the poets' dream who was at that moment leaving the hut.

Mouse uttered a snort, muttering. "My tutor used to talk of an emperor who said," and here she switched from the common speech to scholarly Imperial, *"the world is my bedroom and I'm the only one allowed to snore in it."*

"Huh?" Mo Fuin, who had only been half-listening, asked. "I didn't hear."

But Shigan Fin heard.

An orderly appeared, and swept them all off to the showers and then back again to dress in their new dun cadet clothes. This included a stop at the privy. For the first time, Mouse went with the others, her heart running like a deer in her chest. But everything went as she had expected: no one gave her a second glance.

Rejoicing, she ran with the rest to the next challenge: cadet clothes. Mouse put hers on, noticing the difference at once. As an orderly she'd worn the shapeless tunic, much like the commoner clothing she had worn in Sweetwater—clothing meant to fit any size or shape, as it would be handed down many times until it was worn to rags.

Her new undershirt was made of finer material—linen, she guessed, and sun-dyed the color of cream. The only thing it had in common with commoner clothes was that it tied at the right hip. Most everyone wore clothes that fastened at the right, whether emperor or bond-servant. But this shirt was narrower in cut, fitting more to the body. The brown robe that went over it was long—coming to the top of her boots, though slit up the sides and back for riding. It was still loose once she sashed the robe, but it didn't bunch above the sash; it lay more or less neatly. And there was the headband of the same shade.

She felt her change of status in these clothes. Before she was a servant. Now she was in the military. At the very bottom of the ranks, of course, though above foot-soldiers. Whom she was expected to command one day. This brought its own set of expectations. Threats, if she wasn't careful.

But she knew how to be careful. As she looked around at the others, she noticed what she'd seen when she was in Muin's hut: the brown of their clothes wasn't always quite the same shade, and for the first time she mentally followed the path of her new clothes backward: to the neighboring village where bolts of cloth were turned into robes of various sizes, to the supply ships that carried the cloth, to the island where the cloth was woven, to those whose labors made and dyed the threads. Then a tenth of their labors was saved out for taxes, just as Sweetwater's mats were shipped to wherever the government decided they must be sent.

A noisy gong made her start. "Drill!" someone bawled.

And so they ran out to begin their first day of sword drills.

"The purpose," the drill instructor shouted, "is for all to understand what is expected, so that when the drums begin to beat, the army moves as one. You must know the sequences in your bones before you can command others effectively."

That made sense—but when it came to the actual sequence of the drills, Mouse loathed them. With shield (which meant banging with full strength) or without shield (which meant precision, as they were expected to have control), it was all toilsome, jerky. Clumsy. After a lifetime of being trained to flow with strength tempered by effort, the cadenced step, block, stamp, thrust, retreat, felt like starting and stopping at full strength. She sensed her Essence vanishing uselessly at every jolt.

This must be how strength is built, she told herself grimly. In any case, she had made a vow to do what must be done. No more. No less. Get through each day moving exactly like the others.

But the tedium and toil of those drills made it all the more necessary to find the time, and a place, to work through Heaven and Earth at least twice each day, just to shake her body free of the feel of that clumsy tread of jerk-and-stamp.

Time streamed, turning into a week, two weeks, then three, until the ten beds in the hut had filled. Her feet, now accustomed to shoes, adapted swiftly to boots. Her fellow cadets were an assortment of personalities, but not a Yulin among them. The single jarring note was Shigan Fin, but at least he didn't talk to anyone. He even left the hut as often as he could at the appearance of Cayin, his assigned grunt, a long-faced, glowering boy who had a tendency to quote Kanda in a self-righteously rebuking voice, on the virtues of care and cleanlyness. Shigan was clean—very, actually: he began by bathing twice a day and changing his clothes, until Cayin's quotations got pointed about wastefulness as he brought back fresh clothes—but Shigan shrugged off tears and smudges, as if he'd once had a thousand shirts.

As if he'd *stolen* a thousand shirts, Mo Fuin remarked one morning as Shigan escaped ahead of Cayin's *Avoiding waste is among the humblest of civic virtues, and therefore one of the most meritorious.* "A thief can throw away anything he's tired of, and nip a new one off someone's washing line that catches his eye," Mo Fuin finished, to the satisfaction of all: though there was not a shred of proof, as Shigan did not even glance at anyone's trunk, much less go through it. Still, the hut enjoyed believing he was a criminal who ran from the law, which was far more satisfactory than that he was clumsy with his clothes.

Thief or not, Shigan strutted through the days, aloof, disdainful even. Mouse's detached hate sharpened to personal when it turned out he was an expert at the despised pitch-pot game, which, sure enough, their hut deemed it necessary to play during after-dinner free time. In spite of his sorry initial appearance, he moved like a noble—his posture erect, as if he never had to lower his eyes to anyone, and when he threw the arrows, he looked like a hero. And never missed.

But! Unlike the noble and military sons, he was terrible at nearly everything else.

He wasn't a coward. He waded right in at sword lessons, swinging wildly, but he obviously had no training. His first spear throw caused laughter as it cartwheeled through the air and bounced butt first in the dirt. His first shot at archery sailed over the target to clatter against the hay-storage barn behind it—he was strong enough to pull the bowstring, and he certainly knew how to handle an arrow, but had no concept of aiming, much less shooting.

In short, everyone loved to hate him. Mouse was grateful

that he took all the attention that might come her way.

Yaso appeared and disappeared each day, and though Mouse was careful to be polite and respectful—she knew what life felt like from the grunt's end—she kept her end of conversations strictly about everyday things.

Miraculously, Yaso never brought up the box with the Longevity Root in it, in spite of the disappearance of Mouse's old shirt and the appearance of a new, larger one laid atop the box. Nor did the orderly comment about the occasional extra sock, sometimes damp, that appeared in her things, as she washed her bamboo-holding sock when she bathed.

Yaso offered a weather prediction along with the morning's hot water, speaking in that voice like a reed pipe, or one of those marsh birds that called to one another in mellow hoots. Those predictions were always right; gradually Mouse came to see, even on a clear, cool morning, that if Yaso said afternoon would bring a thunderstorm, the sky would cloud over, usually by Horse Watch, and she prepared for it as well as she could. Meanwhile each day the water was hot, the tea fresh, her clothes mended better than she ever had done for herself.

Days passed.

Mouse had spent two years with a broom in her hand rather than a weapon. She had worked to keep her arm strength with handstands and pullups. Those and sweeping required brute strength, not the type of strength one used in handling a blade, which she discovered required training of muscles in wrists especially.

Invariably Mouse stayed in the back row of any drill, watching everyone. Sometimes Shigan's glossy blue-black head ended up in front of her, and her eyes stayed on him because he moved like water pouring down a stream, yet when he performed the combinations, he kept the same jerky cadence, using much more vitality to stop and start at full strength.

Three weeks in they were put to limited sparring, no more than five moves. She watched her hut mates, who demonstrated more or less familiarity with the military style. Shigan stood out again. Lip curled, with two fast, hard strokes, he knocked the swords out of his opponents' hands.

She was not there to beat anyone. She had only to perform respectably until Muin completed his five years. Still, when it came time to face Shigan Fin, she decided that she was not going to let him have the pleasure of knocking her wooden sword out of her hand.

They squared up, and he came on with his usual fast attack. She let the first strike whoosh past her blade a finger's breadth away, and when he came around for the backhand strike, she angled her blade just enough for his to slide off harmlessly.

At the periphery of her vision, she became aware of everyone staring. She should drop her weapon, she told herself. Stay meek, unnoticed. That was her plan. But there were those black eyes, the contempt plain. She tightened her core, pulling up Essence in readiness. "Strike," he said.

She said nothing.

He struck with the same pattern, only harder.

She sidestepped, then let his blade glance off hers.

"Come at me," he said impatiently. "What are you, scared?"

She said nothing. She would not stand out, but she wasn't going to be anyone's target. Losing might make her a target if this pretty-faced snot was another Yulin.

He attacked a third time, the same combination. This time she beat, deflected, then bound her blade around tightly and tapped him smartly on the wrist. Shigan's eyes widened in surprise, then the tips of his even white teeth showed in a grin that changed his expression so much she didn't recognize him in that moment. Then he retaliated, putting all his strength into the thrust.

She set her foot hard and blocked him, but felt the reverberation all the way up her arm. She snorted away the pain, hating that she'd had to spend half her Essence in warding that clumsy blow.

"Cadet Shigan. If that had landed," came the instructor's voice, "you would have earned ten strokes, and you'd be back to stabbing at a straw target for a month. This exercise is partly about *control*."

"I have control," Shigan began, then stopped.

"And that will be another honor mark, for offering an

unrequested opinion. Begin again."

This time Shigan offered the combination the way they'd been taught, and she retaliated with the expected response. The tassel nodded and looked at the watchers with his brows raised. They hastily got back into their rows, and resumed sparring.

Mouse managed to get Shigan's next bout into the periphery of her vision. She saw his partner grip his sword, mouth determined. And when Shigan struck, the boy kept his sword in his grip.

Mouse smothered a grin, and moved on.

As the day progressed, she became aware of sidled glances full of question. She ought to have guessed that Trickle, though up there with the third years, would have somehow found time to meet and blab with the newcomers.

Later, when they got their turn at the showers, the questions began.

Since her first year she'd gotten very good at sketching the deflection charm on her lower limbs, getting clean in record time with only her back to the rest of the room, then quickly drying and dressing. Most had been raised to be more or less modest, she had discovered, and if you stayed in the middle of the group no one glanced twice your way unless you did something to draw the eye. Like Trickle's clowning during the time they were grunts and orderlies, and now it was the Mo cousins.

She always got in first so that she could claim the last stall, which had the weakest water but was the hardest to see into through all the steam. This particular day, as the rest entered, over the hissing of water and the clouding mist, the questions started.

"Ryu! Did you really take out half the third years with only a practice knife?"

"I heard it was with his hands."

"*I* heard it was our Ryu that tossed Silam in the sweat beds over the wall onto his head because he called him a barefoot rabbit."

"It wasn't half the third years, idiot, it was just one hut."

Mouse hurried through her cleaning, having decided to wait and let them blab until they got bored and switched to some other topic. But then Mo Fuin stuck his head around the divider between them—luckily just as she pulled up her pants. "Ryu?" he said. "Did you really flatten an entire hut, led by Yulin Pel?"

"It wasn't that many," Mouse said, passing by as she wrung her hair out. "And I don't remember. It happened too fast."

"*How* many?" Haleg Vo asked. He was not a bad sort, but in the short time Mouse had known him, she'd seen that he tended to hang onto an idea, or a joke, or whatever interested him, like a small dog with a rope toy.

Mo Fuin bounced up beside her and smacked her on the arm with his wet towel. "How many?"

"Ayah, stop it! You're getting me all wet."

"How many," Mo Fuin said, dancing back and forth in front of her, apparently undisturbed by being completely naked. Modesty did not seem to be a quality shared by the Mo clan.

"Five," Mouse said, and as she shoved her feet into her boots, she said to the damp floor, "It was only luck. They didn't expect me. It won't happen again. Drop it."

"That's *just* what a real hero would say," Mo Fuin chortled in an ecstasy of mirth.

"I'm going to puke." She moaned in nausea.

Then Cayin poked his nose in, carrying a fresh set of clothes for Shigan (who never seemed to remember to bring his own) and muttered to the wall another of Kanda's quotations about creating more labor for others. Since Cayin, in addition to being obnoxious, had proven to be a tell-tale, the room fell silent.

Shigan sighed, and everyone else hastily exited, Mouse among them as she wound her hair up and skewered the topknot with her wooden clasp.

TWENTY-ONE

LIFE FELL INTO A regular round of training, broken by meals. Twice Mouse got that back-of-the-neck prickle sensation, turned sharply, and caught sight of the back of a big boy's head as he walked away. Everybody dressed in dun, and had dark hair worn up in topknots, but the eye is quicker than the mind: There was something in the walk, the angle of shoulder and of head that she recognized as distinctively Yulin's, and that he had been staring at her.

What could she do? He hadn't approached her. He hadn't even been in speaking distance either time. But that crawly sensation determined her never to relax her vigilance, unless the third years went on battle games.

After some inner debate, one morning she followed Yaso out after the grunt's delivery of water and clean clothes. "Yaso, I had some trouble last year. If an orderly named Weed, that is, Orderly Yulin, comes around you, be careful, will you?"

Yaso saluted politely, then responded in that mellow tenor voice, "I know, but thank you for the reminder. I was told about Grunt Yulin."

"Good." Mouse turned away, feeling awkward, and ran back inside the hut to finish getting ready for the day.

Life wasn't bad by any means. Mouse found training much

easier work than being an orderly, at least so far. Of course the training would get harder, but she'd be learning all along, wouldn't she?

In the meantime, with one exception she liked the others in the hut. On rainy nights, the Mo family did Shadow Play, which meant lining up the hut's two lanterns against one wall. One or another of the Mo boys knelt in front of the lanterns, twisting their fingers together to make an astonishing variety of shadow shapes on the opposite wall, as Mo Fuin related tales in a range of voices.

With the exception of Shigan Fin, who lay on his bunk staring upward, his profile unutterably bored, the rest were enthralled—even if Haleg Vo tended to ask, "Why are you laughing? Was that a joke? Why is it funny?"

By the end of the month, the first years were sparring one on one, and Mouse at last achieved an arrow in the pitch-pot mouth. Once she understood the trick of the throw, she got better at it. But no one was as good as Shigan, who finally said he wasn't going to play anymore, as no one would play against him.

They took their first night march, to get accustomed to navigating in the dark. Shigan now spent all his free time at the targets, working on archery, and Mouse sneaked away to practice Heaven and Earth. Just as she was becoming comfortable with the new routine, they announced that strategy and tactics lessons were to begin.

All first years gathered in the hall at last, where Instructor Shaz, he of the mild voice and jug ears, said, "No one is expected to come here an expert in planning and executing battles."

Mouse only heard him with half her attention—there was the sand table Muin had talked about!

The instructor went on, "The rest of this year, we will be looking at the Empire's wars and discussing them according to our understanding of *The Way of the Blade*. You will also soon begin battle games, after which you'll assemble here to discuss what went right, and what went wrong."

A whisper serried through the ranks—*battle game!*—then

Instructor Shaz raised his voice, giving a brief overview of what was known of Liad II's life: born in obscurity, thought to be son of a scholar, promoted rapidly in the army, made a general, nearly executed when the king he served ignored his advice and was defeated, retired to a fishing boat, married the captain of a trading fleet and turned them into a formidable defensive force, which became an armada until peace was made between the marauders and his island.

Mouse listened with part of her attention, having heard all that before from both Father and Ul Keg, and in far more detail. Her eye caught on Shigan, who leaned forward, eyes intent on the instructor, as if this skimpy summary was new.

"Liad II retired to a temple, where he remained until he was invited to advise the new king. He was then promoted to command of both land and sea when the Easterners tried to invade the islands. He won the war, but lost his wife in the battle. He returned his commander's tally and banner, and retired to the temple again . . ."

Mouse glanced around. Many were gazing out the window, or at their hands, or into space, except for Shigan, still intent.

Instructor Shaz went on. "When Liad II died, his daughter came forward with this book; she, and it, were discredited by the king, who did not like the criticisms of kingship that were in it, and ordered it destroyed, but copies turned up elsewhere, until it was adopted by the Second Emperor of the Dai Dynasty. And so it comes to us. Who can give us the first line of *The Way of the Blade*?"

Mo Fuin's cousin, the joker Mo Muin, jumped up eagerly. "War is the failure of peace and order," he shouted, then bowed deeply, grinning.

"Very well! So what does it mean?"

They looked at each other.

Failure, Mouse thought. Ul Keg said, *War is civilization's failure and shame.* But would the military manage to read glory into that line?

Almost as if he read her mind, Instructor Shaz asked, "Is Liad Li glorifying war?" He looked down the rows, the bright morning light slanting in the east windows catching his projecting ears, making them glow reddish.

Mouse watched her fellow cadets sidling glances at each other, clearly wondering which answer the instructor wanted to hear.

Instructor Shaz knew this, and sighed a little. Every year, he had to work to gain their trust. Sometimes it came quickly, and some years, he never succeeded. Though they were all individuals, every year had its mood. He had yet to discern this year's. "There is a hint in the word *failure*."

Mo Fuin leaped to his feet, bowed, and said, "He thinks it's bad."

"Good answer," the instructor said, smiling. "Why?"

A more thoughtful cadet gained enough courage to rise and say slowly, "My tutor said it's because everything else can be fixed, but war destroys everything in its path."

"That's another good answer," Instructor Shaz said. "The destruction begins with your own lives when you face the enemy. It extends to your village and your families if you fall. We're here because we are trying to learn how to limit the destruction, to know when to strike and how to do it most effectively, and when to stop. Once you get into the field, you will discover just how rapidly everything can change, for the worse. This is why emperors keep augurs at their sides to use every method they have to predict the outcome. They choose auspicious days, and hours. They study maps. They send scouts and spies. They choose the best generals. But when enemy meets enemy, it is rare that anyone can always predict the outcome. So, with that in mind, we will evaluate the accounts of land battles."

Mouse looked at the boys around her. Had they been expecting exhortations about glory? Shigan sat back, his profile skeptical.

"Our first lesson will be in how accounts can differ vastly," the instructor said, and Shigan leaned forward again, chin in hand.

Mouse turned away. She had already learned that lesson: she could hear Ul Keg's voice overlying Instructor Shaz's about how difficult it was to get at the absolute truth in any account. Or even what truth might mean—in a war, a great victory, after all, was a miserable defeat to the other side.

When the watch change drums reverberated through the walls, the instructor told them that next time they would discuss the early wars, and begin evaluating the strengths and weaknesses of mounted versus foot warriors, before everyone was dismissed.

In spite of her efforts, Mouse was high in the rankings.

Not first, at least. She never took the initiative in the competitions, keeping strictly to defense. The first ranks went to those both skilled and aggressive.

The only competition she thoroughly enjoyed was tracking, but she was careful to pace herself so that she never came in first. Archery was all right—there, she could aim for the second ring out from the bull's eye, or the third, and feel secret satisfaction when she placed it close to where she aimed. And she was beginning to like riding, as she got used to the silent way horses talked with their entire bodies.

But her tentative competence wasn't a candle to the sun of Shigan's riding. The haughty, obnoxious Shigan was dreadful at every single martial skill except riding. There, he had somehow, somewhere, learned not just to ride, but to make it look as if he and the horse had been born together.

Everyone's heads turned when he leaped up onto the horse's back, and then, without so much as moving his hands, got the horse to spring into a gallop and thunder down the riding field, then come around and soar over the obstacle that the rest of them were not to attempt for weeks yet.

She turned her back, reminding herself that she was there to lose, lose, lose. Which meant *not* learning how to ride like that. If she even could.

The first years were given a week of afternoon battle games in different types of terrain (by now they had memorized all nine, and could recite them in their sleep) before they went on their first overnight. In these they had to get used to chalking their wooden blade to make a mark on their opponents. They were expected to have enough self-control to pull thrusts and strikes — they only used full strength when going at the stuffed targets with actual steel. Those who struck fellow cadets too hard got honor marks.

So far, she hadn't spotted any Yulins. That didn't mean there were none; it's just that those who despised cadets of lower birth hid it better.

The afternoon games were all melees, two on the parade ground, two in the fields on the other side of the north gate, and one on a rocky hill a gong's march away.

Mouse felt everyone watching her on the first one, overtly and covertly. Instead of launching into the enemy and mowing them down right and left, she chose someone randomly and matched his movements, doing no more, no less. The others gradually lost interest in her. By the time they essayed the rocky hill, they were too busy watching their footing as well as each other to pay any attention to her.

So she had leisure to watch the rest of them. The best were the military boys, no surprise there. They'd been scrapping since they were small.

No one stood out. There did not seem to be any Faliks among them. Or Muins, or even Duns. She hoped there wasn't going to be a Yulin — and swept the field, looking for Shigan. He was easy to spot, the graceful way he leaped down the hillside. But his sword work still took too much effort, as if he thought out each move ahead, and then applied all his strength.

"That one has had some kind of training, but it wasn't with weapons."

Mouse jumped, startled — and discovered a gray-haired tassel behind her. Flushing, she bowed.

The tassel, whose name she didn't even know, gave her a thin, approving smile, as he said, "Assessing the field, eh, Cadet Ryu?"

Since she'd been caught flat, she had to admit it. Flushing even more, she said, "Yes, sir."

"Good. That's excellent instinct."

"It's just that I did it for my brother, and it got to be habit, sir," she said, hoping that she'd sound boring that way. Then realized as soon as the words were out that the instructor would probably think it was good practice.

Sure enough. "An excellent habit," he replied, and moved on.

She sighed, and looked around for someone with a red armband to randomly — and badly — attack.

Though she was not first in the rankings, she was still made commander of the green armbands on the first battle game. As yet the division into two armies was simple, west doors against east doors.

After a sleepless night coming up with increasingly wild plans for losing the battle, she had to march at the front, one of her two captains bearing the green banner marching behind her. She carried the wooden tally of command, which she was to display when she issued orders, which made the orders real — that is, there were consequences if not obeyed.

She wanted to hurl the tally away as far as she could. She loathed the responsibility, the expectant faces. She meant to lose, but she couldn't cheat the others, who wanted to do their best. She'd thought she could conveniently forget to send her scouts, as had happened Muin's first year, but the two she was given were both military boys. They hovered around her expectantly, waiting for orders. When she gathered from their eager hints that they expected to be sent to skulk in the shadow of red army, once her army peeled off in the direction of their assigned location, she raised the tally and pointed in tacit command. They took off, whispering their own plans as they disappeared among the tall weeds along the path.

Mouse remembered Muin's first battle game site on a small hill, but to her surprise, the tassel on horseback did not lead them there. They veered eastward, to another site she recollected from much later in Muin's first year, among rolling hills.

The objective was simple: find the other army's camp and take it if they could. She hoped the commander of the red army had remembered his scouts, but she suspected he hadn't. It so happened she had most of the best first year trackers in her army.

All she could do was "forget" to set an outer perimeter patrol to catch any roving scouts, and put up the usual traps to catch spying enemy scouts, as the camp was set up. But she did post sentries around the camp—not to would definitely bring an honor mark. She stood in the door of her tent, peering past the green banner stuck in the ground to the right of the door, and watched the grunts going about duties that for two years had been hers.

Yaso seemed to get along well with the other grunts, even that Cayin, whose tattling and Kanda quotations kept everyone at a prudent distance. Mouse had not once seen anything but cheer from her grunt.

Presently the call went out for the evening meal, which was, as she remembered, already prepared and sent along. After a long march, cold food tasted wonderful. They were all ravenous.

They were halfway through the meal when both her scouts turned up, red in the face from running. "We know where they are, commander," one gasped.

Before Mouse could say a word, the two captains had set aside their wooden bowls and turned her way, reminding her of dogs on the quiver, waiting for the word to run.

"Command meeting," she said to their expectant faces.

They stampeded to the tent that her hut shared, but no one else approached except the two captains—and she was aware of the crunch of footsteps outside as the tassel listened.

She looked at the boys, and then it finally struck her, they were waiting for a clever plan. Maybe the tassel was, too. She said, "Let's hear your ideas."

So much for being a new Falik, she exulted as the two boys' words tumbled over one another. They'd clearly been talking about nothing else.

Mouse only half listened. All she knew about the red army commander was that his voice was often heard in Instructor Shaz's class, discussing past battles' strategy and tactics. He might have forgotten all about scout traps in his excitement to command. She suspected that this boy would do something like set up an elaborate trap to mire an attack once he'd learned his territory. Did he remember to send his scouts as lures instead of spies?

". . . so we can gain most honor merits by a night sneak," one finished. "Isn't that true?"

The question recalled Mouse to the waiting faces.

"Night sneak, most honor merits," she stated, and they grinned. "If red army's scouts fall afoul of warning traps, we should get an idea of the direction of their camp."

Her second captain, an earnest boy, seemed reassured by her stating the obvious. He said eagerly, "We laid plenty of traps for their scouts, and our sentries are on the watch."

She nodded, and all that was left to say was, "We have our plan. Let's do it." There!

Their plan being to leave when Phoenix Moon rose, but by the end of Dragon Watch, the sky was covered with thick clouds. Nevertheless the scouts successfully led them to the enemy camp . . . where they fell into a trap.

Mouse exulted inwardly at having guessed right. From the sound of it, two lines, either side. If her captains each thought to call their own huts into groups, maybe they could rally . . . but they didn't. She copied them, yelling wildly and fighting in every direction. She made as much noise as she could, careful to keep her attacks to that jerky pattern of stamp-thrust, block-retreat until someone *finally* thumped her in the back and yelled, "I killed the commander!"

They returned to the fortress the next day.

When they gathered for their first after-battle session, Mouse was surprised by a skeptical glance from Instructor Shaz. He *couldn't* know what she was doing. Could he? She had better seem serious, and upset at the defeat.

He asked for her assessment. She said, "We let excitement get to us when we fell into the enemy trap. What we should have done is divide, each half under one captain. If we'd done that, we might have rallied and taken the camp."

Instructor Shaz's expression cleared. "Good assessment, Second Ryu. Let's take a look at it in the sand table."

They gathered around, and the instructor pointed out the geographic features they had so recently experienced—and Mouse, looking down, blinked. For a heartbeat or two she was that eagle flying overhead . . . no, what she saw was what the Circle game represented.

As the instructor went over their battle, she saw exactly how the tide of it flowed—and what she ought to have done, what the opposing army ought to have done. It was very much like the Circle game.

The instructor's voice changed, and she caught herself up, turning her attention to him. "Having a secondary plan is always a good idea . . ." and he went on to discuss the army and then individual rankings.

The reds gained two honor merits for use of scouts and the night sneak. The greens nothing, but at least no honor marks.

Mo Fuin was commander on the next battle game. This time they were the red army—and Mouse recognized the site the tassel was leading them to.

She felt sorry for Mo Fuin, who looked grim from sleeplessness. When she was sure the mounted tassel's attention was on the grunts setting up the camp, she sidled up and murmured, "You know, there was something I thought of as we came up that last bit of trail."

Mo Fuin turned such a hopeful, desperate face her way, she knew he didn't have a plan. She said, "What about Chase Tiger Lure Snake?"

Mo Fuin's lips moved, *Chase Tiger Lure Snake*, then he said, "Where's the lure?"

"Didn't you see that little gully below the willows?"

"Why," Shigan interrupted from behind them, "are you listening to that idiot? Ryu *lost* the last battle, in case you forgot."

Mo Fuin glanced back, uncertainty tightening his shoulders.

Mouse sighed. Shigan was irritating, but not wrong. She said, "You can always send your scouts to look at the gully, and decide." She walked away.

TWENTY-TWO

MO FUIN AND HIS captains figured out how to use the gully, and they won.

After that, Mouse enjoyed finding a way to make suggestions to the commanders, if she saw a way to help. She made sure no tassel was around to hear. And no Shigan.

Then around came Shigan's turn to command again. This time they were on a mountain site, different from the ones Mouse remembered. He sent two pairs of scouts—by then commanders were expecting spies and scouts were captured half the time—and established two perimeters. And when it came time for him to make his plan known, he loaded not just the captains but everyone else with so many contingencies that it didn't take much thinking to foresee disaster.

". . . gave us so many orders I forgot most of them when the enemy was on us," Haleg Vo said earnestly in the after-battle discussion back at the fortress.

Several others shot to their feet, bowed, and said, "It was the same for me, too, sir." "And me." "And me as well."

"I tried to remember, sir, but while I was standing there figuring out which one to use, I got whacked from behind," Mo Fuin said plaintively. "No use remembering them all when I was dead!"

As usual, Instructor Shaz presided, along with the instructor who had gone along on the battle game. The two exchanged glances, then Instructor Shaz waved at the cadets to sit down — except for Shigan, who remained standing, color edging the fine ridge of his cheekbones. "I thought we were to plan for all possible variations," he said.

"Indeed." Instructor Shaz gave a nod. "So you should. But . . . remember Liad Li's account of the Battle of Three Islands?"

Shigan flushed all the way to the ears. "No, sir. That must be from a section we have not discussed yet."

Instructor Shaz's eyebrows lifted. "Have you actually read *The Way of the Blade*?"

". . . no, sir."

"Were you not tested on it?" The instructor's voice was mild, but Shigan reddened even more. "Never mind. We're aware that some garrisons are more assiduous than others at the admittance testing, and of course none of you are here to learn scholarship. I will lend you my copy, if you like. It will take us the remainder of the year to work through it. Being familiar with it now will surely aid you in future lessons."

Instructor Shaz turned to the class. "The rest of you might remember the five words that precede the beginning of his account of that battle. 'After two moons of preparation, we embarked in the ships for Fragrant Island . . .' and so on. The important words being *after two moons of preparation*."

The instructor pointed at the sand table as he spoke. "What those five small words translate out to meant hard training for various contingencies, every day, for two moons. They practiced landing the boats and running to the attack, every single day. Both the army and the navy together. We'll discuss landings in detail in a couple of years, but you should know now that the most dangerous moment is when the boats reach the shoreline. Liad Il drilled his warriors in every aspect of his complicated plans, so they knew exactly what to do, without having to stand there trying to recollect orders while hewn down by the enemy."

After being dismissed, Mo Fuin and his cousin Mo Muin walked on either side of Mouse. Mo Muin, who looked very much like Mo Fuin except shorter and wider, said, "I really think that Shigan was the personal servant of a high noble, at least a marquis. Before he got kicked out."

"For?" Mo Fuin asked skeptically.

"Theft?"

"Then his hand would be cut off. Or his head, more likely. The higher you are, the worse it goes."

"Then what, if not theft?"

"His mouthiness. Laziness. Lack of something, you can be sure. Think of it. Who else would speak such high-sounding Imperial, but be so ignorant of *The Way of the Blade*, or strut around like a god come to earth, but arrive in clothes that a beggar would kick into the gutter. Not to mention how he didn't know one end of a sword from the other, but rides like his betters? I think he's a shadow son, definitely of a noble, thrown out for being worthless."

Mouse had seen "shadow children" referred to in scrolls, but neither Ul Keg or Mother would explain what they were outside of the word "illegal," and that severe look on their faces that meant something having to do with marriage-intimacy.

Mouse knew vaguely what happened between adults. You couldn't live around animals and stay ignorant, but she considered the subject boring, as distant as the stars. Yet here was the subject again, and these boys loved to show off what they knew. "What's a shadow son?" she asked.

"You don't know?"

"What are you, five?"

"Blah blah blah." Mouse waved off the expected scoffing. "So you don't know either?"

Mo Muin said with an air of importance, "I've known for *ages*. It's when a woman has a baby without a consort."

"How can you have a baby without a consort?" Mouse asked, eyeing him with extreme skepticism. "It takes two people, and they don't drink any boiled silver milkweed."

"Yes, but the marriage ritual gives the baby a clan *legally*. It's only Spring Festival babies that can be got in spite of the weed, and everyone knows those will be born around New Year Two Moons. And no one ever calls them shadow anything, on account of being gifts from the gods."

"Why would anybody have a baby without a consort?" Mouse asked, sensing that there was a lot missing. "I thought if you don't want a baby, you both drink silver milkweed."

"Ambitious women who didn't get to be consorts, but want a child in hopes the father will be forced to marry her. Or shameless men who made promises, don't bother to drink the weed, and if the woman believes the promises and doesn't drink the weed, a child comes," Mo Fuin said. "Sometimes it works out. Like, after a war or plague when a family is wiped out, and there's the surprise son or daughter growing up in the next village over, and the family isn't ended after all. But every one of those cases goes to the justices, and the augurs and the like get in there to prove or disprove things."

"How?" That was Mo Muin. "I never understood that part."

Mo Fuin waved a hand. "Has to do with charms. Essence. Rituals, and something to do with blood."

"Nothing to do with blood is ever good." Mo Muin shook his head. "Shadow son. Let's call Shigan Shadow from now on."

"You're an idiot," his cousin stated genially.

"Why? What's he going to do? He's terrible at everything except riding."

Both turned to Mouse. "What do you think?"

Mouse hated giving an opinion, lest it make her stand out. She mumbled, "Wouldn't."

"Why not?" Mo Muin asked, looking curious. "It's a great name."

"Don't want to risk honor marks for that," Mouse said. "It gets you nothing."

"Nothing but trouble," Mo Fuin stated.

"But it's *funny*," his cousin said plaintively, as if that mattered most.

"*You're* funny, and I don't mean it in a good way," Mo Fuin retorted. "Funny between the ears."

And so once again the cousins embarked on what Ul Keg had called "three rats with four eyes" squabbling. They did it right across the unwilling Mouse as they led the way toward the dining hall—all three unaware of Shigan three paces behind them, his mouth twisted with a kind of bitter humor that he couldn't even define to himself.

No one in Mouse's hut remarked on Shigan reading *The Way of the Blade* at night, before they put the lantern out, but when he turned up with another book a few days later, Haleg Vo asked, "Where did you get that?"

Shigan looked at him as though he'd grown a second head. "Instructor Shaz. Where else? He has a room full of them."

Haleg Vo's eyes widened. "Can anyone read them?"

Shigan spread his hands, the book in one of them. "What do you think?" he retorted with such sarcasm Haleg Vo retreated hastily.

After their next lecture, Haleg Vo hung back, then later came up to where Mouse sat with Mo Fuin and a couple others from their hut. He looked stunned. "It's that room behind the hall," he muttered softly. "It's got books, *so* many books. And that's not all. It has all our battles, written up by the instructors."

"Right there to be read?"

Haleg Vo nodded solemnly. "All you have to do is go there. You can read right there. Or you can take one, after you write your name down in the scroll. Then when you return it, you sign your name again."

"Did you look up our battles so far?" Mo Fuin whispered, his eyes crinkled in mirth. "Were they terrible?"

"Of course I did, first thing. It doesn't say much beyond what they say in the meetings after." He lowered his voice even more. "But you can read what the fifth years are doing. I saw Falik in there, reading."

"Falik the son of the cavalry general?"

"Yes."

Mo Fuin laid his sticks down and put his chin in his hands. "If it's not forbidden, why are we whispering?"

Haleg Vo glanced around. "If everyone knew, won't they be stampeding over there to get ideas? And we'll get booted out for certain, being first years."

Mo Fuin burst out laughing. "I think most of 'everybody'

would be snoring by the second page if the writing is by the tassels, and not by one of us, with good stuff like 'Haleg Vo was a turtle at leading a charge,' or 'Mo Muin stunk out the entire tent with cabbage farts.'"

"Ayah." Mo Muin hit the back of his cousin's head. "More like you'd be listed as worst in . . ."

As soon as the discussion turned into the typical exchange of insults, Mouse's attention slid away. Interesting that the instructors hadn't told them, yet didn't forbid them to read anything in that room.

She waited a few days, then on a rainy afternoon between a riding drill and a tracking exercise, she slipped over to the building, making sure no instructors were around to see her. She bypassed the military books for the fortress records. In what Mother would call a lower level scholar's neat hand, there were all the cadet battles, listed by year. Mouse leaned against the wall and read rapidly, at first enjoying the sensation of having a book in her hands again. Sniffing the faint smells of paper and dried ink.

She noticed the frequency of types of terrain as well as typical strategies and tactics. In Muin's year, Falik was ahead for wins. No surprise there. But Brother Muin and his friend Dun got mentioned time after time for leadership in charges and breaking lines.

Brother Muin ought to be looking at these! But he had so much trouble with reading, maybe she ought to study them and compile a list of suggestions for him. He was due back any day from a week-long tracking competition.

She read as long as she could, and over the next couple of days, sneaked back to read some more, careful not to be seen. Of course she wouldn't write her name down—she was convinced the tassels counted up who took books and for how long.

Brother Muin turned up at last.

It was another rainy day. He was covered with mud but grinning in triumph. "We not only got in first, but hit the target," he said to her when they met between the huts, as he headed for the bath house.

"Did you know about Tassel Shaz's library?" she asked.

His jerked a shoulder up. "Of course," he said so

indifferently the words she'd been about to speak, offering to give him summaries, dried up. "You know I'm not going to read a lot of stuff if I don't have to. Anyway, Cor and a couple of the nobles all said that we'd get no honor merits for copying old ideas. They want to see fresh ideas."

Mouse frowned. "Isn't Falik using his father's ideas? I saw him written up a lot when I looked there, and more than half the time it said something like, 'modeled on General Falik's action at the Bay of Moths' and so on. That means it's all old ideas."

Muin shrugged. "So? Look, Mouse, I itch all over, and —"

"I wonder if Cor is lying," she said slowly.

Muin had been turning away, but hitched to a stop. "Lying? About those old records? If it was spy reports that would help us now, I could see lying. But why bother about that old stuff that we already heard in our after-action talks . . ."

"I just wonder if the tassels might be seeing who studies there. Like, takes initiative to study past battles. The history ones and the training ones."

Muin's expression altered to uncertainty, then he shrugged again. "Dun goes in there from time to time, and he always tells us what he read. Especially now that we get weekly battle situations that we have to work out solutions for. We talk it over, but mostly what he gets from reading those are things *not* to do." He sighed again. "I guess I should've remembered that you might be interested. You're a reader. But when I was a first year, and we found out Falik was always in there, I couldn't send you because you were a grunt."

"That's very true," she said. "Even if I'd had the free time, which we didn't, they would have noticed me."

Muin whacked her shoulder. "Ayah, everything's all right, then. Now, let me tell you about our win . . ."

Over the next month she went back a couple times out of curiosity, until she noticed that Shigan was there every time they had liberty and it was raining too hard for him to be practicing archery at the targets. He seemed to be reading every book in that library, even the old musty tomes written in the older court hand from right to left instead of from left to right.

She stopped going, squelching her curiosity with a

reminder that she had no interest in what made good or bad commanders, since she would never be one.

And for the rest of that year speeding by, she concentrated on trying to train herself to the two styles: competence in the jerk-stamp rhythm of the army drills and its emphasis on shoulder strength, and her continued labors at gaining strength in combing Essence with Heaven and Earth.

The seasons blended one into the other, the routine the same. Her birthday came and went unnoticed, except when she made her private bow in the evening. Her throat that night closed up and her eyes burned as she thanked her parents in heart for giving her birth, and Ul Keg for his lessons.

TWENTY-THREE

HARVEST AND THE END of the cycle of moons saw a new cycle beginning with the Year of the Rooster. Winter gave way to spring and reassignment, Mouse to the second year, Brother Muin now a fourth year, with crossbow training a regular thing—but only at the targets, and not on war games. For Mouse it meant a lot more riding—including riding while shooting, using blunt arrows on war games.

They also had hut leaders, now, another exercise in leadership meant to encourage everyone to work harder; theirs was Haleg Vo, the only former hut mate Mouse had. At least Shigan was no longer in her hut, and that meant no more of Cayin's nasal whine scolding them with admonishments from the ancients.

Mouse was still aware of Shigan whenever he crossed her periphery. She was both sorry and glad that Mo Fuin was also assigned elsewhere, sorry because he was so much fun to talk to, but glad because now she didn't need to avoid dangerous personal questions.

Late spring brought the first change in the battle games: the instructors began dividing the second years into armies according to abilities. No more west doors against east, unless at festival competitions, which were mostly games.

Still, she was safe enough from having to command after working hard to remain in the middle of the rankings. She stuck to her strategy: do well on one, make a mistake the next time, lose the third, do better the fourth.

Summer ripened and then waned. Mouse's concentrated mediocrity worked until Captain Instructor Fumig returned from a long exercise with the fifth years, and observed them from afar.

He gave the next assignment himself, saying, "We will be appointing commanders and captains from midway in the rankings, to give those cadets a better chance to improve. Those at the top, you will get practice at taking orders, which will be your lot when you leave here. Perhaps for a considerable time, unless you are very lucky."

He paused long enough to let that sink in, then said, "Cadet Shigan, you have been rising steadily in all areas. You will command the green army in the next exercise." He went on to name Shigan's captains, and Mouse had breathed a sigh of relief that she wasn't one of those when the Voice of Doom stated, "And Cadet Ryu, you will command the reds. Your captains are . . ."

Mouse clacked her teeth together against the groan that wanted to rise all the way up from her heels, as hopeful and expectant faces turned her way.

Shigan sent a slack-lidded glance at her, his mouth curled in an expression she couldn't interpret, except that it made her bristle all over. As she walked away, she gave in to a very short struggle. She promised herself she would lose the next five battles she was forced to command, but *this* one, she had to win.

As soon as they were dismissed, she lurked around the side of the building, and sure enough, there went Shigan as if drawn by an invisible rope straight to the library. Of course to find the cleverest plan someone else had dreamed up.

She walked away, brooding, and for the rest of the day, did her mounted archery and sparring practice mechanically as she considered what she'd read so far in her own visits. The problem was, she had no idea what the terrain would be until she was handed her map — for the tassels no longer led them to their positions. Each army was given a map right before they parted, and they'd be expected to find their way to it, the instructors riding behind.

That meant the most elegant plan in the world, one that had caused the poets to write reams of praise, might end up being the stupidest idea for that particular place. Or for her army.

It was while she hustled through the baths, making sure she kept well away from anyone who might look at her, that it struck her she was coming at it all wrong. This was a situation where she ought to consider not just the plans, but the nature of her enemy. Shigan clearly thought he was cleverer than anyone. He also kept aloof. She was willing to wager he never bothered to learn the names of anyone low in the rankings, so he would surely come up with some complex or famous battle plan, without thinking about how to use the people he had.

She would not make that mistake.

Though Mouse didn't talk to anyone except in the course of an exercise, by now she knew everyone in her year, after a year of covert observation to discover if there were any Yulins among them.

She considered her army as she hastened to dress and wrap up her wet hair, until she hit on the perfect person: Mineg was near the bottom of the rankings, strong but slow because of his habit of mixing right and left, which made him stumble in combinations and drills with called cadences. But he was near the top of the rankings in tracking.

In the general chaos after they left the baths, she jogged among her first year peers until she found Mineg.

"About our battle tomorrow," she said, falling in step beside the tall boy. "Would you be willing to run a ruse?"

Mineg's face had lowered, as if he expected something else, but at the word *ruse* he looked up, right at her. "Ruse? *Me?*"

"You. I know you have trouble with the drills, but you're a good tracker."

Mineg flushed, his head dropped again, and he mumbled something about how tracking was easy, no right-left-left-right.

A sudden thought hit Mouse. "Unless you know Shigan?"

Mineg said ruefully, "Everyone knows who he is."

"Oh?" Mouse asked. "Does he give you trouble?"

"No, no, no. I see him at the targets, early morning, late at night. Those of us who want, who *need*, extra practice. But he doesn't talk to any of us. He wouldn't know me to step on me."

"Then it's perfect," Mouse exclaimed. "Tomorrow, when we march, I'll slip you our location and also get you a red armband once we capture one of the real reds."

Mineg's eyes widened. "Can we do that? Start the battle as soon as we leave, like that?"

According to what Mouse had read, yes. "Why not? It would happen in a real battle. You quietly follow the reds to their camp. Once camp is set up, and the night watch changes, you slip away and find us. I know you're good during the day. How are you at night stalks?"

Mineg flashed a grin. "I grew up doing night stalks. We thought it was a game."

"Great. We'll count on you." She meant it to be encouraging, but when his shoulders tightened and his brow furrowed in worry, she added, "Look, Mineg, it's just a battle game. We have the rest of this year and three more to improve. If this plan fails, the Sun God isn't going to smite you. At worst it'll just be an honor mark off. But if we make it work, wouldn't it feel good?"

"I'll do it," he promised. No, it was more of a vow.

Mouse still felt bad as she walked away. This really was a game to her, the goal to win against that Shigan and his haughty looks as if everybody else had come straight from night soil duty. She didn't care at all about the rankings. But she could see that it was important to Mineg. Maybe if she sent an extra pair of scouts as support . . .

By the time they were dismissed for the night she had half her plan in place. All she needed was the location of her position to hold, and its terrain. One look at Shigan and she knew he had some wickedly clever plan all worked out, meant to make her and her army look stupid. Though he, too, didn't know the terrain as yet.

Before she went off to sleep, she pulled aside one of her captains to recruit two trusty friends to waylay a green who needed a bit of a lesson in manners. This target would be taken prisoner along the road, and his armband removed.

Early next morning the second years assembled as usual, the orderlies at the back with their wagons. The two commanders stood facing each other as the tassel in charge handed each a map with their location on it. Mouse's gaze lifted from hers to meet Shigan's challenging gaze.

She turned away, and made a little business of studying the map as Shigan quickly nodded at his waiting banner bearer, raised his tally, and shouted, "March!"

The red army looked disappointed, some annoyed; everyone liked to go first, as the second army inevitably ate the first's dust. Mouse didn't say anything as she waved her tally at her banner bearer to fall in behind the greens.

They proceeded out the north gate, and stayed on the north path toward the higher ridges, hidden by thick trees.

She motioned Mineg over and silently showed him the map so that he could learn the location of red army's defensive position. Then she waited until the marchers began separating into their inevitable clumps, some singing, some chattering, or shying rocks at targets to work on their aim. At a promising turn in the path, with plenty of tree and shrub coverage, she gave the nod to her captain.

Their prisoner was jumped and dragged behind some shrubs, unseen and unmissed, then given a choice of marching between two guards wearing Mineg's red armband, or being tied up, gagged, and stuffed in the supply wagon to broil under the canvas cover.

He made the sensible choice, and though he glowered direfully until the two armies split off, no one noticed he was missing as Mineg—marching until now close to the front of the red army—stealthily edged up to the green stragglers, then joined them, new green armband replacing his red one.

Nothing marred the march to their site, though Mouse had two alert perimeters at all times. She sent two scouts to shadow the greens, because she knew Shigan would expect them. Both were her worst trackers.

When she and her army reached their campsite, she sent another pair of scouts.

One of her captains muttered, "If you send any more, we won't have any army left. Especially with that outer perimeter."

"Just for tonight," Mouse said.

As the camp was in the middle of the chaos of setup, she walked away in the direction of the jakes that had been freshly dug, but veered off to relieve herself alone in the woods. Afterward she ran straight up the side of a steep hill, for she recognized their location, and rejoiced.

There were the redbark trees. She breathed in the heady Essence-drenched air, laughing in her heart.

Before she reached the first tree she stopped and made reverence to this sacred space. Then she made her way under the shelter of the long, thin fingers of the redbark's drooping leaves, and there were all the slow-growing Longevity Herbs she had left, looking as if they had frozen in time. But when she bent close, she made out the buds of new leaves, which made her happy.

She moved away from the purple plants to a flat spot beneath the greatest tree, and began the Heaven and Earth warmups. Then whirled into motion, strong and sure. On each thrust Essence shot from her palm through the wind imps, sending those drooping leaves swinging out as though an invisible hand had pushed them.

Was she getting stronger, or was it just the Essence here, so strong that anyone might use it? Once again, this time faster —

And when she came to a stop, breathing fast, she turned her head and froze in shock, staring into Yaso's face. She bit back an exclamation of anger as Yaso said, "Both your captains are looking for you."

She pressed her lips together, reminding herself that Yaso was an orderly, trained in everything except martial arts. One style would look like another. If she didn't draw attention to what she was doing . . .

She forced her voice to steady. "Next time, can you call out? I, um, might have a weapon in hand, and I would hate to hurt you accidentally, just from being caught by surprise."

Yaso said, "Oh. I felt the Essence, and thought it was safe as you were just making small winds."

Mouse's surprise doubled. "You know about Essence?"

"I am learning. I know that it takes more effort to blow into a wind instrument, which then has to force out the musical sound, than it does to sing," Yaso said cheerily, in that mellow hoot. "You are choosing a more difficult path. That is interesting."

More difficult? That didn't even make sense. But Mouse had been raised by both Mother and Ul Keg—and even Father, who had spent his early life trained to obedience—to avoid denying someone face, and she knew how tough it was to be a grunt. "Thank you," she said, "Ayah, I'm done, so I'll come with you."

When she got back, the captains frowned over the report that the first two scouts had not shown up yet.

"Let's wait until after the watch change and our meal," Mouse suggested.

By the time those were finished, the scouts were still missing.

They began to watch for the second pair of scouts. At last, a gong into Dragon Watch, they straggled in, covered with mud, but triumphant. "We were nearly caught by roving patrols in line-of-sight," one explained.

The other grinned. "But we know where their camp lies."

The first added, "We saw our scouts right out by the campfire, in plain sight. It's like the enemy was showing us up by having them right out in the open, ha ha, see who you lost."

The most eager of Mouse's captains jumped to his feet, his angular face flushed, the fire reflecting in his black eyes. "Let's go!"

Mouse said, "Get everything ready, but wait."

"Wait? Why? Night sneaks get the most honor merits." Both captains looked disappointed, one turning his face away to hide frustration, even anger.

Mouse held out the tally, a silent reminder. They looked back, one biting his lip. She said slowly, "Let's get everything ready. Then take some rest, but be ready to march at a word. If I'm right . . . Ayah! If I'm wrong, we'll leave when Phoenix Moon touches those treetops. That should be the end of Turtle Watch, which is still time for extra honor merits."

The captains agreed, the impatient one still frowning, the other mollified by the reminder about honor merits.

By now, most everyone had lost the urge to play around

while away from Loyalty Fortress and its strict rules about silence after the lanterns were blown out. Night marches were a regular thing, now, and nobody liked the following long day on little rest, too often with a lot of either scrapping or skill tests at the end of it.

The camp was soon silent, except for the crunch of steps as the patrols made their rounds. Mouse tried to stay awake, wondering idly what sort of childhood Yaso had had. She'd assumed the orderly had been raised in the village, but who there would study Essence scholarship? Or maybe that had been a family member who left the island for one of the temples or scholars' houses. In any case, she was not going to ask, because that might invite the sort of questions she didn't want to answer.

Without being aware, she dozed off . . . and jerked awake when one of the sentries poked her and said, "Mineg from East-Three-East is here, insists the green armband is a ruse. We have him tight."

"It's all right," Mouse croaked, her mouth dry. She'd been drooling onto her arm, ugh! "He's ours. Let him in."

Mineg entered the tent, as everyone who'd been asleep began rousing. He said without preamble, "They moved the camp."

"They what?" someone muttered.

"I *thought* it would be something like that," Mouse said.

Mineg grinned in spite of the mud covering him. "Shigan said to put the scouts they grabbed right in front, so the next scouts you sent would see them. Then to make sure the scouts got away, but not to make it too easy. There's a trap waiting at the old site."

Everybody turned to Mouse. She considered her words, remembering that anything she said would get repeated. The military was not as concerned about face as non-military, having its way with steel to settle differences. But Ul Keg's lessons were never far from her thoughts. Instead of giving an opinion of Shigan and his apparent belief in his superior cleverness, she said, "Shigan has been reading in the library. I figured he'd try something tricky like this. We're going to use the Host Becomes the Guest strategy . . ."

"A trap!" Both her captains grinned.

She'd spent the entire day agonizing over what-ifs, but it paid off now. She called for volunteers to spring the greens' trap. "This means you'll get captured. But what you have to do is make a lot of noise, which will be the signal for us to hit the real camp from behind. If we're lucky, we might be able to free you if they don't go for kills, but capture."

Turtle Watch was just ending when they reached the other campsite and caught the greens flat. The reds were led by Mineg, who became the hero of the day. Besides Mouse, but she insisted that the plan would have fallen apart without Mineg, whom the instructor gave a personal honor merit on the spot.

The reds hallooed and yelled, giddy with triumph even after the sun rose, at breakfast everyone telling everyone else which moves they'd made and what the enemy had looked like when they sprang on the green camp out of nowhere.

They remained giddy on the long march back, the green army having gone well ahead so that they wouldn't have to meet the jubilant reds along the way.

At the after-battle assessment, the two tassels and Instructor Shaz listened to the various opinions on the action, but when it came time to award merits, they had the two commanders stand side by side.

Instructor Shaz said, "Red army, you earned the full five honor merits. Green army, the instructors both agree you earned four honor merits, for the plan and the excellence with which it was executed. But for the ruse with the spy going undercover, you might very well have come out the victors."

The red army exchanged glances of glee, then turned their attention back as he went on, "All of you. I am told that your year is ahead of the generality of second years, especially with tracking, so with this battle, we will go right to the next level. On each battle game we will furnish the armies with a map and an objective. It won't always be as simple as find, attack, and defend one another's positions. Dismissed."

The cadets stampeded out, leaving the three instructors awaiting the rest of their number, most of whom had listened from the library's open door at the back.

When all the instructors had gathered, Captain Instructor

Fumig said, "Shigan Fin arrived profoundly ignorant, but with the garrison captain's belief in his potential. I am beginning to respect that far-sightedness. I am impressed with Cadet Shigan's strong gain in all the rankings in the face of quite respectable competition."

Everyone agreed, then Instructor Shaz said, "As for Second Ryu, at last we're seeing the potential we only glimpse now and then. He seems determined to hide his talents in the mid-ranks, though we all know he's more capable."

One of the older instructors said in his slow voice, "It's common in younger brothers. They're raised to think it unfilial to surpass the elder."

"But we've spent considerable time trying to undo that habit. And we've made certain that all the exercises keep the two Ryus well apart," someone else said.

Instructor Shaz spoke up. "What I think I'm seeing is that the other talent, Cadet Shigan, seems to bring out Cadet Second Ryu's sense of competition."

Captain Instructor Fumig nodded. "Let's move them directly to group actions. Put those two in the same troop. At least until Cadet Second Ryu begins to show more initiative."

TWENTY-FOUR

THE BLUE-MIMOSA TREES BLOOMED twice a year, once in spring and around the time of Harvest Festival, when the second tax tribute was due.

The festival was nigh, which filled Yskanda with happiness. There was the hope of seeing Grandmother Anise in the next week or two, who would come by and carry verbal messages from his parents, then return with his own message. There was the festival itself, and no less appealing were those gorgeous blooms, which Yskanda loved for their own sake, and for how much they reminded him of Mouse.

Those blue and lavender blossoms looked spectacular on the tree, and right after they dropped, but if they weren't gathered, by the silk makers and scholars to be leached of their color for paint and fabric dyes, they turned into slime.

It had always been right after Mouse's birthday when Mother sent the two of them out to gather baskets of the blossoms. Invariably, First Brother had gone off with Father to the shoreline to practice with steel, which had left Mouse to Yskanda, just the two of them.

Though he loved First Brother, he'd also loved the times when he was the elder brother. He and Mouse could talk over the better stories in the classics, as they both always remembered everything they read. First Brother's eyes could pick out a bird on the horizon and identify it correctly, but somehow he could not recognize characters on a page, so they saved their talk about reading for when he was out with the fishers, or training with Father. They would talk about stories, and Mouse would listen as Yskanda ventured into his particular delight — paint, color, dyes, and properties of each — as they gathered plants like crimson hibiscus, which made excellent medicine for the stomach and other ailments. Everybody in the village kept some on hand.

The sight of those graceful blue and lavender trees brought Mouse to mind as Yskanda walked about the harbor on his free afternoon. As usual, he sustained a pulse of regret that the spoken reports, brought by Granny Anise along with the tax deliveries, had nothing from Mouse. All Mother ever said was that the family was well. Granny Anise never even named them, for surely Mother worried who might overhear. Granny Anise reported on villagers, and pets, and the seasons, along with exhortations to work hard.

The report brought a week ago had been yet another with no details of what First Brother or Mouse were doing. Yskanda imagined First Brother happy in his training somewhere, and Mouse busy with her studies.

On this free day, as always with no one to visit, he'd walked out of Master Bankan's house with friends — he enjoyed having friends — but they all wanted to drink hot rice wine in a stuffy room, and watch the fan dancers. He worked in stuffy rooms. He needed the outside air he'd grown up with, and the ever-changing stage of the harbor world.

"I'll see you all at supper," he called, and tucked his sketchbook under his arm, steering clear of the little first-year pages busy sweeping up dropped blossoms — his job that first year, when everything was so bewildering.

As he passed the shrine to the Snow Crane, he dipped his head and saluted, sending a wordless burst of gratitude for . . . everything, including having survived that hard first year. He passed beyond the stooping youngsters and their baskets, remembering the careless cruelty of that handful of nobles' sons and daughters who'd invariably kick through the blossoms, scattering them into the street and under cart wheels, then laugh. At least they were all gone now, out into the world—at the bottom of another hierarchy, Yskanda hoped, though the reality for the more wealthy and powerful ones was more likely some sinecure somewhere, where a person like him did all the actual work.

Ayah! Thinking about things he couldn't fix was like drawing water from a basket, as Granny Anise would say. Much better to find new sights to draw. He turned the corner, following the scent of fried dumplings as he considered his own likely future. Bottom of a hierarchy, of course. But if the work included the illustration of manuscripts, maybe even painting, even if something small and out of the way, he knew he could be happy.

Just as he was content to do the grinding and mixing and tending paper through the long, tedious process of making it, to earn a few tinnies from his elders. Tinnies weren't much in themselves, but they added up. A job doing all the work for some rich heir wouldn't be much in itself, but surely there would be times when he would be alone to paint. Everything was wonderful as long as he had time to paint.

He bought a cabbage-leaf full of dumplings, and munched as he walked, his gaze darting about for a likely subject to sketch. The dumplings were crisp on the outside, hot and delicious within, bringing Mouse again to mind. When would she be old enough for Mother to permit her to come and visit him? She would come if she could, he thought wistfully, and looked away, trying to think of something else.

Like the old woman selling ribbons. He had many sketches of her. No sketch would capture her scratchy, compelling voice as she sang those old melodies that had to have been popular in days of old.

Maybe those two girls with tiny dangles dancing at the end of their hair ornaments as they finished hanging up the ribbons they'd written wishes on. Then all three turned and began giggling as they wriggled and posed and twirled locks of their hair. They aimed it at—yes, there were a couple of tall apprentices loitering outside the silversmith's shop, eating their lunches as they watched the girls.

Yskanda thought about sketching the group, but he couldn't get an interesting angle . . . and anyway the hoarse shout from within caused the boys to hastily finish eating and duck back inside. The girls scampered off.

He reached the end of the street and turned the corner at the silversmith's shop, hastening his step as this was the alley between that shop and a warehouse. He was two streets from the riverside. The sun was stronger than the cold wind. He could get in one last walk along the riverbank before winter. There was almost always something interesting to sketch.

He moved to one side as someone came from the other end. Before he lowered his gaze, he caught sight of a vaguely familiar face. Though the man was dressed as an ordinary laborer, and he pulled a cart, there was something of the warrior in his bearing. Yskanda had seen those features before, and recently, too.

Was it in the shop, when he had desk duty? He gave a mental shrug, rolled up the cabbage leaf and ate it as they began to pass one another. The man's step slowed, and Yskanda glanced up, to catch such a searching stare that vague alarm made him hasten his step. Though he scolded himself inwardly, for after all the day was bright, the city busy, and the governor's guards patrolled everywhere. As long as he stayed within this part of the city, it was safe enough.

That was when he heard the hiss of quick steps on stone. From behind, to the side. He clutched his sketchbook tighter against himself. Should he run? Yell for help?

The moment for decision was taken when hands grabbed his arms. He opened his mouth to yell, but a cloth snapped expertly around his face and pulled tight at his mouth, gagging him.

A cloth then rustled over his head, smelling strongly of dust and sweet potatoes. His sketchbook fell away, and then he was lifted, struggling hard, and lowered to a wooden surface. The cart?

Someone said in pure Imperial, "What about his book here?"

"Take it."

A square shape thudded on top of Yskanda; then the light

vanished as a wooden cover scraped over the top of the cart. Yskanda lay there, rope bound around the sacking covering his head. He could hear muffled voices, but only a word or two was clear.

His knees were bent, making it difficult to kick the sides of the cart, but he did his best. The voice rose, arguing back and forth about the price of good wine as he bumped and jolted within the cart.

This went on for a time impossible to gauge, then the cart tipped, and men's voices grunted at the back. Pushing the cart? Up a hill?

A *ramp?*

The wheels jolted onto another wooden surface, as the stench of brine worked its way through the cart slats and the rough hemp of the sack. Now the wheels moved more slowly, but at least smoothly, rocking back and forth . . .

He lay there, furious and terrified by turns, sweating inside the sack and the cart, for what seemed like a full watch. In the distance the now-familiar sound of the governor's enormous brass gong sounded the hour —

Distance?

As if in answer, the wooden cover grated away, and a breeze scoured into the now-open cart, bringing light pinpointing between the loose warp and weft of the hempen sack.

The rope was then loosened, and the sack pulled away, leaving Yskanda face to face with silent men, as he processed the fact that he was on board a ship, moving with every wave and lurch farther from the harbor.

TWENTY-FIVE

TO MOUSE'S DISMAY, SHE had this year succeeded in getting Shigan out of her hut, just to be stuck with him and his scorn with their new assignment in a troop, each of them taking turns leading. At first it was in general scraps and tracking, stalking or infiltration exercises, but gradually they were given objectives that tested not only their attack and defense skills, but their leadership. The dismay began when these exercises occurred several times a week, unlike the battle games once a week or so. That meant more occasions to be pushed into leadership. Mouse didn't think Muin's year had gotten this exercise until his third.

Then she shrugged it off. It didn't matter why it was happening now. What mattered was to endure and keep to her vows.

It was easy to remind herself at night, after she had saluted her family and her tutor and lay staring upward in the dark hut as her hut-mates slept around her. During the day, with eyes on her, it was far more difficult to restrain herself when her eye observed intent and reaction, and she knew what ought to be done. She forced herself to choose one of the other boys and mirror his actions, fighting the twitch of muscles, the instinctive turn of shoulder or pitch of hip to ready for the action that she refused to perform.

It was especially hard when Shigan commanded, because he always put her in front, forcing her to choose between betraying the rest of the troop—who were sweating their eyeballs out doing their best—or standing out. She tried to compromise, sticking to the drill patterns as much as she could until the chaos of the scrapping flowed around her, at which time she could ease herself to the outer edge of the scrum, picking someone to mimic until she was chalked in a "kill."

When she had to command, she used her personal strategy: win one, stumble on the next, lose, lose, lose.

What she did not observe were the observers observing her. She dared not look at the tassels, and she completely missed the occasions when Muin caught sight of her and her mates, and paused to watch.

Mouse's birthday had silently come and gone, shortly after another a startling discovery, her monthly bleed. She had utterly forgotten about girl things, though her mother had taught her what to expect years ago. She had managed to shrug off the recent, occasional tenderness and twinges in her breasts, which at least were still reassuringly flat.

Now she had to face the fact that this state of affairs wasn't going to last.

She retreated up to her spot on the bathhouse roof to think. There were things women could do, of course. The most stringent was the denaturing charm, which apparently men had to suffer if they wanted to serve in the palace—and women in the more ascetic temples also endured. In both cases it was inked into their skin, or even burned, to make it permanent.

Mother had said that centuries before, the men had suffered far worse, knives being used to castrate them, and if they survived that, they were maimed for life. The discovery of the denaturing charm rendered men unable, and uninterested, in the harem—Mouse hadn't understood any of that part, and felt too squirmy about the entire subject to ask—and made internal organs wither, rendering it impossible for women to have the monthly blood, or children.

Both women and men became, Mother said, physically more like children except with adult height, and their passions lit on other aspects of their personalities. This, too, she hadn't really understood, outside of Mother's warning that such charms could ring untold changes in one's nature, which, when done frivolously, went directly against the most fundamental of the Twenty-Five Virtues, being unfilial. One's parents gave one life, in a body that partook of their families. To frivolously alter it for whim was disrespectful. One could, of course, out of necessity, or other causes . . .

She did not know what those were, and right now they were immaterial. She knew she did not want to denature herself. She liked being Mouse, and part of being Mouse was being a girl. Having to keep that a secret wouldn't last forever.

That left the Cramp alternative. An Essence charm along with certain herbs, drunk in a tea, would cause the female part in which babies grew to wring itself out so that the monthly blood, instead of dribbling over a few days, would be pretty much like squatting to pee.

Mother had warned her it would hurt.

And it did.

It left her trembly with cold sweat, but clean down there. She made herself wash out her underthings, so that Yaso would not discover what had happened, and then she claimed a stomach-ache. She was sent to the sweat-beds and had to drink a nasty tonic, but at least she was able to go to bed early.

By the next day, she was fine.

The weather turned steadily colder, the air full of drifting yellow, orange, and scarlet leaves. Presently the fourth years found out that they were slated for an extended infiltration battle game that would involve the fifth years, covering the valley beyond the western ridge.

Knowing the schedule, Muin found the time to isolate Mouse between activities, and pull her aside.

"Mouse, why are you throwing those troop matches? I can't believe you've turned rabbit."

"What?" she exclaimed, dismayed. "I do my best—"

"No, you don't," Muin stated. "Oh, it might look like it, but I can tell. And if I can, the tassels can. They might even blame *me*. There's no other way to explain why you start out strong, then turn turtle in the middle of the scrap."

"What?" Mouse looked aghast, her hands clasped under her chin the way they had when she was very small, and something had frightened her.

Muin looked away, then relented. "I guess not *everyone* would see it. You look fine. To most. You look like the rest of them. But *I* see it, because I know you. I can see when you throw away what we learned from Father, and turn stiff. It would be all right if you put power into it, but you don't."

"I can't," she said miserably. "I know *you* have put the two together."

"But I haven't, not really," Muin countered.

But Mouse swept right on. "To me, they are so different, I can't . . ." She paused, reaching for words: it wasn't just the balance and flow of Heaven and Earth style compared to the jerky stamp-and-thrust of the army's way, it was how her Essence, which she struggled so hard to integrate with Heaven and Earth, broke to pieces in the army style.

Then there was her confusion over Essence, and that odd thing Yaso had said. She kept worrying at it, usually late at night, but it still made no sense — and she was reluctant to ask, lest Yaso ask *her* questions she could not answer.

However, Muin had no interest in the arts of drawing out Essence, so she mentally shook away those thoughts, and looked up into his face. "I don't want to stand out," she said. "I just want to stay in the middle of the ranks until you get promoted away from here, and they give you real army orderlies. It's only one more year after this one."

"So you've said. If that's what you want, I won't say anything to it. But you *could* do better, you know." And at a stubborn look from her, he remembered that she was a girl (it was so easy to forget), and added in a mumble, "If they haven't figured it out, ayah! I don't think they ever will." He finished with a confidence that neither of them thought to question.

Mouse sighed. She didn't know what she wanted, except not to get caught. "I just wish there was a way I could help you."

"I'm doing fine," he said gruffly, ruffling his hand over the top of her head. "Good, in fact. Look, I'll probably never beat Falik, but there's still next year. And beyond that, Father warned me once that the phoenix feather's path might be a long one. That's all right with me. I like what I'm doing. Dun and I talk everything out, and we hold steady at the top, along with Cor, right behind Falik. I can live with that." He grinned. "Especially when I see Yulin's sour face when they read out the rankings."

Yulin's name brought worry-tension to Mouse's forehead. "He hasn't tried anything more, has he?"

He had. This year alone, two fairly vicious fights, both times during sentry duty on battle games. And both times Muin had thrashed him; they were much of a size, and strength, but Father's training had been so much better than Yulin's early training, and the muscles remember. These fights while on battle games, Muin had learned, were how personal feuds were decided among the future army leaders. You took care of your own problems.

He decided that what Mouse didn't know wouldn't worry her. "It's fine," he said. "You're a good, loyal broth-uh, brother," he stated more firmly, then in a lower voice, "Just think about what you want, and do your best, all right? If you do, it makes me look good, too."

In other words, stop making him look bad. Along with making her troop mates look bad.

"Sure," she said unhappily, wondering if now she knew the reason for Shigan's glares of active contempt the few times their eyes met during those battles. The rest of the time he ignored her as if she were invisible.

In any case, there wasn't much time to consider it. The weather auguries had apparently declared that winter might arrive early, and so every year was getting in their last battle games at the farther reaches of the island before the snows came—the fifth years working with boats.

"Your spy," Captain Instructor Fumig said to the gathered second years, "staggered back to your banner with an arrow in his back. Before he dropped dead, he said The Tiger in the Grass."

He looked at the next commander, an earnest military son much like Haleg Vo, but from another hut. "Your objective is to use this clue to defend your border. Here is your map. As you'll see, your border is marked by this stream." He named the two

captains, then pointed at Mouse. "Second Cadet Ryu, you are
Scout One. Cadet Shigan, you're Scout Two."

He then issued a similar map to the commander of the
green army as he told them that they would be attacking, and
then said to them all, "You'll march before sunrise tomorrow
morning."

And he dismissed them. The two commanders looked at
each other and then bolted for the library — it being habit now
for Mouse's year to make themselves familiar with the history
of successes and failures of any classic strategy.

Mouse watched the two commanders jostling one another
in their race to get there first, backed by both sets of captains.
She was familiar enough with both boys to guess that they
would end up taking turns reading aloud the relevant portion
of the books before separating.

She wondered what The Tiger in the Grass might be. Father
had never mentioned it, and of the many tactics and strategies
they'd heard about all last year, that hadn't been among them.
But she wasn't curious enough to follow the commanders to the
library.

As a scout, all she had to do was take orders. She turned
away, her breath clouding, as she ran off to grab time to drill
alone before the drums brought them all together for riding
practice.

The next morning, the sky was clear, the light hard as steel
in cold, dry air. During days like this, Mouse had learned not to
gnaw her lips lest they chap, something she'd never
experienced until coming here.

As the upper levels had all the horses, their task was set in
difficult terrain, which meant going on foot. They marched into
the still, cold air. Most trees had shed leaves, except for the dark
green, smudged line of firs along the higher ridges; here and
there, mostly in gullies, sudden, startling glimpses of brilliant
orange leaves brightened the uniformly brown world. A couple
broad-winged raptors hung on invisible air currents high in the
sky, looking for small animals getting in a last hunt for food
before holing up to hibernate.

As soon as the red army reached the curve in the stream
that their commander chose for their defense, before camp was

even set up, he summoned Shigan and Mouse. The two stood side by side, neither speaking or even looking at the other as the commander rubbed his cold-reddened nose and said in his pedantic way, "We know they'll lose merits if they don't use some version of The Tiger in the Grass, which is number sixteen in the thirty-six strategies, for you who don't remember. It's a sneak-and-surprise attack by infiltrating enemies first, then on a signal, attack from within and without. I need the two of you to scout everywhere on that side of the stream, as fast as you can, before they post watchers."

Mouse sighed—she'd hoped for something hot first—but the sooner she made her scan, the sooner she could get back. She took a wooden sword, mostly to use as a walking stick on hills, but ignored the heavy, cumbersome shields.

She and Shigan jumped from rock to rock across the low stream that already had ice-rime along its edges, but on the other side, as Shigan headed for the meadow strewn with rocks, Mouse made a sharp left and began toiling up the rocky hill leading to the waterfall that fed the stream.

She was surprised by Shigan's voice. "They won't be charging down a hill, Ryu. Even on foot."

She almost turned to retort that she always went high to scan if she could, but suppressed the impulse. She had been told to scan, and she was scanning. She owed nothing to *him*.

It was a longer climb than it looked. She knew she still had trouble estimating size and distance when it came to hills and mountains. Her main focus was to keep fingers and ears warm; she kept her head down and her shoulders up.

Another thing she still had trouble judging was weather, so far in the north. She knew the obvious signs of the seasons, but the subtleties had thus far escaped her, unless pointed out, and so she missed how the light thinned to a glaring white that kept her gaze on the ground ahead of her as she climbed.

When at last she reached the top of the hill she had chosen, which afforded the widest field of vision, she was surprised to discover that the meadow below had hazed into a uniform brown, the stream barely visible.

She rubbed her eyes and frowned. It had been so clear and sharp when they set out! The sunlight was all glare. She shaded her eyes with her hand and peered down, all her attention on her attempt to descry details of the landscape on the enemy's side, without being aware of two dangers: first, how the light had changed, and the second, three figures on her side of the stream, barely discernable — dun clothes and horses against the brown hill.

On that hill, Yulin sat on his horse, hand upraised to keep his two companions still as he stared, lips parted in amazement followed by a rush of angry glee. He knew that small figure, all alone on the next hill. Totally oblivious.

The vital importance of his own search had vanished. Here, at last, was a rare opportunity, not to be missed. But he had to run it right.

Looking at his two companions, both followers, he said, "We're on Jal's trail. We have some time."

"For?"

"Target practice," he said, patting the real arrows, which were only to be used against stationary targets. The blunted ones were reserved for the war games, when the other army had their shields.

Yulin's gaze stayed on that still figure. It would scarcely be still any longer, if he didn't move fast. His followers exchanged questioning looks, but Yulin was captain of this scout team. One of the followers glanced at Yulin fingering the steel arrows, and was glad they weren't allowed to use crossbows on war games.

"We'll ride down the other side of the hill and come around from the back," Yulin said, making it an order.

They moved away — unnoticed by Mouse on her hill, as she leaned out, willing the murk to clear. If anything, it seemed to be *worsening*, or was that just her eyes being tired from early rising? No, over there, ghostly fingers of fog drifted slowly, dreamlike, hiding the scree behind her.

She took a couple steps toward a dangerous tumble of rocks, as if that would help clear her sight —

And two things happened.

Yulin paused his riders at the extreme of shooting distance and, putting arrow to bow, snapped, "Shoot!"

Below, Shigan, who had unwillingly forced himself to follow Mouse in order to warn her that bad weather was on the way, started to shout. The sound was nearly obscured by the hissing zing of arrows.

"Isn't . . . that a person?" one of Yulin's riders asked doubtfully, peering under his hand.

"No," Yulin said. "Hay stuffed into a human shape. Looks real in the murk. Let's fill it with arrows, then ride out. Let those second years think it's an act of the gods."

Target practice, especially at such a distance was fun. Especially riding and shooting. They kicked their heels into their mounts' sides, pulled arrows, and shot.

Yulin's first shot zipped past Mouse's ear, not a hand's breadth away.

Shock burned through her nerves. Hide! But there was nowhere to hide. She stood on a bare, rocky hill.

She yanked the sword from her sash, where she'd put it while climbing, drew in a steadying breath against the tremble of shock in her limbs . . . and as Shigan, panting his way uphill below, stared upward in disbelief, Ryu went in one step from an oblivious target to a figure out of a tapestry, or a dream, wooden sword humming through the mist to beat the arrows into harmlessness.

TWENTY-SIX

BELOW, THE RIDERS GOT close enough to see that their straw target was moving. "Wait, that *is* someone," one exclaimed. "Look at him! Have you ever seen anyone do that? It's like a hero tale come alive!"

"That little runt brother of Muin's, isn't it?" the other said, peering under his hand—then turned a suspicious look at Yulin.

"I thought it was a target," Yulin said—though all three knew he was lying.

The two riders, instead of answering, wheeled their horses and bucketed back in the other direction, where they were supposed to be. Leaving Yulin alone, with no arrows. Which he could collect to hide the evidence, and incidentally, ride that little shit down, and *nobody would know*.

When the arrows stopped, Mouse began to hop from rock to rock downhill, as overhead, the sun—a pale disc of fire, impossibly distant and cold—vanished entirely behind a solid wall of threatening gray.

Yulin kicked the horse, which neighed, objecting to the unstable ground. Even at a slowed pace four legs were faster than Mouse, who glanced back every so often. There was safety, not fifty paces below, in a fold between ridges.

Yulin's path intersected with Shigan's fifteen paces below Mouse, and both recoiled in surprise. Shigan swayed to a stop, raising his hands to cup his mouth and yell a warning. But before he could yell, Yulin—whose only thought was to get rid of witnesses— snarled as he snatched his wooden sword from the saddle sheath. He leaned out, striking down.

Shigan tried to run. The blow glanced off the side of his head, luckily protected a bit by his headband. Instead of cracking his skull, the blow knocked him off balance. He fell hard.

Yulin's horse slipped on a rock gleaming with gathered moisture a heartbeat before the clouds now overhead struck their first blow. A sudden frigid wind rose out of nowhere, shooting needles of sleet down. Yulin rolled off the horse's back, sword in hand, as Mouse tried to slow her running descent. Shigan steadied himself on a boulder, dizzy, blood running into one eye. He watched helplessly as Yulin, a tall silhouette, loomed over Mouse, striking to kill.

Like a reed in the wind, Mouse sidestepped, her sword moving as fast as Yulin's as she blocked and deflected his strike to one side. Yulin took his sword in both hands and grunted as he scythed sideways, but once again Mouse leaned away as the tip whooshed harmlessly a finger's breadth from her, and then struck twice: knee, a hit hard enough to crack on the air, and then, faster than thought, the second blow smashed down on his right wrist.

Yulin spun, fell—and cracked his head on the same rock that his horse had slid on. He was not as lucky as Shigan, as his head struck above the headband, but at least it was a fall and not a blow.

It was hard enough. He lay still.

And the blizzard hit. The horse's looming bulk vanished, horse hooves thudding on the piling snow as the animal followed its instinct to find shelter.

Mouse dropped her sword, her hand throbbing, as her mind caught up with her body. Yulin? Where had he even come from? She stared at his motionless figure before the wind hit her in the back, and numbing snow began to batter her, almost obscuring him and Shigan a few steps away.

Shigan. She was beyond question, fighting to bite back the wail rising from her core. *Shelter.*

Shigan, no more than a silhouette now, roused enough to struggle to hands and knees. Another, stronger gust knocked Mouse to her knees. She looked back over her shoulder, and there it was—not even a cave, but a gigantic slab of rock that had sheered away ages ago and fell against a larger stone, forming a hollow beneath.

"Here," she shouted to Shigan, pointing.

He was already crawling that way.

Mouse backed up to the lichen-dotted boulder, out of the wind, and peered into the lethal white curtain that had come out of nowhere. Like Yulin. And Shigan.

Yulin. Trembling all over, she struggled internally, wanting very badly to leave him lying there in the wind and ice. But she knew what Ul Keg would say. And Mother. And Father, too, though he would put it differently: *Never leave an enemy unwatched.*

But to Mother and Ul Keg an enemy was a person, once someone's child, and it was their voices echoing in her head that drove her back out into the wind. Once again it knocked her down. She crawled to where she thought Yulin lay—and nearly missed him. By now she had no sense of direction. The world had reduced to an arm's length in front of her.

Her knee knocked against Yulin's boot. She scrambled around, felt up his body to his neck. There, under her numbing fingers, was the beat of his pulse: alive.

She knew what she had to do.

She glanced behind her, made out the barest outline of the slab of rock, grabbed Yulin's limp arm, and slowly, one grunt of effort at a time, dragged him what seemed an infinite distance, though it was scarcely the length of two men.

As soon as she got him out of the wind, she let his arm drop and fell back against the huge stone, panting and shivering. Shigan sat close enough that she could make out the pale oval of his face, framed by black hair fallen from its clasp, ruffling snow-dotted over his cloak.

Cloak. Her own was still in her pack, somewhere a world away.

"Back to back," Shigan said.

"Huh?" Her teeth were chattering too hard for words.

"I read it. Back to back. It'll preserve some of our heat. Until this blows past."

Mouse didn't want to move. Already a weird lassitude was stealing over her. But then a hand yanked unpleasantly on her arm, rocking her head on her shoulders. Making an effort that felt impossibly difficult, she sat up, scooted her butt toward Shigan, and then turned. A bony back thumped against her, and she let out a long sigh.

Already it was slightly better, enough that some of the shivering abated. Enough for her to force out a few words, "What about *him*?"

"He's actually in the best spot. We're blocking the worst of the wind," Shigan said. "At least, it should do until the storm blows over."

Mouse squinted upward. "Will it?" she asked in a small voice, very different from the amazing warrior that Shigan was already half-thinking he'd dreamed, as his head throbbed from the rapidly swelling cut.

"This sort of storm, this time of year, moves fast. Generally." Pain cut him free of his usual restraints. Except for the beat of pain, everything else seemed slightly unreal. "You really didn't see it coming? Are you blind, or just stupid?"

She opened her mouth to say, *Where I come from*, but froze. Three and a half years of hard habit reined her: even that much was dangerous, in that it might invite more questions.

So she said nothing.

Shigan heard that silence as superiority. Disdain.

Still sitting back to back, so that neither could see the other's face, he went on conversationally, "I think I despise you the most for how easy everything comes to you. But even you," he added as he flung his straggling hair irritably away from his aching face, "can't outrun a howling storm. Surprise!"

She startled as cool strands of his hair, soft as silk, fanned against her cheek. She jerked away, then mumbled, "I was trying to . . ." She gave up on her justification. She knew — now — she really had been stupid, especially forgetting to be alert in all directions, not just toward where the enemy camp lay. The proof lay three steps away, still unmoving, but now she could see his chest rising and falling beneath his heavy winter robe and his cloak.

Shigan went on, still in that pure court Imperial, like a scholar, "That's not it. That is, if you had respected anything we are learning, or the rest of us, it would not have rankled so much. But you don't. You ignore us as if we didn't exist, and sleep through every exercise, winning when you feel like it. Usually to make me look bad."

In spite of the cold, heat crept up Mouse's neck to burn painfully in her face. "But that's not it *at all*," she protested.

Shigan couldn't see Second Ryu, but he could hear the break of sincerity in that bat squeak of a voice, and he wondered if the runt was younger than anyone had supposed, in spite of those formidable talents. But then even the rare talents, often called *qilin* talents for the mystical creature of luck and light, had to be young once. "Then what is it?" he asked.

Lies spun through her mind, so easy to speak, but difficult to remember, and worse, to have to build upon. "I don't want to say," she muttered. "I *can't* say. It—it—there are reasons."

She heard how weak that sounded, and squirmed with vexation, expecting a blast of sarcasm that she probably deserved, if everyone felt the way he did. It was horrible, to think that they saw her as the sort of snob that she saw in Shigan, when she'd always thought herself safely invisible. Uninteresting.

She braced herself for more withering scorn.

Surprisingly, all he said was, "I suppose something terrible happened, or some such."

"Oh, yes," she breathed.

"So there are reasons," he said to the moaning wind driving the horizontal clots of snow. "I can understand that. Better than whim, anyway. Everyone has reasons they do things."

She said cautiously. "Which is why I'm going to ask you not to tell anyone what happened. That is, any more than that Yulin fell, and cracked his head. Until he tells his side of what happened."

She felt Shigan shake his head. "Why? I could see wanting to hide cowardice, or a bad decision. But your skill—"

"It was all accident," she said quickly. "Panic. Luck."

She knee-walked a little way away, where the wind struck her, and snow whirled wildly around her head, ice gathering in her eyelashes and hair as she put her hands together and faced him.

For a moment they stared at one another in the dim lighting, he with blood fast crusting the side of his face, glossy ribbons of hair spilling down over his cloak. She grubby-faced and absolutely in earnest.

Then she bowed, face to the rock at her knees. "Please."

His hand shot out and caught her wrist, closing tight enough to feel surprisingly small bones inside the thickness of those clothes. "Don't." It was his turn to flush. "Get back in here. You're making both of us colder than we need to be. Take half this cloak. I don't want the honor marks if you freeze to death right here."

Mouse returned and they sat back to back again, with him flinging a fold of the cloak over her.

She held her breath, bracing for a caustic comment. Then another, and another, still dreading the inevitable questions.

But they didn't come. The pause became a silence, during which she stared out at the wall of white, as her eyelids slid heavily down. She pulled her arms tight against her body and her knees up . . . and dropped into a state midway to dream, until she became aware of a new figure in the thinning white wall, bent over Yulin.

That silhouette, familiar. Where did Yaso come from?

Was that a glow in Yaso's hands?

She blinked, weary; the next thing she knew the shelter was full of figures and voices, and someone was trying to pick her up.

"I can walk," she croaked, pushing the hands away. Dizzily, she found her feet. Another thousand-year stumble on numb feet, and there was her tent, and her bedroll beside the others', but nobody else was in the tent. She peeled off her sodden robe and crawled into the bed in shirt and trousers, fending off Yaso's offer to fetch clean things to change into. "I'm fine," she muttered, but as she lay back, and looked up into Yaso's round face, she became aware that they were alone.

"What you did," she murmured. "Did I see the Essence glow?"

Yaso's long eyelashes lowered. "Just a charm I learned. In case that child was in danger."

"Child." That was the way adults usually spoke, but Mouse was beyond questioning it. She sighed, her head aching, her mind already slipping toward dreams. But not quite there. "What you said. That time. About Essence. I don't understand."

Yaso picked up the wet robe before saying, "It's the way you use Essence. So much effort, pulling it to you, then putting it into wind, and then sending the wind to do the work. Twice the effort for one result. Is that an exercise? I am still learning. But I thought, just as in singing, you might try pulling the Essence and sending it directly."

Yaso's head tipped as Mouse mouthed the words, "Sending it directly . . ."

Mouse's eyes closed, and that was the last she knew until morning, when she woke to discover the tent full of her fellow second years. She was too warm, her clothes twisted around her, and she threw back her bedroll, aware of ravenous hunger.

Figures sat upright around her. As usual, once someone woke, everyone did. And here came the questions. "Yulin was really trying to shoot you?"

"Nah," she lied.

"All those arrows they found just happened to be there?" someone else said sarcastically.

"What happened?"

"Why did he come at you?"

Mouse shrugged. "I went to scout, and he was just there. I thought the fours were supposed to be somewhere else."

"They were — on the far side of the ridge. Yulin was chasing someone, *so they say.*"

"But he's lost his memory," someone else added with a sarcastic eye roll. "So *he* says."

"What's going on?" Mouse asked, ignoring all the questions.

And of course the delight of being in the know won over curiosity. "The tassels are all over in the tassel tent," Mo Muin said. "Trying to figure out what to do. The wind blew all the snow down into the valley, hiding the stream, or so it was last night. If we can't find the stream, how can we defend it, and anyway there's Yulin, and maybe another blizzard coming."

A head poked in. "Food's ready."

There was a stampede, but the questions had not abated. In fending them off, Mouse discovered that Shigan seemed not to have said anything about the fight. Everyone seemed to think that Mouse was shot at, dove for cover, and then the storm came, and Yulin's horse fell, dumping him head first onto a rock, where he messed up his knee and wrist.

Mouse went along with that without actually saying anything, letting them talk themselves into what they wanted to believe. She quickly learned that the tassels from both armies, plus the one who had been with the fourth years, had ridden down toward the stream, halting when the horses reached drifts up to their withers.

While they conferred, and the rest of her army gathered for congee (Shigan among them, though with a bandage wrapped around his head), Mouse squashed her appetite and headed for the tent set aside for wounded or sick people, deciding that it would be better to find out whatever Yulin was going to say, and deal with it now.

She found him alone in the tent, lying flat, staring upward. When she entered his view, his eyebrows twitched downward, but more puzzled than angry. It was odd to look into his face and see just a face. Without the sneer he was almost unrecognizable.

"Ryu the Runt," he whispered, then winced, as if that much effort hurt his head. "What are you doing here?"

"Don't you remember?" she asked.

"Remember . . . what?" His voice was a bare thread, his expression completely confused as his fingers wandered up to finger the bandage on the top of his head. "Where's Weed?"

Mouse backed away without answering. His memory would surely return as soon as that bump on his head healed, but at least she had some time. And maybe he'd make up some story when he did remember, to get out of what surely would be a terrible punishment for shooting at her.

She joined the others for congee, felt much better when she'd eaten, and discovered that they were going to have a winter tracking exercise and then return to base. She wasn't allowed to go. The tassels pulled her aside, and she had to face three of them as the senior one said, "Two of the fourth years, acting as scouts along with Cadet Yulin, both testified that they shot at you, having mistaken you for a straw target."

Mouse said, "I saw some arrows, but they were blown by the wind."

One of the tassels gave a nod, and Mouse imagined them finding the arrows scattered all down the hillside, where she had struck them away. Their following questions led to easy answers (Did Yulin's horse slip? Did he fall? You dragged him to safety? Yes, yes, yes) after which one said, "This all corroborates what Cadet Shigan testified. It sounds like Yulin rode out of bounds of the exercise, but the weather might be to blame. We will have to wait until he regains his memory to question him."

And they let her go.

TWENTY-SEVEN

YSKANDA WAS PERMITTED TO wander on the deck.

His inkstone had broken into pieces while he was lying in that cart. But he had learned when young how to make the most out of the least. He mixed the fragments in the bottom of his tea cup, and sat on the deck in the sunlight, covering pages of his sketchbook with tiny impressions of islands, clouds, birds, the ever-changing sea, and the slant of ships under sail.

No one introduced themselves by name. Except for two of the sailors, all were men; there were two groups, the sailors, who dressed for the sea in rough clothing, their speech a dialect that Yskanda half-understood, and the ones with the military bearing who dressed like artisans or laborers, but who all spoke in Imperial. By the second day, the imperials used the bare space on the foredeck for grappling and then sword drill.

Yskanda had learned how to defend himself long enough to run away from an attacker, and he'd worked through forms every day with his siblings, but always with his mind elsewhere; the day he became an apprentice, he stopped doing Heaven and Earth. But he retained enough of Father's teaching to recognize that the imperials fought in a style akin to Father's.

He shrugged that away, as it had nothing to do with why he was *here*. He tried not to let his mind wander to the worst, that the evil emperor so far away had somehow traced Mother and Father at last, after all these years. At least, surely if that were the case, he would at least see them? He could bear edicts, and chains, and those horrible wooden boards called racks that he'd twice seen prisoners put in, that clamped around the neck and hands, if it meant the family would be together again before the execution.

He forced his mind away from that. So far no one had even searched him, so his waist pouch was still hanging at his side in his increasingly grubby clothes. It contained his few coins, and those bits of inkstone plus his smaller sketch brushes.

He decided not to ask, because he did not want to cause them to ask questions in their turn. If they were not cruel, then he could believe it was all a mistake, and as soon as the imperials got wherever they were going they could admit their error, and send him home again.

Days passed, indistinguishable especially when they sailed between islands, surrounded by nothing but the sea. He noticed that when the sailors set certain flags flying among the many mostly red, talisman-covered flags that never came down, other ships veered off, leaving them alone. They let him stand at the side to gaze down into the water, but as always, he could see so very little. He saw little of land, too—they passed islands now and then, but they never drew near enough for him to make out details.

He lost count until the morning he woke up with the taste of iron on his tongue, under a sky bright as steel, the sea a dark gray full of chopping little waves, as though the slow-rolling billows he was used to had been smashed with a hammer and strewn about by an angry god.

When the crew began sending up anxious glances skyward as they conferred about sails, he caught some of their concern, which heightened dramatically when all across the west a white line rose up from the horizon and began rapidly to eat the sky.

By then they were skipping over the sea under full sail, the entire ship a plaintive song of creaks and groans. The deck slanted under wind demons ever colder than the last, until a sudden blast nearly turned the ship on its end.

Yskanda and the imperials were ordered below, out of the

sailors' way. Yskanda thrust his sketchbook inside all his clothes, then tightened his sash over it not two heartbeats before the ship tilted suddenly, smashing them into one of the walls, as their belongings — the only items not bolted or tied down by the sailors — flung about, hitting them. Water oozed between the slats of the hull, then poured down through a hole in the deck.

One of the imperials sprang for the hole, then fell back as the ship plunged in the opposite direction. He splashed into the black, brackish water. The lanterns bolted to the sides guttered, throwing wild shadows about. The world had been swallowed by angry, waters, which Yskanda found bewildering. He had always felt so safe in and around it.

"Wind is too strong," the man gasped, slinging his hand through his dripping hair — his hair clasp had vanished among their things in the ink-dark water.

The ship rose slowly, then pitched forward as if falling into a hole, yawing mercilessly side to side. This went on for an eternity, until Yskanda found himself dozing between the pitches, then waking, his eyes stinging.

He began to hope that this was the worst of it when there was a great, rending crack, and a falling mast smashed through the deck above. Hands yanked Yskanda out of the way as splinters of wood arrowed down, stabbing one of the imperials. Two of his fellows leaped to his aid, but were thrown back by the pitch of the ship.

One of the others heaved himself forward, a rope in hand, and began tying it around the man with the long, jagged splinter buried in his shoulder. "No," he gasped. "Him. Make him fast." A look Yskanda's way.

Another violent heave flung people and contents against the bulkheads, and then another horrible, shrieking smash of wood as an upended tree impaled the side of the ship, broken branches jabbing inward. The ship yawed, and as suddenly as it had appeared, the tree vanished on another surge of night-black waters, which tried to suck the rest of them out with the tree.

By then the biggest man had flipped the rope around Yskanda and one of the sconces bolted to the bulkhead, securing him—he lay helpless in the water as belongings floated out into the blackness of the night through the hole, followed by the man with the bleeding, broken arm.

One of his fellows made a lunge and caught his robe by the hem. The man's body swung around, his good arm scrabbling at the jagged hole in the hull; then another imperial managed to catch him by the ankle, and so they kept him from being flung out into the night.

That seemed to be the storm's final blow. Though the pitch and dive and yaw continued on, water pouring in and surging out, gradually—gradually—the surges seemed to ease, and then did ease, and when the ship righted itself, much of the filthy water poured away somewhere, leaving Yskanda to sink into a kind of sleep, shivering though he was.

He woke abruptly, and saw that he was alone, except for the wounded man, whose shoulder had been bound up. He lay insensible on a slab of wood, head pillowed on a block. Slanting sunlight danced in shards over the water sloshing about on the floor, coming in through that gigantic hole in the side.

Yskanda's tongue moved dryly in his mouth. He was desperately thirsty, but not enough to assay that murky brine. He levered himself from a stack of ruined bags of rice, now swollen to bursting, onto which he had fallen in his stupor.

He looked out the spectacular hole in the hull—and stared down into a smiling face of a girl maybe Mouse's age. She was sculling in a little roundish boat not unlike the ones Yskanda and the village children had played with off their shoreline.

She patted the net beside her in clear invitation, then held up a hand, palm flat.

Instinctively, Yskanda's hand went to his pouch. The girl looked hopeful. Yskanda's fingers worked into the sodden pouch, and came out inky, gripping one of his coins.

He reached out, dropped it into her hand—and she picked up the net, making space for him in her little coracle. He still knew how to get into boats. Tucking his damp sketchpad against his stomach, he got one leg, then the other, past the splintery gouge in the hull, dropped down, and folded up. The girl looked at him in question, and when he pulled the net over himself, she left it that way.

He lay there, pinpoints of sunlight glinting through the holes in the net, until the girl began chattering. Her dialect sounded fuzzy to Yskanda, but he understood half of it: she'd sculled her boat out to check the damage more closely, as their ship was definitely the worst wreck in the harbor, and maybe she'd earn some money.

Yskanda was already sweltering in the bright sunlight, the salt in his dirty clothes chaffing everywhere.

He peeked up cautiously.

"You can come out. We are behind the two traders," the girl said in vernacular, but with an accent Yskanda had never heard before. She held up two fingers before returning to her sculling.

Yskanda sat up, folding the net properly with absent fingers. This earned another smile from the girl. Yskanda smiled back, relieved to be away from the wreckage, breathing sweet, pure air, and gazing at the sparkling waters. Ah, they were safe again!

The girl skimmed them expertly between larger boats, skiffs, and gigs of every imaginable type, then pulled them to the shore under a dock. Yskanda thanked her. Her smile widened to a grin as she blushed. Giddy with hunger and thirst, he stepped onto the sand and began to walk up toward the shore, noticing the wrack left by a very high tide.

Something to drink first. He hoped they had fountains, but if not, a tea shop.

As soon as he stepped up on the boardwalk he staggered, his balance uncertain. He scanned the bright colors and traffic, his gaze fixing on the familiar character for tea. Twenty steps took him to the shop. He had gulped down three cups, and was tipping his head back to get the last drops when he caught sight of a sign two shops over: TAN'S BATHS.

He upended the ink-stained contents of his pouch into his palm. He'd already paid for the tea. Among the bits of soggy ink, there were . . . He squinted, having trouble focusing. Surely there was enough here, if he did not ask for extras like herbs. Or even soap. Maybe he could even get his clothes laundered.

Inside the bathhouse, he held out his palm as he explained his dilemma, his mild voice husky with the exhaustion of extreme hunger. "I do need to have enough left to get something to eat," he confessed at the end. "I don't know when I ate last, except that it was before the storm."

Tan's wife took one look at that beautiful face, that trusting manner, then pinched her huge bull of a husband by the ear and tugged him unceremoniously into the back room before he could speak.

Yskanda waited patiently, too foggy-headed to do anything else, until the proprietor emerged again, ham-like fists on his hips. He cocked his head toward the door that divided them from the women's side. "My wife tells me a pretty thing like you ought to have herbs, and she knows what to bring."

"But I . . ."

"It's her gift," the man said in that same accented vernacular, leading Yskanda to one of the canvas-walled little bath alcoves. "If anyone asks the young lord where you bathed, you must say, at Tan's."

Yskanda agreed a little guiltily, as he wasn't a young lord, and he did not plan on talking to anyone. His main worry was whether or not his clothes would dry in time. "Can you really have these ready?" he asked as a series of brawny young fellows entered and dumped steaming buckets of water into a waiting tub.

"We share our back wall with the baker," Proprietor Tan confided. "It's hot and dry in that back room. Your things will probably be ready before you are."

And so Yskanda laid aside his sketchbook and the bits of ink, stripped down to his skin, and then, oh bliss, climbed into the tub. True to her word, Proprietress Tan sent a small boy in who brought a shell full of soap, then poured fragrant herbs into the water.

Yskanda sank back with a sigh, suddenly almost too tired to move. But he forced himself to immerse his head. He then fingered the soap and herbs through his hair, rubbing and rinsing until his hair squeaked in his fingers.

Then he lay back in the healing waters, eyes closed, unaware of time until the proprietor cleared his throat. "Young lord, it'll be ten tinnies for more hot water, as yours has gone cold. And your things are ready."

That meant someone else wanted the bath, Yskanda translated.

He got out, his body heavy, dried off, wrapped his hair up again, and pulled on clean clothes that smelled of citrus, cinnamon bark, and fennel. He slid his sketchbook inside his dry, clean robe, retied his pouch with the ink, his two brushes, and the last coins, put on his sandals, and walked out.

"Thank you," he said to the proprietor, then blushed when a broad female face appeared in the other doorway, other female faces peeping over her shoulder and around her. "Such a *pretty* young lord." A girl his own age sighed.

Feeling awkward, Yskanda half-bowed, and hurried out, breathing easier when he reached the street, where he discovered the sun had shifted a good way across the sky. Though he'd been hearing such comments on his appearance from strangers ever since his apprenticeship began, it never ceased to be awkward. He was so used to being a "me" moving invisibly through the world, searching for beautiful things to delight his senses. He could not quite come to terms with others thinking him one of those things.

What now?

Food.

He bought filled buns from one vendor, and grilled plantains from another, then walked along as he consumed the food, feeling very much better with each bite. Enough to consider what to do next.

He had given up trying to divine why he had been grabbed like that. It could not possibly be for ransom, but they might be Western slave traders or some sort. Anyway, now he was free. That meant the first thing to do would be earn some money. How? Sketching, of course —

Then his mind blanked when he looked into a shop window, where a very old man was in the midst of painting orchid blossoms around the rim of a moon-pale porcelain vase so pure in line that Yskanda stopped dead, unaware of traffic flowing around him. This vase was the sort of precious art he had copied from books, and had never hoped to see in real life.

A glimpse inside the shop disclosed other exquisite porcelain. Was this a white-clay island, then? Yskanda backed up, then sank down onto the ground, pulled out his sketchpad, and used the moisture still clinging to his brush and a bit of ink to sketch the basic shape . . .

He was so absorbed that he didn't become aware of his surroundings until the street noise went silent, and a human shadow slid over his sketchpad.

He looked up, blinking, into the face of a guard in light blue. Looking around in bewilderment, he discovered he was ringed by guards, all with swords out. Behind them stood two of the imperials he recognized from the ship, both dressed in black warrior robes slashed up the side and sashed at the waist, with black warrior headbands. Both wore bandages, one beneath his headband.

A local guard's face was suffused with the purple of rage. He stamped between two of his fellow blue guards and loomed over Yskanda, fists rising—then one of the familiar ones in black said softly but distinctly in Imperial, "Untouched." The word was freighted with meaning.

As Yskanda blinked up at them, that same man added in a more normal voice, "Besides, he's not exactly halfway across the island, is he?" And tapped the side of his head, drawing a circle. The way people did to mean one of the Snow Crane's abandoned, with an empty head.

Yskanda scrambled to his feet, pausing to look down in regret at his unfinished sketch of the vase. Around him the guards in blue slid their swords back into their sheaths, exchanging meaning looks and smiles, as the imperial said to Yskanda in vernacular, his tone slow and soothing, "Come along, then. We need to go back to the ship."

Yskanda responded in the same language, "I don't understand. And surely, the ship cannot sail with that hole in the side . . ."

"We have another vessel," the man said in a voice a little too loud, a little too smooth. As though Yskanda's mind was not quite all there.

Yskanda flushed, but as two of the ones in black closed in on either side of him, the big one with the purple face breathing heavily in the background, he forbore adding anything more. The men stayed next to him, tight on either side, until they reached the dock, where another ship lay, this one a slightly different shape than the first.

As they mounted the ramp, Yskanda looked down to be sure of his footing in his seawater-ruined sandals, and noticed a tally swinging at the imperial's sash. He couldn't make out the characters among all the carving, except for the claw of a dragon holding a jewel, with gold worked into the frame.

Gold—dragon—jewel. Tiger-eye. Symbol of the Jehan emperors and empresses. Men dressed all in black.

Slowly, too slowly, the truth began to work its way past the mental barrier he had raised without realizing it.

These men were not pirates, or thieves. They were warriors—and not general warriors. Those did not carry tallies with gold or five-toed dragon claws or tiger-eyes. That was the imperial symbol, reserved to the emperor.

And according to gossip among the apprentices of rank who had traveled, there was only one group of warriors who dressed all in black: the emperor's personal guards, called the imperial ferrets.

TWENTY-EIGHT

YULIN'S MEMORY RETURNED—EXCEPT, it seemed, for what happened the day the storm struck. Many thought it convenient, as there were wild whispers about him trying to murder the younger Ryu, but Muin and Mouse both believed it because there was no vengeance talk from Yulin at all. He still scowled at the sight of them—he had not changed that much—but he seemed more confused about recent events than anything.

Gradually, life returned to normal as the days got steadily colder.

Or to the new normal. Mouse cautiously felt her way into an unspoken truce with Shigan Fin, who kept his promise and said nothing of the events of that day. Maybe it was only because his own part wasn't exactly heroic, being knocked down before he could lift a sword. Mouse didn't know his motivations, and didn't care. It was enough that the incident passed on without more comment than had happened on the following day.

A week, then two passed, before they were paired on a stalking mission. They had proceeded in silence, the way she preferred it, when he said abruptly, eyes on the ground, "Will you teach me that style?"

"What style?" she said defensively.

Shigan turned that mocking not-quite-smile her way as he said, "I may only still be a learner, but I am able to discern that style is not what we're being taught."

"What we're being taught is fine," she retorted, feeling on uncertain ground.

"Not if a person wants to save his own life," he shot right back. "You know it's better."

"So you're in danger here?" she said, crossing her arms.

He hissed a sigh, the subject dropped, and they were back to the cold silence.

She shrugged that off. Life was much easier if people didn't talk to her. She had enough to think about with all the extra troop exercises on top of their regular training. The only time she could get away was very early, when it was bitterly cold, or very late, when she was so tired she could scarcely stand.

But she made herself rise, and work through Heaven and Earth as she thought about what Yaso had said. It was either that or lie awake worrying at something she felt she ought to understand — it was almost there — but not quite.

Until the cold, crisp morning she thought she was finally getting it.

It had rained the night before. She hopped over the stream winding between the huts, then paused, watching the water rushing. Essence was there. Her first lesson. Neither good nor evil. She had repeated that so many times the words had almost stripped themselves of meaning.

Essence could be used to enhance heat. It could push the wind imps, the way she had been striving to master it all this time. She had read that those who cultivated the higher paths could even use it to purify water, and to clear poisons from the blood.

But what if the Essence could be a force in itself?

She returned to her old, abandoned site. Most of her seed pods and twigs still hung from the crabapple trees. The air was so cold it almost banished the smell of the kitchen garden fertilized with night soil. She hastened through the warmups, and whirled into Heaven and Earth, but on each thrust, she pushed the Essence directly at the hanging targets.

Nothing. Her effort dissipated into air.

She did it again, and this time she sighted along two fingers, as if shooting Essence like an arrow—and poof, the hanging seed pod swung. It was no different in strength than when she'd pushed Essence into wind imps, then sending the wind imps to strike the seed pods, but she discerned a fundamental difference. It really was as Yaso had said. She had trained herself to make two efforts accomplish one thing.

What would happen if she made one effort? No wind imps. Using Essence itself. But she had to see it as . . . what, wind? No, then it was pretty much the same.

Then she remembered that early lesson, Father saying, "I always thought it was the exaggeration of the storytellers, how we heard about warriors who used Essence as extensions of their hands, their feet, their swords. . ."

How could she have forgotten? Those words had been what set her to experimenting with Essence in the first place. But wind had power, and she hadn't had any, and Mother had trained her to use Essence strictly for good purposes: healing charms, pulling sunlight into stones for warming, and so on. Which she had completely forgotten when she was shivering back to back in that cave with Shigan! Using the power of anger to draw Essence and make it into invisible steel was supposed to be the very definition of evil.

Ayah! What if she thought of Essence as a *defensive* force, not a weapon?

Once again she moved through Heaven and Earth, breathing hard to use that ball of Essence fire in her core, and on the thrust she *pushed*.

The seed pod ripped free of the old string and tumbled to the ground ten paces away. Mouse staggered to a stop, her breathing fast.

She'd done it. She stared at that pod lying on the churned-up soil with the stumps of harvested vegetables pocking the ground, fighting to get her breathing under control. She tried once more, knowing by the tremble in her wrists, and the watery sense in her knees, that this ought to be the last attempt—and that she had a miserably long day ahead.

She forced her breathing to slow, deliberately moved through the drill, and when it came to the swing and thrust, she stamped her foot, tightened her entire body, and . . .

Smack! This time the pod bounced crazily before coming to a stop thirty paces away, its string also broken. But all the Essence in her core was gone. She forced her breathing to slow, and tried to marshal Essence from the air to settle inside her. She badly wanted to sit down somewhere long enough to catch her breath, but there was no time — the brass gong reverberated, calling everyone into motion.

She pushed her way through the day, her head panging, her thoughts back in that stinky grove. She had it — she thought she had it — she had it but was so feeble. All she wanted to do was get back there to practice until she *knew* she had it.

Through that interminable day she thought constantly of going back at bedtime, but when that time came, and she waited for her hut mates to settle down, she fell asleep sitting up, waking with a knot in her neck. She shed her outer garments and crawled under the winter bedding and dropped off.

So it went for a handful more days. Excitement thrilled through her; she had begun to perceive that some of those old poems and tales did not exaggerate the power of Essence. If one could call enough of it inside, then use just enough.

Now she was impatient for a battle game, which would afford her a chance to get away from everyone for a longer session, but unfortunately, the tassels were firm about avoiding games at a distance. Their next was to be right there in Loyalty Fortress, defending it against the fourth years making a night invasion.

Shigan was to command. She was one of the two captains.

As soon as they were dismissed, and the others had stampeded out, Shigan looked past her in the old, aloof way, saying to the other captain, "I want to look at the fourth years' last few night defenses and invasions. Since we're supposed to be sentries caught by surprise, there's no map work to be done, or other preparation. I'll have a plan when we meet at Dragon Watch second gong."

He turned away. By the set of his shoulders she could tell he was annoyed. He was still that much taller than she was. Though Yaso had twice lengthened the hems of her trousers and sleeves a finger's breadth this past year, he'd grown three fingers' breadths.

Irked, she went off to the midday meal. Because they'd be up that night, they had a free half-watch afterward to sleep, or rest, or whatever they wanted.

Mouse knew she'd be tired, but she wanted to practice. The drive to master that Essence . . . *thing*—not a weapon, not, not, not—was stronger than the tiredness that was a part of life.

But when she once again retreated to her old site, she heard voices, one of them Dun's. The fourth years were practicing some kind of maneuver, probably to be used against them that night.

Should she spy, or retreat? Did she want to win? Did she want Shigan in command to win?

Ambivalence wrung through her, then she remembered what she was there for: Heaven and Earth. She retreated to the laundry lines, and there she whirled through the movements, but her ambivalence sharpened into a vague sense of guilt that she couldn't define until Shigan's voice spoke in memory, accusing her of snobbery. She heard a bunch of grunts coming, laden with freshly washed bedding, vaulted to the bath roof and down the other side, and away.

She was *not* a snob. She was *quiet*. There was a difference. *He* was the snob.

She might as well get in that nap.

She didn't think she'd sleep, but the next thing she knew after stretching out was someone punching her shoulder. "Ayah! Get moving."

And so the day went, one hard drill after another, until the second years met again before the watch change from Dragon to Turtle.

The air was bitterly cold as they gathered by the sundial to face Shigan and the other captain. Shigan said, "Patrol by troops." Pointing to troop leaders, "You, northwest tower to midpoint over the back gate, you northeast. You, east gate, both directions, you southeast tower, and you southwest. I'll be over the gate with Niam here." He pointed to the second captain, his gaze passing right by Mouse as if she weren't there. "Any sign of anything, send a runner to us, and we'll defend from there. Go."

They split into their troops, Mouse with lagging steps. She couldn't believe that Shigan had forgotten she was supposed to be his second captain. Or had he? Who cared, she reminded herself fiercely, and ran to catch up with her troop. She would walk the wall, peering assiduously out and down for any sign of sneaking fourth years — of course she would. Did he think she would let them invade?

For one gong, then two, she patrolled as a sentry, walking back and forth along the wall, cloak pulled up to her ears. She paid more attention to the ground far below than she ever had. No one was going to sneak up on her, no chance. But she kept coming back to that deliberately blank gaze passing her, as if she didn't exist. He hadn't forgotten. Even worse, she occasionally caught sight of covert looks from the others, and her sharp ears caught whispers on the frigid air.

Finally she decided to face him and get it over with. As a second captain, she could leave her post, and so she did, running along the walls until she reached the gate, where Shigan leaned out, peering downward, the other captain peering inward at the parade ground in case the fourth years had somehow infiltrated and were attacking from behind.

"Shigan," she said.

He didn't move.

Her heart banged her ribs. She marched up right beside him. "Shigan, I'm supposed to be second captain."

He straightened up and turned to face her, arms crossing as he looked down at her. "Why bother? You'll just find some way to make us lose."

For the first time, she was aware just how much she loathed the advantage that superior height had in moments like this. She turned away from that scornful moral superiority — which she knew was entirely justified — and peered out over the dark sea, starlight peeking between clouds and winking on the water. Neither moon was up yet; one had already sunk, the other would not rise until the end of Turtle Watch.

"I . . ." She blinked, puzzled by smudges on what should be the clean, flat horizon, the black sea a shade deeper than the midnight blue of the southern sky. What *was* that?

She leaned out, as if a hand's breadth or two would bring

her closer to that unmeasurable distance. "What is that? It can't be an island."

Shigan gave a snort of disbelief, and turned to stare. Then he stilled, and he, too, leaned out. "Is that . . . an island?"

"No island. Ships," said Niam, the other captain. "Two? Three? I can't quite tell."

"This is not ship time," Shigan said, his voice rising in question.

"No," Niam added decisively—he liked details, the more, the better. "It's a week too early. The spring ships come at different times, because they go from island to island, but the supply ship always comes once a month from Te Gar Island, never more than two days from mid-month."

All three stared so hard their eyes watered in the cold air.

"And never three ships at once," someone else muttered.

One of the scouts elbowed up, and grinned. "Hey, what if it's pirates?"

"Pirates?" Niam scoffed. "Why would pirates come *here?* There's nothing for them!"

"Except five hundred of us who do nothing but train to fight," the scout said with a kind of anticipatory lilt to his voice. It cracked as he added, "Wouldn't it be fun if it was pirates?"

"Don't be an idiot. There's nothing here that they'd want, and attacking the imperial army is a capital offense," Niam stated.

The scout shrugged. "Pirates don't need an excuse to attack people."

"Maybe they're refugees from that big storm," someone else said doubtfully, as more people crowded up.

By now, a turn in the current had caused all three ships to separate, such that they could be made out a bit more distinctly, though they were still too far away for any details to be seen.

"But that storm was a month ago, and there are two harbors full of supplies within three days and a week in either direction," Shigan said slowly.

The four of them looked at each other, others watching them for clues. Then Niam spoke, placing responsibility squarely on Shigan, "What do you want to do?"

"Where's the tassel?"

No one knew — the entire idea was for the evaluating tassel to stay out of the way, preferably unnoticed.

Shigan said, "If the tassel — "

Quick footsteps approached from both sides. It was the fourth years, wooden swords up, grins on their faces.

TWENTY-NINE

SHIGAN HELD UP HIS hand in the rarely used signal for a halt.

The commanding fourth year slowed to a stop. "What? If you're faking us out . . ."

"Look," Shigan said tersely, pointing. "Have you ever seen that before?"

The two invader teams halted, Muin among them, and in silence everyone stared out.

"Three ships." A flurry of whispers ran among them. "Ever seen that?" "Could be anything . . ." "Surprise inspection from the capital?" "Not *three* ships! Our bay is barely big enough for one!"

The fourth years parted suddenly, and Falik was there. "Shigan, aren't you the second year captain?"

"I think we ought to send for the tassels," Shigan said. "If there's going to be trouble for it, then I'll take it. But I don't like the looks of them."

Falik stared out, and everyone waited for the general's son to speak. Finally he said in his clipped voice, "No one ever gets in trouble for readiness. Shall we plan a defense here, even if it comes to nothing?" He took in the fortress with his hand.

Mouse had been scanning in both directions. She said, "Village."

Everyone turned her way.

Falik had never spoken to her before. "What's that, Second Ryu?"

Everyone stared at her.

She swallowed down nervousness. "In the stories — everything . . ." She was aware she was babbling, justifying herself before anyone objected, and cut herself off, then tried again. "If I was a pirate. I'd go into the village first. Easier to get into. Set fires. And when we go over to fight it, jump on us in the chaos."

"Village." Falik grimaced in the torchlight. "I never thought of it. I never think of it — I've never been there." Though the fourth years could earn liberty there, he always spent free time in the library, or at the targets.

But Mouse remembered the village. During that long first year of night soil duty, she'd seen the farmers on the terrace rice paddies, and glimpsed from across the stream the clusters of cottages built partly of stone and of wood. "It's completely indefensible."

Falik gave her a quick nod. "Fourth years. We'll lay traps before the village — we've been working on that. You second years, you've got to get everyone else roused. Commander Weken might give different orders, but until he does, let's get the third years up. Half can lay traps right below us, which they've been working on. The rest bring all our weapons. That includes crossbows, and real arrows."

Everyone stared, hearts drumming.

"First years will be on bucket duty if there are fires. You seconds, those not rousing everybody else watch up here. Keep your heads low. If they are pirates, and are coming in on the sneak to surprise us, ayah! The best defense we have is surprise . . ."

He waved at his own scouts to get moving, leaving Shigan to send the second year scouts to run to the third and first years' huts. Shigan also ordered his troop to douse the south wall torches, plunging them all into darkness — but their night vision soon came, stronger now without the distraction of those orange flames.

The exercise was forgotten. Mouse remained where she was, on watch; presently a man's silhouette appeared out of the darkness, with a shorter, slimmer boy's at his shoulder. Falik was explaining what orders he'd given, and—as scrupulous and honest as he was utterly humorless—added, "I would have set the defense entirely around the fortress, but it was Second Ryu here who reminded me of the village."

Commander Weken turned his head. "Second Cadet Ryu?"

"Sir," Mouse said, saluting as more instructors joined the commander.

"Good job, Falik," the commander was saying. "We will leave it to the fifth years to defend the village. I concur with your sending the first years to douse fires . . ."

Mouse backed away until she reached her troop, still standing around the southeast tower.

From there she could see below. By the time everyone was in place, the world seemingly asleep, the ships had put down anchors a ways outside the bay. Equally quietly they let down longboats, shapes dropping into them from all three, and then striking for shore. They used no lights, but here and there a needle-strip of cold light gleamed on bare steel, reflecting the starlight above.

"What do you think?" Commander Weken asked softly, his voice barely carrying to Mouse on the still, cold air.

Captain Instructor Fumig said, "We will know more when they land. Pirates usually attack in a mass. Mercenaries use military order."

"Mercenaries?" Commander Weken repeated in a tone of disbelief. There had never, in all the years he was aware of, been any kind of trouble on this island. Now he regretted that their heavy weapons—catapults and gunpowder bombs, and the majority of their crossbows and bolts—were left on the far side of the island where no one lived, and the fourth and fifth years could practice without harming anyone.

They didn't even have enough steel for everyone, only the wooden swords. But what they had was in the hands of the fifth years and the instructors. The best shots among the second and third years crouched below the wall, ready to be sent to wherever the attackers went to breech, and the bigger fourth years waited in the parade ground, ready to be deployed at ground level. Every crossbow had been passed out. Everyone had a full bag of arrows, and shields.

Captain Instructor Fumig looked over at his commander, who went on, "Unless we discover word of a larger war elsewhere, there is no sense in a prince or powerful noble sending mercenaries against us. If these are mercenaries, they've turned pirate," he said, striving to make sense of a scene that made so little sense.

Captain Instructor Fumig grunted. To him their motivation was immaterial. What mattered was their tactical approach. "All we really need to know is how they fight."

The commander, whose single experience of war had been limited to support when he was not much older than his fifth years, agreed, and the two watched in silence as the attackers' oars rose and dipped, then were shipped to allow the rippling breakers to bring them up to the shoreline.

Still silent, the two watched as the attackers assembled into troops, swiftly putting together ladders that had been carried in pieces.

"Mercenaries," Fumig breathed. He turned to Instructor Shaz, bringing up the flat of his hand and then pointing it: wait for the signal, one man, one shot.

Shaz raised his hand in silent salute, and vanished into the tower to repeat the orders to those waiting below.

It wasn't until the dark silhouettes were halfway up the beach, and thus could be counted, that Captain Instructor Fumig and Instructor Biyat, who had been in the navy for half his life, realized that these could not be three ships' worth of mercenaries.

At that same moment, the cold, still air carried faint sounds from the east, where the village lay: screams, like the cries of birds. Shouts. As heads turned in that direction, eyes made out the orange glow of flames here and there. Biyat understood first: the mercenaries had put off boats before the ships arrived on the horizon, and these had come around the point that formed the outer arm of the bay, completely out of sight of the fortress. There had not been a lookout on the point for five centuries.

As if those screams served as their signal, the mercenaries below broke into a run, looming larger at every step. Fumig kept his arm up as every boy on the wall stared, palms sweaty, hearts racing. They all knew the fearful cost if anyone broke order enough to shoot before the signal.

Fumig waited as the ladders slapped against the walls. A soft keening sounded beside Mouse, whose throat seemed to be crowded by her own frantic heart. But no one spoke, or moved . . .

The mercenaries began scrambling up the ladders.

Fumig waited.

Someone's breath hissed, a sound nearly smothered by the clatter of boots and weapons on the other side of the wall.

And then the hand came down.

The archers leaped up and shot a lethal rain of arrows — the foremost pirates fell, several of them with five or six arrows in their bodies.

Two knocked the followers off the ladders. The attackers on the other ladders shoved their fellows away with their swords and scrambled to take their place as the second row of boys shot, the first row cranking crossbows.

Fumig had found a single barrel of gunpowder bombs in storage, to be used as demonstrations. Everything else lay on the other side of the island, out of reach. He put his fist in the air, the signal to the instructors chosen to handle these. As below, the mercenaries began shooting their own lethal rain of arrows up at the walls, the instructors lit the fuses, held the bombs until the glow ate the fuses to a finger's breadth from the fused coconuts containing the gunpowder — and then popped up to drop them, each to a ladder.

Three bombs exploded on climbers. One bounded off the stone as its thrower fell back onto the sentry wall with two arrows in him, shoulder and neck. That bomb landed on its fuse, which was snuffed.

A boy screamed behind Mouse, harrowing her nerves. He fell to the sentry walk, sobbing, "Shit, shit, shit."

Another choked off a cry at the other end of the wall, and Fumig roared, "Shields!"

They hadn't practiced with shields and arrows more than once or twice — that was something the fourth and fifth years did.

Mouse began striking arrows out of the air, her heart thumping frantically. She dared not look to see who was hurt — or worse.

When the smoke cleared, three ladders had burst apart into small flames, pirates lying still on the ground below, or groaning.

But more were coming.

The shooting increased.

"They're waiting for something," Fumig said, his voice nearly lost in the whistle and hum of arrows and the shouts of boys.

"Us to open the gates and rush them?" young Instructor Vin asked, turning from Fumig to the commander.

"Don't. They can't get at us here . . ."

Fumig's words died away when a line of attackers appeared on the strand from the east, each forcing a person to stumble before them. Pitiless starlight reflected off the white sleeping clothes of children, mothers, and silver hair of a man and a woman of venerable age.

These were the people the villagers had tried to send farther up the strand for safety as soon as the boys had made known what might happen. No one had expected attackers to sneak along the farthest reaches of the promontory, and capture them one by one.

A loud voice roared, "Open the door, or we start killing them one by one. Beginning now, so you know we're serious."

And before anyone could move, the mercenary below made a cutting motion across his neck, and the first person in line, a stout woman of some forty years, got shoved away and her throat cut.

"Mama!" a child screamed.

"You're next, brat," the mercenary said. "You can join your mama bowing to the King of Hell, ha ha!"

Fumig turned a blanched face toward Weken.

The agonizing moment seemed to stretch forever, as Mouse's horrified gaze swept over those people in the line, none of them armed, half of them sobbing along with the child whose mother lay motionless, bleeding out her life in the sand.

Mouse's mind seemed to separate from her body, looking

down from a great height. And yet she felt each muscle, each nerve, each thud of her heart sending blood singing through her veins. She looked at the mercenaries grouped at one side, ready to charge the fortress door, the prisoners held a few steps away —

She threw down her crossbow and shield, took up her wooden sword, stepped to the wall, and leaped.

Her small figure, clothed in dun, was the only thing that moved as Essence flowed in and around her, glowing softly like a candle in crystal. The entire world seemed to still.

Between one heartbeat and the next, defenders and mercenaries alike stared.

Then, "Shoot," the mercenary chief shouted.

Arrows arced toward Mouse.

But her muscles knew what to do. Essence burned through her as the sword hummed, knocking the arrows away. Then she landed lightly as the gate-attacking party charged, straight toward her.

Mouse drew in a deep, steadying breath, Father's voice whispering in memory: what to look for to break a line, and keep it broken.

She stamped her foot on the hard path, fury and grief drawing up a mighty fountain of Essence.

Her sword hummed as it swept around in a half-circle too fast to see, and a weird glow, like fire and sunlight combined, flashed up and out in a loud clap of air. Mercenaries and villagers fell flat as if struck by the invisible fist of a god.

The mercenaries closest sat up dizzily. "Kill him! Kill him!" the mercenary chief roared. The mercenaries farther off got to their feet, raising their weapons and shouting in rage as they advanced on Mouse. The villagers mostly began crawling away.

Mouse charged the mercenaries. Her sword came down, too fast to see. It was not a death blow. Her training had honed her to strike joints, to disable and disarm. But the blow hit the chief's right shoulder with the force of a lightning bolt. Then she broke the ribs of the man to his right, shattered the knee of the one to his left, and on the backswing, smashed the right arm of another, all within one heartbeat and the next.

Seeing their leaders stumble back and fall staggered the mercenaries, and struck fear into many, as Mouse stood there, a small, lone figure swaying on her feet.

Later, no one knew who opened the great doors, only that it was one of those rare moments when an act of will is shared: no one watching was going to let Mouse Ryu face the enemies alone.

Seeing their fellows bent over, still trying to breathe against that invisible blow that had hit them mid-chest, the mercenaries farthest away and thus less affected by that invisible blow ran up the beach to attack Mouse.

Her fellow cadets got there first. The bigger ones went straight for the mercenaries in no order, shrieking and screaming in rage. Mouse's head had reeled as an aftereffect of her Essence blow, but when she saw a mercenary cut one fourth year boy, and another gut a third year boy with more courage than strength, once again Essence surged up in her, and she charged, sword whirling. No steel came near her. Essence poured through her, each strike gaining power as she scythed through the enemy, shattering shoulders, elbows, knees, until she became aware that the fighting had broken into scattered battles—too many wounded boys lying still, or writhing in agony.

The mercenaries were still coming on. She shook her aching head, then froze when a roar of triumph brought her attention around, as four or five of them charged . . . Shigan?

Whose sarcastic mouth had obviously worked against him, she thought as she charged toward them. Shigan wielded his wooden sword with both hands, though by now it had chunks missing as he warded steel. He backed up with each block until his back reached the wall—and that was when Mouse was on the attackers from behind.

Once more, she drew on Essence. This surge was far less potent. She was losing strength, but it was enough to send her blade humming among them: she struck elbows and knees, crippling mercenaries who, for all their prowess with steel, never seemed to remember to protect the weakest joints.

That surge was long enough for two instructors to appear, both with steel, and both indiscriminate in killing the fallen attackers, leaving Shigan standing at the wall, hair hanging in his eyes as his ribs rose and fell behind his sweat-soaked clothes. His wide eyes met Mouse's, and she blinked, then looked around, discovering to her amazement that the rest were running, to be shot down by the advancing fourth years, one by one, until the beach was quiet again, except for the groans of the wounded, and the muffled cries of the villagers around the dead woman.

Mouse's sword dropped from nerveless fingers and she sat down abruptly, hollowed like a husk, her vision swimming with blobby shadows, voices a distant roar in her ears. She did not see the wide berth her fellows gave her, the looks of awe, some of fear, that many sent her way.

The first one to reach her was Yaso, smelling of smoke. Until then, she'd forgotten that the orderlies and grunts had also been part of the defense, though none of them had weapons. It was clear from the smoke scent that Yaso had been part of the bucket line, and then had been coopted for other tasks. She looked up dully, suddenly exhausted — all she could see was that pirate, or whatever he was, cutting that woman's throat.

Lightning flared in a suddenly cloudy sky, revealing Yaso's benign smile. "I came to ask if we might use the Longevity Herb? We're going to need it. So many wounded."

Mouse drew in a breath, beyond question. At least it was, for once, an easy question to answer, and she was able to shake loose from the paralysis gripping her. "Of course. Take it —"

Rain struck then, shockingly sudden. She raised her voice, though it seemed to take all her effort just to talk. "Take it. If it will help. Even though it hasn't been ground. Or treated properly for making medicine."

Yaso replied, oblivious to the rain, "Even so, the purple is strong enough that, scalded and left to brew a bit, with a charm or two, it will help with the worst wounds."

Mouse wanted to say, *Don't tell them where you got it,* but that would just bring questions, inevitable as flies on horse droppings. Hoping that in the general chaos no one would think to ask, she said, "It's yours."

Between cracks of thunder Captain Instructor Fumig began

calling out orders, some to help carry the wounded inside, others to accompany the villagers back to their homes. The downpour was already putting out the fires; the younger boys were to gather the spent arrows and any dropped weapons; the instructors, and the tough old dock workers, would begin the grim task of dealing with the dead invaders.

The aimless wandering and chatter ended as people began moving purposefully, bent against the onslaught from the heavens. Those wounded who could walk were sent to get rest. Mouse plodded after them, still isolated in a sea of questions that she barely noticed.

She made it to her hut, managed to strip off her outer robe and her shoes, then crawled into bed, curled up, pulled the quilt overhead, and dropped into a profoundly deep sleep.

THIRTY

YSKANDA'S NEW SHIP HAD to recover all the distance they had been blown off course, and the ferrets began to recover. Every one of them had been injured in that storm, two badly. They pressed the need for speed upon the hired crew as they observed their . . . charge with a growing concern as the days slipped by.

No one had said anything to him—their chief questioned each separately—yet he appeared to have withdrawn into himself. He sat below, exactly where they had put him, staring at nothing, his sketchpad forgotten by his side. He only moved to go to the head, then returned to the same spot. He even slept there, curled up like a small child.

Not even when one of the ferrets discovered a square of rough ink among the sailors and requisitioned it to offer to Yskanda did he react with any more than a polite but vague word of thanks, then withdrew even deeper.

They had meant to keep him below as a safety measure— and in part, a consequence of his near-escape (if that's what it was; he had been briefly left to sleep while they dealt with the injured, and the two least hurt went out to commandeer a new vessel)—but after several days passed and Yskanda barely ate enough to keep a bird alive, they brought him up on deck during a last burst of fine weather, and then tried to coax him into eating. One then another delicacy was brought forth, the last precious hoard of plums, another's private stash of figs, fresh fish grilled with the wine they'd meant to drink. He might eat a bite to be polite, but then his gaze would go diffuse, his profile like an etching of grief in an old scroll. He looked disturbingly ethereal in his quiet melancholy, as if between one breath and another he would transform into an insubstantial ghost, which somehow intensified their growing alarm and sense of helplessness.

Yskanda was aware of none of it. There could be only one reason why the emperor's men had taken him: the emperor had found his family.

His mind had sunk into torturous roils of what-ifs: were the others already dead? Or was it mere accident that he was found? If that was true, and Sweetwater still lay undiscovered, what if the emperor forced him to rat out his parents and siblings before he was executed? He was not at all certain he could withstand torture.

But in a way, herbs might be even worse. He knew from things Mother had said that there were all kinds of herbs that could do strange things to people's minds. In the worst nightmares he listened to his own voice betraying his family as he babbled out The Story, and whatever else was demanded of him.

Should he try to kill himself first, and save his family? How? He had no weapons, and he was never permitted near the ship's rail—he was just conscious of his keepers enough to be aware of how closely they watched him.

They sensed his mood, perhaps catching some of his thoughts when his eyes strayed toward their weapons while the more able practiced. And so the steel vanished from the deck, and one or another slept near him all night long, as their leader used all the suasion of his imperial tally to urge the sailors to maximum speed.

The sailors knew that the infamous and deadly imperial ferrets were granted extraordinary powers, as they took their orders directly from the emperor. The ferrets had promised recompense for requisitioning the ship and its supplies, they were polite and clean in their habits, but that aura of death and danger — the sense of the dragon throne hovering in the air behind the soft-spoken chief — made the ship captain anxious to get to the capital and be well rid of them and their ever frailer . . . charge.

It was the third day of the new month when they perceived the familiar lines of the capital on the horizon, with the great snow-capped mountain behind the city. Yskanda recognized it from scroll drawings (it was a common assignment to copy the great artists of the past, and Mount Lir was a favorite subject) and he roused a bit from his torpor, reflecting that those artists of ancient days had sat aboard a ship approximately where he sat now, in order to get that view.

He even felt the twitch of desire to sketch, then remembered he was most likely doomed to a painful death soon, and sank back with a sigh, closing his eyes.

The imperial ferrets watched him, their emotions a mix from which triumph was notably absent. No one knew why the order had gone out the year before, only that it had taken over a year, by more than ten teams, making this the largest manhunt in memory for the younger ferrets. But nobody believed that this boy, who looked no older than fifteen or sixteen, could have committed murder or treason or fostered a rebellion.

Word winged ahead; when they stepped ashore, a plain cart awaited them, rather than a prison cart. Only the discreet red and gold edging to the plain silk of the window and door covering indicated that this cart had something to do with the imperial palace, and must not be hindered in any way.

Yskanda was helped inside. His head swam unpleasantly, and he sank back on the bench, closing his eyes, as sweat shone on his forehead. Fever marked his cheeks a dull red. The chief of the team — not a man given to fancies — wanted nothing more than to hand off this charge before he expired on the spot.

The driver, having been given her own instructions, took them around to the palace's east gate, where servants and supplies entered. Not to the imperial prison, then.

Inside, a servant in shades of soft gray awaited them, his smooth face dominated by a pair of intelligent eyes below a tall hat with stiff extensions to either side. He carried in the crook of his arm an elaborate object of gold, carved with symbols. Attached to the upper end was a long horsetail, which hung over his arm, the straw-colored hair bright against the gray of his robe.

The servant and the leader bowed to each other. "Chief Bitternail."

"Chief Fai. You are awaited," the servant with the ornamental flywhisk said in a tenor murmur.

Then, to Yskanda, in pure court Imperial, "Come this way."

Yskanda's gaze rose, and took in the features of the denatured man. His artist's eye flicked from detail to detail then away as he was led into a hall of exquisite tiles, tapestries, and complicated wooden structure overhead, gilt and painted.

Even imminent death could not keep Yskanda from lagging his steps, his wondering gaze lingering on the most concentrated gathering of art he had ever seen in his life.

His companion, reading him successfully, murmured, "This is just a side hall." And led him away.

Chief Fai Anbai of the ferrets progressed rapidly along narrow service halls, crossed two courtyards still bright with remaining autumnal blooms, and then into the emperor's own mansion. There he found the emperor alone and prostrated himself, after laying Yskanda's sketchbook on the polished floor next to him.

"Rise. I received report of your success. What can you tell me about him?" the emperor said.

The chief stood. "He appears to be an apprentice scribe or artist, your imperial majesty. He drew constantly, at least until the hurricane. Since then he has done little, not even eating, except a bite now and then."

"Was he harmed during the storm?"

"We did not think so, but at the end, the ship was all but destroyed, and he might have taken a blow to the head. Though we saw no evidence of it."

"Did he resist?"

"No. We were too swift for that."

"After?"

"No, your imperial majesty."

"Did he question you at all? Ask why he was taken?"

"Never."

"Oh?" the emperor asked, brows raised.

Chief Fai picked his way carefully, still—after all this time—unsure whether the boy was a prisoner or a rescue or something else entirely. "We think he might be . . . one of the Snow Crane's innocents." He tapped his right temple.

"Ah," the emperor said, forcibly reminded of Hanu's unwavering gaze, innocent of all the female arts and pretenses. "Well done, Chief Fai."

The emperor smiled, and gestured for Chief Fai to wait in the adjacent alcove, where silent servants soon brought a tray of refreshments. Fai Anbai suppressed a sigh, unsure who might be watching through hidden recesses, and reflected that if he were to be sent out again, at least he would not be called upon to conduct that boy down to the inquisitors. That fate might well await Afan Yskanda, but Chief Fai Anbai would not have to see it.

In the interview hall, Emperor Guiyan was aware of a sharp anticipation that made him very much Enjai again as he awaited the prize he had paid so much to acquire. This still might be an error: in the report carried by pigeon, Chief Fai Anbai had been quite firm about the name, Afan Yskanda.

The personal name meant nothing; it was the "Afan" that could not be explained. Hanu had been inordinately proud of her Alk clan. As for Danno—he'd had no clan name at all. Only thieves, criminals, and those thieves and criminals calling themselves gallant wanderers took names not their own. Even the lowest laborer with any integrity knew how unfilial it was to claim a name one was not born to or was not bestowed. And that long ago Second Imperial Prince Enjai would have sworn that his milk-brother Danno would never make such a claim.

But twenty-five years could change a lot; they had not seen one another for more than half their lives.

The door opened, and Bitternail entered with characteristic noiseless, gliding step, escorting a reed of a boy in a decidedly grubby robe that had once been the dull blue-gray of an apprentice. He appeared to be roughly the same age as Jion, the emperor's exasperating first son.

The boy's wide eyes swept along the cranes painted under the eaves, then took in the Kanda Meets the Dragon in the Bamboo Forest painting on the one wall before lighting on the sketchbook, equally grubby, still lying on the floor.

Yskanda knew he was in danger of his life. He could not yet bear to even look at that man sitting so solitary on a throne, after the briefest glance—and his eyes, always seeking beauty, gloried desperately in this room: everywhere above and to either side of that throne, great hands had taken images from nature and rendered them into art. If he gazed on art, surely there might remain some semblance of good in the world?

The emperor watched with interest as Bitternail brought the boy to the precise fifteen strides from the informal throne, and bowed deeply, while his grubby charge stood there, gazing upward at the golden dragon rising skyward on the wall behind the throne. Arrogance or obliviousness?

Yskanda felt a stirring at his side, and heard a whispered, "Bow."

Ul Keg had said once that, if you find yourself confronted by a demon far more powerful than you are, you can either fight and lose painfully, or you can use your wits and give the demon his due. Then find a way to flee.

Yskanda bowed. But it seemed that was not enough.

The emperor watched with sharpening interest and a surprising spurt of amusement as Bitternail gave the boy a tap from the horsehair flywhisk he carried as his badge of office, and whispered a word.

The boy uttered a soft "Oh," and dropped to his knees, his forehead hitting the polished wood of the floor with a thump.

Give the demon his due, Yskanda thought, breathing in the scent of wood polished with fine oil. And in this posture one doesn't have to look at the demon.

"Lift your head," the emperor said.

Yskanda did—to about shoulder height, so all the emperor saw was the untidy top of his head.

"Farther."

Another hand's width, so the point of the boy's noise was visible.

"Your name?"

Unconsciously his head came up a little more as he said, "Afan Yskanda."

"Where are you from?"

Use your wits, Yskanda reminded himself. He might not have long to live, but until he knew if he was first or last to be captured, he would reveal as little as possible. Find a moment to flee if you can.

He spoke to the polished floor. "We call it 'the island'."

The emperor still couldn't see Afan Yskanda's face, just the long hands pressed against his thighs, and a hint of sharply etched collarbone at the neck of his robe. "I take it you're a hopeful scribe, or painter. Let me see an example of your work."

Surprised — Yskanda was braced for the order to drag him off to execution — he turned his head, glancing down at his sketchbook, one hand stretching out as Enjai assessed every detail: the palm of that hand was smooth, the hand of a scholar, not of a trained warrior.

Then the boy looked up in inquiry at the emperor, who at last got a full look at Yskanda's face.

The emperor bit down on an indrawn breath. Oh, yes, there was Hanu in the intelligent arch of eyebrow over teak-colored eyes like windows to an honest . . . no, here was an ardent soul. A straight nose, a sensitive mouth right now pressed in a thin line of fear.

Those were some of her features, but this was not her face. Yskanda's gaze caught on a soaring qilin, an arrested gaze that Enjai had never seen in Hanu. The emperor had seen similar stares in his irritating maternal cousin Kui Pandan. It was the gaze of the artist, though Pandan had never been this fervent, except about pretty boys or girls.

Ever since the arrival of the pigeon that announced the docking of the ship, the emperor had been forcing his way through his schedule, as he contemplated what would amuse him most. *If* this boy was truly the son of Danno and Alk Hanu.

Bitternail approached and bowed, offering the sketchbook. The emperor took it up, turning over the bent, wrinkled pages. The subjects of the drawings were what you'd expect from a boy that age, not very sophisticated, perhaps even trite, but executed with a bold line and a delicate attention to detail that promised considerable talent. Especially those of human figures. Hands, heads, bodies caught mid-movement, all managed to convey emotion as clearly as if he saw the originals. This was not just aptitude, but a glimpse of Talent.

Neither Dannon nor Hanu had had any aptitude for art.

The emperor set aside the book, and leaned forward. "Do you know why you are here?"

Yskanda had been thinking about little else in the past days. His only weapon was silence: he must give nothing away. If only he was not so very tired!

His pulse stuttered. He was unaware of the fast ticking of an artery above his collarbone as he said softly, but firmly, "No."

"No, your imperial majesty," Bitternail murmured.

"No, your imperial majesty," Yskanda repeated obediently, a tide of color rising then fading in his thin face as his gaze flickered up, met the emperor's, and dropped, long lashes fanning his cheeks.

The emperor studied him closely. There was fear in Afan Yskanda's face, but not craven, more a weary resignation, perhaps; the emperor did not miss the flush of fever.

Resignation indeed. To Yskanda there was no question but that the emperor knew who he was. However, he had made a promise when he was ten, and he would keep that promise as long as he was able to.

Seeing that bleak resignation, the emperor discovered that he was not interested in putting this stripling to the extremes of interrogation. The boy had stated his name with the unconsciousness of lifetime habit; he might not even know the truth of his parents' origins.

The emperor was entirely in command of the situation. Why not amuse himself while he sent Fai Anbai to investigate Afan Yskanda's background? In the meantime, if he really was Danno's son, by now the traitor would surely have heard of his son's disappearance, and every day would be an agony.

The emperor smiled. "I'm minded to try an experiment. I would like to see my court through your eyes." The boy looked up, startled as a deer in the wood. "Bitternail, place him under the court artist, who I believe is between apprentices just now.

Let's see how he does."

Yskanda stared, stunned. It wasn't until a gentle but insistent hand tugged at his arm that he remembered where he was, and struggled to his feet, stepping on his robe hem and stumbling. "This way, young apprentice," the servitor said, leading him away.

The interview room was fifty paces long, constructed so that the emperor could hear a whisper from any corner. Thus he heard, before the two vanished through the door, "What did he mean?" from the boy.

"Exactly what he said. You will study under the court artist," Bitternail replied, with detectable humor. "But first you must learn proper manners, and how we conduct ourselves in the palace. And perhaps a bath, and proper clothing, before we progress further?"

The door shut safely behind them, and they were alone in the corridor.

Bitternail went on, "You will discover that your fellow apprentices will be busy writing their yearly letters home, to arrive in time for the New Year's festival. You may also write one."

Yskanda blinked wearily, trying to discover whether that was a threat or not. This Bitternail was acting as if Yskanda had been awarded a place after a test or competition. Were they really pretending he wasn't a prisoner?

All he knew for certain was, he was not yet dead. So he ventured a question. "Do you know why I'm here?"

Bitternail looked down at him, and in an inhumanly detached voice, said, "It was so ordered."

THIRTY-ONE

MOUSE SLEPT THROUGH TWO days of wild storm, waking briefly to either Yaso or an empty hut, for everyone else was busy repairing and rebuilding in spite of the terrible weather.

The first time she woke to pungent medicine pressed to her lips, she was vaguely aware of Yaso's soft voice. "You will have to learn how to be a conduit for Essence, and to maintain balance and harmony. As you are discovering."

Mouse woke once more to the medicine, slept again, then wakened with the rest of her hut one morning to a clean, if dripping, world. When they saw her eyes open, they clamored to tell her the news, leading with the grim fact that four boys had died, and one master while defending villagers, plus the one she had seen die on the wall. Others had been severely maimed and hovered between the worlds of the living and the dead.

The following day dawned golden bright. The memorial tablets had been prepared; the weather was so fine that the day was considered auspicious. A selected group had already borne the dead up to the tomb high on the hill behind the village, overlooking the waterfall, where Loyalty Fortress had buried its dead for centuries. There had been many in the earlier, rougher days.

Down below, everyone able to walk entered the parade ground for the funeral ritual, offering prayers both to the Sun God for thanks in their victory and the Ghost Moon God to ease the fallen's paths to the underworld, and then to the Phoenix Moon on behalf of the families of the dead, begging their souls to return to their clans in the next life. At the end of which, Commander Weken returned to his office to write a letter to each family.

No one performed rites for the dead mercenaries. All they got were talismans sketched over each burial to ward ghosts.

From the village, nearly a dozen had died. The gongs for their burial rituals reverberated on the cold air, a brassy, mournful sound, all through that day.

Everyone was busy, the normal schedule completely thrown over. There were so many wounded, and there was also the damage to the cottages in the village, which must be repaired before winter struck in earnest.

The cadets rotated between repair work and a new patrol schedule, which included a posting at the promontories in case the mercenaries returned — though their losses had been heavy, enough of them had been able to retreat to sail their ships away. And ships that had attacked once for some reason no one knew could come again.

Once she was awake, Mouse was assigned to an outer perimeter guard — the first line of defense — which was in a way was a relief, for it kept her from being pestered by questions. At the same time the fact that she, a second year, was among those fourth and fifth year cadets posted, armed to the teeth, served as silent reminder that she had been marked out and there was no turning back.

For two days she paced the promontory as waves crashed endlessly against the rocks below, mind and heart knotted as she dreaded the inevitable summons.

But the first one to talk to her was Brother Muin, who caught her between buildings before she went out to patrol that second day. Muin spoke urgently in their home tongue. "Mouse, I'm not saying you're wrong. I think a lot more of us would be on the road to the Ghost Moon God right now if you hadn't done . . . that. But they know I didn't teach you to glow like a lantern, or leap from a fifty arm-span wall."

Mouse's mouth opened, but no words emerged.

"You have to tell them that the swordmaster taught you when I was out with the fishers. Got that, Mouse? You hear me? They already know I can spear-fish. I've done it out at the other bay, me and the others who know boats. Swordmaster taught you that Essence-stuff. I wasn't there."

"Swordmaster. Boats," she repeated obediently, then halted, hating the lies with a visceral suddenness. In memory her mother said, *You might have the Alk Gift*. To deny it, to lie about it, seemed criminally unfilial.

No, no, no, even if she did have the Alk Gift, even if the Essence went away and never came back, she could never tell anyone about the Alk Gift, because that would lead to . . .

She licked her dry lips. "First Brother, I think that I have to go."

He nodded. "I know, I tried to catch you before the patrol leaves . . ." Then her brother understood her tone, and he halted, eyeing her.

"I think I have to go *away*." Her voice caught.

He bent and peered into her face. "You mean . . . leave? Loyalty Fortress?"

She had no idea why her throat had seized up. She'd always intended to leave, once Muin finished his fifth year. But somehow the notion that her departure was not a year and some away, but now — it *hurt*.

He searched her gaze, his emotions in turmoil.

They had been in turmoil for two days, actually. He was aware that part of his turmoil was due to seeing Mouse in action. Not just hearing about it, but seeing her wield that sword like something out of a hero tale. "I never thought Essence was real," he said, picking his words one at a time. "That is, not in such a form. Part of charms of healing and the like, sure. But I thought that Essence and martial skills together, like a charmed weapon, were a lot like the dragon tales of ancient days — maybe true, maybe not, but in any case no longer part of life now. I think Father did, too."

"I know," Mouse said. "Father didn't teach me any of that. It was mostly putting together what Mother said. And Ul Keg.

And, ayah! Things in the books. It just seemed to fit together, and if only I practiced hard enough, I might get it. I went about it the wrong way," she added, forestalling his next question, *Why didn't you show me?* "I didn't really get it until recently. A few days ago, in truth. And I didn't know it would be . . . like that. It emptied me like a pitcher. My head still hurts a little." She rubbed her forehead.

He sighed, looking away. "It's not just the Essence. It's also the way you've managed to keep at Heaven and Earth. I didn't even try. I saw, too late, why I should. I think . . . I think I need to find out how to make Heaven and Earth work in *our* training. . ." He sounded both confused and sad.

"It's not too late," she retorted quickly. "Why would it be too late?"

"Too late for the other day," he said grimly. "Too late for four of us, one I was a scout with and shared a hut with."

Mouse's eyes stung. "But you can do it now," she whispered. "Easier, if I go away. They'll forget about me."

Muin's past few nights had been shadowed by nightmares, the basis of which he understood quite well. And he rejected jealousy. It was unworthy, unvirtuous, unfilial. But in the middle of the night, the demons hold stronger sway, and he woke from a sweat after a vivid dream of a golden feather dissipating like glowing ash when he snatched at it, yet when he turned his head, he saw the feather floating in the air, bright and new, to Mouse's outstretched hands.

Because he was innately honest, he forced the words out. "Do you think . . . the Phoenix Feather was for you after all?"

"No," she said violently, hands up in repudiation. Then she struggled to find the right words. "The way Mother and Father and Ul Keg talked, the phoenix feather comes to . . . a leader. I'm not a leader. I can't be a leader." The idea of that much responsibility, of deciding for others — maybe deciding for their lives — chilled her to the soul. "Mother said some in her clan had the Alk Gift. But they were scholars. Not leaders."

Muin let out a breath of relief. The envy still knotted in his heart, but guilt made it ache. He was not being a good older brother. He had pulled his little sister onto his own path. She had followed him uncomplaining. Now the path was leading her somewhere he could not go—it had to be fate, and who could argue with that?

He had already made a vow to himself that he was going to resume Heaven and Earth, somehow, and bring it to his army style. He was already a good leader when it came to tactics—the other boys followed him willingly. He wanted to be able to talk it all out with Mouse. Always, talking with her, and even with Second Brother, who (when he wasn't dreaming) saw things clearly, had helped him be a better big brother.

But she was *leaving*. "Where will you go?"

"Home," she said without thinking. Where else?

Then she saw in his shifted gaze, and in the way he'd moved a little back, that in his mind he had already let her go, which hurt terribly. And yet it might be the right time anyway. She was already having to do that monthly Cramp herb. The disguise as a boy wasn't going to last forever, and what would the army do with her, boy or girl? There was no Essence training here. And she did *not* want to be sent to the imperial capital to train to guard princesses! What if she ran straight into the evil emperor?

"They say the supply ship ought to come in a few days. I will ask if I can go on it."

His eyes stung at the unshed tears he saw her trying to fight, but he knew he was not going to argue. He closed the distance between them, hugged her fiercely as she whispered, "Be careful, First Brother. Remember, swords do not have eyes. Captains and generals can fall. You have to watch for yourself, too."

They let go, and each turned away to begin their separate paths, not looking back.

She walked, breathing hard, all the way to the promontory, and spent a miserable day watching the gray sky and sea, and thinking about that conversation over and over. Was she wrong? Selfish? Should she . . .

When her duty watch was over, her replacement approached. They saluted and he said, "Commander wants you,

Second Ryu."

She saluted again, and bent into the bitter wind that
smelled wet. Weather on the way, Yaso had said.

Here come the questions, she thought as she plodded back
to the fortress. It seemed to take forever, she was so weary.

The commander was waiting for her, his only concession
to the cold a tea urn, which steamed gently. He was alone
except for Steward Pand, standing silently in the background.
She walked in, saluted crisply, and he said, "Sit down, Cadet
Second Ryu."

She dropped on the visitor's mat on the other side of his
table.

He said, "First of all, I wish to commend you for your
actions in the attack. We have been discussing an appropriate
merit . . . Is something wrong?"

Mouse had recoiled. She blushed. "Please don't. I . . . I
know that what I learned isn't . . . that is, I can't really explain.
I had trouble explaining to my brother . . ."

She had the lies ready, but couldn't speak them. There
would be more lies behind them, and more lies, and where
would it end? She said quickly, "I think . . . I think I have to go
away."

Commander Weken's eyes rounded. "Leave your training?"

Training . . . a sudden idea gripped her. "I think I need to
find a master in Essence training."

"Ah?" The Commander looked up at the map of the island
on the wall, with its little flags for various game sites as he
considered this new idea. Between dealing with everything
else, he had been pondering what to do with Second Ryu. In all
his years he had not faced this situation. He had no orders for
it.

The best thing would be to pass the situation up the chain
of command. "I believe I can understand that. For we cannot
provide that here," he said earnestly — and perhaps a little
relieved, only because he was so far outside of his experience.
"I hate to lose a promising captain, but you do need to find
training for your gift. All I can offer you is my highest
recommendation, should the commander at Te Gar, or whoever

he sends you to, seek such."

Mouse said, "I don't really understand it, either. Not *well*."

The Commander frowned into the distance. "I will give you a tally to show at Te Gar Garrison. The commander there will know what to do, or will send you to the imperial capital, where surely they will have proper training for one such as you."

Mouse scrambled to her feet to hide a shudder she could not suppress. She knew the commander was doing what he saw as the right thing—though she also knew she was not going to go anywhere near the capital.

But she didn't have to say so. She bowed, and as she let herself out, she heard him say to Steward Pand, "*Very* glad I didn't send it."

Send what, Mouse was thinking as she walked out. Then she realized it no longer mattered. She breathed deeply, feeling as if a great weight had been lifted from her heart.

Back in the commander's office, he and his most trusted steward looked at one another, then both checked that the doors and windows were shut. The commander said, "In all my years I've never seen an Essence talent. But I do know training. Second Ryu might have been only a small child, but someone gave him at least a little Essence training along with the imperial guard style. Which means that the mysterious swordsman who trained those two brothers could not have been the infamous Danno of all those years ago, who definitely knew nothing of Essence."

Stewart Pand bowed his agreement, silent as becomes a steward.

The commander did not want silence just then. He said, "In my long experience, it has *always* been prudent to avoid the invocation of names from capital lists unless double and triple sure of evidence."

Steward Pand comprehended that his commander did not want silence so much as reassurance. He said slowly, "There will be an investigation. Maybe even the imperial ferrets. A mercenary attack on an imperial training fortress will demand no less."

He paused as the dreaded word *ferrets* hung there, an echo

in their ears. The lowest ferret—bearing the famous golden tiger-eye tally—could supersede the orders of a general.

Commander Weken lifted a hand to this acknowledgment of what they had both been thinking. "Falik, Ryu, and Dun are shaping up to be the best I've trained in ten years. One day Falik will bring merit to the empire, especially with his two most trusted captains at right and left hand."

Steward Pand understood that when they told each other things they well knew, there was something beneath that dared not be uttered in words.

He said, "But not if one must be sent away to the capital."

"Exactly," Commander Weken said, tapping his fingers on his desk. "I would lose Ryu to the capital, which would be inevitable on mentioning a capital list name, however irrelevant it turns out to be. I know the army. Once the question is resolved satisfactorily—as I have every reason to believe will be—Ryu Muin would be handed off to the local commander, who would keep him tight. *I* would," he admitted.

And thus claim the credit when Ryu Muin inevitably won competitions, they both understood that. And depriving the future Glorious General Falik of one of his captains, trained together since youth.

"I should return to my duties now," Steward Pand said, his gaze resting somewhere over the commander's head.

Commander Weken nodded permission. Steward Pand left to oversee his own command. When everything was as it ought to be, he went to the archive, a locked room directly behind his desk.

With the door shut, he leafed back through the intake records until he found the tidy copy he had made from the typically wrinkled, sweat- and water-stained paper that had passed from hand to hand from the garrison at Imai Island to the ship: there, among six other names, Ryu Muin and his brother as orderly, from a small island north of Imai. "A small island." No name.

He stared down at it, breathing out in relief. There would be hundreds of small islands. No one actually knew what went through the heads of the imperial ferrets, but it was unlikely that they would fault Commander Weken, with years of blameless, excellent service, for not dispatching someone (such as a senior steward!) on a long, fatiguing journey to an obscure southern island, to clamber over even smaller, more obscure islands in order to attempt to track down word of a mysterious Essence-trained swordsman who had vanished years ago, according to both boys. Especially as *no sign* of that Essence training had been demonstrated previous to this attack.

The ferrets had who knew how many agents whose entire job was the pursuit of such obscurities. And they probably would send a pack of them searching. That didn't matter. What did matter was that Commander Weken could not be faulted for something he had not known about.

At the other end of the mess hall, Mouse sat with her hut at supper, having decided not to say anything about leaving unless the commander did.

But apparently he left it to her, for the only questions sent her way were about the Essence-martial arts style. "Are you going to teach us?" "Where did you get that—First Ryu doesn't use it." "Why didn't you show us before?"

She told them no one had taught her, and she didn't think she could do it again, and absented herself as quickly as possible—aware of dissatisfaction left behind, as well as disappointment. Let them think she was a snob, or stupid, or ignorant as a frog in a well. She would soon be gone. Even the sight of Yulin crossing the parade ground no longer disturbed her. He had ceased to trouble her after he knocked himself on the head, and soon he would be a mere memory.

The supply ship appeared right on time.

Commander Weken called her in and gave her a packet of letters, saying, "Our usual course is to hand off communications to the ship captain, but since you are going to Te Gar Garrison, you can carry these letters to the garrison commander. This tally will get you directly to him."

She accepted these items with both hands, bowing as she did.

Commander Weken then bowed to her in his turn. She blushed a fiery red and backed to the door as he added, "Go with the Sun God's blessing. We will add your name to the merit roll at New Year's, and next spring."

She bowed again—then, catching sight of her boots, said in dismay, "Ah, my clothes! They belong to Loyalty Fortress."

The commander smiled. "We never send our men away naked. Customarily, it's the blue robe and accoutrements, but that's for our exiting fifth years. Your winter clothes will get you to Te Gar, where you'll be properly kitted out come spring."

"Thank you, sir." She tucked the letters under her arm and the tally into her sash, and exited.

Muin was nowhere in sight. Her throat ached as she crossed to her hut to fetch her second robe and extra shirt and underthings. But when she got there, she discovered her bedding had been taken away to be laundered, and her trunk was empty.

Ayah! She'd arrived in what she stood up in. She could go out the same way.

She slipped out, glancing around for Muin, then remembered he was over at the village helping with repair. She sent him a silent farewell and sped along the seldom used paths until she reached the sundial. Then she marched out through the open gates, and turned toward the docks.

"Where you going, Ryu?" Mo Muin called from the sentry wall.

She turned, smiled, and waved the packet of letters, knowing that he would take the gesture incorrectly, as if she were running a delivery. In her heart she wished him, and the rest, farewell. Then she ran downslope toward the dock—and halted when she rounded the warehouse into which the sailors were putting offloaded supplies.

There was Shigan Fin lounging on a rock.

He looked her way.

She approached cautiously.

As soon as she was in earshot, he straightened up. She had not seen him since the attack, and shock chilled her nerves at the dark circles under his eyes, as if he hadn't slept at all since then.

But there was the old, mocking smile that she thoroughly detested, only with a rueful twist that was new. "Look, Ryu. I was stupid to think it was cowardice keeping you silent. I was an idiot not to see you were hiding something."

She shrugged. "Doesn't matter. I'm leaving."

"So," he said, tipping his chin toward the ship, "am I."

"You're . . ."

"Leaving. On the supply ship, if I can talk my way aboard. I can't tell you what a relief it will be to shed Cayin. I have nothing against the Ancient Master, but if I endure any more of his wise words in Cayin's obnoxious voice, no one can blame me if I turn into something Heaven and reason abhor."

She was too astonished to laugh at Kanda's earnest words about evil. "So you want to go to Te Gar Garrison?"

"No," Shigan said. "I always wanted to join the gallant wanderers. But it's harder than you think, especially if you can't find any of them. I saw the testing site that day, and I was so hungry all I could think of was getting meals. Training, too, yes."

The gallant wanderers! She would surely find an Essence-master among *them*. But if Shigan had never met them . . . "Why?" she asked suspiciously. "You're doing well here. Without me, you'll be first in rank."

He looked away. "Not if there's a warrant out for runaways."

She thought of the Muin cousins' surmises that he was some kind of performer. The way he moved, she'd wondered if he might be a tumbler or dancer. "You're a runaway apprentice?"

His smile deepened. "Yes." The smile vanished. "The army will have inquisitors crawling all over this place soon. Maybe even the ferrets."

"Ferrets?"

"Where have you been all your life? Yes, I know, some flyspeck of an island down south somewhere. I can hear it in your accent. Ayah! Take it from me, you *don't* want to meet up with the emperor's ferrets. They can go anywhere, do anything. They're answerable only to him. And they don't stop ferreting until they find whatever it is the emperor wants found. Then . . ." He drew his finger across his neck.

"Why would the emperor send investigators?" Her heartbeat drummed.

"What do you think is likely to happen when mercenaries

attack an imperial training fortress? Commander Weken will be sending a report about the mercenaries by this very ship — if he hasn't already sent something by one of those pigeons fluttering in and out. Anyone in any kind of trouble will surely be swept up during the questioning."

Mouse had begun to brandish her letters on his words *sending a report*, but a horrible thought hit her, and she turned toward the fortress. "I have to go back. My brother . . ."

Shigan lifted a hand. "Why would anyone trouble with him? It's *you* the ferrets would take an interest in, what with the entire island having witnessed you glowing like Phoenix Moonrise."

"I'd be arrested?"

"No, no, I'm certain they'd waft you along to some imperial training center where people who do whatever it was you did get trained. It's suspicious characters of my sort who'll get collared."

She took out the tally, staring down at it.

"Look, whatever you decide, don't chuck that in the sea. It'll get you free passage on the ship — me, too, if I go as your orderly. We'd better hurry," Shigan said, adding mockingly, "because they won't wait for the likes of us."

She scowled from him to the ground. She didn't want Shigan along, but he was no threat. He had also warned her about those imperial ferrets. And he seemed to have more experience than she did. But then, pretty much anyone would. "All right."

They walked up the ramp, Mouse holding up the tally to the sailors standing at either side on the deck. They were waved aboard. Mouse walked onto the foredeck, then froze. "Yaso?"

Yaso stood at the top of the hatch leading below decks, holding a bundle and smiling as though this were the most natural thing in the world. "I have your things. Both of yours. I'll put them below."

Mouse stared from Yaso to Shigan, whose brows rose. "Are you going to send that grunt back?" he asked, under his breath. "Though he's preferable to Cayin — anyone would be — the first time I laid eyes on him, he was staring at his hands as if trying to figure out how they got attached to his arms." He tapped his forehead and drew a circle.

Mouse looked from the ship to the fortress on the hill, sharply ambivalent. "I didn't ask him to come." Yaso reappeared then, and Mouse raised her voice. "I think they're sailing away soon. You ought to go back quickly."

"I was sent," Yaso said simply.

ABOUT THE AUTHOR

Sherwood Smith writes fantasy, science fiction, and historical fiction. Her full bibliography can be found on her website at https://www.sherwoodsmith.net.

ABOUT BOOK VIEW CAFÉ

Book View Café Publishing Cooperative is an author-owned cooperative of professional writers, publishing in a variety of genres including fantasy, science fiction, romance, mystery, and more.

Its authors include New York Times and USA Today bestsellers as well as winners and nominees of many prestigious awards such as the Agatha Award, Hugo Award, Lambda Literary Award, Locus Award, Nebula Award, RITA Award, Philip K. Dick Award, World Fantasy Award, and many others.

Since its debut in 2008, Book View Café has gained a reputation for producing high quality books in both print and electronic form. BVC's e-books are DRM-free and distributed around the world.

Book View Café's monthly newsletter includes new releases, specials, author news, and event announcements. To sign up, visit https://www.bookviewcafe.com/bookstore/newsletter/

www.ingramcontent.com/pod-product-compliance
Lightning Source LLC
Chambersburg PA
CBHW050525110726
47899CB00005B/1601